TALES FROM THE
SHADOWHUNTER ACADEMY

Also by Cassandra Clare

THE MORTAL INSTRUMENTS

City of Bones

City of Ashes

City of Glass

City of Fallen Angels

City of Lost Souls

City of Heavenly Fire

THE INFERNAL DEVICES

Clockwork Angel

Clockwork Prince

Clockwork Princess

THE DARK ARTIFICES

Lady Midnight

The Shadowhunter's Codex

With Joshua Lewis

The Bane Chronicles

With Sarah Rees Brennan
and Maureen Johnson

Tales from the Shadowhunter Academy

CASSANDRA CLARE

SARAH REES BRENNAN

MAUREEN JOHNSON

ROBIN WASSERMAN

Margaret K. McElderry Books

NEW YORK   LONDON   TORONTO   SYDNEY   NEW DELHI

MARGARET K. McELDERRY BOOKS
An imprint of Simon & Schuster Children's Publishing Division
1230 Avenue of the Americas, New York, New York 10020

For information about special discounts for bulk purchases, please contact Simon & Schuster Special Sales at 1-866-506-1949 or business@simonandschuster.com.
The Simon & Schuster Speakers Bureau can bring authors to your live event.
For more information or to book an event, contact the Simon & Schuster Speakers Bureau at 1-866-248-3049 or visit our website at www.simonspeakers.com.
Also available in a Margaret K. McElderry Books hardcover edition
Interior design by Mike Rosamilia and Nicholas Sciacca
Cover design by Russell Gordon and Nicholas Sciacca
The text for this book was set in Dolly.
Manufactured in the United States of America
First Margaret K. McElderry Books export paperback edition November 2016
2 4 6 8 10 9 7 5 3 1
CIP data for the hardcover edition of this book is available from the Library of Congress.
ISBN 978-1-4814-4325-8 (hc)
ISBN 978-1-4814-4327-2 (eBook)
ISBN 978-1-4814-8514-2 (export pbk)

For all those looking for or looking to be a hero
like Simon: Here's to you, saving entire worlds
(and maybe the galaxy)

TALES FROM THE SHADOWHUNTER ACADEMY

CONTENTS

Welcome to Shadowhunter Academy

By Cassandra Clare and Sarah Rees Brennan

Simon looked at her for a long moment.
She was so overwhelmingly beautiful and impressive,
he found it too much to handle.

—Welcome to Shadowhunter Academy

The problem was that Simon did not know how to pack like a badass.

For a camping trip, sure; to stay at Eric's or overnight at a weekend gig, fine; or to go on a vacation in the sun with his mom and Rebecca, no problem. Simon could throw together a jumble of suntan lotion and shorts, or appropriate band T-shirts and clean underwear, at a moment's notice. Simon was prepared for normal life.

Which was why he was so completely unprepared to pack for going to an elite training ground where demon-fighting half-angel beings known as Shadowhunters would try to shape him into a member of their own warrior race.

In books and movies, people were either whisked away to a magical land in the clothes they were standing up in, or they glossed over the packing part entirely. Simon now felt he had been robbed of critical information by the media. Should he be putting the kitchen knives in his bag? Should he bring the toaster and rig it up as a weapon?

Simon did neither of those things. Instead, he went with the safe option: clean underwear and hilarious T-shirts. Shadowhunters had to love hilarious T-shirts, right? Everyone loved hilarious T-shirts.

"I don't know how they feel about T-shirts with dirty jokes on them in military academy, sport," said his mom.

Simon turned, too quickly, his heart lurching up into his throat. His mom was standing in the doorway, arms folded. Her always-worried face was crumpled slightly with extra worry, but mostly she was looking at him with love. As she always had.

Except that in a whole other set of memories Simon barely had access to, he'd become a vampire and she'd thrown him out of their house. That was one of the reasons Simon was going to the Shadowhunter Academy, why he'd lied to his mom through his teeth that he desperately wanted to go. He'd had Magnus Bane—a warlock with cat eyes; Simon actually knew a warlock with actual cat eyes—fake papers to convince her that he had a scholarship to this fictitious military academy.

He'd done it all so he would not have to look at his mom every day and remember how she had looked at him when she was afraid of him, when she hated him. When she betrayed him.

"I think I've judged my T-shirts pretty well," Simon told her. "I'm a pretty judicious guy. Nothing too sassy for the military. Just good, solid class-clown material. Trust me."

"I trust you, or I wouldn't be letting you go," said his mom.

She walked over to him and planted a kiss on his cheek, and looked surprised and hurt when he flinched, but she did not comment, not on his last day. She put her arms around him instead. "I love you. Remember that."

Simon knew he was being unfair: His mother had thrown him out thinking he was not really Simon anymore but an unholy monster wearing her son's face. Yet he still felt she should have recognized him and loved him in spite of everything. He could not forget what she had done.

Even though she had forgotten it, even though as far as she or almost anybody else in the world was concerned, it had never happened.

So he had to go.

Simon tried to relax in her embrace. "I've got a lot on my plate," he said, curling his hand around his mom's arm. "But I'll try to remember that."

She pulled back. "So long as you do. You sure you're okay getting a lift with your friends?"

She meant Simon's Shadowhunting friends (who he pretended were the military academy buds who had inspired him to join up too). Simon's Shadowhunting friends were the other reason he was going.

"I'm sure," said Simon. "Bye, Mom. I love you."

He meant it. He'd never stopped loving her, in this life or any other.

I love you unconditionally, his mom had said, once or twice, when he was younger. *That's how parents love. I love you no matter what.*

People said things like that, without thinking of potential nightmare scenarios or horrific conditions, the whole world changing and love slipping away. None of them ever dreamed love would be tested, and fail.

Rebecca had sent him a card that said: *GOOD LUCK, SOLDIER BOY!* Simon remembered, even when he'd been locked out of his home, door barred to him in every way it could be, his sister's arm around him and her soft voice in his ear. She had loved him, even then. So there was that. It was something, but it wasn't enough.

He could not stay here, caught between two worlds and two sets of memories. He had to escape. He had to go and become a hero, the way he had been once. Then all of this would make sense, all of this would mean something. Surely it would not hurt anymore.

Simon paused before he shouldered his bag and departed for the Academy. He put his sister's card in his pocket. He left home for a strange new life and carried her love with him, as he had once before.

Simon was meeting up with his friends, even though none of them were going to the Academy. He'd agreed he would come to the Institute and say good-bye before he left.

There was a time when he could have seen through glamours on his own, but Magnus had to help him do it now. Simon looked up at the strange, imposing bulk of the Institute, remembering uneasily that he had passed this place before and seen an abandoned building. That was another life, though. He remembered some kind of Bible passage about how children saw through smudged glass, but growing up meant you could view things clearly. He could see the Institute quite plainly: an impressive structure rising high above him. The sort of building designed to make humans feel like ants. Simon pushed open the filigreed gate, walked down the narrow path that snaked around the Institute, and crossed through to the grounds.

The walls that surrounded the Institute enclosed a garden that struggled to thrive given its proximity to a New York avenue. There were impressive stone paths and benches and even a statue of an angel that gave Simon nervous fits, since he was a *Doctor Who* fan. The angel wasn't weeping, exactly, but it looked too depressed for Simon's liking.

Sitting on the stone bench in the middle of the garden were Magnus Bane and Alec Lightwood, a Shadowhunter who was tall and dark and fairly strong and silent, at least around Simon. Magnus was chatty, though, had the aforementioned cat eyes and magic powers, and was currently wearing a clinging T-shirt in a zebra-stripe pattern with pink accents. Magnus and Alec had been dating for some time; Simon guessed Magnus could talk for both of them.

Behind Magnus and Alec, leaning against a stone wall, were Isabelle and Clary. Isabelle was leaning against the garden wall, looking over it and into the distance. She looked as if she were in the middle of posing for an unbelievably glamorous photo shoot. Then again, she always did. It was her talent. Clary, however, was staring stubbornly up into Isabelle's face and talking to her. Simon thought Clary would get her way and get Isabelle to pay attention to her eventually. That was *her* talent.

Looking at either of them caused a pang in his chest. Looking at both of them started a dull, steady ache.

So instead Simon looked for his friend Jace, who was kneeling by himself in the overgrown grass and sharpening a short blade against a stone. Simon assumed Jace had his reasons for this; or possibly he just knew he looked cool doing it. Possibly he and Isabelle could do a joint photo shoot for *Badass Monthly*.

Everyone was assembled. Just for him.

Simon would have felt both honored and loved, except mostly he felt weird, because he had only a few broken fragments of memory that said he knew these people at all, and a whole lifetime of memories that said they were armed, overly intense strangers. The kind you might avoid on public transportation.

The adults of the Institute and the Clave, Isabelle and Alec's mother and father and the other people, were the ones who had suggested that if Simon wanted to become a Shadowhunter, he should go to the Academy. It was opening its doors for the first time in decades to welcome trainees who could restore the Shadowhunters' ranks that the recent war had decimated.

Clary hadn't liked the idea. Isabelle had said absolutely nothing on the subject, but Simon knew she hadn't liked it either. Jace had argued that he was perfectly capable of training Simon in New York, had even offered to do it all himself and catch Simon up with Clary's training. Simon had thought that was touching, and he and Jace must be closer than he actually remembered them being, but the awful truth was that he didn't want to stay in New York.

He didn't want to stay around *them*. He didn't think he could bear the constant expression on their faces—on Isabelle's and Clary's most of all—of disappointed expectation. Every time they saw him, they recognized him and knew him and expected things of him. And every time he came up blank. It was like watching someone digging where they knew they'd buried something precious, digging and digging and realizing that whatever it was—was gone. But they kept digging just the same, because the idea of losing it was so terrible and because maybe.

Maybe.

He was that lost treasure. He was that maybe. And he hated it. That was the secret he was trying to keep from them, the one he was always fearing he would betray.

He just had to get through this one last good-bye, and then he would be away from them until he was better, until he was closer to the person they all actually wanted to see. Then they would not be disappointed in him, and he would not be strange to them. He would belong.

Simon did not try to alert the whole group to his presence at once. Instead he sidled up to Jace.

"Hey," he said.

"Oh," Jace said carelessly, as if he hadn't been waiting out here for the express purpose of seeing Simon off. He looked up, golden gaze casual, then looked away. "You."

Being too cool for school was Jace's thing. Simon supposed he must have understood and been fond of it, once.

"Hey, I figured I wasn't going to get the chance to ask this again. You and me," Simon said. "We're pretty tight, aren't we?"

Jace looked at him for a moment, face very still, and then bounded to his feet and said: "Absolutely. We're like this." He crossed two of his fingers together. "Actually, we're more like this." He tried to cross them again. "We had a little bit of ini-tial tension, as you may later recall, but that was all cleared up when you came to me and confessed that you were struggling with your feelings of intense jealousy over my—these were your words—stunning good looks and irresistible charm."

"Did I," said Simon.

Jace clapped him on the shoulder. "Yeah, buddy. I remember it clearly."

"Okay, whatever. The thing is . . . Alec's always really quiet around me," Simon said. "Is he just shy, or did I tick him off and I don't remember it? I wouldn't like to go away without trying to make things right."

Jace's expression took on that peculiar stillness again. "I'm glad you asked me that," he said finally. "There is something more going on. The girls didn't want me to tell you, but the truth is—"

"Jace, stop monopolizing Simon," said Clary.

She spoke firmly, as she always did, and Jace turned and answered to it, as he always did, responding to her call as he did to no one else's. Clary came walking toward both of them, and Simon felt that pang in his chest again as her red head drew near. She was so small.

During one of their ill-fated training sessions, in which Simon had been relegated to an observer after a sprained wrist, Simon had seen Jace throw Clary into a wall. She'd come right back at him.

Despite that, Simon kept feeling as if she needed to be protected. Feeling this way was a particular kind of horror, having the emotions without the memories. Simon felt like he was insane to have all these feelings about strangers, without having them properly backed up by familiarity and experiences he could actually recall. At the same time, he knew he wasn't feeling or expressing enough. He knew he wasn't giving them what they wanted.

Clary didn't need to be protected, but somewhere within

Simon was the ghost of a boy who had always wanted to be the one to protect her, and he was only hurting her by staying around unable to be that guy.

Memories came, sometimes in an overwhelming and terrifying rush, but mostly in tiny shards, jigsaw pieces Simon could hardly make sense of. One piece was a flash of walking to school with Clary, her hand so little and his barely bigger. He'd felt big then, though, big and proud and responsible for her. He had been determined not to let her down.

"Hey, Simon," she said now. Her eyes were bright with tears, and Simon knew they were all his fault.

He took Clary's hand, small but calloused from both weapons and art. He wished he could find a way back to believing, even though he knew better, that she was his to protect.

"Hey, Clary. You take care of yourself," he said. "I know you can." He paused. "And take care of Jace, that poor, helpless blond."

Jace made an obscene gesture, which actually did feel familiar to Simon, so he knew that was their thing. Jace hastily lowered his hand when Catarina Loss walked around the side of the Institute.

She was a warlock like Magnus, and a friend of his, but instead of having cat eyes she was blue all over. Simon got the feeling she did not like him very much. Maybe warlocks only liked other warlocks. Though Magnus did seem to like Alec quite a lot.

"Hello there," said Catarina. "Ready to go?"

Simon had been dying to go for weeks, but now that the time had come he felt panic clawing at his throat. "Almost," he said. "Just a second."

He nodded to Alec and Magnus, who both nodded to him.

Simon felt he had to clear up whatever was weird between himself and Alec before he ventured much more.

"Bye, guys, thanks for everything."

"Believe me, even partially releasing you from a fascist spell was my pleasure," said Magnus, lifting a hand. He wore many rings, which glittered in the spring sunshine. Simon thought he must dazzle his enemies with his magical prowess, but also his glitter.

Alec just nodded.

Simon leaned down and hugged Clary, even though it made his chest hurt more. The way she felt and smelled was both strange and familiar, conflicting messages running through his brain and his body. He tried not to hug her too hard, even though she was kind of hugging him too hard. In fact, she was pretty much crushing his rib cage. He didn't mind, though.

When he let go of Clary, he turned and hugged Jace. Clary watched, tears running down her face.

"Oof," said Jace, sounding extremely startled, but he patted Simon quickly on the back.

Simon supposed they usually fist-bumped or something. He did not know the warrior way of being bros: Eric was a big hugger. He decided it would probably be good for Jace, and ruffled his hair a little for emphasis before stepping away.

Then Simon gathered up his courage, turned, and walked over to Isabelle.

Isabelle was the last person he had to say good-bye to; she would be the hardest. She wasn't like Clary, openly tearful, or like any of the others, sorry to see him go but basically all right. She seemed more indifferent than anyone, so indifferent Simon knew it was not real.

"I'm going to come back," said Simon.

"No doubt," Isabelle said, staring off into the distance beyond his shoulder. "You always do seem to turn up."

"When I do, I'm going to be awesome."

Simon made the promise, not sure if he could keep it. He felt as if he had to say something. He knew it was what she wanted, for him to return to her the way he had been, better than he was now.

Isabelle shrugged. "Don't think I'll be waiting around, Simon Lewis."

Just like her pretense of indifference, that sounded like a promise of the complete opposite. Simon looked at her for a long moment. She was so overwhelmingly beautiful and impressive, he found it too much to handle. He could barely believe any of his new memories, but the idea that Isabelle Lightwood had been his girlfriend seemed more unbelievable than the fact that vampires were real and Simon had been one. He didn't have the faintest idea how he had made her feel that way about him once, and so he didn't have the faintest idea how to make her feel that way about him again. It was like asking him to fly. He'd asked her to dance once, to have coffee with him twice in the months since she and Magnus had come to him and given back as much of his memory as they could, but not enough. Each time Isabelle had watched him carefully, expectantly, waiting for some miracle he knew he could not perform. It meant he was tongue-tied around her all the time, so sure he was going to say the wrong thing and shatter everything that he could scarcely say anything.

"Okay," he said. "Well, I'll miss you."

Isabelle's hand shot out, grasping his arm. She still wasn't looking at him.

"If you need me, I'll come," she said, and released him as abruptly as she had grabbed him.

"Okay," Simon said again, and retreated to Catarina Loss's side as she made the Portal to go through to Idris, the country of the Shadowhunters. This parting was so painful and awkward and welcome that he could not quite appreciate how awesome it was to have magic done right in front of him.

He waved good-bye to all these people he barely knew and somehow loved anyway, and he hoped they could not tell how relieved he was to be going.

Simon had remembered snatches about Idris, towers and a prison and stern faces and blood in the streets, but all of it was from the city of Alicante.

This time, he found himself outside the city. He was standing in the lush countryside, on one side a valley and on the other meadows. There was nothing to be seen for miles but different shades of green. There were the jade-green stretches of meadows upon meadows right down to the crystalline dazzle on the horizon that was the City of Glass, its towers blazing in the sunlight. On the other side, there were the emerald depths of a forest, dark green abundance cloaked in shadows. The tops of the trees ruffled in the wind like viridescent feathers.

Catarina looked around, then took one step, so she was standing right on the lip of the valley. Simon followed her, and in that one step the shadows of the forest lifted, as if shadows could become a veil.

Suddenly there were what Simon recognized as training grounds, stretches of clear ground cut into the earth with fences around them, markings indicating where Shadowhunters would run or throw etched so deep in the earth Simon could see them from where he stood. At the center of the grounds and in the very heart of the forest, the jewel to which all the rest was background setting, was a tall gray building with towers and spires. Simon was suddenly searching for architectural words like "buttress" to describe how stone could carry the shape of a swallow's wings and support a roof. The Academy had a stained-glass window set in its very center. In the window, darkened with age and years, an angel wielding a sword could still be seen, celestial and fierce.

"Welcome to Shadowhunter Academy," said Catarina Loss, her voice gentle.

They began their descent together. At one point Simon's sneakers slid in the soft, crumbling earth of the steep slope, and Catarina had to grab hold of his jacket to steady him.

"I hope you brought some hiking boots, city boy."

"I did not bring hiking boots even slightly," said Simon. He'd known he was packing wrong. His instincts had not led him astray. Nor had they been at all helpful.

Catarina, probably disappointed by Simon's demonstrable lack of intelligence, was silent as they walked under the shadow of the boughs, in the green dusk created by the trees, until the trees became sparse and the sunlight flooded back into the space around them and Shadowhunter Academy loomed in the distance before them. As they drew closer, Simon began to notice certain small flaws with the Academy that he had not observed when he was awestruck and far away. One of the tall, skinny towers was leaning at an alarming angle. There were large bird nests in the arches, and cobwebs hanging as long and thick as curtains fluttered in a few of the windows. One of the panes in the stained-glass window was gone, leaving a black space where the angel's eye should have been so that he looked like an angel turned to piracy.

Simon did not feel good about any of these observations.

There were people walking in front of the Academy, under the gaze of the pirate angel. There was a tall woman with a mane of strawberry-blond hair, and behind her two girls who Simon figured were Academy students. They both looked about his age.

A twig snapped under Simon's clumsy foot and all three of the strolling women looked around. The strawberry blonde leaped into action, running full tilt toward them and falling on Catarina as if she was a long-lost blue sister. She seized Catarina by the shoulders and Catarina looked extremely discomposed.

"Ms. Loss, thank the Angel you're here," she exclaimed. "Everything is chaos, absolute chaos!"

"I don't believe I've had the . . . pleasure," Catarina observed, with a significant pause.

The woman collected herself and released Catarina, nodding so her bright hair flew around her shoulders. "I'm Vivianne Penhallow. The, ah, dean of the academy. Delighted to make your acquaintance."

She might speak formally, but she was awfully young to be spearheading the effort to reopen the Academy and prepare all the new, desperately needed trainees for the Shadowhunter forces. Then again, Simon supposed that was what happened when you were second-cousins-in-law with the Consul. Simon was still trying to work out how Shadowhunter government and also Shadowhunter family trees worked. They all seemed to be related to each other and it was very disturbing.

"What seems to be the problem, Dean Penhallow?"

"Well, not to put too fine a point on it, the weeks allotted to renovating the Academy seem to have been, ah . . . 'wildly insufficient' are the words that perhaps best describe the situation," said Dean Penhallow, her words rushing out. "And some of the teachers have already—er—left abruptly. I do not believe they intend to return. In fact some of them informed me of this in very strong language. Also, the Academy is a trifle chilly and, to be perfectly honest, more than a trifle structurally unsound. Moreover, in the interest of thoroughness I must tell you there is a problem with the food supplies."

Catarina raised an ivory eyebrow. "What's the problem with the food supplies?"

"There aren't any food supplies."

"That *is* a problem."

The dean's shoulders sagged and her chest deflated somewhat, as if holding all that in had been confining her in an invisible corset of distress. "These girls with me are two of the older students and of good Shadowhunter families—Julie Beauvale and Beatriz Velez Mendoza. They arrived yesterday and have really been proving themselves invaluable. And this must be young Simon," she said, favoring him with a smile.

Simon was briefly startled and not sure why, until he dimly recalled that very few adult Shadowhunters had ever shown any signs of pleasure at having a vampire in their midst. Of course, she had no reason to hate him on sight now. She'd also seemed eager to meet Catarina, Simon thought; maybe she was all right. Or maybe she was just eager to have Catarina help her.

"Right," said Catarina. "Well, what a surprise that the building left vacant after an upheaval almost two decades ago isn't running entirely smoothly after a few weeks. You'd best show me some of the worst trouble spots. I can shore them up so we don't have all the fuss of a baby Shadowhunter breaking their little neck."

Everyone stared at Catarina.

"The inestimable tragedy, I meant," Catarina amended, and smiled brightly. "Can one of the girls be spared to show Simon to his room?"

She seemed eager to get rid of Simon. She really did not like him. Simon could not think what he could possibly have done to her.

The dean stared at Catarina for a moment longer, and then snapped out of it. "Oh yes, yes, of course. Julie, would you please see to it? Put him in the tower room."

Julie's eyebrows shot up. "Really?"

"Yes, really. The first room as you enter the east wing," the dean said, her voice strained, and turned back to Catarina. "Ms. Loss, I am once again most thankful you have arrived. Can you truly fix some of these irregularities?"

"There is a saying: *It takes a Downworlder to clear up a Shadowhunter mess*," Catarina observed.

"I . . . hadn't heard that saying," said Dean Penhallow.

"How odd," said Catarina, her voice fading as they walked away. "Downworlders say it often. Very often."

Simon was left abandoned and staring at the remaining girl, Julie Beauvale. He'd liked the look of the other girl better. Julie was very pretty, but her face and nose and mouth were all oddly narrow, giving the impression that her entire head was pursed with disapproval.

"Simon, was it?" she asked, and her prepursed mouth seemed to purse further. "Follow me."

She turned, her movements sharp as a drill sergeant's, and Simon followed her slowly across the threshold of the Academy into an echoing hall with a vaulted ceiling. He tilted his head and tried to make out if the greenish cast of the ceiling was bad lighting from the stained-glass window or actual moss.

"Please keep up," said Julie's voice, floating from one of the six dark, small doorways cut into the stone wall. Its owner had already vanished, and Simon plunged into the darkness after her.

The darkness turned out to be only a dim stone stairway, which led up into a dim stone corridor. There was still hardly any light, because the windows were tiny slits in the stone. Simon remembered reading about windows like that, made so nobody could fire in at you but so you could fire arrows out.

Julie led him down one passage, down another, up a short flight of stairs, down still another passage, made her way through a small circular room, which was nice for a change but which led to yet another passage. All the dark, close stone and the funny smell, combined with all the corridors, were making Simon think the words "passage tomb." He was trying not to think of the words, but there they were.

"So you're a demon hunter," said Simon, shifting his bag on his shoulders and hurrying after Julie. "What's that like?"

"Shadowhunter, and that's what you're here to find out," the girl told him, and then stopped at one of many doors, stained oak with black iron fittings, the handle carved to look like an angel's wing. She clasped the handle, and Simon saw that it must have been turned so often over the centuries that the details of the angel's wing had been worn almost smooth.

Inside was a small stone room, containing two narrow

beds—a suitcase open on one—with carved wooden bedposts, a diamond-paned window blurred with dust, and a large wardrobe tilted to one side as if missing a leg.

There was also already a boy in there, standing on a stool. He revolved slowly on the stool to face them, regarding them from on high as if he were a statue on a plinth.

He did not look unlike a statue, if someone had dressed a statue up in jeans and a colorful red-and-yellow rugby shirt. The lines of his face were clean and statue-reminiscent, and he was broad-shouldered and athletic-looking, as most Shadowhunters were. Simon suspected the Angel did not choose the asthmatic or anyone who had ever gotten hit in the face by a volleyball in gym. The boy had a golden summer tan, dark brown eyes, and curly light-brown hair tumbling over his brow. The boy smiled at the sight of them, a dimple creasing one cheek.

Simon did not consider himself much of a judge of male beauty. But he heard a small sound behind him and glanced over his shoulder.

The small sound had been a sigh bursting in an irrepressible gust from Julie, who also, as Simon watched, performed a simultaneous sigh and slow, involuntary wriggle. Simon thought the siggle was probably an indication that this guy was something out of the ordinary when it came to looks.

Simon rolled his eyes. Apparently, all Shadowhunter dudes were underwear models, including his new roommate. His life was a joke.

Julie seemed occupied regarding the dude on the stool. Simon had several questions, like "who is that?" and "why is he on a stool?" but he didn't want to be a bother.

"I'm really glad you guys are here. Now . . . don't panic," the guy on the stool whispered.

Julie backed up a step.

"What's wrong with you?" Simon demanded. "Saying 'don't panic' is guaranteed to make everyone panic! Be specific about the problem."

"Okay, I get what you're saying and you make a fair point," continued the new boy. He had an accent, his voice light yet rumbling over certain syllables. Simon was fairly sure he was Scottish. "It's just that I think there's a demon possum in the wardrobe."

"By the Angel!" said Julie.

Simon said: "That's ridiculous."

There was a sound from within the wardrobe. A dragging, grunting, hissing sound that raised the hairs on the back of Simon's neck.

Quick as a flash and with Shadowhunter grace, Julie leaped onto the bed that did not have an open suitcase on it. Simon supposed that was his bed. The fact that he'd been here only two minutes and already had a girl hurling herself onto his bed would have been thrilling, except that of course she was fleeing infernal rodents.

"Do something, Simon!"

"Yes, Simon—are you Simon? Hi, Simon—please do something about the demonic possum," said the guy on the stool.

"I'm sure it's not a demonic possum."

The sound of scuffling within the wardrobe was very loud, and Simon did not feel entirely sure. It did sound like there was something enormous lurking in there.

"I was born in the City of Glass," said Julie. "I am a Shadowhunter and I can handle the demonic. But I was also raised in a nice house that was not infested with filthy wildlife!"

"Well, I'm from Brooklyn," said Simon, "and not to bad-mouth my beloved city or call it a verminous garbage heap with good music or anything, but I know rodents. Also, I believe I was a rodent, but that was only for a little while—I don't remember it clearly and I don't want to discuss it. I think I can handle a possum . . . which again, I'm sure is not demonic."

"I saw it and you guys didn't!" exclaimed the guy on the stool. "I'm telling you, it was suspiciously large! *Fiendishly* large."

There was another rustle, and some menacing snuffling. Simon sidled over to the open suitcase on the other bed. There were a lot more rugby shirts in there, but on top of them was something else.

"Is that a weapon?" Julie asked.

"Uh, no," said Simon. "It's a tennis racket."

The Shadowhunters needed more extracurricular activities.

He suspected the racket was going to be a truly terrible weapon, but it was what he had. He edged back toward the wardrobe, and threw the door open. There, in the splintered, gnawed-on recesses of the wardrobe, was a possum. Its red eyes shone and its small mouth opened, hissing at Simon.

"How disgusting," said Julie. "Kill it, Simon!"

"Simon, you're our only hope!" said the boy on the stool.

The possum made a movement, as if to dart forward. Simon brought the racket down with a thwack against the stone. The possum hissed again and moved in a different direction. Simon had the wild idea that it was feinting, just before it actually ran between his legs. Simon let out a sound that was too close to a squawk, stumbled back, and hit wildly in several directions, striking flagstones every time. The other two screamed. Simon spun to try to locate the possum, seeing a flash of fur out of the corner of his eye and spinning again. The boy on the stool—either looking for reassurance or in a misguided effort to be helpful—grabbed at Simon's shoulders and tried to turn him, using a handful of his shirt for leverage.

"There!" he yelled in Simon's ear, and Simon whirled of his own accord, was turned against his will, and walked backward into the stool.

He felt the stool tip and tilt against his legs, and the boy on it snatched at Simon's shoulders again. Simon, already dizzy, lurched and then saw the possum's furry little body creeping over his own sneaker and made a fatal mistake. He hit his own foot with the racket. Very hard.

Simon, the stool, the boy on the stool, and the racket all went tumbling onto the stone floor.

The possum streaked out of the doorway. Simon thought it cast him a red-eyed look of triumph as it went.

Simon was in no condition to give chase, since he was in a jumble of chair legs and human legs, and had knocked his head against the bedpost.

He was trying to sit up, rubbing his head and feeling a little dizzy, when Julie jumped off the bed. The bedpost swayed with the force of her movement, and knocked against the back of Simon's head once more.

"Well, I'll leave you guys before the creature returns to his nest!" Julie announced. "Er . . . I mean, I'll leave you guys . . . to it." She paused in the doorway, staring in the direction the possum had gone. "Bye now," she added, and bolted in the opposite direction.

"Ow," Simon said, giving up on sitting up straight and

leaning back on his hands. He grimaced. "Very ow. Well . . . that was . . ."

He gestured to the stool, the open doorway, the disgusting wardrobe, and his supine self.

"That was . . . ," he continued, and found himself shaking his head and laughing. "Just *such* an impressive display from three future awesome demon hunters."

The boy no longer on the stool looked startled, no doubt because he thought his new roommate was deranged and giggled over possums. Simon could not help it. He could not stop laughing.

Any of the Shadowhunters he knew back in New York would have dealt with the situation without blinking an eye. He was sure Isabelle would have cut off the possum's head with a sword. But now he was surrounded by people who panicked and screamed and stood on stools, flailing disasters of human beings who could not cope with a single rodent, and Simon was one of them. They were all just normal kids.

It was such a relief, Simon felt dizzy with it. Or maybe that was because he'd hit his head.

He kept laughing, and when he looked over at his roommate again, the other boy met his eyes.

"What a shame our teachers didn't see that awesome performance," Simon's new roommate said seriously. Then he burst out laughing too, hand against his mouth, laugh lines fanning out from the corners of his eyes, as if he laughed all the time and his face had just grown used to it. "We are gonna slay."

After the slight burst of possum-related hysterics, Simon and his new roommate got up off the floor and got to unpacking and introducing themselves.

"Sorry about all that. I'm not great with scuttling little things. I'm hoping to fight demons a bit higher off the ground. I'm George Lovelace, by the way," said the boy, sitting on the bed beside his open suitcase.

Simon stared at his own bag, full of its many hilarious T-shirts, and then suspiciously at the wardrobe. He didn't know if he trusted the possum wardrobe with his T-shirts.

"So you're a Shadowhunter, then?"

He'd worked out how Shadowhunter names were constructed by now, and he'd already figured George for a Shadowhunter at first sight. Only that had been before Simon thought George might be cool. Now he was disappointed. He knew what Shadowhunters thought of mundanes. It would have been nice to have someone new to all this to go through school with.

It would be nice to have a cool roommate again, Simon thought. Like Jordan. He could not remember Jordan, his roommate when he was a vampire, all that well, but what he remembered was good.

"Well, I'm a Lovelace," said George. "My family quit Shadowhunting due to laziness in the 1700s, then went and settled outside Glasgow to become the best sheep thieves in the land. The only other branch of the Lovelaces gave up Shadowhunting in the 1800s—I think they had a daughter who came back, but she died, so we were all that was left. Shadowhunters used to come knocking to past generations, and my brave ancestors were all like, 'Nope, think we'll stick with the sheep,' until finally the Clave stopped coming around because they were tired of our layabout ways. What can I tell you? The Lovelaces are quitters."

George shrugged and made a *what can you do?* gesture with his tennis racket. The strings were broken. It was still their only weapon in case the possum returned.

Simon checked his phone. Idris had no reception, big surprise, and he tossed it in the suitcase among his T-shirts. "That's a noble legacy."

"Can you believe, I didn't know anything about it until a few weeks ago? The Shadowhunters came to find us again, telling us they needed new, uh, demon hunters in the fight against evil because a bunch of them had died in a war. Can I just say, the Shadowhunters, man, they really know how to win over hearts and minds."

"They should make flyers," Simon suggested, and George grinned. "Just a bunch of them looking very cool and wearing black. The flyer could say 'READY TO BE A BADASS?' Put me in touch with the Shadowhunter marketing department, I have more gems where that came from."

"I have some bad news to break to you about most Shadowhunters and their abilities with a photocopier," George told him. "Anyway, it turned out my parents had known the whole time and just not informed me. Because why would I be interested in a little thing like that? They said my grandma was insane when she talked about dancing with the faeries! I made myself very clear on the subject of keeping intensely cool secrets from me before I left. Dad said, in fairness, that Gran *is* completely out of her tree. It's just that faeries are also real. Probably not her four-inch-tall faerie lover called Bluebell, though."

"I'd bet against it," said Simon, thinking over all he remembered about faeries. "But I wouldn't bet a lot."

"So, you're from New York?" said George. "Pretty glam."

Simon shrugged: He didn't know what to say, when he had been casually comfortable with New York his whole life, and then found that the city and his own soul had turned traitor. When he had been so painfully eager to leave.

"How did you find out about all this? Do you have the Sight?"

"No," Simon said slowly. "No, I'm just ordinary, but my best friend found out she was a Shadowhunter, and the daughter of this really bad guy. And the sister of this other really bad guy. She has the worst luck with relatives. I got mixed up in it, and to tell you the truth, I don't really remember everything, because—"

Simon paused and tried to think of some way to explain demon-related amnesia that would not convince George that Simon had the same problems as George's grandma. Then he saw George was looking at him, his brown eyes wide.

"You're Simon," he breathed. "Simon *Lewis*."

"Right," Simon said. "Hey. Is my name on the door, or—is there some sort of register I'm meant to be signing—"

"The vampire," said George. "Mary Morgenstern's best friend!"

"Uh, Clary," said Simon. "Uh, yeah. I like to think of myself as the ex-undead."

The way George was looking at him, as if he was seriously impressed rather than disappointed or expectant, was a little embarrassing. Simon had to admit, it was also a little nice. It was so different from the way anyone else had looked at him, in his old life or his new one.

"You don't understand. I arrived in this freezing hellhole full of slime and rodents, and the whole Academy was buzzing with people talking about these heroes who are my age and actually went to a hell dimension. It gave real perspective to the fact that the toilets don't work here."

"The toilets don't work? But what do we—how do we—"

George coughed. "We commune with nature, if you know what I'm saying."

George and Simon looked out of their casement window to the forest below, leaves gently swaying in the wind beyond the diamond-shaped panes of glass. George and Simon looked, darkly, sadly, back at each other.

"Seriously, you and your hero group is all anybody talks about," George said, returning to a more cheerful subject. "Well, that and the fact we have pigeons living in the ovens. You saved the world, didn't you? And you don't remember it. That's got to be weird."

"It is weird, George, thanks for mentioning that."

George laughed, tossed his broken racket on the floor, and kept looking at Simon as if he was someone amazing. "Wow. Simon Lewis. I guess I have someone at Spinechilling Academy to thank for getting the cool roommate."

George led Simon down to dinner, for which Simon was deeply grateful. The dining hall looked a lot like all the other square stone rooms in the Academy, except on one end it had a massive carved mantelpiece, displaying crossed swords and a motto so worn that Simon could not read it.

There were several round tables, with wooden chairs of varying sizes assembled around them. Simon was starting to genuinely believe they had furnished the Academy from an old person's garage sale. The tables were crowded with kids. Most of them were at least two years younger than Simon. Quite a few were younger than that. Simon had not realized he was on the elderly side for a trainee demon hunter, and it made him nervous. He was deeply relieved when he saw some mildly familiar faces his own age.

Julie of the pursed face, Beatriz, and another boy saw them and waved them over. Simon assumed the wave was for George, but when he sat down Julie actually leaned into him.

"I can't believe you didn't say you were Simon *Lewis*," she said. "I thought you were just a mundane."

Simon leaned slightly away. "I am just a mundane."

Julie laughed. "You know what I mean."

"She means we all owe you a debt, Simon," said Beatriz Mendoza, smiling at him. She had a great smile. "We don't forget that. It's a pleasure to meet you, and it's a pleasure to have you here. We might even be able to get sensible conversation out of a boy for once. No chance of that with Jon here."

The boy, who had biceps the size of Simon's head, reached across the table and offered a hand. Despite his extreme arm intimidation, Simon shook it.

"I'm Jonathan Cartwright. Pleasure."

"Jonathan," Simon repeated.

"It's a very common name for Shadowhunters," said Jon. "After Jonathan Shadowhun—"

"Er, no, I know, I have my copy of the *Codex*," said Simon. Clary had given him hers, actually, and he'd had fun reading the scribbling of practically everybody in the Institute on the pages. He'd felt he was getting to know them, safely away from them where they could not see him fail and expose his gaps of knowledge. "It's just . . . I know some people called Jonathan.

Not that any of them call themselves Jonathan. Called themselves Jonathan."

He did not remember much about Clary's brother, but he knew his name. He did not particularly want to remember more.

"Oh, right, Jonathan Herondale," said Jon. "Of course you know him. I'm actually pretty good friends with him myself. Taught him a trick or two that probably helped you all out in the demon realms, am I right?"

"Do you mean—Jace?" Simon asked dubiously.

"Yeah, obviously," said Jon. "He's probably mentioned me."

"Not that I recall . . . ," said Simon. "But I do have demon amnesia. So there's that."

Jon nodded and shrugged. "Right. Bummer. He's probably mentioned me and you forgot, on account of the demon amnesia. Not to brag, but we're pretty close, me and Jace."

"I wish I was close to Jace Herondale," Julie sighed. "He is *so* gorgeous."

"He is foxier than a fox fur in a fox hole on fox hunting day," Beatriz agreed dreamily.

"Who's this?" asked Jon, squinting at George, who was leaning back in his chair and looking rather amused.

"Speaking of people being foxy, do you mean? I'm George Lovelace," said George. "I say my surname without shame, because I am secure in my masculinity like that."

"Oh, a Lovelace," said Jon, his brow clearing. "Yeah, you can sit with us."

"I've got to say, my surname has never actually been a selling point before, though," George remarked. "Shadowhunters, go figure."

"Well, you know," said Julie. "You're going to want to hang out with people in your own stream."

"Come again?" Simon asked.

"There are two different streams in the Academy," Beatriz explained. "The stream for mundanes, where they inform the students more fully about the world and give them badly needed basic training, and the stream for real Shadowhunter kids, where we're taught from a more advanced curriculum."

Julie's lip curled. "What Beatriz's saying is, there's the elite and there's the dregs."

Simon stared at them, with a sinking feeling. "So . . . I'm going to be in the dregs course."

"No, Simon, no!" Jon exclaimed, looking shocked. "Of course you won't be."

"But I'm a mundane," Simon said again.

"You're not a regular mundane, Simon," Julie told him. "You're an exceptional mundane. That means exceptions are going to be made."

"If anyone tried to put you in with the mundanes, I'd have words with them," Jon continued loftily. "Any friend of Jace Herondale's is, naturally, a friend of mine."

Julie patted Simon's hand. Simon stared at his hand as if it did not belong to him. He did not want to be put in the stream for losers, but he didn't feel comfortable about being assured he would not be either.

But he did think he remembered Isabelle, Jace, and Alec saying some sketchy things about mundanes, now and then. Isabelle, Jace, and Alec weren't so bad. It was just the way they were brought up: They didn't mean what it seemed like they meant. Simon was pretty sure.

Beatriz, who Simon had liked on sight, leaned in across Julie and said: "You've more than earned your place."

She smiled shyly at him. Simon could not help smiling back.

"So . . . I'm going to be in the dregs course?" George asked slowly. "I don't know anything about Shadowhunters and Downworlders and demons."

"Oh no," said Jon. "You're a Lovelace. You'll find it will all come very easily to you: It's in your blood."

George bit his lip. "If you say so."

"Most students in the Academy will be in the elite course," Beatriz said hastily. "Our new recruits are mostly like you, George. Shadowhunters are searching all over the world for lost and scattered people with Shadowhunter blood."

"So it's Shadowhunter blood that gets you into the elite stream," George clarified. "And not knowledge at all."

"It's perfectly fair," Julie argued. "Look at Simon. Of course he's in the elite stream. He has proven himself worthy."

"Simon had to save the world, and the rest of us get in because we have the right surname?" George asked lightly. He winked at Simon. "Hard luck on you, mate."

There was an uncomfortable silence around the table, but Simon suspected nobody felt as uncomfortable as he did.

"Sometimes those of Shadowhunter blood are put in the dregs stream, if they disgrace themselves," Julie said shortly. "Mainly, yes, it is reserved for mundanes. That's the way the Academy always worked in the past; it's how it will work in the future. We take some mundanes, those with the Sight or with remarkable athletic promise, into the Academy. It's a wonderful opportunity for them, a chance to become more than they could have ever dreamed. But they cannot keep up with real Shadowhunters. It would hardly be fair to expect them to. They can't all be Simon."

"Some of them simply will not have the aptitude," Jon remarked in a lofty tone. "Some of them won't live through Ascension."

Simon opened his mouth, but before he could ask any further questions he was interrupted by the sound of a lone clap.

"My dear students, my present and future Shadowhunters," said Dean Penhallow, rising from her chair. "Welcome, welcome! To Shadowhunter Academy. It is such a joy to see you all here at the auspicious official opening of the Academy, where we will be training a whole new generation to obey the Law laid down by the Angel. It is an honor to have been chosen to come here, and a joy for us to have you."

Simon looked around. There were about two hundred students here, he thought, uncomfortably crammed around rickety tables. He noticed again that several of them were very young, and grubby and desolate. Simon's heart went out to them, even as he wondered exactly what the running water situation at the Academy was.

Nobody looked as if they felt honored to be here. Simon found himself wondering again about the Shadowhunters' recruiting methods. Julie talked about them as if they were noble, searching for lost Shadowhunter families and offering mundanes amazing opportunities, but some of these kids looked about twelve. Simon had to wonder what your life must be like, if you were ready to leave it all and go fight demons at twelve.

"There have been a few unexpected losses from the staff, but I'm certain we will do splendidly with the excellent personnel we have remaining," Dean Penhallow continued. "May I introduce Delaney Scarsbury, your training master."

The man sitting next to her got up. He made Jon Cartwright's biceps look like grapes held up to a grapefruit, and he actually had an eye patch, like the angel in the stained-glass window.

Simon turned slowly and looked at George, who he hoped would feel him on this one. He mouthed: *No way.*

George, who obviously did feel him on this one, nodded and mouthed: *Pirate Shadowhunter!*

"I look forward to crushing you all into a pulp and molding that pulp into ferocious warriors," announced Scarsbury.

George and Simon exchanged another speaking glance.

A girl at the table behind Simon began to cry. She looked about thirteen.

"And this is Catarina Loss, a very estimable warlock who will be teaching you a great deal about—history and so on!"

"Yay," said Catarina Loss, with a desultory wave of her blue fingers, as if she'd decided to try clapping without bothering to lift both hands.

The dean soldiered on. "In past years at the Academy, because Shadowhunters come from all over the globe, every day of the week we would serve a delicious dish from a different nation. We certainly intend to keep up that tradition! But the kitchens are in a slight state of disrepair and for now we have—"

"Soup," said Catarina flatly. "Vats and vats of murky brown soup. Enjoy, kids."

Dean Penhallow continued her one-woman applause. "That's right. Enjoy, everyone. And again, welcome."

There really was nothing on offer but huge metal vats full of very questionable soup.

Simon lined up for food, and peered into the greasy depths of the dark liquid. "Are there alligators in there?"

"I won't make you any promises," said Catarina, inspecting her own bowl.

Simon was exhausted and still starving when he crawled into bed that night. He tried to cheer himself up thinking again about how lately a girl had been on the bed. A girl on his bed for the first time ever, Simon thought, but then memories came like a wisp of cloud over the moon, dimming all certainty. He remembered Clary sleeping in his bed, when they were so little their pajamas had trucks and ponies on them. He remembered kissing Clary, and how she had tasted like fresh lemonade. And he remembered Isabelle, her dark hair flowing over his pillow, her throat bared to him, her toenails scratching his leg, like a sexy vampire movie aside from the bit about the toenails. The other Simon had been not only a hero but a lady-killer. Well, more of a lady-killer than Simon was now.

Isabelle. Simon's mouth moved to form the shape of her name, pressing it into his pillow. He'd told himself he wasn't going to think about her, not until he was really getting somewhere in the Academy. Not until he was on his way to being better, being the person she wanted him to be.

He turned so he was flat on his back and stared up at the stone ceiling.

"Are you awake?" George whispered. "Me too. I keep worrying that the possum will come back. Where did it even come from, Simon? Where did it go?"

The trials of transforming himself into a Shadowhunter became apparent to Simon the very next day.

First, because Scarsbury was measuring them for their gear, which was a terrifying experience on its own. Second, because it involved hurtful personal comments about Simon's physique.

"You have such narrow shoulders," Scarsbury said thoughtfully. "Like a lady."

"I'm lithe," Simon informed him, with dignity.

He looked bitterly over at George, who was lounging on a bench waiting for Simon to finish being measured. George's gear was sleeveless; Julie had already come over to compliment him on how good the fit was and touch his arms.

"Tell you what," said Scarsbury. "I have some gear here meant for a girl—"

"Fine," said Simon. "I mean, terrible, but fine! Give it to me."

Scarsbury shoved the folded black material into Simon's arms. "It's meant for a tall girl," he said in a voice that was possibly intended to be comforting, and definitely too loud.

Everyone looked around and stared at them. Simon prevented himself from taking a sarcastic bow, and stomped off to put on his gear.

After they got gear, they were given weapons. Mundane students could not wear runes or use steles or most Shadowhunter weapons, so they were all given mundane weapons; it was meant to broaden the Shadowhunter kids' weapons knowledge. Simon feared his own weapons knowledge was as broad as spaghetti.

Dean Penhallow brought around giant boxes of terrifying knives, which seemed very strange in an academic setting, and asked them to select a dagger that suited them.

Simon picked a dagger completely at random, then sat at his desk waggling it about.

Jon nodded to it. "Nice."

"Yeah," Simon said, nodding back and gesturing with it. "That's what I thought. Nice. Very stabby."

He stabbed the dagger into the desk, where it got stuck and Simon had to pry it out of the wood.

Simon thought being trained could not possibly be as bad as being prepared to be trained, but as it turned out it was much worse.

The Academy days were half physical activity. It was like half the day was gym. Stabby, stabby gym.

When they were learning the basics of swordplay, Simon was paired up with the girl he'd noticed in the dining hall, the one who had cried when Scarsbury was introduced.

"She's from the dregs stream, but I understand you're not particularly experienced with swordplay," Scarsbury told him. "If she's not enough of a challenge, let me know."

Simon stared at Scarsbury instead of doing what he wanted to do, which was saying he could not believe an adult was calling someone "dregs" to their face.

He looked at the girl, her dark head bowed, her sword shining in her trembling hand.

"Hey. I'm Simon."

"I know who you are," she muttered.

Right, apparently Simon was a celebrity. If he had all his memories, maybe this would seem normal to him. Maybe he would know that he deserved it, instead of knowing he did not.

"What's your name?" he asked.

"Marisol," she told him reluctantly. She was not shaking anymore, he noted, now that Scarsbury had retreated.

"Don't worry," he said encouragingly. "I'll go easy on you."

"Hmm," said Marisol. She did not look like she was going to cry now; her eyes were narrowed.

Simon was not used to much younger kids, but they were both mundanes. Simon had an awkward fellow feeling. "You settling in okay? Do you miss your parents?"

"I don't have parents," Marisol said in a small, hard voice.

Simon stood stricken. He was such an idiot. He'd thought about it, why mundane kids might come to the Academy. Mundanes would have to choose to give up their parents, their families, their former lives. Unless, of course, they already had no parents and no families. He'd thought about that, but he'd forgotten, obsessing about his own memories and how he would fit in, thinking only about himself. He had a home to go back to, even though it wasn't perfect. He'd had a choice.

"What did the Shadowhunters tell you, when they came to recruit you?"

Marisol stared at him, her gaze clear and cold. "They told me," she said, "that I was going to fight."

She had been taking fencing classes since she could walk, as it turned out. She cut him off at the knees and left him literally in the dust, stumbling as a tiny, swordy whirlwind came at him across the practice grounds, and falling.

He also stabbed himself in the leg with his own sword as he fell, but that was a very minor injury.

"Went a little too easy on her," Jon said, passing by and helping Simon up. "The dregs won't learn if they're not taught, you know."

His voice was kind; his glance at Marisol was not.

"Leave her alone," Simon muttered, but he did not say that

Marisol had beaten him fairly. They all thought he was a hero.

Jon grinned at him and walked on. Marisol did not even look at him. Simon studied his leg, which stung.

It was not all stabbing. Some of it was regular stuff, like running, but as Simon tried to run and keep up with people a lot more athletic than he had ever been, he was constantly plagued by memories of how his lungs had never burned for lack of air, how his heart had never pounded from overexertion. He had been fast, once, faster than any of these Shadowhunter trainees, cold and predatory and powerful.

And dead, he reminded himself as he fell behind the others yet again. He didn't want to be dead.

Running was still a lot better than horseback riding. The Academy introduced them to horseback riding on their first Friday there. Simon thought it was supposed to be a treat.

Everyone else acted as if it was a treat. Only those of the elite stream were allowed to go riding, and at mealtimes they had been mocking the dregs for missing out. It seemed to cheer Julie and Jon up, in the face of the endless terrible soup.

Simon, precariously balanced on top of a huge beast that was both rolling its eyes and apparently trying to tap-dance, did not feel this was any sort of treat. The dregs had been sent off to learn elementary facts about Shadowhunting. They had most of their classes apart from the elite, and Jon assured Simon they were boring. Simon felt he could really do with being bored, right about now.

"Si," said George in an undertone. "Quick tip. Riding works better if you keep your eyes open."

"My previous riding experience is the carousel at Central Park," Simon snapped. "Forgive me for not being Mr. Darcy!"

George was, as several of the ladies were remarking, an excellent horseman. He barely had to move for the horse to respond to him, both of them moving smoothly together, sunlight rippling off his stupid curls. He looked right, made it all look easy and graceful, like a knight in the movies. Simon remembered reading books about magic horses that read their rider's every thought, books about horses born of the North Wind. It was all part of being a magical warrior, having a noble steed.

Simon's horse was defective, or possibly a genius that had worked out that Simon could not possibly control it. It went off for a wander in the woods, with Simon on its back alternately pleading, threatening, and offering bribes. If Simon's horse could read his every thought, then Simon's horse was a sadist.

As night drew in and the evening grew cold, the horse wandered back to its stall. Simon had no choice in the matter, but he did manage to tumble off the horse and stagger into the Academy, his fingers and knees gone entirely numb.

"Ah, there you are," said Scarsbury. "George Lovelace was beside himself. He wanted to assemble a search party for you."

Simon regretted his spiteful thoughts about George's horsemanship.

"Let me guess," said Simon. "Everyone else said, 'Nah, being left for dead builds character.'"

"I was not concerned you were going to be eaten by bears in the deep dark woods," said Scarsbury, who did not look as if he had ever been concerned about anything in his life, ever.

"Of course you weren't, that would be abs—"

"You had your dagger," added Scarsbury casually, and walked away, leaving Simon to call after him.

"My—my *bear-killing* dagger? Do you really think me killing bears with a dagger is a plausible scenario? What information do you have about bears in these woods? I think it's your responsibility as an educator to tell me if there are bears in the woods."

"See you at javelin practice bright and early, Lewis," said Scarsbury, and marched on without looking back.

"Are there bears in the woods?" Simon repeated to himself. "It's a simple question. Why are Shadowhunters so bad at simple questions?"

The days passed in a blur of horrible violent activity. If it wasn't javelin practice, Simon was getting thrown around a room (George was very apologetic later, but that did not help). If it wasn't dagger work, it was more swordplay and humiliating defeat before the blades of tiny, evil trainee Shadowhunters. If it wasn't swordplay, it was the obstacle course, and Simon refused to speak of the obstacle course. Julie and Jon were growing noticeably cool at mealtimes, and a few comments about mundies were passed.

At last Simon staggered wearily to the next exercise in futility and sharp objects, and Scarsbury placed a bow in his hands.

"I want everyone to try to hit the targets," said Scarsbury. "And, Lewis, I want you to try not to hit any of the other trainees."

Simon felt the weight of the bow in his hands. It had a nice balance, he thought, easy to lift and manipulate. He nocked the arrow, and felt the tautness of the string, ready to release, primed to let it fly along the path Simon wanted.

He drew his arm back, and it was that easy: bull's-eye. He fired once more, and then again, arrows flying to find their targets, and his arms burned and his heart pounded with something like joy. He was glad to be able to feel his muscles working and his heart thumping. He was so glad to be alive again, and able to feel every moment of this.

Simon lowered his bow to find everybody staring at him.

"Can you do that again?" asked Scarsbury.

He'd learned to shoot arrows in summer camp, but standing here holding a bow, he remembered something else. He remembered breathing, his heart beating, Shadowhunters watching him. He'd still been human then, a mundane they all despised, but he'd killed a demon. He remembered: He'd seen something had to be done, and he'd done it.

A guy not so different from who he was now.

Simon felt a smile spread across his face, hurting his cheeks. "Yeah. I think I can."

Julie and Jon were both much more friendly over dinner than they had been for the last few days. Simon told them about killing the demon, what he remembered, and Jon offered to teach him some swordplay tricks.

"I would really love to hear more about your adventures," said Julie. "Whatever you can remember. Especially if they involve Jace Herondale. Do you know how he got that sexy scar on his throat?"

"Ah," said Simon. "Actually . . . yes. Actually . . . that was me."

Everybody stared at him.

"I might have bitten him. A tiny bit. It was more like a nibble, really."

"Was he delicious?" asked Julie, after a thoughtful pause. "He *looks* like he would be delicious."

"Um," said Simon. "He's not a juice box."

Beatriz nodded earnestly. Both the girls seemed very interested in this discussion. Too interested. Their eyes were glazed.

"Did you maybe climb on top of him slowly and then lower your head to his tender, pulsing throat?" Beatriz said. "Could you feel the heat radiating off his body and into yours?"

"Did you lick his throat before you bit him?" Julie asked. "Oh, and did you get a chance to feel his biceps?" She shrugged. "I'm just curious about, you know, vampire techniques."

"I imagine Simon was both gentle and commanding during his special moment with Jace," said Beatriz dreamily. "I mean, it was special, wasn't it?"

"No!" said Simon. "I can't stress that enough. I've bitten several Shadowhunters. I bit Isabelle Lightwood and Alec Lightwood; biting Jace was not a tender and unique moment!"

"You bit Isabelle and Alec Lightwood?!" asked Julie, who was starting to sound freaked-out. "What did the Lightwoods ever do to you?"

"Wow," said George. "I imagined the demon realms were fearsome and terrifying, but seems like it was pretty much nonstop nom nom nom."

"That is not how it was!" Simon said.

"Can we stop talking about this?" Jon demanded, his voice sharp. "I'm sure you all did what you had to do, but the idea of Shadowhunters being prey for a Downworlder is disgusting."

Simon did not love the way Jon said "Downworlder," as if the words "Downworlder" and "disgusting" were more or less the same thing. But maybe it was natural for Jon to be disturbed. Simon could remember being disturbed about it himself. Simon hadn't wanted to make his friends into his prey either.

Today had gone pretty well. Simon didn't want to ruin it. He decided he was in a good enough mood to let it go.

Simon felt better about the Academy until that night, when he woke from a doze to a deluge of memory.

The memories hit like that sometimes, not in sharp tiny jabs but in an insistent and terrible cascade. He had thought of his former roommate before. He'd known he'd had a friend, a roommate, named Jordan, and that Jordan had been killed. But he hadn't recalled the *feelings* of it—the way Jordan had taken him in when his mother had barred her door, talking about Maia with Jordan, hearing Clary laugh that Jordan was cute, talking to Jordan, patient and kind and always seeing Simon as more than a job, more than a vampire. He remembered seeing Jordan and Jace snarl at each other and then play video games like idiots, and Jordan finding him sleeping in a garage, and Jordan looking at Maia with such regret.

And he remembered holding Jordan's Praetor Lupus pendant in his hands, in Idris, after Jordan was dead. Simon had held that pendant again since then, once he had regained some of his memories, feeling the weight of it and wondering what the Latin motto meant.

He had known Jordan was his roommate, and known he was one of the many casualties of the war.

He had never truly felt the weight of it, until now.

The sheer weight of memory made him feel as if stones were being piled on his chest, crushing him. Simon couldn't breathe. He erupted from his sheets, swinging his legs over the side of the bed, his feet hitting the stone floor with a shock of cold.

"Wuzz—wuzzit?" mumbled George. "Did the possum come back?"

"Jordan's dead," Simon said bleakly, and put his face in his hands.

There was a silence.

George did not ask him who Jordan had been, or why he suddenly cared. Simon would not have known how to explain the tangle of grief and guilt in his chest: how he hated himself for forgetting Jordan, even though he could not have helped it, how this was like finding out Jordan was dead for the first time and like having a scarred-over wound reopened, both at once. There was a bitter taste in Simon's mouth, like old, old blood.

George reached out and put a hand on Simon's shoulder. He kept it there, grip firm, hand warm and steady, something to anchor Simon in the cold, dark night of memory.

"I'm sorry," he whispered. Simon was sorry too.

At dinner the next day, it was soup again. It had been soup for every meal for many days now. Simon did not remember a life before soup, and he despaired of ever achieving a life after soup. Simon wondered if the Shadowhunters had runes to protect against scurvy.

Their usual group was clustered around their usual table, chatting, when Jon said: "I wish we were being taught about demons by someone with less of an agenda, if you know what I mean."

"Uh," said Simon, who mostly sat through their classes on demons through the ages in deep relief that he was not being asked to move. "Don't we all have the same . . . demon-hunting . . . agenda?"

"You know what I mean," Jon said. "We've got to be taught

about the past crimes of warlocks as well. We have to fight the Downworlders, too. It's naive to pretend they're all tame."

"The Downworlders," Simon repeated. The soup turned to ashes in his mouth, which was actually an improvement. "Like vampires?"

"No!" said Julie hastily. "Vampires are great. They have, you know, class. Compared to the other Downworlders. But if you're talking about creatures like werewolves, Simon, you must see they're not exactly our kind of people. If you can call them people at all."

She said "werewolves" and Simon could not help but think of Jordan, flinching as if he'd been struck and unable to keep his mouth shut a moment longer.

Simon pushed his bowl of soup away and shoved his chair back.

"Don't tell me about what I must, Julie," he said coldly. "I must inform you there are werewolves worth a hundred of your and Jon's Shadowhunter asses. I must say that I am sick to the teeth of you insulting mundanes and telling me I'm your special pet exception, as if I want to be the pet of people who bully kids younger and weaker than they are. And I must tell you, you'd better hope this Academy works out and mundanes like me Ascend, because from all I can see of you, the next generation of Shadowhunters is going to be nothing without us."

He looked toward George, the way he looked to George to share jokes in class and over meals, to see if George agreed with him at all.

George was staring at his plate.

"Come on, man," he muttered. "Don't—don't do this.

They'll make you move rooms. Just sit down, and everybody can apologize, and we can go on as we were."

Simon took a deep breath, absorbed the disappointment, and said: "I don't want things to go on as they were. I want things to change."

He turned away from the table, from all of them, marched over to where the dean and Scarsbury were sitting, and announced at the top of his voice: "Dean Penhallow, I want to be placed in the stream for mundanes."

"What?" Scarsbury exclaimed. "The dregs?"

The dean dropped her spoon into her soup with a noisy splash. "The mundane course, Mr. Scarsbury, if you please! Do not refer to our students in that manner. I'm glad you came to me with this, Simon," she said after a moment of hesitation. "I understand you may be having difficulties with the course, given your mundane nature, but—"

"It's not that I'm having difficulty," said Simon. "It's that I'd rather not associate with the elite Shadowhunter families. I just don't think they're my kind of people."

His voice rang out against the stone ceiling. There were a lot of young kids staring at him. One was little Marisol, regarding him with a startled, thoughtful expression. Nobody said anything. They just looked.

"Okay, I've said all I had to say, I'm feeling bashful, and I'm gonna go now," Simon said, and fled the room.

He almost walked right into Catarina Loss, who had been watching from the doorway.

"Sorry," he mumbled.

"Don't be," Catarina said. "In fact, I'm going to come with you. I'll help you pack."

"What?" Simon asked, hurrying after her. "I actually have to move?"

"Yeah, they put the dregs in the underground level," Catarina said.

"They put some kids in the dungeons, and nobody has ever pointed out that this is a disgusting system before now?"

"Is it?" asked Catarina. "Do tell me more about the Shadowhunters, and their occasional tendency to be unfair. I will find it fascinating and surprising. Their excuse is that the lower levels are easier to defend, for the kids who cannot fight as well as their fellow students."

She strode into Simon's room and looked around for his things.

"I actually haven't unpacked very much," Simon said. "I was afraid of the possum in the wardrobe."

"The what?"

"George and I found it very mysterious too," Simon told her earnestly, picking up his bag and stuffing in the few things he had left lying out. He wouldn't want to forget his lady gear.

"Well," Catarina said. "Whatever about possums. The point I want to make is . . . I may have gotten you wrong, Simon."

Simon blinked. "Oh?"

Catarina smiled at him. It was astonishing, like a blue sunrise. "I was not looking forward to coming to teach here. Shadowhunters and Downworlders do not get along, and I try to keep myself more separated from the Nephilim even than most others of my kind. But I had a dear friend called Ragnor Fell, who used to live in Idris and taught in the Academy for decades before it was closed. He never had the greatest opinion of Shadowhunters, but he was fond of this place. I—lost him recently, and I knew this place could not operate without teachers. I wanted to do something in memory of him, even though I hated the idea of teaching a pack of arrogant Nephilim brats. But I loved my friend more than I hate Shadowhunters."

Simon nodded. He thought of his remembrance of Jordan, thought of how it hurt to even look at Isabelle and Clary. Without memory, they were lost. And nobody wanted someone they loved to be lost.

"So I may have been a little cranky about coming," Catarina admitted. "I may have been a little cranky about you, because— from all I know, you didn't think much of being a vampire. And now you're cured, what a miracle, and the Shadowhunters are so quick to pull you into the fold. You truly get to be one of them, what you always wanted. You had the stain of being one of us wiped away."

"I didn't . . . ," Simon said, and swallowed. "I can't remember it all. So it's like defending the actions of someone else sometimes."

"Must be frustrating."

Simon laughed. "You have no idea. I don't—I didn't want to be a vampire, I don't think. I wouldn't want to be made one again. Being stuck at age sixteen when all my friends and my family would've grown up without me; having the urge to—to hurt people? I didn't want any of that. But—look, I don't remember much, but I remember enough. I remember I was a person back then, just as much as I am now. Becoming a Shadowhunter won't change that, if I ever do become a Shadowhunter. I've forgotten enough. I will not forget that."

He lifted his bag onto his shoulder, and gestured for Catarina to lead the way to his new room. She did, descending down stone steps Simon had figured were to the basement. He had not figured they kept kids in the basement.

It was dark on the stairs. Simon put a hand to the wall to steady himself, and then snatched it back.

"Oh, disgusting!"

"Yes, most of the subterranean surfaces are coated in black slime," said Catarina, in a matter-of-fact tone. "Watch yourself."

"Thank you. Thanks for that warning."

"You're welcome," said Catarina, a hint of a laugh in her voice. For the first time, it occurred to Simon that Catarina might actually be nice. "You said—if you ever do become a Shadowhunter. Are you thinking about leaving?"

"Now that I've touched the slime, I am," Simon muttered. "No. I don't know what I want, except that I don't want to give up yet."

He almost reconsidered when Catarina led him to his room. It was much darker than the last room, though laid out in the same way. The wooden bedposts of the two narrow beds looked decayed, and in the corners of the room the black slime had grown almost viscous, turning into tiny black slime waterfalls.

"I don't remember hell all that well," Simon said. "But I think I recall it was nicer than this."

Catarina laughed, then shocked Simon by leaning in and giving him a peck on the cheek. "Good luck, Daylighter," she told him, laughing at his expression. "And whatever you do, don't use the bathrooms on this floor. Not on any floor, obviously, but especially on this one!"

Simon did not ask her to explain, because he was terrified. He sat down on his new bed, and then stood hastily back up at the resulting long creak and cloud of dust. Hey, at least this time he didn't have a roommate—he was king of this claustrophobic, slimy domain. He set his mind to unpacking. The wardrobe in this room was actually clean and empty, which was a definite improvement. Simon might go live in the wardrobe with his funny T-shirts.

He was long finished unpacking by the time George sauntered in, dragging his suitcase behind him and bearing his broken racket on his shoulder like a sword. "Hey, man."

"Hey," Simon said cautiously. "Er, what—what are you doing here?"

George dumped his suitcase and his racket on the slimy floor, and threw himself down on the bed. He stretched luxuriously, ignoring the ominous creak of the bed beneath him.

"The thing is, the advanced course is actually pretty hard," George said, as Simon started to smile. "And you may have heard: Lovelaces are quitters."

Simon was even more relieved to have George the next day, so they could sit together rather than at one of the tables of thirteen-year-old mundanes, who were all giving them the side-eye when they were not whispering brokenly about their phones.

The day brightened further when Beatriz plopped down at their new table as well.

"I'm not going to drop out of advanced training to follow you around like Curlytop here," Beatriz announced, "but we can still be friends, right?"

She pulled George's hair affectionately.

"Be careful," George said in a tired, humble voice. "I did not sleep in our small, slimy room. There is, I believe, a creature living in our walls. I hear it. Scuttling. I have to admit, I may not have made the brightest decision in following Simon. It's possible I'm not that bright. It's possible that looks are all I have."

"Actually . . . even though I'm not willing to follow you into boring classes and the endless disrespect of my classmates . . . I think it was a very cool thing you did, Simon," said Beatriz.

She smiled, teeth flashing white against her brown skin, and her smile was warm and admiring—about the nicest thing Simon had seen all day.

"You're right, our morals are sound even though our walls are infested. And we'll still have some interesting classes, Si," George said. "Plus, don't worry, we still get sent on missions to fight demons and rogue Downworlders."

Simon choked on his soup. "I was not worrying about that. Are any of our teachers at all worried that sending out people with no superpowers to fight demons might prove just a teeny bit, not to put too fine a point on it, fatal?"

"They have to face trials of courage before they must face Ascension," said Beatriz. "Better for them to drop out because they are scared, or even because a demon ate their leg, than to have them try to Ascend without being suitable, and die in the attempt."

"That's a cool, cheerful, and normal thing to say," Simon said. "Shadowhunters are great at saying normal things."

"Well, I'm looking forward to the missions," said George. "And tomorrow a Shadowhunter is coming in to give a guest lecture on the lesser-utilized weapons. I hope there'll be a practical demonstration."

"Not in a classroom," said Beatriz. "Think of what one heavy-duty crossbow could do to the walls."

That was all the warning Simon got before he clattered happily into class the next day, George on his heels, and found Dean Penhallow already there, talking with nervous good cheer. The classroom was very full—both the regular stream and the mundane stream were in attendance.

"—despite her tender years, a Shadowhunter of some renown and noted expertise with less-used weapons such as the whip. May I welcome to Shadowhunter Academy our first guest lecturer: Isabelle Lightwood!"

Isabelle turned, sleek black hair flaring around her shoulders and black skirt flaring around her pale legs. She was wearing glittery plum lipstick, so dark it looked almost black. Her eyes did look black, but another small knife of memory pierced Simon, of course at the worst time possible: He remembered the colors of her eyes from close up, very dark brown, like brown velvet, so close to black as to make no difference, but with paler rings of color. . . .

He stumbled over to his desk, and folded into his chair with a thump.

When the dean left, Isabelle turned and regarded her class with absolute contempt.

"I am not actually here to instruct any of you idiots," she told them, walking up and down the rows of desks. "If you want to use a whip, train with one, and if you lose an ear, don't be a big whiny baby."

Several of the boys nodded, as if hypnotized. Almost all the boys were watching Isabelle as if they were a nest of snakes intent on being charmed. Some of the girls were watching her that way too.

"I am here," Isabelle announced, finishing her prowl of the perimeter and turning to face them all again with snapping eyes, "to determine my relationship."

Simon goggled. She couldn't be talking about him. Could she?

"Do you see that man?" Isabelle asked, pointing at Simon. Apparently she *was* talking about him. "That's Simon Lewis, and he is *my boyfriend.* So if any of you think about trying to hurt him because he's a mundie or—may the Angel have mercy on your soul—pursuing him romantically, I will come after you, I will hunt you down, and I will crush you to powder."

"We're just bros," said George hastily.

Beatriz edged her desk away from Simon's.

Isabelle lowered her hand. The flush of excitement was receding from her face as well, as though she had come to say what she had said, and now that she was out of adrenaline she was actually processing what had come out of her mouth.

"I am going to go now," Isabelle announced. "Thank you for your attention. Class dismissed."

She turned and walked out of the room.

"I have to—" Simon began, rising from his desk on legs that felt a little unsteady. "I have to go."

"Yeah, you do," George said.

Simon went out the door, and ran down the stone corridors of the Academy. He knew Isabelle was fast, so he ran, faster than he'd ever run on the training grounds, and he caught up to her in the hall. She stopped in the dim light of the stained-glass window as he called her name.

"Isabelle!"

She stood waiting for him. Her lips parted and gleamed, like plums under a winter frost, ready to be tasted. Simon could see himself running up to her, catching her in his arms, and kissing her mouth, knowing what it had taken for her to do that—his brave, brilliant Isabelle—and carried away in a whirl of love and joy, but he saw it as if through a pane of glass, as if looking into another dimension, one he could see but not quite touch.

Simon felt a hot pang of grief through his whole body, not just through his chest, as if he had been struck by lightning. But he had to say it.

"I'm not your boyfriend, Isabelle," he called out.

She went white. Simon was horrified by how badly his words had come out.

"I mean, I can't be your boyfriend, Isabelle," he said. "I'm not him—that guy who was your boyfriend. That guy you want."

He almost said: *I wish I could be.* He had wished he could be. That was why he had come to the Academy, to learn how to be that guy they all wanted back. He'd wanted to be that way, be an awesome hero like in a game or a movie. He'd been so sure, at first, that was what he wanted.

Except wishing he could be that guy was like wishing to obliterate the guy he was now: the normal, happy guy in a band, who could still love his mother, who did not wake up in the coldest, darkest hour of the night weeping for dead friends.

And he did not know if he could be that guy she wanted, whether he wished it or not.

"You remember everything, and I—I don't remember enough," Simon went on. "I hurt you when I don't mean to, and I thought I could come to the Academy and come back better, but it's not looking good. The whole game has changed. My skill level has decreased and the difficulty level has been jacked up to impossible—"

"Simon," Isabelle interrupted, "you're talking like a nerd."

She said it almost fondly, but it freaked Simon out more. "And I don't know how to be smooth, sexy vampire Simon for you, either!"

Isabelle's perfect mouth curved, like a dark half-moon in her pale face. "You were never that smooth, Simon."

"Oh," said Simon. "Oh, thank God. I know you've had a lot of boyfriends. I remember there was a faerie, and"—another flash of memory, this time most unwelcome—"a . . . Lord Montgomery? You dated a member of the nobility? How am I ever going to compete with that?"

Isabelle still looked fond, but it was diluted with a good deal of impatience. "You're Lord Montgomery, Simon!"

"I don't understand," said Simon. "When you're made a vampire, are you also given a title?"

Maybe that made sense. Vampires were aristocratic.

Isabelle put her fingers up to touch her brow. It was a gesture that seemed like disdainful weariness, like Isabelle was tired of all this, but Simon saw the way her eyes closed, as if she could not look at him when she spoke. "It was just a joke between you and me, Simon."

Simon was tired of all this: of knowing pieces of her so well and others not at all, of knowing he was not what she wanted.

"No," he said. "It was a joke between you and him."

"You are him, Simon!"

"I'm not," Simon told her. "I don't—I don't know how to be, that's what I've been realizing all this time. I thought I could learn to be him, but since I got to the Academy I learned that I can't. I can't experience everything we did over again. I'm never going to be the guy who did all that. I'm going to do different things. I'm going to be a different guy."

"Once you Ascend, you'll get all your memories back!" Isabelle shouted at him.

"If I Ascend, it will be in two years. I'm not going to be the same guy in two years, even if I do get all the memories back, because there will be so many other memories. You're not going to be the same girl. I know you believed in me, Isabelle, I know you believed because you—you cared about him. That means more than I can tell you. But, Isabelle, Isabelle, it isn't fair of me to take advantage of your belief. It isn't fair to keep you waiting for him, when he isn't ever coming back."

Isabelle had her arms crossed, fingers curled into the dark plum velvet of her own jacket as if she was offering herself comfort. "None of this is fair. It isn't fair that part of your life was ripped from you. It's not fair that you were ripped away from me. I'm so angry, Simon."

Simon took a step toward her and took one of her hands, uncurling her fingers from her jacket. He did not take her in his arms but he stood a little distance away from her, their hands linked across the distance. Her trembling mouth sparkled, and so did her eyelashes. He did not know if this was indomitable Isabelle crying, or whether it was sparkly mascara. All he knew was that she shone, like a constellation in the shape of a girl.

"Isabelle," he said. "Isabelle."

She was so much herself, and he had scarcely any idea who he was.

"Do you know why you're here?" she demanded.

He just looked at her. There were so many things that question could mean, and so many ways to answer.

"I mean at the Academy," she said. "Do you know why you want to be a Shadowhunter?"

He hesitated. "I wanted to be that guy again," he said. "That hero that you all remember . . . and this seems like a training school for heroes."

"It's not," Isabelle said flatly. "It's a training school for Shadowhunters. And yeah, I think that's a pretty cool thing, and yeah, I think protecting the world is pretty heroic. But there are cowardly Shadowhunters and evil Shadowhunters and hopeless Shadowhunters. If you're going to get through the Academy, you have to figure out why *you* want to be a *Shadowhunter* and what that means to *you*, Simon. Not just why you want to be special."

He winced, but it was true. "You're right. I don't know. I know that I want to be here. I know I need to be here. Believe me, if you'd seen the bathrooms, you'd know I didn't make this decision lightly."

She gave him a withering look.

"But," he said, "I don't know why. I don't know myself well enough yet. I know what I said to you, at first, and I know what you hoped. That I could turn back into who I was before. I was really wrong and I am really sorry."

"*Sorry?*" Isabelle demanded. "Do you know what a big deal it was for me to come here, to make a fool of myself in front of all these people? Do you know—of course you don't. You don't want me to believe in you? You don't want me to choose you?"

Isabelle pulled her hands away from him, turned her face away as she had in the garden of the Institute that was her home. This time Simon knew it was absolutely his fault.

She was already leaving as she said:

"Have it your way, Simon Lewis. I won't."

Simon was so depressed after Isabelle had gone—after he had driven her away—that he didn't think he'd ever move off his cot bed again. He lay there, listening to George chatter and scrub the walls. He'd removed an impressive amount of the slime.

Simon retreated to where he believed nobody would ever find him. He went and sat in the bathroom. The stone flags were cracked in the bathrooms; there was something dark in one of the toilets. Simon hoped it was just a result of people throwing away the soup.

He had half an hour of peace in the bathroom, alone with the horrible toilets, until George poked his head around the door.

"Hey, buddy," said George. "Do not use these bathrooms. I cannot stress that enough."

"I'm not going to use the bathroom," Simon said drearily. "I'm a mess, but I'm not an idiot. I just wanted to be alone and think depressing thoughts. You want to know a secret?"

George was silent for a moment. "If you want to tell me. You don't have to. We all have secrets."

"I chased away the most amazing girl I have ever met, because I'm too much of a loser to manage being myself. That's my secret: I want to be a hero, but I'm not one. Everybody thinks I'm some amazing warrior who summoned angels and rescued Shadowhunters and saved the world, but it's a joke. I can't even remember what I did. I can't imagine how I did it. I'm no one special, and no one's going to be fooled for long, and I don't even know what I'm doing here. So. You have a secret that can beat that?"

There was a low gurgle from one of the toilets. Simon did not even look toward it. He was not interested in investigating that sound.

"I'm not a Shadowhunter at all," George said in a rush.

Sitting on a bathroom floor was not an ideal way to receive monumental revelations. Simon frowned. "You're not a Lovelace?"

"No, I'm a Lovelace." George's normally lighthearted voice was stern. "But I'm not a Shadowhunter. I'm adopted. The Shadowhunters who came to recruit me didn't even think of that—of people with Shadowhunter blood wanting mundane children, giving them Shadowhunter names and thinking of them as their own. I was always planning to tell the truth, but I figured it would be easier when I got here—less trouble to decide to let me stay than to work out whether they wanted to bring me. And then I met the others, and I started the course, and I figured out I could keep up with them pretty easily. I saw what they thought of mundanes. I figured it wouldn't do any harm to keep the secret and stay in the elite class and be like the rest of the guys, just for a while."

George shoved his hands in his pockets, and stared at the floor.

"But I'd met you, too, and you didn't have any special powers, and you'd already done more than all the rest of them put together. You do things now, like transfer to the mundane class when you didn't have to, and that made me man up and tell the dean I was a mundie and get transferred too. You did that.

The way you are now, okay? So stop talking about what a loser you are, because I wouldn't follow a loser into a slime-covered bedroom or a slime-covered bathroom, and I've followed you into both." George paused and said aggressively: "And I would really like to change the phrasing of that last sentence, because it sounded so bad, but I'm not sure how."

"I'll take it in the spirit it was meant," said Simon. "And I—I'm really glad you told me. I was hoping for a cool mundie roommate from the start."

"Wanna know another secret?" George asked.

Simon was slightly terrified of another revelation, and worried George was a secret agent, but he nodded anyway.

"Everybody in this academy, Shadowhunters and mundanes, people with the Sight and without it, every one of them is looking to be a hero. We are all hoping for it, and trying for it, and soon we will be bleeding for it. You're just like the rest of us, Si. Except there's one thing about you that's different: We all want to be heroes, but you know you can be one. You know in another life, in an alternate universe, however you want to think of it, you were a hero. You can be one again. Maybe not the same hero, but you have it in you to make the right choices, to make the big sacrifices. That's a lot of pressure. But it's a lot more hope than any of the rest of us have. Think about it that way, Simon Lewis, and I think you're pretty lucky."

Simon had not thought about it that way. He'd just kept thinking that a switch was going to be flipped, and he was going to be special again. But Isabelle was right: This could not just be about being special. He remembered seeing the Academy for the first time, how glamorous and impressive it had looked from a distance, and how different it had looked close up. He was starting to think the process of becoming a Shadowhunter was the same way. He was starting to believe it would all be cutting himself with a sword and having his horse run away with him, eating terrible soup and scraping slime off the walls, and figuring out slowly and awkwardly who he really wanted to be, this time around.

George leaned against the bathroom wall, which was an obviously rash and dangerous move, and grinned at him. Seeing that grin, seeing George refuse to be serious for more than a second, reminded Simon of something else about his first day at the Academy. It reminded him of hope.

"Speaking of luck, Isabelle Lightwood is a total babe. Actually, she's better than a babe: She's a hero. She came all the way here to tell the world you were hers. You're telling me she doesn't know another hero when she sees one? You're going to figure out what you're doing here. Isabelle Lightwood believes in you, and for what it's worth, I do too."

Simon stared up at George.

"It's worth a lot," he said finally. "Thanks for saying all that."

"You're welcome. Now please get up off the floor," George implored. "It is so nasty."

Simon did get up off the floor. He left the bathroom, George ahead of him, and both of them almost plowed into Catarina Loss, who was dragging a huge covered tureen over the flagstones with a scraping sound.

"Ms. Loss . . . ," said Simon. "Can I ask you—what you're doing?"

"Dean Penhallow has decided that she is not going to order fresh food supplies until all this delicious, nutritious soup has been consumed. So I am going to bury this soup in the woods," announced Catarina Loss. "Grab the other handle."

"Huh. Okay, good plan," said Simon, grabbing the other handle of the tureen and falling in with Catarina. George followed them as they went, unsteadily balancing the soup tureen between them. As they walked through the drafty, echoing corridors of the Academy, Simon added: "I just have one quick question about the woods. And bears."

The Lost Herondale

By Cassandra Clare and Robin Wasserman

Simon was about to argue, again, when a shining whip
lashed out of the shadows and wrapped around the girl's neck.
It yanked her off her feet and she landed hard, head
cracking against the cement floor.

—The Lost Herondale

There was a time, not long ago, when Simon Lewis had been convinced that all gym teachers were actually demons escaped from some hell dimension, nourishing themselves on the agonies of uncoordinated youth.

Little did he know he'd been almost right.

Not that Shadowhunter Academy had *gym* class, not exactly. And his physical trainer, Delaney Scarsbury, wasn't so much a demon as a Shadowhunter who probably thought lopping the heads off a few multiheaded hellbeasts comprised an ideal Saturday night—but as far as Simon was concerned, these were technicalities.

"Lewis!" Scarsbury shouted, looming over Simon, who lay flat on the ground, trying to will himself to do another push-up. "What are you waiting for, an engraved invitation?"

Scarsbury's legs were as thick as tree trunks, and his biceps were no less depressingly huge. This, at least, was one difference between the Shadowhunter and Simon's mundane gym teachers, most of whom could barely have bench-pressed a bag of potato chips. Also, none of Simon's gym teachers had worn an eye patch or carried a sword carved with runes and blessed by angels.

But in all the ways that counted, Scarsbury was exactly the same.

"Everyone get a look at Lewis!" he called to the rest of the class, as Simon levered himself into a shaky plank position, willing himself not to do a belly flop into the dirt. Again. "Our hero here might just defeat his evil spaghetti arms after all."

Gratifyingly, only one person laughed. Simon recognized the distinctive snicker of Jon Cartwright, eldest son of a distinguished Shadowhunter family (as he'd be the first to tell you). Jon believed he was born for greatness and seemed especially irritated that Simon—a hapless mundane—had managed to get there first. Even if he could no longer remember doing it. Jon, of course, was the one who'd started calling Simon "our hero." And like all evil gym teachers before him, Scarsbury had been only too happy to follow the popular kid's lead.

Shadowhunter Academy had two tracks, one for the Shadowhunter kids who'd grown up in this world and whose blood destined them for demon-fighting, and one for the mundanes, clueless, lacking in genetic destiny, and scrambling to catch up. They spent most of the day in separate classes, the mundanes studying rudimentary martial arts and memorizing the finer points of the Nephilim Covenant, the Shadowhunters focusing on more advanced skills: juggling throwing stars and studying Chthonian and Marking themselves up with runes of obnoxious superiority and who knew what else. (Simon was still hoping that somewhere in the Shadowhunter manual was the secret of the Vulcan death grip. After all, as his instructors kept reminding them: All the stories are true.) But the two tracks began every day together: Every student, no matter how inexperienced or advanced, was expected to report to the training field at sunrise for a grueling hour of calisthenics. *Divided we stand*, Simon thought, his stubborn biceps refusing to bulge. *United we do push-ups.*

When he'd told his mother he wanted to go to military school so he could toughen up, she'd given him a strange look. (Not as strange as if he'd said he wanted to go to demon-fighting school so he could drink from the Mortal Cup, Ascend to the ranks of Shadowhunter, and just maybe get back the memories that had been stolen from him in a nearby hell dimension, but close.) The look said: *My son, Simon Lewis, wants to sign up for a life where you have to do a hundred push-ups before breakfast?*

He knew this, because he could read her pretty well—but also because once she'd regained the ability to speak, she'd said, "My son, Simon Lewis, wants to sign up for a life where you have to do a hundred push-ups before breakfast?" Then she'd asked him teasingly if he was possessed by some evil creature, and he'd pretended to laugh, trying for once to ignore the tendrils of memory from that other life, his *real* life. The one where he'd been turned into a vampire and his mother had called him a monster and barricaded him from the house. Sometimes, Simon thought he would do anything to get back the memories that had been taken from him—but there were moments when he wondered whether some things were better left forgotten.

Scarsbury, more demanding than any drill sergeant, made his young charges do *two hundred* push-ups every morning . . . but he did, at least, let them eat breakfast first.

After the push-ups came the laps. After the laps came the lunges. And after the lunges—

"After you, hero," Jon sneered, offering Simon first shot at the climbing wall. "Maybe if we give you a head start, we won't have to wait around so long for you to catch up."

Simon was too exhausted for a snarky comeback. And definitely too exhausted to claw his way up the climbing wall, one impossibly distant handhold at a time. He made it up a few feet, at least, then paused to give his shrieking muscles a rest. One by one, the other students scrambled up past him, none of them seeming even slightly out of breath.

"Be a hero, Simon," Simon muttered bitterly, remembering the life Magnus Bane had dangled before him in their first meeting—or at least, the first one Simon could remember. "Have an adventure, Simon. How about, turn your life into one long agonizing gym class, Simon."

"Dude, you're talking to yourself again." George Lovelace, Simon's roommate and only real friend at the Academy, hoisted himself up beside Simon. "You losing your grip?"

"I'm talking to myself, not little green men," Simon clarified. "Still sane, last I checked."

"No, I mean"—George nodded toward Simon's sweaty fingers, which had gone pale with the effort of holding his weight—"your grip."

"Oh. Yeah. I'm peachy," Simon said. "Just giving you guys a head start. I figure in battle conditions, it's always the red shirts who go in first, you know?"

George's brow furrowed. "Red shirts? But our gear is black."

"No, *red shirts*. Cannon fodder. *Star Trek*? Any of this ringing a . . ." Simon sighed at the blank look on George's face. George had grown up in an isolated rural pocket of Scotland, but it wasn't like he'd lived without Internet and cable TV. The problem, as far as Simon could tell, was that the Lovelaces watched nothing but soccer and used their Wi-Fi almost exclusively to monitor Dundee United stats and occasionally to buy sheep feed in bulk. "Forget it. I'm fine. See you at the top."

George shrugged and returned to his climb. Simon watched his roommate—a tan, muscled Abercrombie-model type—swing himself up the plastic rock handholds as effortlessly as Spider-Man. It was ridiculous: George wasn't even a Shadowhunter, not by blood. He'd been adopted by a Shadowhunting family, which made him just as much a mundane as Simon. Except that, like most of the other mundanes—and very *un*like Simon—he was a near-perfect specimen of humanity. Repulsively athletic, coordinated, strong and swift, and as close to a Shadowhunter as you could get without the blood of the angels running through your veins. In other words: a jock.

Life at Shadowhunter Academy was lacking in a lot of things Simon had once believed he couldn't survive without: computers, music, comic books, indoor plumbing. Over the past couple of months, he'd gotten mostly used to doing without, but there was one glaring absence he still couldn't wrap his head around.

Shadowhunter Academy had no nerds.

Simon's mother had once told him that the thing she loved most about being Jewish was that you could step into a synagogue anywhere on earth and feel like you'd come home. India, Brazil, New Zealand, even Mars—if you could rely on *Shalom,*

Spacemen!, the homemade comic book that had been the highlight of Simon's third-grade Hebrew school experience. Jews everywhere prayed with the same language, the same melodies, the same words. Simon's mother had told her son that as long as he could always find people who spoke the language of his soul, he would never be alone.

And she'd turned out to be right. As long as Simon could find people who spoke his language—the language of Dungeons & Dragons and World of Warcraft, the language of *Star Trek* and manga and indie rockers with songs like "Han Shot First" and "What the Frak"—he felt like he was among friends.

These Shadowhunters in training, on the other hand? Most of them probably thought manga was some kind of demonic athlete's foot. Simon was doing his best to educate them to the finer things in life, but guys like George Lovelace had about as much aptitude for twelve-sided dice as Simon did for . . . well, anything more physically complex than walking and chewing gum at the same time.

As Jon had predicted, Simon was the last one left on the climbing wall. By the time the others had ascended, rung the tiny bell at the top, and rappelled to the ground again, he'd made it only ten meters off the ground. The last time that had happened, Scarsbury, who had an impressive flair for sadism, had made the entire class sit and watch as Simon painstakingly made his way to the top. This time, their trainer cut the torture session mercifully short.

"Enough!" Scarsbury shouted, clapping his hands together. Simon wondered whether there was such a thing as a runed whistle. Maybe he could get Scarsbury one for Christmas. "Lewis, put us all out of our misery and get down from there.

The rest of you, hit the weapons room, pick yourself out a sword, then pair up for scrimmage." His iron grip closed over Simon's shoulder. "Not so fast, hero. You stay behind."

Simon wondered whether this was it, the moment that his heroic past was finally overpowered by his hapless present, and he was about to be kicked out of school. But then Scarsbury called out other names—among them Lovelace, Cartwright, Beauvale, Mendoza—most of them Shadowhunters, all of them the best students in the class, and Simon let himself relax, just a little. Whatever it was Scarsbury had to say, it couldn't be that bad, not if he was also saying it to Jon Cartwright, gold medalist in sucking up.

"Sit," Scarsbury boomed.

They sat.

"You're here because you're the twenty most promising students in the class," Scarsbury said, pausing to let the compliment settle over them. Most of the students beamed. Simon willed himself to disappear. More like the nineteen most promising students and the one still coasting on the achievements of his past self. He felt like he was eight years old again, overhearing his mother bully the Little League coach into letting him take a turn at bat. "We've got a Downworlder that broke the Law and needs taking care of," Scarsbury continued, "and the powers that be have decided it's the perfect opportunity for you boys to become men."

Marisol Rojas Garza, a scrawny thirteen-year-old mundane with a permanent *I will kick your ass* expression, cleared her throat loudly.

"Er . . . men and women," Scarsbury clarified, looking none too happy about it.

Murmurs rippled across the students, excitement mixed with alarm. None of them had expected a real training mission this soon. Behind Simon, Jon faked a yawn. "Boring. I could kill a rogue Downworlder in my sleep."

Simon, who actually *did* kill rogue Downworlders in his sleep, along with the terrifying tentacled demons and Endarkened Shadowhunters and other bloodthirsty monsters that crawled through his nightmares, didn't feel much like yawning. He felt more like throwing up.

George raised his hand. "Uh, sir, some of us here are still"— he swallowed, and, not for the first time, Simon wondered whether he regretted admitting the truth about himself; the Academy was a much easier place to be when you were on the elite Shadowhunter track, and not just because the elites didn't have to sleep in the dungeon—"mundanes."

"I noticed that myself, Lovelace," Scarsbury said dryly. "Imagine my surprise when I discovered some of you dregs are worth something after all."

"No, I mean . . ." George hesitated, substantially more easily intimidated than any six-foot-five Scottish sex god (Beatriz Velez Mendoza's description, according to her bigmouthed best friend) had a right to be. Finally, he squared his shoulders and plowed forward. "I mean we're *mundanes*. We can't be Marked, we can't use seraph blades or witchlight or anything, we don't have, like, superspeed and angelic reflexes. Going after a Downworlder when we've only had a couple months of training . . . isn't that dangerous?"

A vein in Scarsbury's neck began to throb alarmingly, and his good eye bulged so far out of his head Simon feared it might pop. (Which, he thought, could finally explain the mysterious eye patch.) "Dangerous? *Dangerous?*" he boomed. "Anyone else here afraid of a little *danger*?"

If they were, they were even more afraid of Scarsbury, and so kept their mouths shut. He let the silence hang, thick and angry, for an agonizing minute. Then he scowled at George. "If you're afraid of dangerous situations, boy, you're in the wrong place. And as for the rest of you dregs, best you find out now whether you've got what it takes. If you don't, then drinking from the Mortal Cup will kill you, and trust me, mundies, getting bled dry by a bloodsucker would be a much kinder way to go." He'd fixed his gaze on Simon, maybe because Simon had once *been* a bloodsucker, or maybe because he now seemed the most likely to get drained by one.

It occurred to Simon that Scarsbury could be hoping for that outcome—that he'd selected Simon for this mission in hopes of getting rid of his biggest problem student. Though surely no Shadowhunter, even a Shadowhunting gym teacher, would stoop so low?

Something in Simon, some ghost of a memory, warned him not to be so sure.

"Is that understood?" Scarsbury said. "Is there anyone here who wants to go running to mommy and daddy crying 'please save me from the big, bad vampire'?"

Dead silence.

"Excellent," Scarsbury said. "You have two days to train. Then just keep reminding yourself how impressed all your little friends will be when you come back." He chuckled. "If you come back."

The student lounge was dark and musty, lit by flickering candlelight and watched over by the glowering visages of

Shadowhunters past, Herondales and Lightwoods and even the occasional Morgenstern peering down from heavy gilt frames, their bloody triumphs preserved in fading oil paint. But it had several obvious advantages over Simon's bedroom: It wasn't in the dungeon, it wasn't splattered with black slime, it didn't carry the faint whiff of what might have been moldy socks but might have been the bodies of former students decaying under the floorboards, it didn't have what sounded like a large and boisterous family of rats scrabbling behind the walls. But the one notable advantage of his room, Simon was reminded that night, while camped out in a corner playing cards with George, was the guarantee that Jon Cartwright and his Shadowhunter-track groupies would never, ever deign to cross the threshold.

"No sevens," George said, as Jon, Beatriz, and Julie swept into the lounge. "Go fish."

As Jon and the two girls approached, Simon suddenly got *very* interested in the card game. Or, at least, he did his best. At a normal boarding school, there'd be a TV in the lounge, instead of a gigantic portrait of Jonathan Shadowhunter, his eyes blazing as bright as his sword. There'd be music leaking out of the dorm rooms and mingling in the corridor, some of it good, some of it Phish; there'd be e-mail and texting and Internet porn. At the Academy, after-hours options were more limited: There was studying the *Codex*, and there was sleep. Playing cards was about as close as he could get to gaming, and when he went too long without gaming, Simon got a little itchy. It turned out that when you spent all day training to defeat actual, real-world monsters, Dungeons & Dragons questing lost a bit of its luster—or at least, so claimed George and every other student Simon had tried to recruit for a campaign—which left him with old half-forgotten summer camp standards: Hearts, Egyptian Ratscrew, and, of course, Go Fish. Simon stifled a yawn.

Jon, Beatriz, and Julie stood beside them, waiting to be acknowledged. Simon hoped if he waited long enough, they'd just go away. Beatriz wasn't so bad, at least not on her own. But Julie could have been carved out of ice. She had suspiciously few physical flaws—the silky blond hair of a Barbie doll, the porcelain skin of a cosmetics model, better curves than any of the bikini-girl posters papering Eric's garage—and wore the hawkish expression of someone on a search-and-destroy mission for any weakness whatsoever. All that, and she carried a sword.

Jon, of course, was Jon.

Shadowhunters didn't practice magic—that was a fundamental tenet of their beliefs—so it was unlikely that the Academy would teach Simon a way to make Jon Cartwright vanish into another dimension. But a guy could dream.

They didn't go away. Finally, George, congenitally incapable of being rude, set down his cards.

"Can we help you?" George asked, a sliver of ice cooling his Scottish brogue. Jon's and Julie's friendliness had melted away once they learned the truth about George's mundane blood, and though George never said anything about it, he clearly had neither forgiven nor forgotten.

"Actually, yes," Julie said. She nodded at Simon. "Well, *you* can."

Finding out about the imminent vampire-killing mission hadn't exactly tied a bright yellow ribbon around Simon's day; he wasn't in the mood. "What do you want?"

Julie looked awkwardly at Beatriz, who stared down at her feet. "You ask," Beatriz murmured.

"Better if you do," Julie shot back.

Jon rolled his eyes. "Oh, by the Angel! I'll do it." He pulled himself up to his full, impressive height, rested his hands on his hips, and peered down his regal nose at Simon. It had the look of a pose practiced in the mirror. "We want you to tell us about vampires."

Simon grinned. "What do you want to know? Scariest is Eli in *Let the Right One In*, cheesiest is late-era Lestat, most underrated is David Bowie in *The Hunger*. Sexiest is definitely Drusilla, though if you ask a girl, she'll probably say Damon Salvatore or Edward Cullen. But . . ." He shrugged. "You know girls."

Julie's and Beatriz's eyes were wide. "I didn't think you'd know so many!" Beatriz exclaimed. "Are they . . . are they your friends?"

"Oh, sure, Count Dracula and I are like this," Simon said, crossing his fingers to demonstrate. "Also Count Chocula. Oh, and my BFF Count Blintzula. He's a real charmer. . . ." He trailed off as he realized no one else was laughing. In fact, no one seemed to realize he was joking. "They're from TV," he prompted them. "Or, uh, cereal."

"What's he talking about?" Julie asked Jon, perfect nose wrinkling up in confusion.

"Who cares?" Jon said. "I told you this was a waste of time. Like he cares about anyone but himself?"

"What's that supposed to mean?" Simon asked, starting to get irritated.

George cleared his throat, visibly uncomfortable. "Come on, if he doesn't want to talk about it, that's his business."

"Not when it's *our* lives at stake." Julie was blinking hard, like she had something in her eye or—Simon caught his breath. Was she blinking back *tears*?

"What's going on?" he asked, feeling more clueless than usual, which was saying a lot.

Beatriz sighed and gave Simon a shy smile. "We're not asking you for anything personal or, you know, painful. We just want you to tell us what you know about vampires from, um . . ."

"From being a bloodsucker," Jon filled in for her. "Which, as you may recall, you were."

"But I *don't* recall," Simon pointed out. "Or have you not been paying attention?"

"That's what you say," Beatriz argued, "but . . ."

"But you think I'm *lying*?" Simon asked, incredulous. The black hole at the center of his memories was such a central fact of his existence, it had never even occurred to him someone might question it. What would be the point of lying about that—and what kind of person would do so? "You all think that? Really?"

One by one, they began to nod . . . even George, though at least he had the grace to look sheepish.

"Why would I pretend not to remember?" Simon asked.

"Why would they let someone like *you* in here, if you really didn't have a clue?" Jon retorted. "It's the only thing that makes sense."

"Well, I guess it's a mad, mad, mad world," Simon snapped. "Because what you see is what you get."

"A whole lot of nothing, then," Jon said.

Julie elbowed him, sounding uncharacteristically angry—usually she was happy to go along with whatever Jon said. "You said you'd be *nice*."

"What's the point? Either he doesn't know anything or he doesn't want to tell us. And who cares, anyway? It's just one Downworlder. What's the worst that could happen?"

"You really don't know, do you?" Julie said. "Have you ever even been in battle? Have you ever seen anyone get hurt? Die?"

"I'm a Shadowhunter, aren't I?" Jon said, though Simon noticed that wasn't much of an answer.

"You weren't in Alicante for the war," Julie said darkly. "You don't know how it was. You didn't lose anything."

Jon reared on her. "Don't you tell me what I've lost. I don't know about you, but I'm here to learn how to *fight*, so that next time—"

"Don't say that, Jon," Beatriz pleaded. "There won't be a next time. There can't be."

Jon shrugged. "There's always a next time." He sounded almost hopeful about it, and Simon understood that Julie was probably right. Jon talked like someone who'd been kept very far away from death of any kind.

"I've seen dead sheep," George said brightly, clearly trying to lighten the mood. "That's about it."

Beatriz frowned. "I don't really want to have to fight a vampire. Maybe if it were a faerie . . ."

"You don't know anything about faeries," Julie snapped.

"I know I wouldn't mind killing a couple of them," Beatriz said.

Julie deflated abruptly as if someone had pricked her and let all the air out. "Me neither. If it were that easy . . ."

Simon didn't know much about Shadowhunter-Downworlder relations, but he'd figured out pretty quickly that faeries were public enemy number one in Shadowhunterland these days.

The *actual* enemy number one, Sebastian Morgenstern, who'd started the Dark War and Turned a bunch of Shadowhunters into evil Sebastian-worshipping zombies, was long dead. Which left his secret allies, the Fair Folk, to bear his consequences. Even Shadowhunters like Beatriz, who seemed to honestly believe that werewolves were like anyone else, if a little hairier, and had a bit of a fangirl crush on the infamous warlock Magnus Bane, talked about the faeries like they were a roach infestation and the Cold Peace like it was merely a pit stop to extermination.

"You were right this morning, George," Julie said. "They shouldn't be sending us out like this, not any of us. We're not ready."

Jon snorted. "Speak for yourself."

As they bickered among themselves about exactly how hard it would be to kill one vampire, Simon stood up. Bad enough that they all thought he was a liar—even worse that, in a way, he sort of was. He couldn't remember anything about being a vampire—nothing useful, at least—but he remembered enough to be extremely uncomfortable with the idea of killing one.

Or maybe it was just the idea of killing *anything*. Simon was a vegetarian, and the only violence he'd ever committed was on-screen, blowing up pixelated dragons and sea slugs.

That's not true, a voice in his head reminded him. *There's plenty of blood on your hands.* Simon shrugged it off. Not remembering something might not mean it never happened, but sometimes pretending that made things easier.

George grabbed his arm before he could leave. "I'm sorry about—you know," he told Simon. "I should have believed you."

"Yeah. You should have." Simon sighed, then assured his roommate there were no hard feelings, which was mostly true.

He was halfway down the shadowed corridor when he heard footsteps chasing after him.

"Simon!" Julie cried. "Wait a second."

In the last few months, Simon had discovered the existence of magic and demons, he'd learned that his memories of the past were as flimsy and fake as his sister's old paper dolls, and he'd given up everything he'd ever known to move to a magically invisible country and study demon-hunting. And still, nothing surprised him quite as much as the ever-increasing list of hot girls who urgently wanted something from him. It wasn't nearly as much fun as it should have been.

Simon stopped to let Julie catch up. She was a few inches taller and had the kind of gold-flecked hazel eyes that changed in every light. Here in the dim corridor, they flashed amber in the candelabra's glow. She moved with an easy grace, like a ballet dancer, if ballet dancers habitually sliced people to ribbons with a silver runed dagger. In other words, she moved like a Shadowhunter, and from what Simon had seen of her on the training field, she was going to be a very good one.

And like any good Shadowhunter, she had no inclination to bond with mundanes, much less mundanes who used to be Downworlders—even mundanes who, in a life they could no longer remember, had saved the world. But ever since Isabelle Lightwood had descended on the Academy to stake her claim on Simon, Julie had looked at him with special fascination. Less like someone she wanted to throw into bed and more like someone she wanted to examine under a microscope as she plucked off his limbs, excavated his interior, and sought some glimmer of what might possibly attract a girl like Isabelle Lightwood.

Simon didn't mind letting her look. He liked the sharp

curiosity in her gaze, the lack of expectation. Isabelle, Clary, Maia, all those girls back in New York, they claimed to know and love him, and he believed them—but he also knew they didn't love *him*, they loved some bizarro-world version of him, some Simon-shaped doppelgänger, and when they looked at Simon, all they saw, all they wanted to see, was that other guy. Julie may have hated him—okay, clearly hated him—but she also *saw* him.

"It's really true?" she asked him now. "You don't remember any of it? Being a vampire? The demon dimension? The Dark War? None of it?"

Simon sighed. "I'm tired, Julie. Can we just pretend that you asked me that a million more times and I gave you the same answer, and call it a day?"

She brushed at her eye, and Simon wondered again whether it was possible that Julie Beauvale had actual human feelings and, for whatever reason, was blinking back actual human tears. It was too dark in the corridor to see anything but the smooth lines of her face, the glint of gold where her necklace disappeared into her cleavage.

Simon pressed a hand to his collarbone, suddenly remembering the weight of a stone, the flash of a ruby, the steady pulse so like a heartbeat, the look on her face when she'd given it to him for safekeeping, said good-bye, shards of confused memory impossible to piece together, but even as he asked himself *whose* face, *whose* frightened farewell, his mind offered up the answer.

Isabelle.

It was always Isabelle.

"I believe you," Julie said. "I don't get it, but I believe you. I guess I was just hoping . . ."

"What?" There was an unfamiliar note in her voice, something gentle and uncertain, and she looked almost as surprised as he did to hear it.

"I thought you, of all people, might understand," Julie said. "What it's like, to fight for your life. To fight Downworlders. To think you're going to die. To"—her voice didn't waver and her expression didn't change, but Simon could almost feel her blood turn to ice as she forced the words out—"see other people fall."

"I'm sorry," Simon said. "I mean, I know about what happened, but . . ."

"But it's not the same as being there," Julie said.

Simon nodded, thinking about the hours he'd spent sitting beside his father's bed, long after the heart monitor had flatlined, knowing he'd never wake up. He'd thought: *Okay, I know how this goes.* He'd seen plenty of movies where the hero's father dies; he'd pictured the look on Luke Skywalker's face, returning to find his aunt's and uncle's bodies smoldering in the Tatooine ruins, and thought he understood grief. "There are some things you can't understand unless you've been through them yourself."

"Did you ever wonder why I was here?" Julie asked him. "Training at the Academy, rather than in Alicante or some Institute somewhere?"

"Actually . . . no," Simon admitted, but maybe he should have. The Academy had been shut down for decades, and he knew in that time, Shadowhunter families had gotten used to training their children themselves. He also knew that most of them, in the wake of the Dark War, were still doing so, not wanting to let their loved ones too far out of their sight.

She looked away from him then, and her fingers knit together, needing something to hold on to. "I'm going to tell you something now, Simon, and you won't repeat it."

It wasn't a question.

"My mother was one of the first Shadowhunters to be Turned," she said, her voice deadened. "So she's gone now. After, we evacuated to Alicante, just like everyone else. And when they attacked Alicante . . . they locked all the children up in the Accords Hall. They thought we'd be safe there. But there wasn't anywhere safe that day. The faeries got in, and the Endarkened—they would have killed us all, Simon, if it weren't for you and your friends. My sister, Elizabeth. She was one of the last to die. I saw him, this faerie with silver hair, and he was so beautiful, Simon, like liquid mercury, that's what I was thinking when he brought down his sword. That he was beautiful." She shook herself all over. "Anyway. My father's useless now. So that's why I'm here. To learn to fight. So next time . . ."

Simon didn't know what to say. *I'm sorry* felt so inadequate. But Julie seemed to have run out of words.

"Why are you telling me this?" he asked gently.

"Because I want someone to understand that it *is* a big deal, what they're sending us out to do. Even if it's just one vampire against all of us. I don't care what Jon says. Things happen. People—" She nodded sharply, like she was dismissing not just him but everything that had passed between them. "Also, I wanted to thank you for what you did, Simon Lewis. And for your sacrifice."

"I really don't remember doing anything," Simon said. "You shouldn't thank me. I know what happened that day, but it's like it all happened to someone else."

"Maybe that's how it seems," Julie said. "But if you're going to be a Shadowhunter, you have to learn to see things how they *are*."

She turned away then, and started to head for her room. He was dismissed.

"Julie?" he called softly after her. "Is that why Jon and Beatriz are at the Academy too? Because of the people they lost in the war?"

"You'll have to ask them," she said, without turning back. "We all have our own story of the Dark War. All of us lost something. Some of us lost everything."

The next day, their history lecturer, the warlock Catarina Loss, announced that she was handing the class over to a special guest.

Simon's heart stopped. The last guest lecturer to honor the students with her presence had been Isabelle Lightwood. And the *"lecture"* had consisted of a stern and humiliating warning that every female in a ten-mile radius should keep her grubby little hands off Simon's hot bod.

Fortunately, the tall, dark-haired man who strode to the front of the classroom looked unlikely to have any interest in Simon or his bod.

"Lazlo Balogh," he said, his tone implying that he should have needed no introduction—but that perhaps Catarina should have done him the honor of supplying one.

"Head of the Budapest Institute," George whispered in Simon's ear. In spite of his self-proclaimed laziness, George had memorized the name of every Institute head—not to mention every famous Shadowhunter in history—before arriving at the Academy.

"I have come to tell you a story," Balogh said, eyebrows

angling into a sharp, angry V. Between the pale skin, dark widow's peak, and faint Hungarian accent, Balogh looked more like Dracula than anyone Simon had ever met.

He suspected Balogh wouldn't have appreciated the comparison.

"Several of you in this classroom will soon face your first battle. I have come to inform you what is at stake."

"We're not the ones who need to be worrying about *stakes*," Jon said, and snickered from the back row.

Balogh lasered a furious glare at him. "Jonathan Cartwright," he said, his accent giving the syllables a sinister shadow. "Were I the son of your parents, I would hold my tongue in the presence of my betters."

Jon went sheet white. Simon could feel the hatred radiating from him, and thought that it was likely Balogh had just made an enemy for life. Possibly everyone in the classroom had, too, because Jon wasn't the type to appreciate an audience to his humiliation.

He opened his mouth, then shut it again in a thin, firm line. Balogh nodded, as if agreeing that, *yes*, it was right that he should shut up and burn with silent shame.

Balogh cleared his throat. "My question for you, children, is this. What is the worst thing a Shadowhunter can do?"

Marisol raised her hand. "Kill an innocent?"

Balogh looked like he'd smelled something bad. (Which—given that the classroom had a bit of a stinkbug infestation—wasn't entirely unlikely.) "You're a mundane," he said.

She nodded fiercely. It was Simon's favorite thing about the tough thirteen-year-old: She never once apologized for who or what she was. To the contrary, she seemed proud of it.

"There was a time when no mundane would have been allowed in Idris," Balogh said. He glanced at Catarina, who was hovering at the edge of the classroom. "And no Downworlders, for that matter."

"Things change," Marisol said.

"Indeed." He scanned the classroom, which was filled with mundanes and Shadowhunters alike. "Would any of the . . . more informed students like to hazard a guess?"

Beatriz's hand rose slowly. "My mother always said the worst thing a Shadowhunter could do was forget her duty, that she was here to serve and protect mankind."

Simon caught Catarina's lips quirking up into a half smile.

Balogh's turned noticeably in the other direction. Then, apparently deciding that the Socratic method wasn't all it was cracked up to be, he answered his own question. "The worst thing any Shadowhunter can do is betray his fellows in the heat of battle," he intoned. "The worst thing any Shadowhunter can *be* is a coward."

Simon couldn't help but feel like Balogh was speaking directly to him—that Balogh had peered inside his head and knew exactly how reluctant Simon was to wield his weapon in battle conditions, against an actual living thing.

Well, not exactly *living*, he reminded himself. He'd fought demons before, he knew that, and he didn't think he'd lost sleep over it. But demons were just monsters. Vampires were still people; vampires had souls. Vampires, unlike the creatures in his video games, could hurt and bleed and die—and they could also fight back. In English class the year before, Simon had read *The Red Badge of Courage*, a tedious novel about a Civil War soldier who'd gone AWOL in the heat of battle. The book, which at the time had seemed even more irrelevant than calculus, had put him to sleep, but one line had burrowed itself into his brain: "He was a craven loon." Eric was in the class too, and for a few weeks they'd decided to call their band the Craven Loons, before forgetting all about it. But lately Simon couldn't drive the phrase out of his head. "Loon" as in: nuts for ever thinking he could be a warrior or a hero. "Craven" as in: Spineless. Frightened. Timid. A big fat coward.

"The year was 1828," Balogh declaimed. "This was before the Accords, mind you, before the Downworlders were brought into line and taught to be civilized."

Out of the corner of his eye, Simon saw their history lecturer stiffen. It didn't seem wise to offend a warlock, even one as seemingly unflappable as Catarina Loss, but Balogh continued unheeded.

"Europe was in chaos. Unruly revolutionaries were fomenting discord across the continent. And in the German states, a small cabal of warlocks took advantage of the political situation to visit the most unseemly miseries upon the local population. Some of you mundanes may be familiar with this time of tragedy and havoc from the tales told by the Brothers Grimm." At the surprised look on several students' faces, Balogh smiled for the first time. "Yes, Wilhelm and Jacob were in the thick of it. Remember, children, all the stories are true."

As Simon tried to wrap his head around the idea that, somewhere in Germany, someone's dear old grandmother might actually be a wolf in a hat, Balogh continued his story. He told the class of the small band of Shadowhunters that had been dispensed to "deal with" the warlocks. Of their journey into a dense German forest, its trees alive with dark magic, its birds and beasts enchanted to defend their territory against the forces of justice. In the dark heart of the forest, the warlocks had summoned a Greater Demon, planning to unleash its might on the people of Bavaria.

"Why?" one of the students asked.

"Warlocks don't need a reason," Balogh said, with another look at Catarina. "The summons of dark magic is always heeded by the weak and easily tempted."

Catarina murmured something. Simon found himself hoping it was a curse.

"There were five Shadowhunters," Balogh continued, "which was more than enough might to take on three warlocks. But the Greater Demon came as a surprise. Even then, right would have triumphed, were it not for the cowardice of the youngest of their party, a Shadowhunter named Tobias Herondale."

A murmur rippled across the classroom. Every student, Shadowhunter and mundane alike, knew the name Herondale. It was Jace's last name. It was the name of heroes.

"Yes, yes, you've all heard of the Herondales," Balogh said impatiently. "And perhaps you've heard good things—of William Herondale, for instance, or his son James, or Jonathan Lightwood Herondale today. But even the strongest tree can have a weak branch. Tobias's brother and sister-in-law died noble deaths in battle before the decade was out. For some, that was enough to wipe away the stain on the name Herondale. But no amount of Herondale glory or sacrifice will make us forget what Tobias did—nor should it. Tobias was inexperienced and distracted, on the mission under duress. He had a pregnant wife at home, and labored under the delusion that this should excuse him from his duties. And when the demon launched its attack, Tobias Herondale, may his name be blackened for the rest of time, turned on his heel and ran away." Then Balogh repeated that last, cracking his hand against the desk with each word. *"Ran. Away."*

He went on to describe, in gruesome, painful detail, what happened next: How three of the remaining Shadowhunters were slaughtered by the demon—one disemboweled, one burned alive, one doused with acidic blood that dissolved him into dust. How the fourth survived only by the intercession of the warlocks, who returned him—disfigured by demonic burns that would never fade—to his people as a warning to stay away.

"Of course, we returned in even greater force, and repaid the warlocks tenfold for what they'd done to the villagers. But the far greater crime, that of Tobias Herondale, still called for vengeance."

"The greater crime? Greater than slaughtering a bunch of Shadowhunters?" Simon said before he could stop himself.

"Demons and warlocks can't help what they are," Balogh said darkly. "Shadowhunters are held to a higher standard. The deaths of those three men sit squarely on the shoulders of Tobias Herondale. And he would have been punished in kind, had he ever been foolish enough to show his face again. He never did, but debts need repaying. A trial was held in absentia. He was judged guilty, and punishment was carried out."

"But I thought you said he never came back?" Julie said.

"Indeed. So the punishment was carried out on his wife, in his stead."

"His *pregnant* wife?" Marisol said, looking like she was about to be sick.

"*Sed lex, dura lex*," Balogh said. The Latin phrase had been hammered into them from the first day at the Academy, and Simon was coming to hate the sound of it—so often was it used as an excuse for acting like monsters. Balogh steepled his fingers and contemplated the classroom, watching in satisfaction as his message came clear. This was how the Clave treated cowardice on the battlefield; this was justice under the Covenant. "The Law is hard," Balogh translated for the hushed students. "But it is the Law."

"Choose wisely," Scarsbury warned, watching the students sift through the many pointy options the weapons room had to offer.

"How are we supposed to choose wisely when you won't even tell us what we're going up against?" Jon complained.

"You know it's a vampire," Scarsbury said. "You'll learn more when you arrive on site."

Simon slung a bow over his shoulders and selected a dagger for melee fighting; it seemed the weapon he was least likely to accidentally stab himself with. As the Shadowhunter students Marked themselves with runes of strength and agility and tucked witchlights into their pockets, Simon hooked a slim flashlight to one side of his belt and a portable flamethrower to the other. He touched the Star of David hanging on the same chain as Jordan's pendant around his neck—it wouldn't help much unless this vampire happened to be Jewish, but it made him feel just a little better. Like someone was looking out for him.

There was an electric charge of anticipation in the air that reminded Simon of being a little kid, preparing to go on a field trip. Of course, a visit to the Bronx Zoo or the sewage treatment center carried with it less chance of disembowelment, and instead of lining up to board a school bus, the students assembled themselves in front of a magical Portal that would transdimensionally carry them thousands of miles in the blink of an eye.

"You ready for this?" George asked him, grinning. Decked out in full gear with a longsword slung over his shoulder, Simon's roommate looked every inch the warrior.

For a brief moment, Simon imagined himself saying no. Raising his hand, asking to be excused. Admitting that he didn't know what he was doing here, that every fighting tactic he'd been taught had evaporated from his mind, that he would like to pack up his suitcase, Portal home, and pretend none of this had ever happened.

"As I'll ever be," he said—and stepped through the Portal.

From what Simon remembered, traveling by school bus was a filthy, undignified experience, rife with foul smells, spitballs, and the occasional embarrassing bout of motion sickness.

Traveling by Portal was significantly worse.

Once he'd regained his balance and his breath, Simon looked around—and gasped. No one had mentioned where they were Portaling *to*, but Simon recognized the block immediately. He was back in New York City—and not just New York but Brooklyn. Gowanus, to be specific, a thin stretch of industrial parks and warehouses lining a toxic canal that was less than a ten-minute walk from his mother's apartment.

He was home.

It was exactly as he'd remembered it—and yet, wholly different. Or maybe it was just that he was wholly different, that after only two months in Idris, he'd forgotten the sounds and smells of modernity: the low, steady hum of electricity and the thick haze of car exhaust, the honking trucks and pigeon crap and piles of garbage that had for sixteen years formed the fabric of his daily life.

On the other hand, maybe it was because now that he could see through glamours, he could see the mermaids swimming in the Gowanus.

It was home and not home all at the same time, and Simon felt the same disorientation he had after his summer in the mountains at Camp Ramah, when he'd found himself unable to fall asleep without the sound of cicadas and Jake Grossberg's snoring in the upper bunk. Maybe, he thought, you couldn't know how much going away had changed you until you tried to go home.

"Listen up, men!" Scarsbury shouted, as the final student came through the Portal. They were assembled in front of an abandoned factory, its walls streaked with graffiti and its windows boarded up tight.

Marisol cleared her throat, loudly, and Scarsbury sighed. "Listen up, men and *women*. Inside this building is a vampire who's broken the Covenant and killed several mundanes. Your mission is to track her down, and execute her. And I suggest you do so before sunset."

"Shouldn't the vampires be allowed to deal with this themselves?" Simon asked. The *Codex* had made it pretty clear that Downworlders were trusted to police themselves. Simon wondered whether that involved giving alleged rogue vampires a trial before they were executed.

How did I get here? he wondered—he didn't even believe in the death penalty.

"Not that it's any of your concern," Scarsbury said, "but her clan has handed her over to us, so that you children can get a little blood on your hands. Think of it as a gift, from the vampires to you."

Except "it" wasn't an *it* at all, Simon thought.

"*Sed lex, dura lex*," George murmured beside him, with an uneasy look, as if he was trying to convince himself.

"There's twenty of you and one of her," Scarsbury said, "and in case even those odds are too much for you, experienced Shadowhunters will be watching, ready to step in when you screw up. You won't see them, but they'll see you, and ensure that you come to no harm. Probably. And if any of you are tempted to turn tail and run, remember what you've learned. Cowardice has its price."

When they were standing on the curb in the bright sunlight, the mission had sounded more than a little unsporting. Twenty Shadowhunters in training, all of them armed to the gills; one captured vampire, trapped in the building by steel walls and sunshine.

But inside the old factory, in the dark, imagining the flicker of motion and the glimmer of fangs behind every shadow, was a different story. The game no longer felt rigged in their favor—it no longer felt like much of a game at all.

The students split up into pairs, prowling through the darkness. Simon volunteered to guard one of the exits, hoping very much that this would prove similar to those gym class soccer games, where he'd spent hours guarding the goal and only a handful of times had to fend off a well-aimed kick.

Of course, each of those times, the ball had sailed over his head and into the net, losing the game for his team. But he tried not to think about that.

Jon Cartwright was stationed at the door beside him, a witchlight stone glowing in his hand. Time passed; they did their best to ignore each other.

"Too bad you can't use one of these," Jon said finally, holding up the stone. "Or one of these." He tapped the seraph blade hanging from his belt. The students hadn't been taught how to fight with them yet, but several of the Shadowhunter kids had brought their own weapons from home. "Don't worry, hero. If the vamp shows up, I'm here to protect you."

"Great, I can hide behind your massive ego."

Jon wheeled on him. "You want to watch yourself, mundane. If you're not careful, you'll . . ." Jon's voice trailed off. He backed up until he was pressed against the wall.

"I'll what?" Simon prompted him.

Jon made a noise that sounded suspiciously like a whimper. His hand floundered at his belt, fingers stretching for the seraph blade but coming nowhere near it. His eyes were riveted on a spot just over Simon's shoulder. "Do something!" he squeaked. "She's going to get us!"

Simon had seen enough horror movies to get the picture. And the picture was enough to make him want to bolt for the door, slip through it into the daylight, and keep running until he was back home, doors locked, safely under the bed, where he'd once hidden from imaginary monsters.

Instead, slowly, he turned around.

The girl who melted out of the shadows looked to be about his age. Her brown hair was pulled back into a high ponytail, her glasses were dark pink and horn-rimmed vintage, and her

T-shirt featured a bloody, crimson-shirted *Star Trek* officer and read, LIVE FAST, DIE RED. She was, in other words, exactly Simon's type—except for the fangs glinting in his flashlight beam and the inhuman speed with which she streaked across the room and kicked Jon Cartwright in the head. He crumpled to the ground.

"And then there were two," the girl said, and smirked.

It had never occurred to Simon that the vampire would be his age, or at least look it.

"You want to be careful with that thing, Daylighter," she said. "I hear you're alive again. Presumably you want to keep it that way."

Simon looked down to realize he had taken the dagger into his hand.

"You going to let me out of here, or what?" she asked.

"You can't go out there."

"No?"

"Sunshine, remember? Makes vampires go poof?" Simon couldn't believe his voice wasn't shaking. Honestly, he couldn't believe he hadn't peed his pants. He was alone with a *vampire*. A cute, girl vampire . . . that he was supposed to kill. Somehow.

"Check your watch, Daylighter."

"I don't wear a watch," Simon said. "And I'm not a Daylighter anymore."

She stepped closer to him, close enough to stroke his face. Her finger was cold, her skin as smooth as marble. "Is it true you don't remember?" she said, peering curiously at him. "You don't even remember me?"

"Did I . . . do I know you?"

She brushed her fingertips across her lips. "The question is, how *well* did you know me, Daylighter? I'll never tell."

Clary and the others had said nothing about Simon having vampire friends, or . . . more-than-friends. Maybe they'd wanted to spare him the details of that part of his life, the part where he'd thirsted for blood and walked in the shadows. Maybe he'd been so embarrassed that he'd never told them.

Or maybe she was lying.

Simon hated this, the not knowing. It made him feel like he was walking on quicksand, every unanswered question, every new discovery about his past sucking him farther down into the muck.

"Let me go, Daylighter," she whispered. "You would never have hurt one of your own."

He'd read in the *Codex* that vampires had the ability to mesmerize; he knew he should be guarding himself against it. But her gaze was magnetic. He couldn't look away.

"I can't do that," he said. "You broke the Law. You killed someone. Many someones."

"How do you know?"

"Because . . ." He stopped, realizing how feeble it would sound: *because someone told me so.*

She guessed at the answer anyway. "You always do what you're told, Daylighter? You never think for yourself?"

Simon's hand tightened on the dagger. He'd been so worried about discovering he was a coward, too frightened to fight. But now that he was here, facing the supposed monster, he wasn't afraid—he was reluctant.

Sed lex, dura lex.

Except maybe it wasn't so simple; maybe she'd just made a mistake, or someone else had, maybe he'd gotten the wrong information. Maybe she was a cold-blooded killer—but even so, who was he to punish her?

She angled past him toward the door. Without thinking, Simon moved to block her. His dagger swung up, slicing a dangerous arc through the air and whistling past her ear. She danced backward, laughing as she lunged for him, fingers curled like claws. Simon felt it then, for the first time, the adrenaline surge he'd been promised, the clarity of battle. He stopped thinking in terms of techniques and moves, stopped thinking at all, and simply acted, blocking and ducking her attack, aiming a kick at her ankles to sweep her legs out from under her, slashing the dagger across pale skin, drawing blood, and as his mind kicked into gear again, a step behind his body, he thought, *I'm doing it. I'm fighting. I'm* winning.

Until she wrapped a hand around his wrist in an iron grip, flipped him over onto his back as if he were a small child, and straddled him. She'd been playing with him, he realized. Pretending to fight, until she got bored.

She lowered her face toward his, close enough that he would have felt her breath—if she'd been breathing.

He remembered, suddenly, how cold he had been, when he was dead. He remembered the stillness in his chest, where his heart no longer beat.

"I could give it all back to you, Daylighter," she whispered. "Eternal life."

He remembered the hunger, and the taste of blood.

"That wasn't life," he said.

"It wasn't death, either." Her lips were cold on his neck. Everything about her was cold. "I could kill you now, Daylighter. But I'm not going to. I'm not a monster. No matter what they told you."

"I told you, I'm not a Daylighter anymore." Simon didn't

know why he was arguing with her, especially now, but it seemed important to say it out loud, that he was alive, that he was human, that his heart beat again. Especially now.

"You were a Downworlder once," she said, rising over him. "That will always be a part of you. Even if you forget, they never will."

Simon was about to argue, again, when a shining whip lashed out of the shadows and wrapped around the girl's neck. It yanked her off her feet and she landed hard, head cracking against the cement floor.

"Isabelle?" Simon said in confusion, as Isabelle Lightwood charged at the vampire, blade gleaming.

He'd never before realized what a horrible crime against nature it was that he had lost his memories of Isabelle in action. It was clear that it was her natural state. Isabelle standing still was beautiful; Isabelle leaping through the air, carving death into cold flesh, was unworldly, burning as brightly as her golden whip. She was like a goddess, Simon thought, and then silently corrected himself—she was like an avenging angel, her vengeance swift and deadly. Before he could lever himself off the ground, the vampire girl's throat was split wide open, her undead eyes rolling back in her head, and like that, it was over. She was dust; she was gone.

"You're welcome." Isabelle extended her hand.

Simon ignored it, rising to his feet without her help. "Why did you do that?"

"Um, because she was about to kill you?"

"No, she wasn't," he said coldly.

Isabelle gaped at him. "You're not seriously mad at me? For saving your ass?"

It wasn't until she asked that he realized he was. Angry at her for killing the vampire girl, angry at her for assuming he *needed* his ass saved and being pretty much right, angry at her for hiding in the dark, waiting to save him, even though he'd made it painfully clear that there couldn't be anything between them anymore. Angry that she was a supernaturally sexy, raven-haired warrior goddess and apparently against all odds still in love with him— and he was apparently going to have to break up with her, *again*.

"She didn't want to hurt me. She just wanted to *go*."

"And what? I should have *let* her? Is that what you were planning to do? There are more people in the world than you, Simon. She killed children. She ripped out their throats."

He couldn't answer. He didn't know what to feel or think. The vampire girl had been a murderer. A cold-blooded murderer, in every sense of the word. But he'd felt a kinship with her as she'd embraced him, a sort of whispering in the back of his mind that said *we are lost children together.*

He wasn't sure there was a place in Isabelle's life for someone lost.

"Simon?" Isabelle was like a tightly coiled spring. He could see how much effort it was taking her just to keep her voice steady, her face free of emotion.

How can I know that? Simon wondered. Looking at her was like seeing double: one Isabelle a stranger he barely knew, one Isabelle the girl that other, better Simon loved so much he would have sacrificed everything for her. There was a part of him—a part beneath memories, beyond rationality—desperate to close the space between them, to take her in his arms, smooth back her hair, lose himself in her bottomless eyes, her lips, her fierce, protective, overwhelming love.

"You can't keep doing this!" he shouted, unsure whether he was yelling at her or himself. "It's not your job to choose for me anymore, to decide what I should do or how I should live. Who I should be. How many times do I have to tell you before you hear me? *I'm not him.* I will never be him, Isabelle. He belonged to you, I get that. But *I don't.* I know you Shadowhunters are used to having everything your way—you set the rules, you know what's best for the rest of us. But not this time, okay? Not with me."

With deliberate calm, Isabelle coiled her whip around her wrist. "Simon, I think you've mistaken me for someone who cares."

It wasn't the emotion in her voice that cracked his heart, but the lack of it. Behind the words was nothing: no pain, no suppressed anger, only a void. Hollow and cold.

"Isabelle—"

"I didn't come here for you, Simon. This is my job. I thought you wanted it to be your job too. If you still feel that way, I'd suggest you reconsider some things. Like how you speak to your superiors."

"My . . . *superiors?*"

"And for the record, since you brought it up? You're right, Simon. I don't know this version of you at all. And I'm pretty sure I don't want to." She stepped past Simon, her shoulder brushing against his for the briefest of moments, then slipped out of the building.

Simon stared after her, wondering if he should follow, but he couldn't seem to make his feet move. At the sound of the door slamming shut, Jon Cartwright blinked his eyes open and woozily eased himself upright. "We got her?" he asked Simon, catching sight of the small pile of dust where the vampire girl had been.

"Yeah," he said wearily. "You could say that."

"Oh yeah, that's right, bloodsucker!" Jon pumped his fist in the air, then made devil fingers. "You mess with a Cartwright bull—you get the horns."

"I'm not saying she *didn't* break the Law," Simon explained, for what seemed like the hundredth time. "I'm just saying, even if she did, why did we have to kill her? I mean—what about, I don't know, *jail*?"

By the time they'd Portaled back to the Academy, dinner was long over. But as a reward for their labors, Dean Penhallow had opened up the dining hall and the kitchen for the twenty returning students. They huddled around a couple of the long tables, gnawing hungrily at stale egg rolls and mercifully flavorless shawarma. The Academy had returned to its traditional policy of serving international food—but unfortunately, all of these foods were prepared by a single chef, who Simon suspected was a warlock, because nearly everything they ate seemed enchanted to taste like dog food.

"Because that's what we do," Jon said. "A vampire—any Downworlder—violates the Covenant, someone has to kill it. Have you not been paying attention?"

"So why isn't there a Downworlder jail?" Simon said. "Why aren't there Downworlder trials?"

"That's not how it *works*, Simon," Julie said. He'd thought she might be friendlier after their conversation in the corridor the other night, but if anything, her edges had gotten sharper, more liable to draw blood. "This isn't your stupid mundane law. This is the Law. Handed down from the Angel. Higher than everything else."

Jon nodded proudly. *"Sed lex, dura lex."*

"Even if it's wrong?" Simon asked.

"How could it be wrong, if it's the Law? That's an oxymoron."

Takes one to know one, he thought childishly, but stopped himself before saying it out loud. Anyway, Jon was more of your garden-variety moron.

"You realize you all sound like you're in some kind of cult," Simon complained. He touched the star that was still hanging at his neck. His family had never been particularly religious, but his father had always loved helping him try to figure out the Jewish perspective on questions of right and wrong. "There's always a little wiggle room," he'd told Simon, "a little space to figure these things out yourself." He'd taught Simon to ask questions, to challenge authority, to understand and believe in rules before he followed them. There was a noble Jewish heritage of arguing, his father liked to say, even when it came to arguing with God.

Simon wondered now what his father would think of him, at this school for fundamentalists, swearing fealty to a higher Law. What did it even mean to be Jewish in a universe where angels and demons walked the earth, practiced miracles, carried swords? Was thinking for yourself an activity better suited to a world without any evidence of the divine?

"The Law is hard, but it's the Law," Simon added in disgust. "So freaking what? If the Law is wrong, why not change it? Do you know what the world would look like if we were all still following the laws made up back in the Dark Ages?"

"You know who else used to talk like that?" Jon asked ominously.

"Let me guess: Valentine." Simon scowled. "Because apparently in all of Shadowhunter history only one guy has bothered to ask any questions. Yeah, that's me, charismatic, evil supervillain about to lead a revolution. Better report me."

George shook his head warningly. "Simon, I don't think—"

"If you hate it so much, why are you even here?" Beatriz cut in, an uncharacteristically hostile note in her voice. "*You* get to pick the life you want to live." She stopped abruptly, leaving something unspoken hanging in the silence. Something, Simon suspected, like: *Unlike the rest of us.*

"Good question." Simon set down his fork and pushed his chair back.

"Come on, you didn't even finish your . . ." George waved toward the plate, as if he couldn't bring himself to actually describe it as *food.*

"I just lost my appetite."

Simon was halfway to the dungeons when Catarina Loss stopped him in the hallway.

"Simon Lewis," she said. "We need to talk."

"Can we do it in the morning, Ms. Loss?" he asked. "It's been a long day, and—"

She shook her head. "I know about your day, Simon Lewis. We talk now."

The sky was bright with stars. Catarina's blue skin glowed in the moonlight, and her hair burned silver. The warlock had insisted that they both needed some fresh air, and Simon had to admit she was right. He felt better already, just breathing in the grass and trees and sky. Idris had seasons, but so far, at least, they weren't like the seasons he was used to. Or rather, they were like the best possible versions of themselves: each fall day crisp and bright, the air rich with the promise of bonfires and apple orchards, the approach of winter marked by only a startlingly clear sky and a new sharp bite to the air that was almost pleasurable in its icy pain.

"I heard what you said at dinner, Simon," Catarina said as they strolled across the grounds.

He looked at his teacher with surprise and a bit of alarm. "How could you?"

"I'm a warlock," she reminded him. "I *can* a lot of things."

Right. Magic school, he thought in despair, wondering if he'd ever have any privacy again.

"I want to tell you a story, Simon," she said. "It's something I've told a very few, trusted people, and I hope that you'll choose to keep it to yourself."

It seemed like a strange thing for her to risk on a student she barely knew—but then, she was a warlock. Simon had no idea what they were capable of, but he was getting better at imagining. If he broke her confidence, she'd probably know it.

And act accordingly.

"You were listening in class to the story of Tobias Herondale?"

"I always listen in class," Simon said, and she laughed.

"You're very good at evasive answers, Daylighter. You'd make a good faerie."

"I'm guessing that's not a compliment."

Catarina offered him a mysterious smile. "I'm no Shadowhunter," she reminded him. "My opinions on faeries are my own."

"Why do you still call me Daylighter?" Simon asked. "You know that's not what I am anymore."

"We are all what our pasts have made us," Catarina said. "The accumulation of thousands of daily choices. We can change ourselves, but never erase what we've been." She held up a finger to silence him, as if she knew he was about to argue. "Forgetting those choices doesn't unmake them, Daylighter. You'd do well to remember that."

"Is that what you wanted to tell me?" he asked, his irritation more visible than he'd intended. Why did everyone in his life feel the need to tell him who he was, or who he should be?

"You're impatient with me," Catarina observed. "Fortunately, I don't care. I'm going to tell you another story of Tobias Herondale now. Listen or not—that's your decision."

He listened.

"I knew Tobias, knew his mother before he was born, watched him as a child struggling to fit into his family, find his place. The Herondales are a rather infamous line, as you probably know. Many of them heroes, some of them traitors, so many of them brash, wild creatures consumed by their passions, whether it be love or hate. Tobias was . . . different. He was mild, sweet, the kind of boy who did as he was told. His older brother, William—now, *there* was a Shadowhunter fit to be a Herondale, just as brave and twice as headstrong as the grandson who later bore his name. But not Tobias. He had no special talent for Shadowhunting, and not much love for it either. His father was a hard man, his mother a bit of a hysteric, though few could blame her with a husband like that. A bolder boy might have turned from his family and its traditions, decided he was unfit for the Shadowhunter life and struck out on his own. But for Tobias? That was unthinkable. His parents taught him the Law, and he knew only to follow it. Not so unusual among humans, even when their blood is mixed with the Angel's. Unusual for a Herondale, maybe, but if anyone thought that, Tobias's father made sure they kept their mouths shut. And so he grew up. He married, a match that surprised everyone, for Eva Blackthorn was the opposite of mild. A raven-haired spitfire, somewhat like your Isabelle."

Simon bristled. She wasn't *his* Isabelle, not anymore. He wondered if she ever truly had been. Isabelle didn't seem like the type of girl to *belong* to someone. It was one of the things he liked best about her.

"Tobias loved her more than he'd loved anything—his family, his duty, even himself. There, perhaps, the Herondale blood ran true. She was carrying her first child when he was called to the mission in Bavaria—you've heard how that story ended."

Simon nodded, heart clenching all over again at the thought of the punishment visited on Tobias's wife. Eva. And her unborn child.

"Lazlo Balogh knows only the version of this story as it's been handed down to him by generations of Shadowhunters. Tobias is no longer a person to them, or an ancestor. He's nothing but a cautionary tale. There are few of us left to remember him as the kind boy he once was."

"How did you know him so well?" Simon asked. "I thought back then, warlocks and Shadowhunters weren't exactly . . . you know. On speaking terms." Actually, Simon had thought it was more like killing terms; from what he'd learned from the *Codex* and his history classes, the Shadowhunters of the past had gone after warlocks and other Downworlders the way big-game hunters went after elephants. Sportingly and with bloodthirsty abandon.

"That's a different story," Catarina chided him. "I'm not telling you my story, I'm telling you Tobias's. Suffice it to say, he was a kind boy, even to Downworlders, and his kindness was remembered. What you know, what all Shadowhunters today think they know, is that Tobias was a coward who abandoned his fellows in the heat of battle. The truth is never so simple, is it? Tobias hadn't wanted to leave behind his wife when she was ill and pregnant, but he went anyway, doing as he was told. Deep in those Bavarian woods, he encountered a warlock who knew his greatest fear, and used it against him. He found the chink in Tobias's armor, found a way into his mind by convincing him his wife was in terrible danger. He showed him a vision of Eva, bloody and dying and screaming for Tobias to save her. Tobias was held spellbound and stricken, and the warlock hurled vision after vision of all the horrors in the world Tobias could not bear. Yes, Tobias ran away. His mind broke. He abandoned his fellows and fled into the woods, blinded and tormented by waking nightmares. Like all Herondales, his ability to love without measure, without end, was both his great gift and his great curse. When he thought Eva was dead, he shattered. I know who I blame for the destruction of Tobias Herondale."

"They can't have known he was driven mad!" Simon protested. "No one could punish him for that!"

"They did know," Catarina told him. "That didn't matter. What mattered was his treason against his duty. Eva was never in danger, of course—at least, not until Tobias abandoned his post. That was the last cruel irony of Tobias's life: that he doomed the woman he would have died to save. The warlock had shown him a glimpse of the future, a future that would never have come to pass if Tobias had been able to resist him. He could not resist. He could not be found. The Clave came for Eva."

"You were there," Simon guessed.

"I was," she agreed.

"And you didn't try to stop them?"

"I did not waste my time trying, no. The Nephilim do not pay heed to interfering Downworlders. Only a fool would try to get between the Shadowhunters and their Law."

There was something about the way she said it, wry and sorrowful at the same time, that made him ask, "You're a fool, aren't you?"

She smiled. "It's dangerous to call a warlock names like that, Simon. But . . . yes. I tried. I looked for Tobias Herondale, using ways the Nephilim do not have access to, and found him wandering mad in the forest, not even knowing his own name." She lowered her head. "I couldn't save him or Eva. But I saved the baby. I managed that much."

"But how? Where—?"

"I used a certain amount of magic and cunning to make my way into the prison of the Shadowhunters, where you were held once," said Catarina, nodding to him. "I made the baby come early, and cast a spell to make it seem as if she was still carrying the child. Eva was steel that night, relentless and bright in the darkness that had come upon her. She did not falter and she did not flinch and she did not betray herself by any sign as she walked to meet her death. She kept our secret to the very end, and the Shadowhunters who killed her never suspected a thing. After that, it was almost easy. The Nephilim seldom have any interest in the doings of Downworlders—and Downworlders often find their blindness very convenient. They never noticed when I sailed away to the New World with a baby. I stayed there for twenty years, before I went back to my people and my work, and raised the child until he was grown. He has been dust for years, but I can close my eyes and see his face when he was as young as you are now. Tobias and Eva's child. He was a sweet boy, kind as his father and fierce as his mother. The Nephilim believe in living by hard laws and paying high prices, but their arrogance means they do not fully understand the cost of what they do. The world would have been poorer without that boy in it. He had a mundane love, and a mundane life filled with small acts of grace, which would have meant very little to a Shadowhunter. They did not deserve him. I left him as a gift to the mundane world."

"So you're saying there's another Herondale out there somewhere? Maybe generations of Herondales that no one knows anything about?" There was a line from the Talmud Simon's father had always liked to quote: *He who saves a single life, it is as if he has saved an entire world.*

"It's possible," Catarina said. "I made sure the boy never knew what he was—it was safest that way. If indeed his line lives on, his descendants surely believe themselves mundane. It's only now, with the Shadowhunters so depleted, that the Clave might welcome their lost sons or daughters back to the fold. And perhaps there are those of us who might help that along. When the time is right."

"Why are you telling me this, Ms. Loss? Why now? Why ever?"

She stopped walking and turned to him, silver-white hair billowing in the wind. "Saving that child, that's the biggest crime I've ever committed. At least, according to Shadowhunter

Law. If anyone knew, even now . . ." She shook her head. "But it's also the bravest choice I've ever made. The one I'm most proud of. I'm bound by the Accords just like everyone else, Simon. I do my best to live by the rule of Law. But I make my own decisions. There's always a higher law."

"You say that like it's so easy to know what it *is*," Simon said. "To be so sure of yourself, that you're right, no matter what the Law says."

"It's not easy," Catarina corrected him. "It's what it means to be alive. Remember what I said, Simon. Every decision you make, makes *you*. Never let other people choose who you're going to be."

When he returned to his room, his mind spinning, George was sitting on the ground in the hallway, studying his *Codex*.

"Um, George?" Simon peered down at his roommate. "Wouldn't it be easier to do that inside? Where there's light? And no disgusting slime on the ground? Well . . ." He sighed. "Less slime, at least."

"She said I have to wait out here," George said. "That you two need your privacy."

"Who said?" But the question was superfluous, because who else? Before George could answer, he was already opening the door and charging inside. "Isabelle, you can't just throw my roommate—"

He stopped short, so suddenly that he nearly tripped over himself.

"It's not Isabelle," said the girl perched on his bed. Her fire-red hair was pulled into a messy bun and her legs were folded beneath her; she looked utterly at home, as if she'd spent half her life lounging around in his bed. Which, according to her, she had.

"What are you doing here, Clary?"

"I Portaled in," she said.

He nodded, waiting. He was glad to see her, but it also hurt. Just as it always did. He wondered when the pain would go and he would be able to feel the joy of friendship that he knew was still there, like a plant under frozen ground, waiting to grow again.

"I heard what happened today. With the vampire. And Isabelle."

Simon lowered himself onto George's bed, across from her. "I'm fine, okay? No bite marks or anything. It's nice of you to worry about me, but you can't just Portal in and—"

Clary snorted. "I can see your ego's unharmed. I'm not here because I'm worried about you, Simon."

"Oh. Then . . . ?"

"I'm worried about *Isabelle*."

"I'm pretty sure Isabelle can take care of herself."

"You don't know her, Simon. I mean, not anymore. And if she knew I was here, she'd murder me, but . . . can you just try to be a little nicer to her? Please?"

Simon was appalled. He knew that he'd disappointed Isabelle, that his very existence was a constant disappointment to her, that she wanted him to be someone else. But it had never occurred to him that he, the non-vampire, non-heroic, non-sexy iteration of Simon Lewis, could have the power to hurt her.

"I'm sorry," he blurted. "Tell her I'm sorry!"

"Are you kidding me?" Clary said. "Did you not hear the part about how she'd murder me if she knew I was talking to you about this? I'm not telling her anything. I'm telling *you*. Be careful with her. She's more fragile than she seems."

"She seems like the strongest girl I've ever met," Simon said.

"She's that, too," Clary allowed. She shifted uncomfortably then, and hopped to her feet. "Well, I should . . . I mean, I know you don't really want me around here, so . . ."

"It's not that, I just—"

"No, I get it, but—"

"I'm sorry—"

"I'm sorry—"

They both laughed, and Simon felt something loosening in his chest, a muscle he hadn't even known was clenched.

"It didn't used to be like this, huh?" he asked. "Awkward?"

"No." She gave him a sad smile. "It was a lot of things, but it was never awkward."

He couldn't imagine it, feeling so at ease with a girl, much less a girl like her, pretty and confident and so filled with light. "I bet I liked that."

"I hope so, Simon."

"Clary—" He didn't want her to leave, not yet, but he wasn't sure what to say to her if she stayed. "Do you know the story of Tobias Herondale?"

"Everyone knows that story," she said. "And, obviously, because of Jace . . ."

Simon blinked, remembering: *Jace* was a Herondale. The last of the Herondales. Or so he thought.

If he had family out there, lost for generations, he would want to know, wouldn't he? Was Simon supposed to tell him? Tell Clary?

He imagined a lost Herondale out there, some golden-eyed

girl or boy who didn't know anything about the Shadowhunters or their sordid legacy. Maybe they would welcome finding out who they really were—but maybe, if Clary and Jace came knocking at their door, telling them stories of angels and demons and a noble tradition of death-defying insanity, they would run screaming in the opposite direction.

Sometimes, Simon wondered what would have happened if Magnus had never found him, never offered him the chance to reenter the Shadowhunter world. He would have been living a lie, sure . . . but it would have been a happy lie. He would have gone to college, kept playing with his band, flirted with some non-terrifying girls, lived on the surface of things, never guessing at the darkness that lay beneath.

He guessed that in his other life, telling Clary what he knew wouldn't even have been a question; he guessed that they were the kind of friends who told each other everything.

They weren't any kind of friends now, he reminded himself. She was a stranger who loved him, but she was still a stranger.

"What do you think of it?" he asked her. "What the Clave did to Tobias's wife and child?"

"What do you *think* I think?" Clary asked. "Given who my father was? Given what happened to Jace's parents, and how he survived it? Isn't it obvious?"

It may have been obvious to someone who knew them and their stories, but not to Simon.

Her face fell. "Oh."

His confusion must have been visible. As was her disappointment—like she was remembering all over again who he was, and who he wasn't.

"It doesn't matter. Let's just say that I do think the Law

matters—but it's not the only thing that matters. I mean, if we followed the Law without thinking, would you and I ever have—"

"What?"

She shook her head. "No, I promised myself I wasn't going to keep doing this. You don't need a bunch of stories about what happened to us, who you used to be. You have to figure out who you are *now*, Simon. I want that for you, that freedom."

It amazed him, how well she understood. How she knew what he wanted without him having to ask.

It gave him the nerve to ask her something he'd been wondering ever since he got to the Academy. "Clary, back when we were friends, before you knew about Shadowhunting or anything, were you and I . . . the same?"

"The same how?"

He shrugged. "You know, into weird music and comics and, like, really *not* into gym."

"You mean, were we both klutzy nerds?" Clary asked, laughing again. "That's affirmative."

"But now you're—" He waved a hand at her, indicating the taut biceps, the graceful, coordinated way she moved, everything he knew of her past and present. "You're like this Amazon warrior."

"Thanks? I think? Jace is a good trainer. And, you know, there was incentive to get up to speed pretty quick. Fending off the apocalypse and all. Twice."

"Right. And I guess it's in your blood. I mean, it makes sense that you'd be good at all this stuff."

"Simon—" She narrowed her eyes, suddenly seeming to understand what he was getting at. "You do realize Shadowhunting isn't just about how big your muscles are, right? They don't call it Bodybuilding Academy."

He rubbed his aching biceps ruefully. "Maybe they should."

"Simon, you wouldn't be here if the people in charge didn't think you had what it takes."

"They think *he* had what it takes," Simon corrected her. "The guy with the vampy superstrength and—whatever else it is vampires bring to the table."

Clary got close enough to poke him in the chest, and then she did. Hard. "No, *you*. Simon, do you know how we got as far as we did in that demon dimension? How we managed to get ourselves close enough to Sebastian to take him down?"

"No, but I'm guessing it involved a lot of demon killing?" Simon asked.

"Not as much as there might have been, because *you* came up with a better strategy," Clary said. "Something you figured out from all those years playing D&D."

"Wait, seriously? Are you telling me that stuff actually worked in real life?"

"I'm telling you that. I'm telling you that you saved us, Simon. You did it more than once. Not because you were a vampire, not because of anything you've lost. Because of who you were. Who you still are." She stepped away then and took a deep breath. "I promised myself I wouldn't do this," she said fiercely. "I promised."

"No," he said. "I'm glad you did. I'm glad you came."

"I should get out of here," Clary said. "But try to remember about Izzy, okay? I know you can't understand this, but every time you look at her like she's a stranger, it's like . . . it's like someone pressing a hot iron to her flesh. It hurts that much."

She sounded so certain, like she *knew*.

Like maybe they weren't just talking about Isabelle anymore.

Simon felt it then, not the twinge of fondness he often experienced when Clary smiled at him, but a forceful rush of love that nearly swept him off his feet and into her arms. For the first time, he looked at her, and she wasn't a stranger, she was *Clary*—his friend. His family. The girl he'd sworn always to protect. The girl he loved as fiercely as he loved himself.

"Clary—" he said. "When we were friends, it was great, right? I mean, I'm not just imagining things, feeling like this is where we belong? We got each other, we supported each other. We were good together, right?"

Her smile turned from sad to something else, something that glowed with the same certainty that he felt, that there was something real between them. It was as if he'd switched on a light inside her. "Oh, Simon," she said. "We were absolutely amazing."

The Whitechapel Fiend

By Cassandra Clare and Maureen Johnson

She lunged for the fire; Will caught her and hauled her back. Everything seemed to have gone dark and silent in Tessa's ears. All she could think about was her baby. His soft laugh, his storm-black hair like his father's, his sweet disposition, the way he put his arms around her neck, his lashes against his cheeks.

Somehow, she had fallen to the floor. It was hard against her knees. James, she thought desperately.

—The Whitechapel Fiend

"I spy," George said, "with my little eye, something that begins with *S*."

"It's slime, isn't it?" Simon said. He was lying on his back on the cot in his dorm room. His roommate, George, was lying on the opposite cot. Both of them were staring up thoughtfully into the darkness, which involved staring at the ceiling, which was unfortunate because the ceiling was gross. "It's always slime."

"Not so," George said. "One time it was mold."

"I'm not sure we can really make the distinction between slime and mold, and I hate that I have to care about that."

"It wasn't 'slime,' anyway."

Simon considered for a moment.

"Is it . . . a snake? Please tell me it's not a snake."

Simon curled up his legs involuntarily.

"It's not a snake, but now that's all I will be able to think about. Are there snakes in Idris? It seems like the kind of place where they'd drive the snakes out."

"Isn't that Ireland?" Simon said.

"I don't think there are limitations on snake driving. Surely they got rid of the snakes. Must have done. Oh God, this place has to have snakes. . . ."

There was a faint tremor to George's soft Scottish brogue now.

"Are there raccoons here in Idris?" Simon said, trying to change the subject. He adjusted himself on the hard, narrow bed. There was no point in adjusting. Every position was just as uncomfortable as the last. "We have raccoons in New York. They can get in anywhere. They can open doors. I read online that they even know how to use keys."

"I don't like snakes. Snakes don't need keys."

Simon paused for a moment to recognize the fact that "Snakes don't need keys" was a good album name: It sounded deep for a second, but then completely shallow and obvious, which made you go back to the first thought and think it might be deep.

"So what was it?" Simon asked.

"What was what?"

"What did you spy that begins with *S*?"

"Simon."

This was the kind of game you played when you lived in a sparsely decorated room located in the basement of the Shadowhunter Academy—or, as they had started to refer to it—the floor of ultimate moisture. George had commented many times how it was a shame they weren't slugs, because it was perfectly set up for the slug lifestyle. They had come to an uneasy acceptance of the fact that many creatures had made the Academy their home after it was closed down. They no longer panicked when they heard skittering noises in the wall or under the bed. If the noises were *in* the bed, they allowed themselves some panic. This had happened more than once.

In theory, the mundanes (or dregs, as they were often called) were down in the basement because it was the most secure floor. Simon was sure there was probably some truth to that. But there was probably a lot more truth to the fact that Shadowhunters tended to have a natural snobbery that ran in the blood. But Simon had asked to be here, both with the dregs and in Shadowhunter Academy itself, so there was no point in complaining. With no Wi-Fi, no phones, no television—nights could be long. Once the lights went out, Simon and George often talked to each other across the darkness like this. Sometimes they lay in their respective beds in a companionable silence, each knowing the other was there. It was something. It was everything, really, just to have George in the room. Simon wasn't sure if he would be able to bear it otherwise. And it wasn't just the cold or the rats or anything else about the place physically—it was what was in his head, the ever-increasing noises, slices of memories. They came to him like bits of forgotten songs, tunes he couldn't place. There were remembrances of tremendous joys and fears, but he often couldn't connect them to events or people. They were just feelings, batting him around in the dark.

"Do you ever notice," George said, "how even the blankets feel wet, when you know they're dry? And I come from Scotland. I know wool. I know sheep. But *this* wool? There's something demonic about this wool. I cut my knuckles on it making the bed the other morning."

Simon *mmm*'ed a reply. There was no need for any real attention. He and George had these same conversations every night. The slime and the mold and the creatures in the walls and the rough blankets and the cold. Every night, these were the topics. Simon's thoughts drifted. He'd had two visitors recently, and neither of the visits had gone well.

Isabelle and Clary, two of the most important people in his life (as far as he could tell), had both come to the Academy. Isabelle had appeared to stake her claim on Simon, and Simon—in a move that astonished him still—told her to back off. It couldn't just go back to the way it was. Not like this, not when he couldn't remember what *it* was. And then in the training exercise, Isabelle had shown up and slain a vampire that was about to take Simon down, but she had done so coolly. There was a distressing deadness to the way she spoke. Then Clary had popped up. *Be careful with her,* Clary had said. *She's more fragile than she seems.*

Isabelle—with her whip and her ability to slice a demon in half—was more fragile than she seemed.

The guilt had been keeping him awake at night.

"Isabelle again?" George asked.

"How did you know?"

"Educated guess. I mean, she showed up and threatened to cut anyone to ribbons who got near you, and now you don't seem to be talking, and your friend Clary showed up to talk to you about her, and you also mumble her name when you sleep."

"I do?"

"On occasion. You're either saying 'Isabelle' or 'fishy smell.' Could be either, to be fair."

"How do I fix this?" Simon asked. "I don't even know what I'm fixing."

"I don't know," George said. "But morning comes early. Best try to sleep."

There was a long pause and then . . .

"There must be snakes," George said. "Isn't this place everything a snake could want? Cool, made of stone, lots of holes to slither in and out of, lots of mice to eat . . . Why am I still talking? Simon, make me stop talking. . . ."

But Simon let him go on. Even talk of possible nearby snakes was better than what was currently going through his head.

Idris did its seasons properly, in general. It was like New York in that manner—you got each one, distinct and clear. But Idris was more pleasant than New York. The winter wasn't just frozen garbage and slush; the summer wasn't just boiling garbage and air-conditioner drippings that always felt like spit coming from overhead. Idris was greenery in the warm weather, crisp and tranquil in the cold, the air always smelling of freshness and burning log fires.

Mostly. Then there were mornings like the ones this week, which were all bluster. Winds with little fishhooks at the end of every gust. Cold that got inside the clothes. Shadowhunter gear, while practical, wasn't necessarily very warm. It was light, easy to move in, like fighting gear should be. It was not made for standing outside on a boggy stretch at seven in the morning when the sun was barely up. Simon thought of his puffy jacket from home, and his bed, and heating in general. Breakfast, which had been a glue substitute under the banner of porridge, sat heavily in his stomach.

Coffee. That's what this morning needed. Idris had no coffee places, nowhere to pop in and get a cup of the hot, steaming, and awake-making. The breakfast drink at the Academy was a thin tea that Simon suspected was not tea at all, but the watery runoff of one of the many noxious soups that emerged from the back of the kitchen. He swore he'd found a bit of potato skin in his mug that morning. He *hoped* it was potato skin.

One cup from Java Jones. Was that so much to want from life?

"Do you see this tree?" shouted Delaney Scarsbury, pointing at a tree.

Of the many questions their physical trainer had put to them over the last few months, this was one of the most logical and direct and yet confusing. Everyone could clearly see the tree. It was the only tree in this particular patch of field. It was tall, slightly tilted to the left.

Mornings with Scarsbury sounded like the name of a call-in radio show for cranks, but it was, in reality, just physical punishment designed to condition and train them to fight. And to be fair, Simon was more in shape now than he had been when he arrived.

"Do you see this tree?"

The question had been so weirdly obvious that no one had replied. Now they all mumbled a yes, they saw the tree.

"Here is what you are going to do," Scarsbury said. "You are going to climb this tree, walk along that branch"—he pointed to one heavy main branch, maybe fifteen feet from the ground—"and jump off."

"No, I'm not," Simon muttered. Similar sounds of discontent rumbled around the class. No one seemed excited about the prospect of climbing up a tree and then deliberately falling out of it.

"Morning," said a familiar voice.

Simon turned to see Jace Herondale behind him, all smiles. He looked relaxed and rested and utterly comfortable in his gear. Shadowhunters could draw runes for warmth. They didn't need hypoallergenic down-substitute puffy coats. Jace wasn't wearing a hat, either, which allowed his perfectly tousled golden hair to wave attractively in the breeze. He was keeping back and had not yet been noticed by the others, who were still listening to Scarsbury yelling over the wind while pointing at the tree.

"How did you get roped into this?" Simon asked, blowing into his hands to warm them.

Jace shrugged. "Just lending a graceful and athletic hand," he said. "It would be remiss of me to deny the newest generation of Shadowhunters a glimpse of what they could become if they were very, very, very lucky."

Simon closed his eyes for a moment. "You're doing this to impress Clary," he said. "Also checking up on me."

"By the Angel, he's gone telepathic," Jace said, pretending to stagger back. "Basically, everyone's pitching in since all your teachers ran away. I'm assisting with training. Like it or not."

"Hmm," said Simon. "Not."

"Come on now," Jace said, clapping him on the arm. "You used to love doing this."

"Did I?"

"Maybe," Jace said. "You didn't scream. Wait. No. Yes, you did. My mistake. But it's easy. This is just a training exercise."

"The last training exercise involved killing a vampire. In the training exercise before that, I watched someone get an arrow in the knee."

"I've seen worse. Come on. This is a fun exercise."

"There is no fun here," Simon said. "This is not Fun Academy. I should know. I was in a band once called Fun Academy."

"To assist you this morning," Scarsbury yelled, "we have an expert and highly physically able Shadowhunter—Jace Lightwood Herondale."

There was an audible gasp and titters of nervous laughter as every head turned in Jace's direction. There were suddenly a lot of female sighs from the class, and some male ones too. It reminded Simon of standing in line for a rock concert—at any moment, he felt, the crowd might burst into a squeeing noise most unbecoming to future demon hunters.

Jace smiled wider and stepped forward to lead the group. Scarsbury nodded his greeting and stepped back, arms folded. Jace eyed the tree for a moment and then leaned casually against it.

"The trick to falling is not to fall," Jace said.

"Wonderful," Simon said under his breath.

"You are not falling. You are choosing to descend using the most direct means possible. You remain in control of your decent. A Shadowhunter doesn't fall—a Shadowhunter drops. You've been trained in the basic mechanics of how to do this . . ."

Simon recalled Scarsbury shouting a few things over the wind several days before that may have been training instructions on falls. Phrases like "avoid rocks" and "not on your back" and "unless you're a complete idiot, which some of you are."

". . . so now we'll take the theory and put it into practice."

Jace took hold of the tree and scampered up it with the ease of a monkey, then made his way to the branch, where he stood freely and easily.

"Now," he called down to the group, "I look at the ground. I choose my landing site. Remember—protect the head. If there's any way to break momentum, any other surface you can use to lessen the length of the fall, use it—unless it's dangerous. Don't aim for sharp rocks or branches that could pierce or break you. Bend the knees. Keep relaxed. If your hands take the impact, be sure to make contact with the entire palm, but avoid this. Feet down, then roll. Keep that momentum going. Spread out the force of the impact. Like so . . ."

Jace delicately stepped off the branch and dropped to the ground, striking with a subdued thud. He instantly rolled and was up on his feet again in a moment.

"Like that."

He gave his hair a little shake. Simon watched several people flush as he did so. Marisol had to cover her face with her hands for a moment.

"Excellent," said Scarsbury. "That's what you will do. Jace will assist."

Jace took this as his cue to climb the tree again. He made it look so simple, so elegant—just hand over hand, feet firmly gripped the entire way up. At the top, he took a casual seat in the nook of the branch and swung his legs.

"Who's first?"

There was no movement for a moment.

"Might as well get it over with," George said in a low voice, before holding up his hand and stepping forward.

Though George was not as nimble as Jace, he did make it up

the tree. He used a lot of clutching, and his feet slipped several times. Some of the phrases he used were lost to the wind, but Simon was pretty sure they were obscene. Once George reached the branch, Jace leaned back dangerously to make room. George considered the branch for a moment—the lone, unsupported beam stretching over the ground.

"Come on, Lovelace!" Scarsbury shouted.

Simon saw Jace lean in and offer a few words of advice to George, who was still gripping the trunk of the tree. Then, with Jace nodding, George released the tree and took a few careful steps out onto the branch. He hesitated again, teetering a bit in the wind. Then he looked down, and with a pained expression, he stepped off the branch and fell heavily to the ground. The thud he made was much louder than Jace's, but he did roll and manage to get back on his feet.

"Not bad," Scarsbury said as George hobbled back to Simon. He was rubbing his arm.

"You do not want to do that," he said to Simon as he approached.

Simon had already worked that out. The confirmation didn't help his spirits.

Simon watched his classmates go up the tree one by one. For some, that took up to ten minutes of grunting and clawing and occasionally falling off halfway up. This got a loud "I told you, not on your back" from Scarsbury. Jace stayed in the tree the entire time, like some kind of rakish bird, at points smiling at the students below. Sometimes he looked elegantly bored and walked up and down the branch for fun.

When there was simply no avoiding it anymore, Simon approached for his turn. Jace smiled at him from above.

"It's easy," Jace said. "You probably did it all the time as a child. Just do that."

"I'm from Brooklyn," Simon replied. "We don't climb trees."

Jace shrugged, suggesting that these things were not to be helped.

The first thing Simon learned about the tree was that while it appeared to lean to the side, it was really just straight up. And while the bark was rough and cut into the meat of the hands, it was also slippery, so every time he tried to get a foothold, he lost it. He tried to do it the way he'd seen Jace and George do it—they seemed to grip the tree very lightly. Simon tried this, realized it was futile, and grabbed the tree in a hug so intimate, he wondered if they were now dating. Using this awkward clutching method and some froglike leg pushes, he managed to get up the trunk, scraping his face along the way. About three-quarters of the way up, he felt his palms slick with sweat and he started to lose his grip. The falling feeling filled him with a sudden panic and he gripped harder.

"You're doing fine," Jace said in a voice that suggested Simon was not doing fine, but that was the kind of thing Jace was supposed to say.

Simon made it to the branch using a few desperate moves he knew looked very bad from below. There was almost definitely a moment or two when his butt must have been on display in a less-than-flattering manner. But he made it. Standing up was the next trick, which he accomplished with more fevered gripping of the trunk.

"Good," Jace said, giving a quirky little smile. "Now just walk to me."

Jace walked backward down the branch. *Backward.*

Now that Simon was on the branch, it didn't look like it was fifteen feet off the ground. It looked like it was in the sky. It was round and uneven and slippery as ever and it wasn't meant to be walked on, especially not in the sneakers Simon had chosen to wear that morning.

But he'd gotten this far and he wasn't going to let Jace just do his magic backward walk while he clung to the trunk. He had gotten up there. Climbing down was a bad prospect, so there was really just the one option, and at least it was quick.

Simon took his first step. His body immediately began to shake.

"Look up," Jace said sharply. "Look at me."

"I need to see—"

"You need to look up to keep your balance. *Look at me.*"

Jace had stopped smirking. Simon looked at him.

"Now step again. Don't look down. Your feet will find the branch. Arms out for balance. Don't worry about down yet. Eyes on me."

Somehow, this worked. Simon made it six steps out onto the branch and was amazed to find himself standing there, arms rigid and out like airplane wings, the wind blowing hard. Just out on a tree branch with Jace.

"Now turn to face the Academy. Keep looking out. Use it as a horizon. That's how you stay balanced—you choose a fixed point to concentrate on. Keep your weight forward—you don't want to go over backward."

No. Simon really didn't want to do that. He moved one foot to meet the other, and then he was standing facing the pile of rocks that formed the Academy, and his fellow students below, all looking up. Most did not look impressed, but George gave him a thumbs-up.

"Now," Jace said, "bend a bit at the knees. And then I want you to just step off in one large stepping motion. Don't jump with both feet. Just step. And as you go down, bring your legs together and keep yourself relaxed."

This should not have been the hardest thing he'd ever done. Simon knew he'd done more. He knew he'd fought demons and come back from the dead. Jumping out of a tree should not have felt this terrifying.

He stepped into the air. He felt his brain react to this new information—*There's nothing there, don't do it, there's nothing there*—but momentum had already pulled his other leg off the branch and then . . .

The good thing that could be said about the experience was that it was quick. Points to gravity on that one. A few seconds of almost blissful fear and confusion and then a hammering feeling as his feet met the earth. His skeleton juddered, his knees buckled in submission, his aching skull lodged a formal complaint, and he fell over sideways in what would have been a roll if he had rolled and not, in fact, just remained there on the ground in a shrimp position.

"Get up, Lewis!" Scarsbury yelled.

Jace landed beside him, like a large killer butterfly, barely making a noise.

"The first one is always the hardest," he said, offering Simon a hand. "The first few dozen, really. I can't remember."

It hurt, but he didn't appear to *be* hurt. The wind was knocked out of his lungs, and he needed a moment to take a few deep breaths. He staggered back to where George was waiting, a sympathetic look on his face. The last two students completed the task, each looking as miserable as Simon, and then they were free to go for lunch. Most of the group was limping as they made their way back across the field.

Since Catarina had buried the soup in the woods, the kitchens of the Academy had been forced to try to come up with some other kind of foodstuff. As usual, an attempt was made to feature food from around the world, to reflect the many nations the students had come from. Today, Simon was informed, featured Swedish cuisine. There were meatballs, a vat of lingonberry sauce, mashed potatoes, smoked salmon, fish balls, beet salad, and at the very end, a strong-smelling item that Simon was informed was a special pickled herring from the Baltic region. Simon got the sense that, prepared by people who knew what they were doing, everything on offer would have looked a lot more delicious—except possibly the pickled herring from the Baltic region. In terms of what a vegetarian could eat, there wasn't much. He got some potatoes and lingonberry sauce and scraped one portion's worth of beet salad out of the practically empty container. Some kind Shadowhunter from Alicante had clearly taken pity on the students and provided bread rolls, which were eagerly snatched up. By the time Simon limped up to the basket, it was empty. He turned to make his way to a table and found Jace in his path. He had a roll in his hand and had already taken a bite.

"How about you sit with me?"

The Academy cafeteria looked less like a school dining hall and more like a terrible, cheap restaurant that had gotten its furnishings out of Dumpsters. There were big tables, and tiny, intimate ones. Simon, still too sore to make jokes about lunch dates, followed Jace to one of the small, rickety tables on the side of the room. He was aware of everyone watching them go. He gave George a nod, hoping to convey that he just had to do this—no offense in not sitting with him. George nodded back.

Jon, Julie, and the others in the elite course, who had been devastated to miss Falling Out of Trees with Jace Herondale 101, all stared over as if ready to leap up and save Jace from the bad company he'd fallen into, carry him away in a litter made of chocolate and roses, and bear his children.

Once they sat, Jace tucked into his lunch and didn't say a word. Simon watched him eat and waited, but Jace was all about the food. He had taken large helpings of most things, including the pickled Baltic herring. Now that he was even closer to it, Simon began to suspect that this fish had not been pickled at all. Someone at the famed Shadowhunter Academy kitchens had *attempted* to pickle fish—something that took skill and precise adherence to instructions—and had probably just invented a new form of botulism. Jace shoveled it back. Then again, Jace was the sort of *Man vs. Wild* guy who would probably be happy to fish a trout out of a stream with his bare hands and eat it while it was still flopping.

"Did you want to talk to me about something?" Simon finally asked.

Jace forked up a meatball and looked at Simon meditatively. "I've been doing research," he said. "Into my family."

"The Herondales?" Simon supplied, after a short pause.

"You might not remember, but I have kind of a complicated family history," Jace said. "Anyway, I only found out I was a

Herondale a little while ago. It took me a while to adjust to the idea. They're kind of a legendary family."

Back to the food for a few minutes. When his plates and bowls were empty, Jace sat back and regarded Simon for a moment. Simon considered asking if Jace was kind of a big deal, but decided he wouldn't get the joke.

Jace went on. "Anyway, the whole thing, it started to remind me—well, of you. It's like there are these important things in my history but I don't know all of them, and I'm trying to pull together an identity that has all these holes in it. The Herondales—some of them were good people, and some of them were monsters."

"None of that needs to affect you," Simon said. "The choices you make are what matter, not your bloodline. But I imagine you have a lot of people in your life to tell you that. Clary. Alec." He looked at Jace sideways. "Isabelle."

Jace's eyebrows went up. "You want to talk about Isabelle? Or Alec?"

"Alec hates me and I do not know why," Simon said. "Isabelle hates me and I do know why, which is almost worse. So no, I do not want to talk about the Lightwoods."

"It's true you have a Lightwood problem," Jace said, and his golden eyes glinted. "It started with Alec. As you astutely observed, you two have a history. But I shouldn't get in the middle of that."

"Please tell me what's going on with Alec," Simon said. "You are really freaking me out."

"No," Jace said. "There are so many deep feelings involved. There's so much hurt. It wouldn't be right. I didn't come here to stir up trouble. I came here to show potential Shadowhunters how to drop from heights without breaking their necks."

Simon stared at Jace. Jace stared back with wide, innocent golden eyes.

Simon decided that the next time he saw Alec, he would have to ask Alec himself about the secrets that lay between them. This was obviously something he and Alec had to work out on their own.

"But I will say this about your Lightwood problem," Jace said, very casually. "Isabelle and Alec both have difficulty showing when they feel pain. But I can see it in both of them, especially when they try to hide it. She's in pain."

"And I made it worse," Simon said, shaking his head. "This is my fault. Me, with my memory wiped out by some kind of demon king. Me, with no concept of what happened in my life. Me, the guy with no special abilities who's probably going to get killed *in school*. I'm a monster."

"No," Jace said evenly. "No one blames you for not being able to remember. You offered yourself as a sacrifice. You were brave. You saved Magnus. And you saved Isabelle. You saved me. You need to bend your knees more."

"What?"

Jace was standing up now.

"When you first step off. Bend the knees right away. Otherwise you did pretty well."

"But what about Isabelle?" Simon asked. "What do I do?"

"I have no idea," Jace said.

"So you just came here to torture me and talk about yourself?" Simon demanded.

"Oh, Simon, Simon, Simon," said Jace. "You may not remember, but that's kind of our thing."

With that, he walked away, clearly aware of the admiring glances that followed his every step.

After lunch they had a history lecture. Usually they met in a classroom, but today everyone was assembled in the main hall. There was no grandeur to the hall—just some crooked benches, and not enough of them. The chairs from the cafeteria were dragged in to supplement, but there still weren't enough seats. So some students (the elites) had chairs and benches, and the dregs sat on the floor at the front, like the little kids in middle school. After this morning, though, a few hours of sitting on a bare, cold, stone floor was luxury.

Catarina took her place at the wobbly lectern.

"We have a special guest lecturer today," she said. "She is visiting us to talk about the role Shadowhunters play in writing history. As you are likely aware, though I don't want to make any overly optimistic assumptions, Shadowhunters have been involved in many prominent moments in mundane history. Because Shadowhunters must also guard mundanes from knowing about our world, you must also sometimes take control of the writing of that history. By this I mean you have to cover things up. You need to provide a plausible explanation for what's happened—one that does not involve demons."

"Like *Men in Black*," Simon whispered to George.

"So please give your full attention to our esteemed guest," Catarina went on. She stepped aside, and a tall young woman took her place.

"I am Tessa Gray," she said in a low, clear voice. "And I believe in the importance of stories."

The woman at the front of the room looked like she might

be a sophomore in college. She was elegantly dressed in a short black skirt, cashmere sweater, and paisley scarf. Simon had seen this woman once before—at Jocelyn and Luke's wedding. Clary had said she had played a very important role in Clary's life when she was a child. She had also informed Simon that Tessa was about a hundred and fifty years old, though she certainly didn't look it.

"For you to understand this story, you have to understand who and what I am. Like Catarina, I am a warlock—however, my mother was not human but a Shadowhunter."

A murmur from around the room, which Tessa glossed over.

"I am not able to bear Marks, but I once lived among Shadowhunters—I was a Shadowhunter's wife, and my children were Shadowhunters. I was witness to much that no other Downworlder ever saw, and now I am almost the only person alive who recalls the truth behind the stories mundanes made up to explain away the times their world brushed ours. I am many things. One is a living record of Shadowhunter history. Here is one story you may have heard of—Jack the Ripper. What can you tell me about that name?"

Simon was ready for this one. He'd read *From Hell* six times. He'd been waiting all his life for someone to ask him an Alan Moore question. His hand shot up.

"He was a murderer," Simon burst out. "He killed prostitutes in London in the late 1800s. He was probably Queen Victoria's doctor, and the whole thing was a royal cover-up to hide the fact that the prince had had an illegitimate child."

Tessa smiled at him. "You are right that Jack the Ripper is the name given to a murderer—or at least, to a series of murders. What you refer to is the royal conspiracy, which has been disproven. I believe it is also the plot of a graphic novel and film called *From Hell.*"

Simon's love life was complicated, but there was a pang, just for a moment, for this woman talking graphic novels with him. Ah, well. Tessa Gray, foxy nerd, was probably dating someone already.

"I will give you the simple facts," Tessa said. "Once, I was not called Tessa Gray but Tessa Herondale. In that time, in 1888, in East London, there was a string of terrible murders. . . ."

London, October 1888

"It's not appropriate," Tessa said to her husband, Will.

"He likes it."

"Children like all sorts of things, Will. They like sweets and fire and trying to stick their head up the chimney. Just because he likes the dagger . . ."

"Look how steadily he holds it."

Little James Herondale, age two, was in fact holding a dagger quite well. He stabbed it into a sofa cushion, sending out a burst of feathers.

"Ducks," he said, pointing at the feathers.

Tessa swiftly removed the dagger from his tiny hand and replaced it with a wooden spoon. James had recently become very attached to this wooden spoon and carried it with him everywhere, often refusing to go to sleep without it.

"Spoon," James said, tottering off across the parlor.

"Where did he find the dagger?" Tessa asked.

"It's possible I took him to the weapons room," Will said.

"Is it?"

"It is, yes. It's possible."

"And it's possible he somehow got a dagger from where it is secured on the wall, out of his reach," Tessa said.

"We live in a world of possibilities," Will said.

Tessa fixed a gray-eyed stare on her husband.

"He was never out of my sight," Will said quickly.

"If you could manage it," Tessa said, nodding to the sleeping figure of Lucie Herondale in her little basket by the fire, "perhaps you won't give Lucie a broadsword until she's actually able to stand? Or is that asking too much?"

"It seems a reasonable request," Will said, with an extravagant bow. "Anything for you, my pearl beyond price. Even withholding weaponry from my only daughter."

Will knelt down, and James ran to him to show off his spoon. Will admired the spoon as if it were a first edition, his scarred hand large and gentle against James's tiny back.

"Spoon," James said proudly.

"I see, Jamie *bach*," murmured Will, who Tessa had caught singing Welsh lullabies to the children on their most sleepless nights. To his children, Will showed the same love he had always shown to her, fierce and unyielding. And the same protectiveness he had only ever showed to one other person: the person James had been named after. Will's *parabatai*, Jem.

"Uncle Jem would be so impressed," she told Jamie with a smile. It was what she and Will called James Carstairs around their children, though between the two of them he was just Jem, and in public he was Brother Zachariah, a feared and respected Silent Brother.

"Jem," echoed James, quite clearly, and her smile grew. Will and James both tilted up their heads as one to look at her, their storm-cloud-black hair framing their faces. Jamie's was small and round, baby fat obscuring the bones and angles of a face that would one day be as like Will's as his hair. Two pairs of eyes, one darkly brilliant blue and one celestial gold, looked up at her with absolute trust and more than a little mischief. Her boys.

The long, long London summer days that Tessa was still getting used to, even after several years, were now starting to shorten rather rapidly. No more sunlight at ten at night— now the night was gathering at six, and the fog was heavy, and faintly yellow, and it pressed against the windows. Bridget had drawn the curtains, and the rooms were dim but cozy.

It was a strange thing, being a Shadowhunter and a parent. She and Will had been living lives that constantly involved danger, and then suddenly, two very small children had joined them. Yes, they were two very small children who occasionally got hold of daggers and would one day start training to become warriors—if they wished to do so. But now they were simply two very small children. Little James, wobbling around the Institute with his spoon. Little Lucie napping in her cradle or basket or in one of many pairs of willing arms.

These days Will was, Tessa was glad to note, a bit more careful about taking risks. (Usually. She would really have to make sure there were no more daggers for the children.) Bridget could usually keep the children well in hand, but Tessa and Will liked to be at home as much as they could. Cecily and Gabriel's little Anna was a year older than James, and had already blazed her way through the Institute. She sometimes made attempts to go for walks on her own in London, but was always blocked by Auntie Jessamine, who stood guard by the door. Whether or not Anna knew that Auntie Jessamine was a ghost was unclear. She was simply the loving, ethereal force by the doorway who shooed her back inside and told her to stop taking her father's hats. Anna's younger brother, Christopher, James's age, was a quiet boy, more given to taking apart the clocks in the parlor than to talking.

It was a good life. There was a feeling of safety about it that reminded Tessa of a more peaceful time, back when she was in New York, back before she knew all the truths about herself and the world she lived in. Sometimes, when she sat with her children by the fire, it all felt so . . . normal. Like there were no demons, no creatures in the night.

She allowed herself these moments.

"What are we having this evening?" Will asked, tucking the dagger into a drawer. "It smells a bit like lamb stew."

Before Tessa could answer, she heard the door open and Gabriel Lightwood came hurrying in, the smell of the cold fog trailing in his wake. He didn't bother to remove his coat. From the way he was walking and the look on his face, Tessa could tell that this little moment of domestic tranquility was over.

"Something wrong?" Will asked.

"This," Gabriel said. He held up a broadsheet newspaper called the *Star*. "It's awful."

"I agree," Will said. "Those halfpenny rags are terrible. But you seem to be more upset about them than is appropriate."

"They may be halfpenny rags, but listen to this."

He stepped under a gaslight, unfolded the paper, and snapped it once to straighten it.

"*The terror of Whitechapel,*" he read.

"Oh," Will said. "That."

Everyone in London knew about the terror in Whitechapel.

The murders had been extraordinarily horrible. News of the killings now filled every paper.

"... has walked again, and this time has marked down two victims, one hacked and disfigured beyond discovery, the other with her throat cut and torn. Again he has got away clear; and again the police, with wonderful frankness, confess that they have not a clue. They are waiting for a seventh and an eighth murder, just as they waited for a fifth, to help them to it. Meanwhile, Whitechapel is half mad with fear. The people are afraid even to talk with a stranger. Notwithstanding the repeated proofs that the murderer has but one aim, and seeks but one class in the community, the spirit of terror has got fairly abroad, and no one knows what steps a practically defenceless community may take to protect itself or avenge itself on any luckless wight who may be taken for the enemy. It is the duty of journalists to keep their heads cool, and not inflame men's passions when what is wanted is cool temper and clear thinking; and we shall try and write calmly about this new atrocity."

"Very lurid," said Will. "But the East End is a violent place for mundanes."

"I do not think this is a mundane."

"Wasn't there a letter? The killer sent something?"

"Yes, a very odd letter. I have that as well."

Gabriel went over to a desk in the corner and opened it, revealing a neat stack of newspaper cuttings.

"Yes, here it is. *Dear Boss, I keep on hearing the police have caught me but they won't fix me just yet. I have laughed when they look so clever and talk about being on the right track. That joke about Leather Apron gave me real fits. I am down on whores and I shan't quit ripping them till I do get buckled. Grand work the last job was. I gave the lady no time to squeal. How can they catch me now. I love my work and want to start again. You will soon hear of me with my funny little games. I saved some of the proper red stuff in a ginger beer bottle over the last job to write with but it went thick like glue and I can't use it. Red ink is fit enough I hope. Ha. Ha. The next job I do I shall clip the lady's ears off and send to the police officers just for jolly wouldn't you. Keep this letter back till I do a bit more work, then give it out straight. My knife's so nice and sharp I want to get to work right away if I get a chance. Good luck. Yours truly, Jack the Ripper.*"

"That's quite a name he's given himself," Tessa said. "And quite horrific."

"And almost certainly false," Gabriel said. "A bit of nonsense made up by newspapermen to keep selling the story. And good for us as well, as it gives a human face—or at least the appearance of a human hand—to it. But come, I'll show you."

He waved them over to the table in the middle of the room and removed a map from inside his coat. He spread this out.

"I have just come from the East End," he said. "Something about the stories disturbed me, for more than the obvious reasons. I went there to have a look about for myself. And what happened last night proves my theory. There have been many murders recently—all of women, women who . . ."

"Prostitutes," Tessa said.

"Quite," Gabriel said.

"Tessa has such an extensive vocabulary," Will said. "It is one of the most attractive things about her. Shame about yours, Gabriel."

"Will, listen to me." Gabriel allowed himself a long sigh.

"Spoon!" James said, running at his uncle Gabriel and jabbing him in the thigh. Gabriel mussed the boy's hair affectionately.

"You're such a good boy," he said. "I often wonder how you could possibly be Will's."

"Spoon," James said, leaning against his uncle's leg lovingly.

"No, Jamie," Will urged. "Your honorable father has been impugned. Attack, attack!"

"Bridget," Tessa said. "Could you take James to have his supper?"

James was ushered from the room, caught up in Bridget's skirts.

"The first murder," Gabriel said, "was here. Buck's Row. That occurred on August the thirty-first. Very vicious, with a number of long cuts to the abdomen. The second was on Hanbury Street on September eighth. Her name was Annie Chapman, and she was found in the courtyard behind a house. This murder had a very similar set of incisions, but was very much worse. The contents of the abdomen were simply removed. Some organs were placed on her shoulder. Some organs were simply gone. All of the work was done with a surgical precision, and would have taken a skilled surgeon some time to do. This was done in minutes, outdoors, without much light to work by. This was the work that got my attention. And now the last murders, which were only a few nights ago—these were fiendish works indeed. Now, observe closely. The first murder of that night took place here."

He pointed to a spot on the map marked Dutfield's Yard.

"This is right off of Berner Street, you see? This was Elizabeth Stride, and she was found at one in the morning. Similar injuries, but seemingly incomplete. Just forty-five minutes later, the body of Catherine Eddowes is found in Mitre Square."

Gabriel traced his finger along the route from Berner Street to Mitre Square.

"It's a distance of over half a mile," he said. "I've just walked it several times. This second murder was much more terrible in nature. The body was utterly dismembered and organs were removed. The work was very delicate in nature, very skilled. And it was done in darkness, in no more than a few minutes. Work that would have taken a surgeon much more time and certainly some light. It's simply not possible, and yet, it happened."

Tessa and Will considered the map in front of them for a moment while the fire crackled gently behind them.

"He could have had a carriage," Will said.

"Even with a carriage, there would simply not be time to commit these acts. And they are most certainly acts committed by the same being."

"Not the work of werewolves?"

"Definitely not," Gabriel said. "Nor vampires. The bodies have not been drained. They haven't been consumed or torn. They have been cut, with organs removed and arranged, as if by design. This"—Gabriel tapped the map for emphasis—"is demonic in nature. And it has set London into a panic."

"But why would a demon target only these poor women?" Will asked.

"There must be something they require. The fiend does seem to take . . . childbearing organs. I propose we patrol the East End, beginning at once. This area."

Gabriel drew a circle around Spitalfields with his finger.

"This is the center of the activity. This is where it must be. Are we agreed?"

"Where's Cecily?" Will asked.

"She has already started the work. She is there now, speaking to some of the women on the street. They find it easier speaking to her. We must start at once."

Will nodded.

"I have one further suggestion. As the beast seems to be attracted to a certain class of woman, we should use glamours . . ."

"Or shape-shifters," Tessa said.

". . . to attract the demon."

Will's eyes caught blue fire. "You are suggesting using my wife and my sister to lure the thing out?"

"It is the best way," Gabriel said. "And your sister is *my* wife. Both Tessa and Cecily are more than capable, and we would be there as well."

"It is a good plan," Tessa said, forestalling Will and Gabriel's next argument. (They would always have time for another one.)

Gabriel nodded. "Again, are we agreed?"

Tessa looked into her husband's bright blue eyes.

"Agreed," she said.

"Agreed," said Will. "On one condition."

"And what condition is—" Gabriel broke off with a sigh. "Ah," he said. "Brother Zachariah."

"This monster is violent," said Will. "We might need a healer. Someone with the power of a Silent Brother. This is a special situation."

"I cannot recall a situation you did *not* think was special and required his presence," said Gabriel dryly. "You have been known to call upon Brother Zachariah for a broken toe."

"It was turning green," said Will.

"He's right," said Tessa. "Green doesn't suit him. Makes him look bilious." She smiled at Gabriel. "There is no reason for Jem not to accompany us. We may yet need him and it does no harm to have him there."

Gabriel opened his mouth and then closed it again with a click. He hadn't known Jem Carstairs that well before Jem had become a Silent Brother, but he had liked him. Still, unlike his wife, Gabriel was one of the people who (clearly) thought it odd that even though Tessa had once been engaged to Jem, she and Will considered him part of their family and tried to include him in everything they did.

There were few people in the world who understood how much Will and Jem had loved each other, *did* love each other, and how much Will missed him. But Tessa did.

"If we might be able to save one of these poor women, we must try," said Tessa. "If Jem can help, that would be wonderful. If not, Cecily and I will do all we can. I hope you do not think either of us lack the courage."

Will stopped glaring at Gabriel, and turned to Tessa. He looked at her and his face softened: The traces of the wild, broken boy he had been vanished, replaced with the expression often worn by the man he was now, who knew what it was to love and be loved. "Dear heart," he said. He took her hand and kissed it. "Who knows your courage better than I?"

"That October," Tessa Gray said, "there were no Ripper murders reported. The London Institute made sure to patrol every evening, right through until sunrise. It was believed that this kept the demon at bay."

It had gotten dark outside, even though it was only around three in the afternoon. The hall had gotten considerably colder as the sun had faded, and all of the students were hunkered down in the seats, arms wrapped around themselves to keep warm, but utterly alert. Tessa had been talking for some time, showing maps of London, describing truly horrific murders. It was the kind of thing that kept you awake.

"I think," she said, rubbing her hands together, "that it is time for a short break. We'll resume in half an hour."

During long lecture classes, the Academy was merciful enough to allow one bathroom break every few hours, along with some more of the murky tea, which was put out in one of the large halls in steaming, ancient urns. Simon was cold enough to take a cup. Again, some benevolent Shadowhunter had provided a tray of small cakes. Simon was able to get a fleeting look at them before they were snatched up by elites, who were excused first. Some sad little biscuits were left on the side. They looked like they were made of packed sand.

"Good stuff today," George said, picking up a dry biscuit. "Well, not good, but more interesting than usual. I like the new teacher as well. You wouldn't think she was—how old is she?"

"I think a hundred and fifty or something. Maybe older," said Simon. His mind was elsewhere. Tessa Gray had mentioned two names: *Jem Carstairs* and *Brother Zachariah*. Apparently they were the same person. Which was interesting, because somewhere in Simon's shifting memories, he knew those names. And he remembered Emma Carstairs, facing Jace—he couldn't remember why, but he knew it had happened—and saying, *The Carstairs owe the Herondales.*

Simon glanced over at Jace, who was seated in an armchair, being waited on hand and foot by students.

"Miss Gray looks very good for a hundred and fifty," said George, looking over at where Tessa was examining the tea suspiciously. As she moved away from the table, she cast a quick glance toward Jace. There was a wistful sadness in her expression.

At that moment Jace stood up from his chair, scattering hangers-on. The elites all moved to make way for him, and there was a quiet chorus of "Hi, Jace" and a few wheezing sighs as he made his way over to Simon and George.

"You did really well today," he said to George, who was flushed and appeared speechless.

"I . . . oh. Right. Yeah. Thanks, Jace. Thanks."

"Are you still sore?" Jace asked Simon.

"Mostly my pride."

"That's supposed to goeth before a fall anyway."

Simon winced at the joke. "Really?"

"I've been waiting to say that for a while."

"That's not possible." Jace's expression showed that it was indeed possible. Simon sighed. "Look, Jace, if I could talk to you for a second—"

"Anything you want to tell me can be said around my good buddy George here."

You're going to regret that, Simon thought. "Fine," he said. "Go talk to Tessa."

Jace blinked. "Tessa Gray? The warlock?"

"She used to be a Shadowhunter," said Simon carefully. "Look, she was telling us a story—more a piece of history, really—and do you remember what Emma said? About the Carstairs owing the Herondales?"

Jace put his hands in his pockets. "Sure, I remember. I'm surprised *you* remember."

"I think you should talk to Tessa," said Simon. "I think she could tell you about the Herondales. Things you don't know already."

"Hm," Jace said. "I'll think about it."

He walked off. Simon looked after him, frustrated. He wished he could remember enough about how he and Jace interacted normally to know whether this meant Jace was going to ignore his advice or not.

"He treats you like a friend," George said. "Or an equal. You really did know each other. I mean, I knew that, but . . ."

Unsurprisingly, Jonathan Cartwright sidled up to them.

"Just talking to Jace, huh?" he said.

"Are you a detective?" Simon replied. "Your powers of observation are amazing."

Jonathan acted like Simon had never spoken.

"Yeah—Jace and I will catch up later."

"Are you really going to keep up the pretense that you know Jace?" Simon asked. "Because you know that's not going to work now, right? Eventually Jace will just come over and say he doesn't know you."

Jonathan looked glum. Before he could say anything, though, the signal was given for everyone to return to the hall, and Simon shuffled in with the others. They took their seats again, and settled in to listen to Tessa.

"We continued to do nightly patrols of the area," Tessa began. "Our duty as Shadowhunters is to protect the mundane world from the influence of demons. We walked, we watched, and we warned all those we could. As much as it was possible, women working in the East End tried to take more care and not walk alone as much. But for women in that profession, safety was rarely a consideration. I had always assumed their lives were hard, but I had no idea. . . ."

London, November 9, 1888

Tessa Herondale certainly knew what poverty was, that it existed. In the time when her aunt had died and she was a young girl left friendless and defenseless in New York, she had felt the cold breath of poverty like a monster stalking at her back. But in the month she and Cecily spent walking the streets of East London under the guise of prostitutes, she knew what it would have been if poverty had caught her and torn at her with its claws.

They dressed the part—old, tattered clothes, heavy rouge on the cheeks. They had to use glamours for the rest, for the true mark of the prostitute was want. Missing teeth. Jaundiced skin. Bodies tight from malnourishment and bent from disease. Women who walked and walked all night long because there was nowhere to sleep, nowhere to sit. They sold themselves for pennies to buy gin because the gin kept them warm, took away the pain for an hour, numbed them to the terrible, brutal reality of their lives. If these women could get the money to have a place to sleep for the night, that didn't mean a bed. It could mean a spot on a floor, or even just a bit of wall to sit against, with a rope run around the room to keep the sleepers from falling over. By the crack of dawn, they'd be tossed out on the street again.

Walking among them, Tessa felt dirty. She felt the remains of her supper in her belly. She knew that her bed in the Institute was warm and contained someone who loved her and would protect her. These women had bruises and cuts. They fought over corners and bits of cracked mirror and scraps of cloth.

And there were children as well. They sat in the fetid streets, no matter their age. Their skin was so dirty as to never be clean. She wondered how many of them had ever had a hot meal in their lives, served on a plate. Had they ever known a home?

Over it all, the smell. The smell was what really ground itself into Tessa's soul. The tang of urine, the night soil, the vomit.

"I'm getting tired of this," said Cecily.

"I think everyone here is tired," Tessa replied.

Cecily sighed sadly.

"One carriage ride away and the streets are quiet and spotless. It's a different world in the West End."

A drunken man approached them and made an overture. Since they had to play the part, Cecily and Tessa smiled and led him to an alley, where they inserted him into an empty oyster barrel and left him.

"A month of this and no sign," Tessa said as they walked away from the flailing, upturned legs of the man. "Either we're keeping it away, or . . ."

"Or this simply isn't working."

"Magnus Bane would be useful at a time like this."

"Magnus Bane is enjoying New York," Cecily replied. "You're a warlock."

"I don't have Magnus's experience. Anyway, it's nearly dawn. Another hour and we can go home."

Will and Gabriel had taken to posting themselves in the Ten Bells pub, which seemed to be the central place for news of the killer. Indeed, many locals said they had seen him there with the victims before the murders. Sometimes Jem would come by with news from the Silent City. It wasn't unusual for Cecily and Tessa to return exhausted to the pub at the crack of dawn, and find Gabriel gone and Will asleep, wrapped up in Brother Zachariah's parchment robes, head on the table.

Jem would be reading a book, or quietly looking out the window. He could see, in his own fashion, despite his closed eyes. He was glamoured, so that his appearance would not shock the tavern's denizens. Tessa could always feel Cecily tense when she first saw Jem: black runes scored his cheeks, and there was a single white streak in his dark hair.

Sometimes, after Cecily and Gabriel left, Tessa would sit with her hand in Jem's and Will sleeping against her shoulder, listening to the rain on the windows. It never did last for long, though, since she did not like leaving the children alone so much, though Bridget was an excellent nurse.

It was hard on both families. The children would wake to find four exhausted parents who drew endless runes for wakefulness and yet still could barely keep up with Anna, running about in her uncle's waistcoat, or James, waving his spoon and trying to find the dagger he had seen and loved. Lucie woke at all hours needing milk and embraces.

And here it was, another dawn walking the streets of the East End, and for what? And the dawn was coming later and later. The nights were so very long. As the sun rose over Christ Church in Spitalfields, Cecily turned to Tessa again.

"Home," she said.

"Home," Tessa replied wearily.

They had arranged for a carriage to come for them that morning on Gun Street. They met Will and Gabriel there. They looked a bit worse for wear, as they often had to drink gin all night in order to blend in with the locals. There had been no Jem that night, and Will seemed restless.

"Did you find out anything?" Tessa asked.

"The same as usual," Gabriel said, slurring a little. "All the victims were seen with *a man*. He varies in stature and all manner of appearance."

"So likely an Eidolon," Will said. "It's so generic that it might even be a Du'sien, but I don't think a Du'sien could get that close and convince a woman he was an actual human male, no matter how drunk she was."

"But that tells us nothing," Cecily said. "If it's an Eidolon, it could be anyone."

"It's being remarkably consistent, though," Will said. "It always comes as a man and it always takes women. We're getting nowhere with this."

"Or we're getting everywhere," Gabriel replied. "It hasn't come back."

"We can't do this *forever*."

They'd been having this same conversation every night for the past week. This one ended as it usually did, with the two couples leaning against each other in the back of the carriage and falling asleep until they reached the Institute. They greeted their children, who were having their breakfast with Bridget, and they listened with half-closed eyes as Anna rambled on about her many plans for the day and James banged his spoon.

Tessa and Will started the climb up the steps to their bedroom. Cecily waited for Gabriel, who was lingering in the front parlor.

"I'll be up shortly," he said, his eyes bloodshot. "I just want to read the morning papers."

Gabriel always did this—always checked, every morning. So Tessa, Will, and Cecily returned to bed. Once in their bedroom, Tessa cleaned her face in the basin with the hot water Bridget had left. Their fire was burning, and the bed was turned back, waiting for them. They fell into it gratefully.

They had barely fallen asleep when Tessa heard a fevered banging at the door and Gabriel admitted himself.

"It's happened again," he said, breathless. "By the Angel, this is the worst one yet."

The carriage was recalled, and within the hour, they were on their way back to the East End, this time dressed in gear.

"It happened in a place called Miller's Court, off Dorset Street," Gabriel said.

Of all the terrible streets in East London, Dorset Street was the worst. It was a short road, just off Commercial Street. Tessa had learned much of the goings-on of Dorset Street in the last few weeks. A pair of abusive slum landlords controlled much of the street. There was so much screaming, so much poverty and stench crowded into a small space that it felt like it could push the air out of the lungs. The houses there were subdivided into tiny rooms, each little space rented away. This was a street where everyone had an empty stare, where the prevailing feeling was of desperation.

On the way, Gabriel told them what he'd managed to find out from the morning papers—the address (number thirteen), the victim's name (Mary Kelly). There was a parade moving through the city for Lord Mayor's Day. News of the crime had spread, though, and was making its way along the parade route. Newspaper boys were chanting about the murder and selling papers like mad. Cecily peered out from the curtain of the carriage.

"They seem to be celebrating it," she said. "They're smiling and running to buy the newspapers. My God, how can people celebrate such a thing?"

"It's interesting," Will said, with a dark grin. "Danger is appealing. Especially to those with nothing to lose."

"It's going to be madness down there," Gabriel said.

Indeed, crowds had already gathered all along the road to Dorset Street. The residents were all out watching the police. The police were attempting to hold people back from a small, dark doorway halfway up the road.

"There," Gabriel said. "Miller's Court. We won't be able to get near it unless you can get in, Tessa. There's a detective down there called Abberline from Scotland Yard. If we can get him over here, or one of the constables working inside the room . . ."

"I'll get one of them," Will said, breaking through the crowd.

He returned a few minutes later with a man of middling age, with a kindly appearance. He did appear to be very busy, and his forehead was creased with consternation. Whatever Will had told him, it was enough to lure him away from the place of the crime.

"Where is it?" he said, following Will. "You're quite sure . . ."

"Quite sure."

It was hard to keep people from following them, so Cecily, Tessa, and Gabriel had to block the way while Will led the inspector down an alley. He whistled a few moments later. He was standing in the doorway of a cheap rented room.

"In here," Will said. The inspector was in the corner, looking quite asleep. His clothes were missing. "He'll be fine, but he'll likely wake up soon. Put these on."

While Tessa took the clothes and changed herself into the

form of Abberline, Will filled her in on a few more facts he had gotten from people in the street. Mary Kelly was probably last seen at two thirty in the morning, but one person claimed to have seen her as late as eight thirty. No matter what, whatever had killed her had probably long since vanished.

Once Tessa was ready, Will helped her push her way back through the crowd, down Dorset Street, to the small entry-way that was Miller's Court. Tessa stepped through the dark passageway into a very small courtyard, barely wide enough to turn around in. There were several houses here, cheaply whitewashed. Dozens of faces peered at her from dirty, broken windows.

Room thirteen was barely a room—it was clearly part of a larger space in which a cheap partition had been constructed. It was mostly empty, containing only a few pieces of broken furniture. It was very, very hot, as if a fire had blazed all night.

In all her time fighting demons, Tessa had never seen any-thing like this.

There was blood.

It was in such a large amount that Tessa wondered how one small body could contain so much. It had turned part of the floor black, and the bed, on which the woman rested, was utterly stained. There was no other color. As for the woman herself—she was no more. Her body was destroyed in a way that could barely be comprehended. This had taken time. Her face—there was nothing much left to speak of. Many parts of her were removed. They could be seen in many places, around her on the bed. Some parts of her were on a table.

A man was leaning over her. There was a doctor's bag on the floor, so Tessa steadied herself and then spoke.

"Well, doctor?"

The doctor turned.

"I think we'll have to move her soon. They're trying to break in. We'll have to move her carefully."

"Summarize for me the general situation. I need a concise report."

The doctor stood and wiped his bloodstained hands on his trousers.

"Well, a very deep cut across the throat. The head is nearly off. You can see the nose is gone, much of the skin. There are so many slashes and incisions in the abdomen I barely know where to start. The abdominal cavity is empty and her hands have been placed inside the opening. You can see he's left some of the contents here in this room, but some are missing. The heart is gone. The skin on the table I believe to be from the thighs. . . ."

Tessa could not really take in much more of the information. This was enough.

"I see," she said. "There's someone I have to speak to."

"Make the arrangements for her to be moved," the doctor said. "We can't keep her here. They're going to get in. They want to see."

"Constable," Tessa said to a policeman by the door, "see to it that a cart is brought."

Tessa walked away quickly, back down through the crowd, breathing in as deeply as she could to get the smell of blood and entrails out of her nose. She felt a queasiness she had not experienced since her pregnancies. Will took one look at her and embraced her. Cecily came forward and put smelling salts under her nose. They had learned that smelling salts were necessary.

"Bring out the detective," Tessa said, when she had recovered. "He's needed."

The inspector was retrieved and dressed. The smelling salts were applied, and he slowly came around. Once they had him on his feet and assured him that he had simply fainted, they left the area quickly and walked toward White's Row.

"Whatever it was," Gabriel said, "it's likely long gone. It happened hours ago. By having the body indoors, it went unnoticed for some time."

He took out his Sensor, but it showed no activity.

"I suggest we return to the Institute," he said. "We've learned what we can here. It's time to apply ourselves to the problem in a different way. We have to look at the clues it leaves behind."

"The people," Tessa said.

"The people," Gabriel corrected himself.

They were more awake now. Tessa wondered if she would ever sleep again. She found the transition from East to West London more repugnant this time—the clean buildings, the space, the trees, the parks, the lovely carriages, and the lovely clothes and shops. And just a mile or so away . . .

"What is done cannot be undone," Will said, taking her hand.

"You didn't see her."

"But we will catch the thing that attacked her."

As soon as they turned onto Fleet Street, Tessa felt something wasn't right. She couldn't figure out what it was. The street was utterly quiet. One of the servants from a neighboring property was sweeping leaves from the step. There was a coal cart and a wagon from a greengrocer delivering vegetables. She sat upright, every nerve tense, and when the carriage stopped, she swung the door open quickly and bounded out. Seeing her reaction, the other three followed in a similar fashion.

The first thing that confirmed her fears was that Bridget did not greet them at the door.

"Bridget?" Tessa called.

Nothing.

She looked up at their windows—clean, unbroken, dark. The curtains had been drawn. Will pushed open the door.

They found Bridget at the foot of the staircase. Cecily rushed to her.

"Unconscious," she said. "But breathing. The children! Who is with the children?"

As one, they raced up the stairs. Every light was out, every door closed, every curtain drawn. They all went in separate directions, running to the nursery, to the bedrooms, to every room on the upper floors. Nothing.

"*Shadowhunters . . .*"

The voice was neither male nor female, and it seemed to come from everywhere. Will and Tessa met in the corridor, and Will held a witchlight high.

"What are you?" he yelled. "Where are the children?"

"*Shadowhunters . . .*"

"Where are the children? You can't have an interest in them. Show yourself."

"*Shadowhunters . . .*"

Gabriel and Cecily appeared, seraph blades ready. Will and Tessa reached for theirs. They walked down the steps, watching in every direction.

"*I follow you,*" hissed the voice, which now seemed to come from below them. *"Shadowhunters. I follow you home. Play my game."*

"What is your game?" Will called back. "I'll play any game you like if you show yourself."

"The game is to hide. I like to hide. I like to take . . . the pieces. I hide. I take the pieces."

"I know you have form," Will said. "You've been seen. *Show yourself.*"

"Spoon!"

The cry came from the direction of the dining room. All four ran toward the voice. When they opened the door, they found James standing at the far end of the room, spoon held aloft.

"James!" Tessa cried. "Come to Mama! Come now, James!"

James laughed and, instead of running to Tessa, turned in the direction of the great fireplace, within which a tremendous fire burned high. He ran directly into it.

"James!"

Will and Tessa both ran for him, but halfway there, the fire flared up in a multitude of colors: blue and green and black. Heat poured from it, sending them stumbling back.

It subsided as quickly as it had arisen. They dashed again for the fireplace, but there was no sign of James.

"No, *no!*" Tessa screamed. *"Jamie!"*

She lunged for the fire; Will caught her and hauled her back. Everything seemed to have gone dark and silent in Tessa's ears. All she could think about was her baby. His soft laugh, his storm-black hair like his father's, his sweet disposition, the way he put his arms around her neck, his lashes against his cheeks.

Somehow, she had fallen to the floor. It was hard against her knees. *James*, she thought desperately.

A cool hand closed about her wrist. There were words in her head, soft and silent, cool as water. *I am here.*

Her eyes flew open. Jem was kneeling over her. The hood of his robes was thrown back, his black-and-silver hair disarrayed. *It's all right. That was not James. That was the demon itself, tricking you. James is in the house.*

Tessa gasped. "My God! Is that the truth?"

Strong arms were suddenly around her, hugging her tight. "It's true. Jem's had a tracking spell on Lucie and James since they were born. They're alive, they just need us to find them. Tess—Tessa—" She felt Will's tears against her shoulder.

Jem was still holding her hand. *I called for James*, she thought, *and he came.*

Tessa stayed where she was. It was the first time in her life, she thought, that her legs had felt so weak that she couldn't rise. Will had his arms around her and her hand was in Jem's. That was enough to keep her breathing. *The Silent City believes the demon to be a sort of trickster. It means for you to chase it around the Institute. Its motives are unclear, but they seem to be those of a child.*

"If it is a child . . . ," Tessa began, almost to herself.

The others turned to her.

"If it's a child, it thinks it's playing a game. It plays with women. I think it wants . . . a mother."

Suddenly it was as if a great wind shook the room.

"*I will play*," called a different voice.

"Jessamine!" Will said. "She's inside the house."

"I will play with you," said Jessamine's voice, louder now.

It seemed to come from every room. "I have toys. I have a doll-house. Play with *me*."

There was a long silence. Then all of the gas jets flared, sending columns of blue flame almost to the ceiling. Just as quickly, they were sucked back down to the jets and the room was dark again. The fire went out.

"My dollhouse is wonderful," Jessamine's voice went on. "It is very small."

"*Very small?*" came the reply.

"Bring the children and we shall play."

There was another great whoosh of wind through the room.

"Jessamine's room," Will said.

They made their way carefully to Jessamine's room, where the door stood open. There was Jessamine's dollhouse, her pride and joy, and next to it, the transparent, gossamer figure of Jessamine. A moment later, something came down the chimney, a kind of fog that splintered into pieces and floated about the room like bits of cloud. Jessamine was busy moving about the dolls in one of the rooms and paid attention to no one.

"We need more of us to play," she said.

"*It is very small. So many pieces.*"

The fog drifted toward the dollhouse, but Jessamine suddenly flared. She became like a web, wrapping herself around the dollhouse.

"We need more of us to play," Jessamine hissed. "The children."

"*They are in the walls.*"

"In the walls?" Gabriel said. "How can they . . ."

"The chimneys," Cecily said. "It uses the chimneys."

They ran from room to room. Each child was found, sound

asleep, tucked up into a chimney. Anna was in one of the empty Shadowhunter rooms. James was in the kitchen, Christopher in the parlor. Lucie was in Cecily and Gabriel's bedroom. Once they were secured, along with Bridget, the two sets of parents returned to Jessamine's room, where the shimmering figure of Jessamine was playing with a small girl. Jessamine appeared to be utterly engrossed in the game until she saw the others, who nodded to her.

"Now we will play a new game," Jessamine said.

The small girl turned toward Jessie, and Tessa caught sight of her face. It was pale and smooth, a child's face, but her eyes were entirely black, with no whites to them at all. They looked like specks of ash. *"No. This game."*

"You must close your eyes. It is a very good game. We are going to hide."

"Hide?"

"Yes. We shall play hide-and-seek. You must close your eyes."

"I like to hide."

"But first you must seek. Close your eyes."

The demon child, a small girl, barely five years of age in appearance, closed her eyes. As she did, Will brought the seraph blade down on her and the room was splattered with ichor.

"And it was gone," Tessa said. "The problem, of course, was that the rest of London couldn't be told that it was over. Jack the Ripper had been conjured up out of thin air, and now there was no Jack the Ripper to put in the dock. There would be no capture, no trial, no public hanging. The killings simply stopped. We considered trying to stage something, but there was so much scrutiny by that point that we felt this might complicate matters. But as it turned out, we didn't need to do anything. The public and the newspapers carried the story. New things were published every day, even though we knew there was nothing to report. It turned out people were willing to make up many theories of their own, and they've continued to do so since 1888. Everyone wants to catch the uncatchable killer. Everyone wants to be the hero of the story. And this has remained true in many cases since. In the absence of facts, the media will often make up stories of their own. It can save us a lot of work. In many ways, modern media is one of our greatest assets when it comes to covering up the truth. Do not discount mundanes. They weave their own stories, to make sense of their world. Some of you mundanes will help us make better sense of ours. Thank you for your attention this afternoon," Tessa finished. "I wish you all the luck in the world as you continue your training. What you do is brave and important."

"A round of applause for our esteemed guest," Catarina said.

This was given, and Tessa stepped down and went over to a man, who kissed her lightly on the cheek. He was slender, and very elegant, dressed in black and white. His black hair had one single white streak in it, completing the dichromatic look.

Memories assailed Simon, some easy to access, some hidden behind the frustrating web of forgetfulness. Jem had been at Luke and Jocelyn's wedding as well. The way that he smiled at Tessa, and she back at him, made it clear what their relationship was—they were in love, of the realest, truest kind.

Simon thought of Tessa's story, of the Jem who had been a Silent Brother, and had been a part of her life so long ago. Silent Brothers did live a long time, and Simon's foggy memory did recall something about one who had been returned to normal mortal life by heavenly fire. Which meant that Jem had lived in the Silent City for more than a hundred years, until his service was over. He had returned to life to live with his immortal love.

Now that was a complicated relationship. It made a little memory loss and former vampire status seem almost normal.

Dinner that night was a new culinary terror: Mexican food. There were roast chickens, or *pollo asado*, with the feathers still on, and square tortillas.

Jace didn't appear. Simon didn't have to look around for him, as the entire cafeteria was on alert. Had there been a sighting of his mighty blond head, Simon would have heard the intake of breath. Dinner was followed by two hours of mandatory study in the library. After all that, Simon and George returned to their room, only to find Jace standing by the door.

"Evening," he said.

"Seriously," Simon said. "How long have you been lurking here?"

"I wanted to talk to you." Jace had his hands stuffed in his pockets and was leaning against the wall, looking like an advertisement for a fashion magazine. "Alone."

"People will say we're in love," Simon said.

"You could come into our room," George said. "If you want to talk. If it's private, I can put earplugs in."

"I'm not going in there," Jace said, glancing in the open doorway. "That room is so damp you could probably hatch frogs on the walls."

"Ah, that'll be in my head now," George said. "I hate frogs."

"So what do you want?" Simon said.

Jace smiled lightly.

"George, go inside the room," Simon said, a bit apologetically. "I'll be right in."

George ducked into their bedroom and shut the door behind him. Simon was now alone with Jace in a long corridor, which was a situation he felt like he'd been in before.

"Thank you," Jace said, surprisingly directly. "You were right about Tessa."

"She's related to you?"

"I went to talk to her." Jace looked shyly pleased, as if a small light inside him had been turned on. It was the sort of expression that would, Simon suspected, have slain adolescent girls in their tracks. "She's my great-great-great-something-grandmother. She was married to Will Herondale. I've learned about him before. He was part of stopping a massive demon invasion into Britain. She and Will were the first Herondales to run the London Institute. I mean, it isn't anything I didn't know, historically, but it's— Well, as far as I know, there isn't anyone alive who shares blood with me. But Tessa does."

Simon leaned back against the wall of the corridor. "Did you tell Clary?"

"Yeah, I was on the phone with her for a couple of hours. She said Tessa hinted at some of this stuff during Luke and Jocelyn's wedding, but she didn't come right out and say it. She didn't want me to feel burdened."

"Do you?" Simon said. "Feel burdened, that is."

"No," Jace said. "I feel like there's someone else who understands what it means to be a Herondale. Both the good parts and the bad. I worried because of my father—that maybe being a Herondale meant I was weak. And then I learned more and thought maybe I was expected to be some kind of hero."

"Yeah," Simon said. "I know what that's like."

They shared a small moment of bizarre, companionable silence—the boy who'd forgotten everything about his history, and the boy who'd never known it.

Simon broke the silence. "Are you going to see her again? Tessa?"

"She says she's going to take me and Clary on a tour of the Herondale house in Idris."

"Did you meet Jem, too?"

"We've met before," said Jace. "In the Basilias, in Idris. You don't remember, but I—"

"Stopped him being a Silent Brother," said Simon. "I do remember that."

"We talked in Idris," said Jace. "A lot of what he said makes more sense to me now."

"So you're happy," Simon said.

"I'm happy," said Jace. "I mean, I've been happy, really, since the Dark War ended. I've got Clary, and I've got my family. The only dark spot's been you. Not remembering Clary, or Izzy. Or me."

"So sorry to mess up your life with my inconvenient amnesia," Simon muttered.

"I didn't mean it that way," Jace said. "I meant I wish you remembered me because—" He sighed. "Forget it."

"Look, Herondale, you owe me one now. Wait out here."

"For how long?" Jace looked aggrieved.

"As long as it takes." Simon ducked into his room and shut the door. George, who had been lying in bed studying, looked glum when Simon informed him that Jace was lurking in the hall.

"He's making *me* nervous now," George said. "Who'd want

Jace Herondale following them around, being all mysterious and taciturn and blond. . . . Oh, right. Probably loads of people. Still, I wish he wouldn't."

Simon didn't bother to lock the bedroom door, partially because there were no locks at Shadowhunter Academy, and partially because if Jace decided to come in and stand over Simon's bed all night, he was going to do that, lock or no.

"He must want something?" George said, stripping off his rugby shirt and throwing it into the corner of the room. "Is this a test? Are we going to have to fight Jace in the middle of the night? Si, not to bag on our awesome demon-fighting prowess, but I do not think that is a fight we can win."

"I don't think so," Simon said, dropping down onto his bed, which dropped much farther than it should have. That was definitely at least two springs breaking.

They got ready for bed. As usual, in the dark, they talked about the mold and the many zoological possibilities crawling around them in the dark. He heard George turn toward the wall, the signal that he was about to sleep and the nightly chat was over.

Simon was awake, hands behind his head, body still achingly sore from the fall out of the tree.

"Do you mind if I turn on a light?" he asked.

"Nae, go ahead. I can barely see it anyway."

They still said "turn on a light" like they were flicking a switch. They had candles at the Academy—nubby little candles that seemed to have been specially made to produce as little light as possible. Simon fumbled around on the small stand next to his bed and found his matches and lit his candle, which he pulled into the bed with him, balancing it on his lap in a way that was probably unsafe. One good thing about the floor of ultimate moisture was that it was unlikely to catch fire. He could still be burned, if the candle overturned in his lap, but it was the only way he would be able to see to write. He reached again for some paper and a pen. No texting here. No typing. Real pen to paper was required. He made a makeshift desk out of a book and began to write:

Dear Isabelle . . .

Should he start with "dear"? It was the way you started letters, but now that he saw it, it looked weird and old-fashioned and maybe too intimate.

He got a new piece of paper.

Isabelle . . .

Well, that looked stark. Like he was angry, just saying her name like that.

Another paper.

Izzy,

Nope. Definitely not. They were not at pet names yet. How the hell did you start a letter like this? Simon considered a casual "Hey . . ." or maybe just forgetting the salutation and getting right to the message. Texting was *so much easier* than this.

He picked up the paper that started with "Isabelle" again. It was the middle choice. He would have to go with that.

Isabelle,

I fell out of a tree today.

I'm thinking of you while I'm in my moldy bed.

I saw Jace today. He may develop food poisoning. Just wanted you to know.

I'm Batman.

I'm trying to figure out how to write this letter.

Okay. That was a possible start, and true.

Let me tell you something you already know—you're amazing. You know it. I know it. Anyone can see that. Here's the problem—I don't know what I am. I have to figure out who I am before I can accept that I'm someone who deserves someone like you. It's not something I can accept just because I've heard it. I need to know that guy. And I know I am that guy you loved—I just have to meet him.

I'm trying to figure out how that happens. I guess it happens here, in this school where they try to kill you every day. I think it takes time. I know things that take time are annoying. I know it's hard. But I have to get there the hard way.

This letter is probably stupid. I don't know if you're still reading. I don't know if you're going to rip this up or slice it in half with your whip or what.

All of that came out in one solid flow. He tapped the pen against his forehead for a minute.

> *I'm going to give this to Jace to give to you. He's been trailing me around all day like some kind of Jacey shadow. He's either here to make sure I don't die, or to make sure I die, or maybe because of you. Maybe you sent him.*
>
> *I don't know. He's Jace. Who knows what he's doing? I'm going to give this to him. He may read it before it gets to you. Jace, if you're reading this, I'm pretty sure you're going to get food poisoning. <u>Do not use the bathrooms.</u>*

It wasn't romantic, but he decided to leave it in. It might make Isabelle laugh.

> *If you are reading this, Jace, stop now.*
>
> *Izzy—I don't know why you would wait for me, but if you do, I promise to make myself worth that wait. Or I'll try. I can promise I am going to try.*
>
> *—Simon*

Simon opened the door and was not surprised to find Jace standing outside of it.

"Here," Simon said, handing him the letter.

"Took you long enough," Jace said.

"Now we're even," said Simon. "Go party in the Herondale house with your weird family."

"I plan to," said Jace, and smiled a sudden, strangely endearing smile. He had a chipped tooth. The smile made him seem like he was Simon's age, and maybe they were friends after all. "Good night, Wiggles."

"Wiggles?"

"Yes, *Wiggles*. Your nickname? It's what you always made us call you. I almost forgot your name was Simon, I'm so used to calling you Wiggles."

"*Wiggles?* What does that . . . even mean?"

"You would never explain," Jace said with a shrug. "It was the big mystery about you. As I said, good night, Wiggles. I'll take care of this."

He held up the letter and used it to make a salute.

Simon shut the door. He knew most people on the hall had probably done everything they could to make sure they heard that exchange. He knew that in the morning he would be called Wiggles and there was nothing he would ever be able to do about it.

But it was a small price to pay to get a letter to Isabelle.

Nothing but Shadows

By Cassandra Clare and Sarah Rees Brennan

The world transformed into sliding grayness, everything still moving slower than James was. Everything was sliding and insubstantial: The battering ram came at him and through him, unable to hurt him; it was like being splashed with water. James lifted a hand and saw the gray air full of stars.

—Nothing but Shadows

I knew nothing but shadows, and I thought them to be real.
—Oscar Wilde

Shadowhunter Academy, 2008

The afternoon sunlight was streaming warm through the arrow-slit windows of their classroom, painting the gray stone walls yellow. The elites and the dregs alike were sleepy from a long morning of training with Scarsbury, and Catarina Loss was giving them a history lesson. History applied to both the elites and the dregs, so they could all learn of the glory of the Shadowhunters and aspire to be a part of that glory. In this class, Simon thought, none of them seemed that different from each other—not that they were all united in aspiring to glory, but they were all equally glazed with boredom.

Until Marisol answered a question correctly, and Jon Cartwright kicked the back of her chair.

"Awesome," Simon hissed behind his book. "That's really

cool behavior. Congratulations, Jon. Every time a mundie answers a question wrong, you say it's because they can't rise to the level of Shadowhunters. And every time one of us answers a question right, you punish them. I have to admire your consistency."

George Lovelace leaned back in his chair and grinned, feeding Simon his next line. "I don't see how that's consistent, Si."

"Well, he's consistently a jackass," Simon explained.

"I can think of a few other words for him," George remarked. "But some of them cannot be used around ladies, and some of them are Gaelic and cannot be understood by you mad foreigners."

Jon looked upset. Possibly he was upset that their chairs were too far away to kick.

"I just think she shouldn't speak out of turn," he said.

"It's true that if you mundies listened to us *Shadowhunters*," said Julie, "you might learn something."

"If you Shadowhunters ever listened," said Sunil, a mundie boy who lived down the (slimy) hall from George and Simon, "you might learn a few things yourself."

Voices were rising. Catarina was beginning to look very annoyed. Simon gestured to Marisol and Jon to be quiet, but they both ignored him. Simon felt the same way as when he and Clary had set a fire in his kitchen by trying to toast grapes and create raisins when they were six: amazed and appalled that things had gone wrong so fast.

Then he realized that was a new memory. He grinned at the thought of Clary with exploded grape in her red hair, and let the classroom situation escalate.

"I'll teach you some lessons down in the training grounds,"

Jon snapped. "I could challenge you to a duel. Watch your mouth."

"That's not a bad idea," remarked Marisol.

"Oh, hey now," said Beatriz. "Duels with fourteen-year-olds *are* a bad idea."

Everyone looked with scorn upon Beatriz, the voice of reason.

Marisol sniffed. "Not a duel. A challenge. If the elites beat us in a challenge, then they get to speak out first in class for a week. If we beat them, then they hold their tongues."

"I'll do it, and you'll be sorry you ever suggested it, mundie. What's the challenge?" Jon asked. "Staff, sword, bow, dagger work, a horse race, a boxing match? I'm ready!"

Marisol smiled sweetly. "Baseball."

Cue mass puzzlement and panicked looks among the Shadowhunters.

"I'm not ready," George whispered. "I'm not American and I don't play baseball. Is it like cricket, Si? Or more like hurling?"

"You have a sport called hurling in Scotland?" Simon whispered back. "What do you hurl? Potatoes? Small children? Weird."

"I'll explain later," said George.

"I'll explain baseball," said Marisol with a glint in her eye.

Simon had the feeling Marisol was going to be a terrifying, tiny expert on baseball, the same way she was at fencing. He also had the feeling the elite stream was in for a surprise.

"And I will explain how a demonic plague almost wiped out the Shadowhunters," said Catarina loudly from the front of the class. "Or I would, if my students would stop bickering and listen for one minute!"

Everybody went very quiet, and listened meekly about

the plague. It was only when the lesson ended that everyone started talking about the baseball game again. Simon had at least played before, so he was hurrying to put away his books and go outside when Catarina said: "Daylighter. Wait."

"Really, 'Simon' would be fine," Simon told her.

"The elite kids are trying to replicate the school they have heard about from their parents," Catarina said. "Mundie students are meant to be seen and not heard, to soak up the privilege of being among Shadowhunters and prepare for their Ascension or death in a spirit of humility. Except you really have been stirring up trouble among them."

Simon blinked. "Are you telling me not to be so hard on the Shadowhunters, because it's just the way they were raised?"

"Be as hard on the smug little idiots as you like," said Catarina. "It's good for them. I'm just telling you so you realize what an effect you're having—and what an effect you could have. You're in an almost unique position, Daylighter. I only know of one other student who dropped from the elites to the dregs—not counting Lovelace, who would have been in the dregs from the beginning if the Nephilim didn't make smug assumptions. But then, smug assumptions are their favorite thing."

That had the effect Catarina must have known it would. Simon stopped trying to fit his copy of *The Shadowhunter's Codex* into his bag and sat down. The rest of the class would take some time to prepare before they actually had the baseball game. Simon could spare a little while.

"Was he a mundane too?"

"No, he was a Shadowhunter," Catarina said. "He went to the Academy more than a century ago. His name was James Herondale."

"A Herondale? Another Herondale?" Simon asked. "Herondales without cease. Do you ever get the feeling you are being chased around by Herondales?"

"Not really," Catarina said. "Not that I'd mind. Magnus says they tend to be a good-looking lot. Of course, Magnus also says they tend to be strange in the head. James Herondale was a bit of a special case."

"Let me guess," Simon said. "He was blond, smug, and adored by the populace."

Catarina's ivory eyebrows rose. "No, he had dark hair and spectacles. There was another boy at school, Matthew Fairchild, who did answer to that description. They did not get along particularly well."

"Really?" said Simon, and reconsidered. "Well then, Team James Herondale. I bet that Matthew guy was a jackass."

"Oh, I don't know," said Catarina. "I always thought he was a charmer, myself. Most people did. Everybody liked Matthew."

This Matthew guy *must* have been a charmer, Simon thought. Catarina rarely spoke about any Shadowhunters with anything like approval, but here she was smiling fondly over a boy from a hundred years ago.

"Everybody except James Herondale?" Simon asked. "The Shadowhunter who got thrown out of the Shadowhunter course. Did Matthew Fairchild have anything to do with that?"

Catarina stepped out from behind her teacher's desk and went to an arrow-slit window. The rays of the dying sun struck through her hair in brilliant white lines, almost giving her a halo. But not quite.

"James Herondale was the son of angels and demons," she said softly. "He was always fated to walk a difficult and painful path, to drink bitter water with sweet, to tread where there were thorns as well as flowers. Nobody could save him from that. People did try."

Shadowhunter Academy, 1899

James Herondale told himself that he was feeling sick only because of the jolting of the carriage. He was really very excited to be going to school.

Father had borrowed Uncle Gabriel's new carriage so he could take James from Alicante to the Academy, just the two of them.

Father had not asked if he could borrow Uncle Gabriel's carriage.

"Don't look so serious, Jamie," Father said, murmuring a Welsh word to the horses that made them trot faster. "Gabriel would want us to have the carriage. It's all between family."

"Uncle Gabriel mentioned last night that he had recently had the carriage painted. Many times. And he has threatened to summon the constabulary and have you arrested," said James. "Many times."

"Gabriel will stop fussing about it in a few years." Father winked one blue eye at James. "Because we will all be driving automobiles by then."

"Mother says you can never drive an automobile," said James. "She made me and Lucie promise that if you ever did, we would not climb into it."

"Your mother was just joking."

James shook his head. "She made us swear on the Angel."

He grinned up at his father. Father shook his head at Jamie, the wind catching at his black hair. Mother said Father and

Jamie had the same hair, but Jamie knew his own hair was always untidy. He had heard people call his father's hair *unruly*, which meant being untidy with charisma.

The first day of school was not a good day for James to be thinking about how very different he was from his father.

During their drive from Alicante, several people stopped them on the road, calling out the usual exclamation: "Oh, Mr. Herondale!"

Shadowhunter ladies of many ages said that to his father: three words that were both sigh and summons. Other fathers were called "Mister" without the "Oh" prefix.

With such a remarkable father, people tended to look for a son who would be perhaps a lesser star to Will Herondale's blazing sun, but still someone shining. They were always subtly but unmistakably disappointed to find James, who was not very remarkable at all.

James remembered one incident that made the difference between him and his father starkly apparent. It was always the tiniest moments that came back to James in the middle of the night and mortified him the very most, like it was always the almost invisible cuts that kept stinging.

A mundane lady had wandered up to them at Hatchards bookshop in London. Hatchards was the nicest bookshop in the city, James thought, with its dark wood and glass front, which made the whole shop look solemn and special, and its secret nooks and hidey-holes inside where one could curl up with a book and be quite quiet. James's family often went to Hatchards all together, but when James and his father went alone ladies quite often found a reason to wander over to them and strike up a conversation.

Father told the lady that he spent his days hunting evil and rare first editions. Father could always find something to say to people, could always make them laugh. It seemed a strange, wondrous power to James, as impossible to achieve as it would be for him to shape-shift like a werewolf.

James did not worry about the ladies approaching Father. Father never once looked at any woman the way he looked at Mother, with joy and thanksgiving, as if she was a living wish, granted past all hope.

James did not know many people, but he was good at being quiet and noticing. He knew that what lay between his parents was something rare and precious.

He worried only because the ladies approaching Father were strangers James would have to talk to.

The lady in the bookshop had leaned down and asked: "And what do you like to do, little man?"

"I like—books," James had said. While standing in the bookshop, with a parcel of books under his arm. The lady had given him a pitying look. "I read—erm—rather a lot," James went on, dreary master of the obvious. King of the obvious. Emperor of the obvious.

The lady was so unimpressed that she wandered off without another word.

James never knew what to say to people. He never knew how to make them laugh. He had lived thirteen years of his life, mainly at the Institute in London, with his parents and his little sister, Lucie, and a great many books. He had never had a friend who was a boy.

Now he was going to Shadowhunter Academy, to learn to be as great a warrior as his father, and the warrior bit was not half as worrying as the fact he was going to have to talk to people.

There were going to be a lot of people.

There was going to be a lot of talking.

James wondered why the wheels did not fall right off Uncle Gabriel's carriage. He wondered why the world was so cruel.

"I know that you are nervous about going to school," Father said at length. "Your mother and I were not sure about sending you."

James bit his lip. "Did you think I would be a disaster?"

"What?" Father said. "Of course not! Your mother was simply worried about sending away the only other person in the house who has any sense."

James smiled.

"We've been very happy, having our little family all together," Father said. "I never thought I could be so happy. But perhaps we have kept you too isolated in London. It would be nice for you to find some friends your own age. Who knows, you might meet your future *parabatai* at the Academy."

Father could say what he liked about it being his and Mother's fault for keeping them isolated; James knew it was not true. Lucie had gone to France with Mother and met Cordelia Carstairs, and in two weeks they had become what Lucie described as bosom companions. They sent each other letters every week, reams and reams of paper crossed out and containing sketches. Lucie was as isolated as James was. James had gone on visits too, and never made a bosom companion. The only person who liked him was a girl, and nobody could know about Grace. Perhaps even Grace would not like him, if she knew any other people.

It was not his parents' fault that he had no friends. It was some flaw within James himself.

"Perhaps," Father went on casually, "you and Alastair Carstairs will take a liking to each other."

"He's older than me!" James protested. "He won't have any time for a new boy."

Father smiled a wry little smile. "Who knows? That is the wonderful thing about making changes and meeting strangers, Jamie. You never know when, and you never know who, but someday a stranger will burst through the door of your life and transform it utterly. The world will be turned upside down, and you will be happier for it."

Father had been so happy when Lucie befriended Cordelia Carstairs. Father's *parabatai* had once been called James Carstairs, though his official name now that he belonged to the Silent Brothers—the order of blind, runed monks that aided the Shadowhunters in the darkness—was Brother Zachariah. Father had told James a thousand times about meeting Uncle Jem, how for years Uncle Jem had been the only one who believed in him, who saw his true self. Until Mother came.

"I have spoken to you often of your mother and your uncle Jem and all they did for me. They made me a new person. They saved my soul," Father said, serious as he rarely was. "You do not know what it is, to be saved and transformed. But you will. As your parents, we must give you opportunities to be challenged and changed. That was why we agreed to send you to school. Even though we will miss you terribly."

"Terribly?" James asked, shyly.

"Your mother says she will be brave and keep a stiff upper

lip," said Father. "Americans are heartless. I will cry into my pillow every night."

James laughed. He knew he did not laugh often, and Father looked particularly pleased whenever he could make James do it. James was, at thirteen, a little old for such displays, but since it would be months and months until he saw Father again and he was a little frightened to be going to school, he nestled up against Father and took his hand. Father held the reins in one hand and put his own and James's linked hands into the deep pocket of his driving coat. James rested with his cheek against Father's shoulder, not minding the jolting of the carriage as they went down the country roads of Idris.

He did want a *parabatai*. He wanted one badly.

A *parabatai* was a friend who had chosen you to be their best friend, who had made their friendship permanent. They were that sure about how much they liked you, that sure they would never want to take it back. Finding a *parabatai* seemed to James the key to everything, the essential first step to a life where he could be as happy as his father was, be as brilliant a Shadowhunter as his father was, find a love as great as the love his father had found.

Not that he had any particular girl in mind, James told himself, and crushed all thoughts of Grace, the secret girl; Grace, who needed to be rescued.

He wanted a *parabatai*, and that made the Academy a thousand times more terrifying.

James was safe for this little time, resting against his father, but all too soon they reached the valley where the school rested.

The Academy was magnificent, a gray building that shone among the gathered trees like a pearl. It reminded James of the

Gothic buildings from books like *The Mysteries of Udolpho* and *The Castle of Otranto.* Set in the gray face of the building was a huge stained-glass window shining with a dozen brilliant colors, showing an angel wielding a blade.

The angel was looking down on a courtyard teeming with students, all talking and laughing, all there to become the best Shadowhunters they could possibly be. If James could not find a friend here, he knew, he would not be able to find a friend in all the world.

Uncle Gabriel was already in the courtyard. His face had turned an alarming shade of puce. He was shouting something about thieving Herondales.

Father turned to the dean, a lady who was unquestionably fifty years old, and smiled. She blushed.

"Dean Ashdown, would you be so very kind as to give me a tour of the Academy? I was raised in the London Institute with just one other pupil." Father's voice softened, as it always did when he spoke of Uncle Jem. "I never had the privilege of attending myself."

"Oh, Mr. Herondale!" said Dean Ashdown. "Very well."

"Thank you," said Father. "Come on, Jamie."

"Oh no," said James. "I'll—I'll stay here."

He felt uneasy as soon as Father was out of his sight, sailing off with the dean on his arm and a wicked smile at Uncle Gabriel, but James knew he had to be brave, and this was the perfect opportunity. Among the crowd of students in the courtyard, James had seen two boys he knew.

One was tall for almost-thirteen, with an untidy shock of light brown hair. He had his face turned away, but James knew the boy had startling lavender eyes. He had heard girls at parties saying those eyes were wasted on a boy, especially a boy as strange as Christopher Lightwood.

James knew his cousin Christopher better than any other boy at the Academy. Aunt Cecily and Uncle Gabriel had spent a lot of time in Idris over the past few years, but before that both families had been together often: They had all gone down to Wales together for a few holidays, before Grandma and Grandpa died. Christopher was slightly odd and extremely vague, but he was always nice to James.

The boy standing beside Christopher was small and thin as a lath, his head barely coming up to Christopher's shoulder.

Thomas Lightwood was Christopher's cousin, not James's, but James called Thomas's mother Aunt Sophie because she was Mother's very best friend. James liked Aunt Sophie, who was so pretty and always kind. She and her family had been living in Idris for the past few years as well, with Aunt Cecily and Uncle Gabriel—Aunt Sophie's husband was Uncle Gabriel's brother. Aunt Sophie came to London on visits by herself, though. James had seen Mother and Aunt Sophie walk out of the practice rooms giggling together as if they were girls as little as his sister, Lucie. Aunt Sophie had once called Thomas her shy boy. That had made James think he and Thomas might have a lot in common.

At the big family gatherings when they were all together, James had sneaked a few glances at Thomas, and found him always hanging quiet and uneasy on the fringes of a bigger group, usually looking to one of the older boys. He'd wanted to go over to Thomas and strike up a conversation, but he had not been sure what to say.

Two shy people would probably be good friends, but there

was the small problem of how to reach that point. James had no idea.

Now was James's chance, though. The Lightwood cousins were his best hope for friends at the Academy. All he had to do was go over and speak to them.

James pushed his way through the crowd, apologizing when other people elbowed him.

"Hullo, boys," said a voice behind James, and someone pushed past James as if he could not see him.

James saw Thomas and Christopher both turn, like flowers toward the sun. They smiled with identical radiant welcome, and James stared at the back of a shining blond head.

There was one other boy James's age at the Academy who he knew a little: Matthew Fairchild, whose parents James called Aunt Charlotte and Uncle Henry because Aunt Charlotte had practically raised Father, when she was the head of the London Institute and before she became Consul, the most important person a Shadowhunter could be.

Matthew had not come to London the few times Aunt Charlotte and his brother, Charles, had visited. Uncle Henry had been wounded in battle years before any of them were born, and he did not leave Idris often, but James was not sure why Matthew did not come visit. Perhaps he enjoyed himself too much in Idris.

One thing James was certain of was that Matthew Fairchild was *not* shy.

James had not seen Matthew in a couple of years, but he remembered him very clearly. At every family gathering where James hung on the edges of crowds or went off to read on the stairs, Matthew was the life and soul of the party. He would talk with grown-ups as if he were a grown-up. He would dance with old ladies. He would charm parents and grandparents, and stop babies from crying. Everybody loved Matthew.

James did not remember Matthew dressing like a maniac before today. Matthew was wearing knee breeches when everyone else was wearing the trousers of the sane, and a mulberry-colored velvet jacket. Even his shining golden hair was brushed in a way that struck James as more complicated than the way other boys brushed their hair.

"Isn't this a bore?" Matthew asked Christopher and Thomas, the two boys James wanted for friends. "Everybody here looks like a dolt. I am already in frightful agony, contemplating my wasted youth. Don't speak to me, or I shall break down and sob uncontrollably."

"There, there," said Christopher, patting Matthew's shoulder. "What are you upset about again?"

"Your face, Lightwood," said Matthew, and elbowed him.

Christopher and Thomas both laughed, drawing in close to him. They were all so obviously already friends, and Matthew was so clearly the leader. James's plan for friends was in ruins.

"Er," said James, the sound like a tragic social hiccup. "Hello."

Christopher gazed at him with amiable blankness, and James's heart, which had already been around his knees, sank to his socks.

Then Thomas said, "Hello!" and smiled.

James smiled back, grateful for an instant, and then Matthew Fairchild turned around to see who Thomas was addressing. He was taller than James, his fair hair outlined by the sun as he looked down on him. Matthew gave the impression that he was looking down from a much greater height than he actually was.

"Jamie Herondale, right?" Matthew drawled.

James bristled. "I prefer James."

"I'd prefer to be in a school devoted to art, beauty, and culture rather than in a ghastly stone shack in the middle of nowhere filled with louts who aspire to nothing more than whacking demons with great big swords," said Matthew. "Yet here we are."

"And *I* would prefer to have intelligent students," said a voice behind them. "Yet here I am teaching at a school for the Nephilim."

They turned and then started, as one. The man behind them had snowy-white hair, which he looked too young to have, and horns poking out among the white locks. The most notable thing about him, however, the thing James noted right away, was that he had green skin the color of grapes.

James knew this must be a warlock. In fact, he knew who it must be: the former High Warlock of London, Ragnor Fell, who lived part-time in the countryside outside Alicante, and who had agreed this year that he would teach in the Academy as a diversion from his magical studies.

James knew warlocks were good people, the allies of the Shadowhunters. Father often talked about his friend Magnus Bane, who had been kind to him when he was young.

Father had never mentioned whether Magnus Bane was green. James had never thought to inquire. Now he was rather urgently wondering.

"Which one of you is Christopher Lightwood?" Ragnor Fell asked in a stern voice. His gaze swept them all, and landed on the most guilty-looking person in the group. "Is it you?"

"Thank the Angel, no," Thomas exclaimed, and went red

under his summer tan. "No offense, Christopher."

"Oh, none taken," said Christopher airily. He blinked up at Ragnor, as if the tall, scary green man had entirely escaped his notice up until this moment. "Hello, sir."

"Are you Christopher Lightwood?" Ragnor asked, somewhat menacingly.

Christopher's wandering attention became focused on a tree. "Hm? I think so."

Ragnor glared down at Christopher's flyaway brown hair. James was beginning to be afraid he would erupt like a green volcano.

"Are you not certain, Mr. Lightwood? Did you perhaps have an unfortunate encounter when you were an infant?"

"Hm?" said Christopher.

Ragnor's voice rose. "Was the encounter between your infant head and a floor?"

That was when Matthew Fairchild said, "Sir," and smiled.

James had forgotten about The Smile, even though it was often broken out to great effect at family parties. The Smile won Matthew extra time before bed, extra Christmas pudding, extra anything he wanted. Adults were helpless to resist The Smile.

Matthew gave his all to this particular smile. Butter melted. Birds sang. People slipped about dazed amid the butter and birdsong.

"Sir, you will have to forgive Christopher. He's a trifle absentminded, but he is definitely Christopher. It would be very difficult to mistake Christopher for anyone else. I vouch for him, and he can't deny it."

The Smile worked on Ragnor, as it worked on all adults. He unbent a tiny bit. "Are you Matthew Fairchild?"

Matthew's smile became more playful. "I could deny it if I liked. I could deny anything if I liked. But my name certainly is Matthew. It has been Matthew for years."

"What?" Ragnor Fell looked as if he had fallen into a pit of lunatics and could not get out.

James cleared his throat. "He's quoting Oscar Wilde, sir."

Matthew glanced over at him, his dark eyes suddenly wide. "Are you a devotee of Oscar Wilde?"

"He's a good writer," James said coldly. "There are a lot of good writers. I read rather a lot," he added, making it clear that he was certain Matthew did not.

"Gentlemen," Ragnor Fell put in, his voice a dagger. "If you could tear yourselves away from your fascinating literary conversation for a moment and listen to one of the instructors in the establishment where you have supposedly come to learn? I have a letter here about Christopher Lightwood and the unfortunate incident that caused the Clave such concern."

"Yes, that was a very unfortunate accident," said Matthew, nodding earnestly as if he was sure of Ragnor's sympathy.

"And that was not the word I used, Mr. Fairchild, as I am sure you are aware. The letter says that you have volunteered to take full responsibility for Mr. Lightwood, and that you solemnly promise to keep any and all potential explosives out of his reach for the duration of his time at the Academy."

James looked from the warlock to Matthew to Christopher, who was regarding a tree with dreamy benevolence. In desperation, he looked to Thomas.

Explosives? he mouthed.

"Don't ask," said Thomas. "Please."

Thomas was older than James and Christopher, but much

smaller. Aunt Sophie had kept him at home an extra year because he was sickly. He did not look sickly now, but he was still rather undersized. His tan, combined with his brown hair and brown eyes and his short stature, made him look like a small, worried horse chestnut. James found himself wanting to pat Thomas on the head.

Matthew patted Thomas on the head.

"Mr. Fell," he said. "Thomas. Christopher. Jamie."

"James," James corrected.

"Do not worry," Matthew said with immense confidence. "I mean, certainly, worry that we are trapped in an arid warrior culture with no appreciation for the truly important things in life. But do not worry about things exploding, because I will not permit anything to explode."

"That was all you needed to say," Ragnor Fell told him. "And you could have said it in far fewer words."

He walked off, in a swirl of green skin and bad temper.

"He was green!" Thomas whispered.

"Really," said Matthew, very dry.

"Oh, really?" asked Christopher brightly. "I didn't notice."

Thomas gazed sadly at Christopher. Matthew ignored him superbly. "I rather liked the unique hue of our teacher. It reminded me of the green carnations that Oscar Wilde's followers wear to imitate him. He had one of the actors in, um, a play of his wear a green carnation onstage."

"It was *Lady Windermere's Fan*," James said.

Matthew was clearly showing off, trying to sound superior and special, and James had no time for it.

Matthew turned The Smile on him. James was unsurprised to find he was immune to its deadly effects.

"Yes," he said. "Of course. Jamie, I can see that as a fellow admirer of Oscar Wilde—"

"Uh," said a voice to James's left. "You new boys have barely been here five minutes, and all you can find to talk about is some *mundane* who got sent to prison for indecency?"

"So you know Oscar Wilde too, Alastair?" Matthew asked.

James looked up at the taller, older boy. He had light hair but dark brows, strongly marked, like very judgmental black brushstrokes.

So this was Alastair Carstairs, the brother of Lucie's best friend, whom Father hoped James would make friends with. James had pictured someone more friendly, more like Cordelia herself.

Perhaps Alastair would be more friendly if he did not associate James with snotty Matthew.

"I know of many mundane criminals," Alastair Carstairs said in chilly tones. "I read the mundane newspapers to find hints of demonic activity. I certainly don't bother reading plays."

The two boys he was with nodded in good Shadowhunter solidarity.

Matthew laughed in their faces. "Naturally. What use do sad, unimaginative little people have for plays?" he asked. "Or paintings, or dancing, or anything that makes life interesting. I am so glad to be at this dank little school where they will try to squeeze down my mind until it is almost as narrow as yours."

He patted Alastair Carstairs on the arm. James was amazed that he was not immediately struck in the face.

Thomas was staring at Alastair with as much panic as James felt.

"Run along now," Matthew suggested. "Do. Jamie and I were talking."

Alastair laughed, his laugh sounding angrier than a sharp word would have. "I was only trying to give you young ones a little guidance about the way we do things in the Academy. If you're too stupid to take heed, that is not my fault. At least you have a tongue in your head, unlike this one."

He turned and glared daggers at James. James was so surprised and dismayed at this turn of events—he hadn't done *anything!*—that he simply stood and stared with his mouth open.

"Yes, you, the one with the peculiar eyes," Alastair snapped. "What are you gawping at?"

"I—" said James. "I—"

He did have peculiar eyes, he knew. He did not truly need eyeglasses, except for reading, but he wore them all the time in order to conceal his eyes. He could feel himself blushing, and Alastair's voice became as sharp as his laugh.

"What's your name?"

"H-Herondale," James stammered out.

"By the Angel, his eyes *are* awful," said the boy to Alastair's right.

Alastair laughed again, this time with more satisfaction. "Yellow. Just like a goat's."

"I don't—"

"Don't strain yourself, Goatface Herondale," Alastair said. "Don't try to speak. You and your friends could perhaps cease obsessing about mundanes and try to think about little matters like saving lives and upholding the Law while you're here, all right?"

He strolled on, his friends laughing with him. James heard the word spreading through the tightly knit crowd with laughter following it, like the ripples from a stone thrown into a pond.

Goatface. Goatface. Goatface.

Matthew laughed. "Well. What an—"

"Thanks so much for dragging me into that," James snapped. He turned on his heel and walked away from the two friends he had hoped for at the Academy, and heard his new name whispered as he went.

James did what he had promised himself he absolutely would not do. He dragged his heavy bag through the courtyard, through the hall, and up several sets of stairs until he found a staircase that seemed private. Then he sat down and opened a book. He told himself that he was only going to read a few pages before he went down again. The Count of Monte Cristo was just descending on his enemies in a balloon.

James emerged hours later, to the sinking realization that the sky had gone dark gray and the sounds from the courtyard had faded away. His mother and Lucie were still in London, far away, and now he was sure his father was gone too.

He was trapped in this Academy full of strangers. He did not even know where he was supposed to sleep tonight.

He wandered around trying to find the bedrooms. He did not discover any, but he did find himself enjoying exploring such a big new place on his own. The Academy was a splendid building, the stone walls shining as if they had been polished. The chandeliers seemed made of jewels, and as James wandered in search of the dining hall, he found many beautiful tapestries depicting Shadowhunters through the ages. He stood looking at an intricate, colorful weaving of Jonathan Shadowhunter fighting during the Crusades, until it occurred to him that dinner must be soon and he did not want to draw any further attention to himself.

The sound of hundreds of strange voices alerted James to where the dining room must be. He fought the impulse to run away, steeled himself, and walked through the doors instead. To his relief, people were still assembling, the older students milling around and chatting to each other with the ease of long familiarity. The new students were hovering, much like James himself.

All except Matthew Fairchild, who was surveying the shining mahogany tables with disdain.

"We have to select a very small table," he told Thomas and Christopher, his satellites. "I am here under protest. I will not break bread with the kind of violent ruffians and raving imbeciles who would attend the Academy willingly."

"You know," James said loudly, "Alastair Carstairs was right."

"That seems very unlikely to me," Matthew responded, then turned. "Oh, it's you. Why are you still carrying your bag?"

"I don't have to answer to you," said James, which he was aware was a bizarre thing to say. Thomas blinked at him in distress, as if he had trusted James not to say bizarre things.

"All right," Matthew said agreeably. "Alastair Carstairs was right about what?"

"People are attending the Academy because they hope to become better Shadowhunters, and save lives. That is a noble and worthy goal. You do not have to sneer at everybody you meet."

"But how else am I going to amuse myself in this place?" Matthew protested. "*You* can sit with us, if you want."

There was an amused glint in his brown eyes. James was certain from the way Matthew was looking at him that he was being made fun of, though he could not quite work out how.

"No thanks," James said shortly.

He looked around at the tables, and saw that the first-year Shadowhunters were now settled around tables in careful, friendly patterns. There were other boys and even a few girls, though, who James could tell were mundanes. It was not so much clothing or build as the way they held themselves: as if they were afraid they might be attacked. Shadowhunters, in contrast, were always ready to attack.

There was one boy in shabby clothes sitting by himself. James crossed the dining room to sit at his table.

"Can I sit here?" he asked, desperate enough to be blunt.

"Yes!" said the other boy. "Oh yes, please. The name's Smith. Michael Smith. Mike."

James reached across the table and shook Mike Smith's hand. "James Herondale."

Mike's eyes widened, clearly recognizing it as a Shadowhunter name. "My mother grew up in the mundane world," James told him quickly. "In America. New York City."

"Your mother was a mundane?" said a girl, coming over and sitting at his table. "Esme Philpott," she added, shaking hands briskly. "I shan't keep it when I Ascend. I'm thinking of changing the Esme too."

James did not know what to say. He did not wish to insult a lady's name by agreeing with her or insult a lady by arguing with her. He was not prepared to be approached by a strange girl. Very few girls were sent to the Academy: of course girls could be just as fine warriors as boys, but not everybody thought that way, and many Shadowhunter families wanted to keep their girls close. Some people thought the Academy had far too many rules, and some far too few. Thomas's sisters, who were very proper, had not come to the Academy. Family legend reported that his cousin Anna Lightwood, who was the least proper person imaginable, had said if they sent her to the Academy, she would run away and become a mundane bullfighter.

"Mmm," said James, a silver-tongued devil with the ladies.

"Did your mother Ascend with no trouble?" Mike asked eagerly.

James bit his lip. He was accustomed to everyone knowing the history of his mother: the child of a stolen Shadowhunter and a demon. Any child of a Shadowhunter was a Shadowhunter. Mother belonged to the Shadowhunter world as much as any of the Nephilim. Only, her skin could not bear Marks, and there had never before been anyone like her in the world. James did not quite know how to explain to people who did not know already. He was afraid he would explain wrong, and the explanation would reflect badly on Mother.

"I know a lot of people who Ascended with no trouble," James said at last. "My aunt Sophie—Sophie Lightwood now—she was a mundane. Father says there never was anyone so brave, before or after Ascension."

"What a relief!" said Esme. "Tell me, I think I've heard of Sophie Lightwood—"

"What a fearful comedown," said one of the boys James had seen with Alastair Carstairs earlier. "Goatface Herondale is actually reduced to sitting with the *dregs*."

Alastair and his other friend laughed. They went to sit at a table with other, older Shadowhunters, and James was certain he heard the word "Goatface" whispered more than once. He felt he was boiling from the inside out with shame.

As for Matthew Fairchild, James looked over at him only once or twice. After James had left him standing in the middle of the dining hall, Matthew had tossed his stupid blond head and chosen a very large table to sit at. He clearly had not meant a word about being so select. He sat with Thomas and Christopher on either side of him like a prince holding court, calling out jokes and summoning people to his side, and soon his table was crowded. He charmed several of the Shadowhunter students away from their tables. Even some of the older students came over to listen to one of Matthew's apparently terribly amusing stories. Even Alastair Carstairs came over for a few minutes. Obviously he and Matthew were great friends now.

James caught Mike Smith looking over at Matthew's table longingly, his face that of an outsider barred from all the fun, doomed to always be at the less exciting table with the less interesting people.

James had wanted friends, but he had not wanted to be the kind of friend who people settled for, because they could not get any better. Except he was, as he had always secretly feared, tedious and poor company. He did not know why books had not taught him how to talk so other people wanted to listen.

James eventually approached the teachers for help finding his bedroom. He found Dean Ashdown and Ragnor Fell in deep conversation.

"I am so terribly sorry," said Dean Ashdown. "This is the first time we have ever had a warlock teacher—and we are delighted to have you! We should have thoroughly cleaned out the Academy and made sure there were no remnants of a less peaceful time."

"Thank you, Dean Ashdown," Ragnor said. "The removal of the mounted warlock's head from my bedroom will be sufficient."

"I am so terribly sorry!" said Dean Ashdown again. She lowered her voice. "Were you acquainted with the—er, deceased gentleman?"

Ragnor eyed her with disfavor. Though that might just be the way Mr. Fell looked. "If you were to happen upon the grotesquely severed head of one of the Nephilim, would you have to be acquainted with him to feel you might perhaps not fancy sleeping in the room where part of his desecrated corpse remained?"

James coughed in the middle of the dean's third frantic apology. "I do apologize," he said. "Could someone direct me to my room? I—got lost and missed all that."

"Oh, young Mr. Herondale." The dean looked quite happy to be interrupted. "Of course, let me show you the way. Your father entrusted me with a message for you that I can relay as we go."

She left Ragnor Fell scowling after them. James hoped he had not made another enemy.

"Your father said—what a charming language Welsh is, isn't it? So romantic!—*Pob lwc, caraid.* What does it mean?"

James blushed, because he was much too old for his father to be calling him by pet names. "It just means—it means good luck."

He could not help smiling as he trailed the dean down the halls. He was sure nobody else's father had charmed the dean into giving a student a secret message. He felt warm, and watched over.

Until Dean Ashdown opened the door of his new room, bid him a cheerful good-bye, and left him to his horrible fate.

It was a very nice room, airy, with walnut bedposts and white linen canopies. There was a carved wardrobe and even a bookcase.

There was also a distressing amount of Matthew Fairchild.

He was standing in front of a table that had about fifteen hairbrushes on it, several mysterious bottles, and a strange hoard of combs.

"Hullo, Jamie," he said. "Isn't it splendid that we are sharing a room? I am certain we will get along swimmingly."

"James," James said. "What are all those hairbrushes for?"

Matthew looked at him pityingly. "You don't think all this"—he indicated his head with a sweeping gesture—"happens on its own?"

"*I* only use one hairbrush."

"Yes," Matthew observed. "I can tell."

James dragged his trunk over to the foot of his bed, took out *The Count of Monte Cristo*, and made his way back to the door.

"Jamie?" Matthew asked.

"James!" James snapped.

Matthew laughed. "All right, all right. James, where are you going?"

"Somewhere else," said James, and slammed the door behind him.

He could not believe the bad luck that had randomly

assigned him to share a room with Matthew. He found another staircase and read in it until he judged that it was late enough that Matthew would certainly be asleep, and he crept back, lit a candle, and resumed reading in bed.

James might have read a little too long into the night. When he woke up, Matthew was clearly long gone—on top of everything else, he was an early riser—and James was late for his first day of class.

"What else can you expect from Goatface Herondale," said a boy James had never seen before in his life, and several more people sniggered. James grimly took his seat next to Mike Smith.

The classes in which the elites were separated from the dregs were the worst. James had nobody to sit with then.

Or perhaps the first class of every day was the worst, because James always stayed up late into the night reading to forget his troubles, and was late every day. No matter what time he rose, Matthew was always gone. James assumed Matthew did this to mock him, since he could not imagine Matthew doing anything useful early in the morning.

Or perhaps the training courses were the worst, because Matthew was at his most annoying during the training courses.

"I must regretfully decline to participate," he told their teacher once. "Consider me on strike like the coal miners. Except far more stylish."

The next day, he said: "I abstain on the grounds that beauty is sacred, and there is nothing beautiful about these exercises."

The day after that, he merely said: "I object on aesthetic principles."

He kept saying ridiculous things, until a couple of weeks

in, when he said: "I won't do it, because Shadowhunters are idiots and I do not want to be at this idiot school. Why does an accident of birth mean you have to either get ripped away from your family, or you have to spend a short, horrible life brawling with demons?"

"Do you want to be expelled, Mr. Fairchild?" thundered one teacher.

"Do what you feel you must," said Matthew, folding his hands and smiling like a cherub.

Matthew did not get expelled. Nobody seemed quite sure what to do with him. His teachers began calling in sick out of despair.

He did only half the work and insulted everyone in the Academy on a daily basis, and he remained absurdly popular. Thomas and Christopher could not be pried away from him. He wandered the halls surrounded by adoring throngs who wanted to hear another amusing anecdote. His and James's room was always completely crowded.

James spent a good deal of time in the stairwells. He spent even more time being called Goatface Herondale.

"You know," Thomas said shyly once, when James had not managed to escape his own room fast enough, "you could pal around with us a little more."

"I could?" James asked, and tried not to sound too hopeful. "I'd . . . like to see more of you and Christopher."

"And Matthew," Thomas said.

James shook his head silently.

"Matthew's one of my best friends," Thomas said, almost pleadingly. "If you spent some time with him, I am sure you would come to like him."

James looked over at Matthew, who was sitting on his bed telling a story to eight people who were sitting on the floor and gazing up at him worshipfully. He met Matthew's eyes, trained in his and Thomas's direction, and looked away.

"I feel I have to decline any more of Matthew's company."

"It makes you stand out, you know," Thomas said. "Spending your time with the mundanes. I think it's why the—the nickname for you has stuck. People are afraid of anybody who is different: It makes them worry everyone else is different too, and just pretending to be all the same."

James stared at him. "Are you saying I should avoid the mundanes? Because they are not as good as we are?"

"No, that's not—" Thomas began, but James was too angry to let him finish.

"The mundanes can be heroes too," James said. "You should know that better than I. Your mother was a mundane! My father told me about all she did before she Ascended. Everyone here knows people who were mundanes. Why should we isolate people who are brave enough to try to become like us—who want to help people? Why should we treat them as if they're less than us, until they prove their worthiness or die? I won't do it."

Aunt Sophie was just as good as any Shadowhunter, and she had been brave long before she Ascended. Aunt Sophie was Thomas's mother. They should know this better than James did.

"I didn't mean it that way," said Thomas. "I didn't think of it that way."

It was as if people didn't think at all, living in Idris.

"Maybe your fathers don't tell you stories like mine does," James said.

"Maybe not everyone listens to stories like you do," Matthew said from across the room. "Not everyone learns."

James glanced at him. It was an unexpectedly nice thing for Matthew, of all people, to say.

"I know a story," Matthew went on. "Who wants to hear it?"

"Me!" said the chorus from the floor.

"Me!"

"Me!"

"Not me," said James, and left the room.

It was another reminder that Matthew had what James would have given anything for, that Matthew had friends and belonged here at the Academy, and Matthew did not care at all.

Eventually there were so many teachers calling in with an acute overdose of Matthew Fairchild that Ragnor Fell was left to supervise the training courses. James wondered why he was the only one who could see this was absurd, and Matthew was ruining classes for everyone. Ragnor could do magic, and was not at all interested in war.

Ragnor let Esme braid ribbons in her horse's mane so it would look like a noble steed. He agreed to let Christopher build a battering ram to knock down trees, because it would be good practice in case they ever had to lay siege to a castle. He watched Mike Smith hit himself over the head with his own longbow.

"Concussions are nothing to be worried about," said Ragnor placidly. "Unless there is severe bleeding of the brain, in which case he may die. Mr. Fairchild, why are you not participating?"

"I think that violence is repulsive," Matthew said firmly. "I am here against my will and I refuse to participate."

"Would you like me to magically strip you and put you in gear?" Mr. Fell asked. "In front of everybody?"

"That would be a thrill for everybody, I'm sure," said Matthew. Ragnor Fell wiggled his fingers, and green sparks spat from his fingertips. James was pleased to see Matthew actually take a step back. "Might be too thrilling for a Wednesday," Matthew said. "I'll go put on my gear then, shall I?"

"Do," said Ragnor.

He had set up a deck chair and was reading a book. James envied him very much.

He also admired his teacher very much. Here was someone who could control Matthew, at last. After all Matthew's lofty talk about abstaining for the sake of art and beauty, James was looking forward to seeing Matthew make an absolute fool of himself on the practice grounds.

"Anyone volunteer to catch Matthew up on what you have all been learning?" Ragnor asked. "As I have not the faintest idea what that might be."

Just then Christopher's team of students actually hit a tree with their battering ram. The crash and the chaos meant there was not the rush of volunteers to spend time with Matthew that there would otherwise have been.

"I'd be happy to teach Matthew a lesson," said James.

He was quite good with the staff. He had beat Mike ten times out of ten, and Esme nine times out of ten, and he had been holding back with them. It was possible he would also have to hold back with Matthew.

Except that Matthew came out wearing gear, and looking—for a change—actually like a real Shadowhunter. More like a real Shadowhunter than James did, truth be told, since James was . . . not as short as Thomas, but not tall yet, and what his mother described as wiry. Which was a kind way to say "no real evidence of muscles in view." Several girls, in fact, turned to look at Matthew in gear.

"Mr. Herondale has volunteered to teach you how to staff fight," Ragnor Fell said. "If you plan to murder each other, go farther down the field where I cannot see you and won't have to answer awkward questions."

"James," said Matthew, in the voice that everyone else liked to listen to so much and that struck James as constantly mocking. "This is so kind of you. I think I do remember a few moves with the staff from training with my mama and my brother. Please be patient with me. I may be a little rusty."

Matthew strolled down the field, the sun brilliant on green grass and his gold hair alike, and weighed the staff in one hand. He turned to James, and James had the sudden impression of narrowed eyes: a look of real and serious intent.

Then Matthew's face and the trees both went sailing by, as Matthew's staff scythed James's legs out from under him and James went tumbling to the ground. He lay there dazed.

"You know," said Matthew thoughtfully. "I may not be so terribly rusty after all."

James scrambled to his feet, clutching at both his staff and his dignity. Matthew moved into position to fight him, the staff as light and easily balanced in his hand as if he were a conductor gesturing with his baton. He moved with easy grace, like any Shadowhunter would, but somehow as if he was playing, as if at any moment he might be dancing.

James realized, to his overwhelming disgust, that this was yet another thing Matthew was good at.

"Best of three," he suggested.

Matthew's staff was a blur between his hands, suddenly. James did not have time to shift position before a jarring blow landed on the arm that was holding his staff, then his left shoulder so he could not defend. James blocked the staff when it came toward his midsection, but that turned out to be a feint. Matthew scythed him off at the knees again and James wound up flat on his back in the grass. Again.

Matthew's face came into view. He was laughing, as usual. "Why stop at three?" he asked. "I can stand around and beat you all day."

James hooked his staff behind Matthew's ankles and tripped him up. He knew it was wrong, but in the moment he did not care.

Matthew landed on the grass with a surprised "Oof!" which James found briefly satisfying. Once there, he seemed happy enough to lie in the grass. James found himself being regarded by one brown eye amid the greenery.

"You know," Matthew said slowly, "most people like me."

"Well . . . congratulations!" James snapped, and scrambled to his feet.

It was the exact wrong moment to stand up.

It should have been the last moment of James's life. Perhaps because he thought it would be the last, it seemed to stretch out, giving James time to see it all: how the battering ram had flown through the hands of Christopher's team in the wrong direction. He saw the horrified faces of the whole team, even Christopher paying attention for once. He saw the great wooden log, sailing directly at him, and heard Matthew scream a warning much too late. He saw Ragnor Fell jump up, his deck chair flying, and lift his hand.

The world transformed into sliding grayness, everything still moving slower than James was. Everything was sliding and insubstantial: The battering ram came at him and through him, unable to hurt him; it was like being splashed with water. James lifted a hand and saw the gray air full of stars.

It was Ragnor who had saved him, James thought as the world tipped from bright, strange grayness into black. This was warlock magic.

He did not know until later that the Academy class had all watched, expecting to see a scene of carnage and death, and instead seen a black-haired boy dissolve and change from one of their own into a shadow cast by nothing, a wicked cutout into the abyss behind the world, dark and unmistakable in the afternoon sun. What had been inevitable death, something the Shadowhunters were used to, became something strange and more terrible.

He did not know until later how right he was. It was warlock magic.

When James woke up, it was night, and Uncle Jem was there.

James reared up from his bed and threw himself into Uncle Jem's arms. He had heard some people found the Silent Brothers frightening, with their silent speech and their stitched eyes, but to him the sight of a Silent Brother's robe always meant Uncle Jem, always meant steadfast love.

"Uncle Jem!" he gasped out, arms around his neck, face buried in his robe, safe for a moment. "What happened? Why do I—I felt so strange, and now you're here, and—"

And the presence of a Silent Brother in the Academy meant nothing good. Father was always inventing excuses for Uncle

Jem to come to them—once he had claimed a flowerpot was possessed by a demon. But this was Idris, and a Silent Brother would be summoned to Shadowhunter children only in a time of need.

"Am I—hurt?" asked James. "Is Matthew hurt? He was with me."

Nobody is hurt, said Uncle Jem. *Thanks be to the Angel. It is only that there is now a heavy burden for you to bear, Jamie.*

And the knowledge spilled out from Uncle Jem to James, silent and cold as a grave opening, and yet with Uncle Jem's watchful care mingled with the chill. James shuddered away from the Silent Brother and clung to Uncle Jem at the same time, face wet with tears, fists clutching his robes.

This was his mother's heritage, was what came from mingling the blood of a Shadowhunter with that of a demon, and then with a Shadowhunter again. They had all thought because James's skin could bear Marks that he was a Shadowhunter and nothing else, that the blood of the Angel had burned away all else.

It had not. Even the blood of the Angel could not burn away a shadow. James could perform this strange warlock trick, a trick no warlock Uncle Jem knew could perform. He could transform into a shadow. He could make himself something that was not flesh or blood—certainly not the blood of the Angel.

"What—what *am* I?" James gasped out, his throat raw with sobs.

You are James Herondale, said Uncle Jem. *As you always were. Part your mother, part your father, part yourself. I would not change any part of you if I could.*

James would. He would have burned away this part of himself, wrenched it out, done anything he could to be rid of it. He was meant to be a Shadowhunter, he had always known he was, but would any Shadowhunter fight alongside him, with this horror about him revealed?

"Am I—are they throwing me out of school?" he whispered in Uncle Jem's ear.

No, said Uncle Jem. A feeling of sorrow and anger touched James and then was pulled back. *But James, I do think you should leave. They are afraid that you will—contaminate the purity of their children. They wish to banish you to where the mundane children live. They apparently do not care what happens to the mundane students, and care even less what happens to you. Go home, James. I will bring you home now if you wish it.*

James wanted to go home. He wanted it more than he could remember wanting anything, with an ache that made him feel as if every bone in his body were broken and could not be put back together until he was home. He was loved there, safe there. He would be instantly surrounded in affection and warmth.

Except . . .

"How would my mother feel," James whispered, "if she knew I had been sent home because of—she'll think it's because of her."

His mother, with her grave gray eyes and her flower-tender face, as quiet as James and yet as ready with words as Father. James might be a stain upon the world, might be something that would contaminate good Shadowhunter children. He was ready to believe it. But not Mother. Mother was kind, Mother was lovely and loving, Mother was a wish come true and a blessing on the earth.

James could not bear to think how Mother would feel if she thought she had hurt him in any way. If he could get through the Academy, if he could make her believe there was no real difference to him, that would spare her pain.

He wanted to go home. He did not want to face anybody at the Academy. He was a coward. But he was not enough of a coward that he would run away from his own suffering, and let his mother suffer for him.

You are not a coward at all, said Uncle Jem. *I remember a time, when I was still James Carstairs, when your mother learned—as she thought then—that she could not have children. She was so hurt by that. She thought herself so changed, from all she had thought she was. I told her the right man would not care, and of course your father, the best of men, the only one fit for her, did not. I did not tell her . . . I was a boy and did not know how to tell her, how her courage in bearing uncertainty of her very self touched me. She doubted herself, but I could never doubt her. I could never doubt you now. I see the same courage in you now, as I saw in her then.*

James wept, scrubbing his face against Uncle Jem's robes as if he were littler than Lucie. He knew Mother was brave, but surely courage did not feel like this; he had thought it would be something fine, not a feeling that could tear you into pieces.

If you saw humanity as I can see it, Uncle Jem said, a whisper in his mind, a lifeline. *There is very little brightness and warmth in the world for me. I am very distant from you all. There are only four points of warmth and brightness, in the whole world, that burn fiercely enough for me to feel something like the person I was. Your mother, your father, Lucie, and you. You love, and tremble, and burn. Do not let any of them tell you who you are. You are the flame that cannot be put out. You are the star that cannot be lost. You are who you have always been, and that is enough and more than enough. Anyone who looks at you and sees darkness is blind.*

"Blinder than a Silent Brother?" James asked, and hiccupped.

Uncle Jem had been made a Silent Brother very young, and strangely: He bore runes on his cheeks, but his eyes, though shadowed, were not stitched shut. Still, James was never sure what he saw.

There was a laugh in James's mind, and he had not laughed, so it must have been Uncle Jem. James clung to him for an instant longer and told himself he could not ask Uncle Jem to take him home after all, or to the Silent City, or anywhere so long as Uncle Jem did not leave him in this academy full of strangers who had never liked him and would hate him now.

They would have to be even blinder than a Silent Brother, Uncle Jem agreed. *Because I can see you, James. I will always look to you for light.*

If James had known how life would be at the Academy from then on, he would have asked Uncle Jem to take him home.

He had not expected Mike Smith to leap to his feet in stark horror when James approached his table.

"Come sit with us," called Clive Cartwright, one of Alastair Carstairs's friends. "You might be a mundie, but at least you're not a *monster*."

Mike had fled gratefully. James had seen Esme flinch once when he walked by her in the hall. He did not inflict his presence on her again.

It would not have been so bad, James believed, if it had been anywhere but the Academy. These were hallowed halls: This was where children were molded to Ascend or grew up learning to serve the Angel.

And this was a school, and this was how schools worked. James had read books about schools before, had read about someone being sent to Coventry, so nobody talked to them at all. He knew how hate could run like wildfire through a group, and that was only among mundanes facing mundane strangeness.

James was stranger than any mundane could ever dream, stranger than any Shadowhunter had believed possible.

He moved out of Matthew's room, and down into the dark. He was given his own room, because even the mundanes were too scared to sleep in the same room as him. Even Dean Ashdown seemed afraid of him. Everybody was.

They acted as if they wanted to cross themselves when they saw him, but they knew he was worse than a vampire and it would do no good. They shuddered when his eyes rested on them, as if his yellow demon's eyes would burn a hole clear through their souls.

Demon's eyes. James heard it whispered again and again. He had never thought he would long to be called Goatface.

He never spoke to anyone, sat at the back of class, ate as quickly as he could, and then ran away so people did not have to look at him while they ate their meals. He crept around the Academy like a loathed and loathsome shadow.

Uncle Jem had been changed into a Silent Brother because he would have died otherwise. Uncle Jem had a place in the world, had friends and a home, and the horror was that he could not be in the place where he belonged. Sometimes after his visits James would find his mother standing at the window, looking out at the street Uncle Jem had long disappeared from, and he would find his father in the music room staring at the violin nobody but Uncle Jem was allowed to touch.

That was the tragedy of Uncle Jem's life; it was the tragedy of his parents' lives.

But how would it be if there was nowhere in the world that you belonged? If you could get nobody to love you? What if you could not be a Shadowhunter or a warlock or anything else?

Maybe then you were worse than a tragedy. Maybe you were nothing at all.

James was not sleeping very well. He kept slipping into sleep and then startling awake, worried he was slipping into that other world, a world of shadows, where he was nothing but an evil shade among shades. He did not know how he had done it before. He was terrified it was going to happen again.

Maybe everyone else was hoping it would, though. Maybe they were all praying he would become a shadow, and simply slip away.

James woke one morning and could not bear the darkness and the feeling of stone above his head, pressing down all around him, for a moment longer. He staggered up the stairs and out onto the grounds.

He was expecting it to still be night, but the sky was bleached by morning, the stars turned invisible against the near-white of the sky. The only color to be found in the sky was the dark gray of clouds, curling like ghosts around the fading moon. It was raining a little, cold pinpricks against James's skin. He sat down on the stone step of the Academy's back door, lifted a palm to the sky, and watched the silvery rain dash down into the hollow of his hand.

He wished the rain would wash him away, before he had to face yet another morning.

He was watching his hand as he wished that, and he saw it happen then. He felt the change creeping over him and saw his hand grow darkly transparent. He saw the raindrops pass through the shadow of his palm as if it was not there.

He wondered what Grace would think, if she could see him now.

Then he heard the crunch of feet running, pounding against the earth, and his father's training made James's head jerk up to see if anyone was being chased, if anyone was in danger.

James saw Matthew Fairchild running as if he was being chased.

Astonishingly, he was wearing gear that he had not, as far as James knew, been threatened into. Even more astonishingly, he was participating in degrading physical exercise. He was running faster than James had seen anyone run in training—maybe faster than James had ever seen anyone run ever—and he was running grimly, face set, in the rain.

James watched him run, frowning, until Matthew glanced up at the sky, stopped, and then began trudging back to the Academy. James thought he would be discovered for a moment, thought of jumping up and racing around to another side of the building, but Matthew did not make for the door.

Instead he went and stood against the stone wall of the Academy, strange and solemn in his black gear, blond hair wild with wind and wet with rain. He tipped his face up to the sky, and he looked as unhappy as James felt.

It made no sense. Matthew had everything, had always had everything, while James now had less than nothing. It made James furious.

"What's wrong with you?" James demanded.

Matthew's whole body jerked with shock. He swung to face James, and stared. "What?"

"You might have noticed life is less than ideal for me at

this time," James said between his teeth. "So give up making a tragic spectacle of yourself over nothing, and—"

Matthew was not leaning against the wall any longer, and James was not sitting on the step. They were both standing up, and this was not a practice on the training grounds. James thought they were really going to fight; he thought they might really hurt each other.

"Oh, I'm terribly sorry, James Herondale," Matthew sneered. "I forgot nobody could do a single thing like speak or breathe in this place without incurring your extremely judgmental judgment. I must be making a spectacle over nothing, if *you* say so. By the Angel, I'd trade places with you in a second."

"You'd trade places with me?" James shouted. "That's rubbish, that's absolute swill, you would never. Why would you do that? Why would you even say it?"

"Maybe it's the fact you have everything I want," Matthew snarled. "And you don't even seem to want it."

"What?" James asked blankly. He was living in opposites land, in which the sky was the earth and the name of every day started with Y. It was the only explanation. "*What?* What do I have that you could possibly want?"

"They will send you home any time you like," Matthew said. "They're trying to drive you away. And no matter what I do, they won't chuck me out. Not the Consul's son."

James blinked. Rain slithered down his cheeks and down the neck of his shirt, but he hardly felt it. "You want . . . to be chucked out?"

"I want to go *home*, all right?" Matthew snapped. "I want to be with my father!"

"What?" James said blankly, one more time.

Matthew might insult the Nephilim, but no matter what he said, he always seemed to be having a marvelous time. James had believed he was enjoying himself at the Academy, as James himself could not. James had never thought he might really be unhappy. He'd never even considered Uncle Henry.

Matthew's face twisted as if he was going to cry. He stared off determinedly into the distance, and when he spoke his voice was hard.

"You think Christopher's bad, but my father is so much worse," Matthew said. "A hundred times as bad as Christopher. A thousand. He's been practicing being terrible for much longer than Christopher. He's so absentminded, and he can't—he can't walk. He could be working on some new device, or writing a letter to his warlock friend in America about a new device, or working out why some old device literally exploded, and he would not notice if his own hair was on fire. I'm not exaggerating, I'm not making a joke—I have put out fires on my own father's head. My mother is always busy, and my brother, Charles Buford, is always running after her and acting superior. I'm the one who takes care of my father. I'm the one who listens to him. I didn't want to go away to school and leave him, and I've been doing all I can to get chucked out and go back."

I don't take care of my father. My father takes care of me, James wanted to say, but he feared it might be cruel to say that, when Matthew had never had that unquestioning security.

It occurred to James that one day there might be a time when his father did not seem all-knowing, able to solve everything and be anything. The thought made him uncomfortable.

"You've been trying to get expelled?" James asked. He spoke slowly. He *felt* slow.

Matthew made an impatient gesture, as if chopping invisible carrots with an invisible knife. "That is what I've been trying to tell you, yes. But they won't. I have been doing the best impression of the worst Shadowhunter in the world, and yet they won't. What is wrong with the dean, I ask you? Does she want blood?"

"The best impression of the worst Shadowhunter," James repeated. "So you don't—believe in all that stuff about violence being repulsive, and truth and beauty and Oscar Wilde?"

"No, I do," Matthew said hastily. "I really like Oscar Wilde. And beauty and truth. I do think it's nonsense that because we are born what we are, we cannot be painters or poets or create anything—that all we do is kill. My father and Christopher are geniuses, do you know that? Real geniuses. Like Leonardo da Vinci. He was a mundane who—"

"I know who Leonardo da Vinci is."

Matthew glanced at him and smiled: it was The Smile, gradual and illuminating as sunrise, and James had the sinking feeling that he might not be immune after all.

"'Course you do, James," said Matthew. "Forgot who I was talking to for a moment there. Anyway, Christopher and my father are truly brilliant. Their inventions have already changed the way Shadowhunters navigate the world, the way they battle demons. And all Shadowhunters everywhere will always look down on them. They will never see what they do as valuable. And someone who wanted to write plays, to make beautiful art, they would throw away like refuse from the streets."

"Do you—want that?" James asked hesitantly.

"No," said Matthew. "I can't draw for toffee, actually. I certainly can't write plays. The less said about my poetry the better. I do appreciate art, though. I'm an excellent spectator. I could spectate for England."

"You could, um, be an actor," James suggested. "When you talk, everyone listens. Especially when you tell stories."

Also there was Matthew's face, which would probably—go over well onstage or something.

"That's a nice thought," said Matthew. "But I think I would rather not get thrown out of my home and still see my father occasionally. Also, I do think violence is terrible and pointless, but—I'm really good at it. In fact, I enjoy it. Not that I'm letting on to our teachers. I wish I was good at something that could add beauty to the world rather than painting it with blood, I really do, but there you have it."

He shrugged.

James did not think they were going to fight after all, so he sat back down on the step. He felt he wanted a sit-down. "I think Shadowhunters can add beauty to the world," he said. "I mean, for one thing—we save lives. I know I said it before, but it's really important. The people we save, any one of them could be the next Leonardo da Vinci, or Oscar Wilde, or just someone who is really kind, who spreads beauty that way. Or they might just be someone who—someone else loves, like you love your father. Maybe you're right that Shadowhunters are more limited, that we do not get the full range of possibilities mundanes get, but—we get to make the mundanes' lives possible. That's what we're born to. It is a privilege. I'm not going to run away from the Academy. I'm not running away from anything. I can bear Marks, and that makes me a Shadowhunter, and that's what I will be whether the Nephilim want me or not."

"You can be a Shadowhunter without going to the Academy,

though," said Matthew. "You can be trained in an Institute, like Uncle Will was. That's what I wanted, so I could stay with Father."

"I could. But—" James hesitated. "I didn't want to be sent home. Mother would have to know why."

Matthew was silent for a little while. There was nothing but the sound of the falling rain.

"I like Aunt Tessa," he said. "I never came to London because I worried about leaving Father. I always wished—she could come to Idris more often."

James had received several shocks this morning that were actually not so bad, but this revelation was unwelcome and inevitable. Of course Mother and Father scarcely ever went to Idris. Of course James and Lucie had been raised in London, a little apart from their families.

Because there were people in Idris, there were arrogant Shadowhunters who thought Mother was not worthy to walk among them, and Father would never have let her be insulted.

Now it would be worse, now people would whisper that she had passed on the taint to her children. People would say horrible things about Lucie, James knew—about his scribbling, laughing little sister. Lucie could never be allowed to come to the Academy.

Matthew cleared his throat. "I suppose I can understand all that. Maybe I will stop being so jealous that you are able to get chucked out of school. Maybe I can understand that your aims are noble. However, I still do not understand why you must make it so clear you detest the sight of me. I know, I know, you're aloof and you wish to be alone with literature all the time, but it's particularly horrible with me. It's very lowering.

Most people like me. I told you that. I don't even have to try."

"Yes, you're very good at Shadowhunting and everybody likes you, Matthew," said James. "Thanks for clarifying that."

"You don't like me!" Matthew exclaimed. "I did try with you! And you still don't."

"The thing is," said James, "I tend to like very modest people? Humble, you know."

Matthew paused, considered James for a moment, and then burst out laughing. James was amazed by how gratifying that was. It made him feel like he could let out the humiliating truth.

He closed his eyes and said: "I was jealous of you."

When he opened his eyes, Matthew looked wary, as if expecting a trick. "Of what?"

"Well, you're not considered an unholy abomination upon this earth."

"Yes, but—no offense, James—nobody but you is," Matthew pointed out. "You are our unique feature in the school, like a sculpture of a warrior chicken. If we had one of those. You disliked me before anybody knew you were an unholy abomination, anyway. Well, I suppose you are simply trying to spare my feelings. Decent of you. I under—"

"I'm not aloof," said James. "I don't know where you got that idea."

"All the aloofness, I think," Matthew speculated.

"I'm a swot," said James. "I read books all the time and I do not know how to talk to people. If I was a girl living in olden times, people would call me a bluestocking. I wish I could talk to people like you do. I wish I could smile at people and make them like me. I wish I could tell a story and have everybody listen, and have people follow me around wherever I went. Well, no, I don't, because I am slightly terrified by people, but I wish I could do all that you can do, just the same. I wanted to be friends with Thomas and Christopher, because I liked them and I thought maybe they were—similar to me, and they might like me back. You were jealous I could get kicked out of school? I was jealous of you first. I was jealous of everything about you, and I still am."

"Wait," said Matthew. "Wait, wait, wait. You don't like me because I am *so very charming?*"

He threw his head back and laughed. He kept laughing. He laughed so much that he had to come and sit beside James on the step, and then he laughed some more.

"Stop it, Matthew," James grumbled. "Stop laughing. I am sharing my innermost feelings with you. This is very hurtful."

"I've been in a bad mood this whole time," said Matthew. "You think I'm charming now? You have *no* idea."

James punched him in the arm. He could not help smiling. He saw Matthew noticing, and looking very pleased with himself.

Sometime later, Matthew ushered James firmly into breakfast and to their table, which James noticed was only Christopher and Thomas, and a rather select table after all.

Christopher and Thomas, in another surprise for James in a morning full of surprises, seemed pleased to see him.

"Oh, have you decided not to detest Matthew any longer?" Christopher asked. "I'm so glad. You were really hurting his feelings. Though we are not supposed to talk about that to you." He gazed dreamily at the bread basket, as if it were a wonderful painting. "I forgot that."

Thomas put his head down on the table. "Why are you the way that you are?"

Matthew reached over and patted Thomas on the back, then rescued Christopher from setting his own sleeves on fire with a candle. He gave James the candle and a smile.

"If you ever see Christopher near an open flame, take him away from it, or take it away from him," Matthew said. "Fight the good fight with me. I must be eternally watchful."

"That must be difficult, when surrounded by, um, your adoring public," said James.

"Well," said Matthew, and paused, "it's possible," he said, and paused again, "I may have been . . . slightly showing off? 'Look, if you don't want to be friends with me, everybody else does, and you are making a big mistake.' I may have been doing that. Possibly."

"Is that over?" Thomas asked. "Thank the Angel. You know large crowds of people make me nervous! You know I can never think of anything to say to them! I am not witty like you or aloof and above it all like James or living in cloud cuckoo land like Christopher. I came to the Academy to get away from being bossed by my sisters, but my sisters make me much less nervous than battering rams flying through the air and parties all the time. Can we please have some peace and quiet occasionally!"

James stared at Thomas. "Does everybody think I'm aloof?"

"No, mostly people think you're an unholy abomination upon this earth," Matthew said cheerfully. "Remember?"

Thomas looked ready to put his head back on the table, but he cheered up when he saw James had not taken offense.

"Why would that be?" Christopher asked politely.

James stared. "Because I can turn from flesh and blood into a ghastly shadow?"

"Oh," said Christopher. His dreamy lavender eyes focused

for a moment. "That's very interesting," he told James, his voice clear. "You should let me and Uncle Henry perform many experiments on you. We could do an experiment right now."

"No, we could not," said Matthew. "No experiments at breakfast time. Add it to the list, Christopher."

Christopher sighed.

And just like that, as if it could always have been that easy, James had friends. He liked Thomas and Christopher as much as he'd always known he would.

Of all his new friends, though, he liked Matthew the best. Matthew always wanted to talk about the books James had read, or tell James a story as good as a book. He made obvious efforts to find James when James was not there, and obvious efforts to protect James when he was there. James did not have many nice things to write letters home about: He ended up writing letters that were full of Matthew.

James knew Matthew probably only felt sorry for him. Matthew was always looking after Christopher and Thomas, with the same painstaking care he must have looked after his father. Matthew was kind.

That was all right. James would absolutely have wanted to share a room with Matthew, now it was out of the question.

"Why do people call you Demon Eyes, James?" Christopher asked one day when they were sitting around a table studying Ragnor Fell's account of the First Accords.

"Because I have golden eyes as if lit by eldritch infernal fires," James said. He had heard a girl whispering that and thought it sounded rather poetic.

"Ah," said Christopher. "Do you look at all like your grandfather aside from that? The demonic one, I mean."

"You cannot simply ask whether people look like their demon grandfather!" Thomas wailed. "Next you will ask Professor Fell if he looks like his demon parent! Please, please do not ask Professor Fell if he looks like his demon parent. He has a cutting tongue. Also, he might cut you with a knife."

"Fell?" Christopher inquired.

"Our teacher," said Matthew. "Our green teacher."

Christopher looked genuinely astonished. "We have a teacher who is green?"

"James looks like his father," said Matthew unexpectedly, then narrowed his laughing dark eyes in James's direction in a musing fashion. "Or he will, when he grows into his face and it stops being angles pointing in all different directions."

James slowly raised his open book to hide his face, but he was secretly pleased.

Matthew's friendship made other friends creep forward too. Esme cornered James and told him how sorry she was that Mike was being an idiot. She also told him that she hoped James did not take this expression of friendly concern in a romantic way.

"I have rather a *tendresse* for Matthew Fairchild, actually," Esme added. "Please put in a good word for me there."

Life was much, much better now that he had friends, but that did not mean anything was perfect, or even mended. People were still afraid of him, still hissing "*Demon Eyes*" and muttering about unclean shadows.

"*Pulvis et umbra sumus*," said James once, out loud in class, after hearing too many whispers. "My father says that sometimes. We are but dust and shadows. Maybe I'm just—getting a head start on all of you."

Several people in the classroom were looking alarmed.

"What did he say?" Mike Smith whispered, clearly agitated.

"It's not a demon language, buffoon," Matthew snapped. "It's Latin."

Despite everything Matthew could do, the whispers rose and rose. James kept expecting a disaster.

And then the demons were let loose in the woods.

"I'll be partners with Christopher," said Thomas at their next training exercise, sounding resigned.

"Excellent. I will be partners with James," said Matthew. "He reminds me of the nobility of the Shadowhunter way of life. He keeps me right. If I am parted from him I will become distracted by truth and beauty. I know I will."

Their teachers seemed extremely pleased that Matthew was actually participating in training courses now, aside from the courses only for the elites, in which Thomas reported that Matthew was still determined to be hopeless.

James did not know why the teachers were so worried. It was obvious that as soon as anyone was actually in danger, Matthew would leap to their defense.

James was glad to be so sure of that, as they walked through the woods. It was a windy day, and it seemed as if every tree was stooping down to howl in his ear, and he knew that Pyxis boxes had been placed throughout the woods by older students—Pyxis boxes with the smallest and most harmless of demons inside, but still real Pyxis boxes with real demons inside, who they were meant to fight. Pyxis boxes were a little outmoded these days, but they were still sometimes used to transport demons safely. If demons could ever be said to be safe.

James's aunt Ella, who he had never seen, had been killed

by a demon from a Pyxis box when she was younger than James was now.

All the trees seemed to be whispering about demons.

But Matthew was at his side, and both of them were armed. He could trust himself to kill a small, almost power-less demon, and if he could trust himself, he could trust Matthew more.

They waited, and walked, then waited. There was a rustle among the trees: It turned out to be a combination of wind and a single rabbit.

"Maybe the upper years forgot to lay out our demon buffet," Matthew suggested. "It is a beautiful springtime day. At such times as these, one's thoughts are filled with love and blossoms, not demons. Who am I to judge—"

Matthew was abruptly quiet. He clutched James's arm, fingers tight, and James stared down at what Matthew had discovered in the heather.

It was Clive Cartwright, Alastair's friend. He was dead.

His eyes were open, staring into nothing, and in one hand he was clutching an empty Pyxis box.

James grabbed Matthew's arm and turned him in a circle, looking around, waiting. He could tell what had happened: Let's give Demon Eyes a scare, a demon won't hurt its own kind, let's chase him away once and for all with a demon larger than he was expecting.

He could not tell what kind of demon it was, but that question was answered when the demon came toward them through the wild woods.

It was a Vetis demon, its shape almost human but not quite, dragging its gray, scaly body through the fallen leaves. James saw the eel-like heads on its arms lifting, like the heads of pointer dogs out hunting.

James slipped from skin to shadow without a thought, like plunging into water to rescue someone, as easy as that. He ran unseen at the Vetis demon and, raising his sword, cleaved one questing head from its arm. He turned to face the head on the other arm. He was going to call to Matthew, but when he glanced back he saw Matthew clearly, despite the sparkling grayness of the world. Matthew already had his bow out, strung and raised. He could see Matthew's narrowed eyes, the determined focus that always lay behind the laughter, and remained when his laughter was stripped away.

Matthew shot the Vetis demon in the red-eyed, sharp-toothed face that sat atop its neck, just as James cut the other head from its remaining arm. The demon lurched, then fell over sideways, twitching.

And James raced through the trees, through the wind and the whispering, afraid of nothing, with Matthew running behind him. He found Alastair and his remaining friend, hiding behind a tree. He crept up to them, a shadow among the whirling shadows of wind-tossed trees, and held his sword to Alastair's throat.

While James was touching the sword, nobody could see it. But Alastair felt the sharpness of the blade and gasped.

"We didn't mean for any of this to happen!" cried Alastair's friend, looking around wildly. Alastair was wise enough to stay quiet. "It was Clive's idea—he said he would finally get you to leave—he only meant to scare you."

"Who's scared?" James whispered, and the whisper came from nowhere. He heard the older boys gasp in fear. "I'm not the one who's scared. If you come after me again, I won't be the one who suffers. Run!"

The pair that had once been a trio stumbled away. James pressed one hand around the hilt of his sword, against the bark of the tree, and willed himself back into a world of solidity and sunshine. He found Matthew looking at him. Matthew had known, all the time, exactly where he was.

"Jamie," Matthew said, sounding unsettled but impressed. "That was terrifying."

"It's James, for the last time," said James.

"No, I'm calling you Jamie for a little while, because you just displayed arcane power and calling you Jamie makes me feel better."

James laughed, shakily, and that made Matthew smile. It did not occur to them until later that a student was dead, and the Shadowhunters feared and distrusted the demonic—that some-body would be blamed. James did not discover until the next day that his parents had been informed of everything that had trans-pired, and that he, James Herondale, was now officially expelled.

They kept him in the infirmary until his father came. They did not say this was because the infirmary had bars on its doors.

Esme came and gave James a hug, and promised to look him up when she Ascended.

Ragnor Fell entered, his tread heavy, and for a moment James thought he was going to be asked for his homework. Instead Ragnor stood over his bed and shook his horned head slowly from side to side.

"I waited for you to ask me for help," Ragnor told him. "I thought perhaps you might make a warlock."

"I never wanted to be anything but a Shadowhunter," James said helplessly.

Ragnor said, sounding disgusted as usual: "You Shadowhunters never do."

Christopher and Thomas visited. Christopher brought a fruit basket, under the mistaken impression that James was in the infirmary because he was unwell. Thomas apologized for Christopher several times.

James did not see Matthew, however, until his father arrived. Father did not come on a mission to charm the dean. His face was grim as he escorted James through the shining gray walls of the Academy, under the flaming colors of the stained-glass angel, for the last time. He stalked down stairs and through halls as if defying someone to insult James.

James knew nobody ever would, not in front of Father. They would whisper behind his back, whisper in James's ear, his whole life long.

"You should have told us, Jamie," said Father. "But Jem explained to us why you did not."

"How is Mother?" James whispered.

"She cried when Jem told her, and said you were her sweet boy," said Father. "I believe she may be planning to strangle you and then bake you a cake afterward."

"I like cake," James said at last.

All that suffering, all that nobly trying to spare her, and for what? James thought, as he walked out the door of the Academy. He had saved her only a month or two of pain. He hoped that did not mean he was a failure: He hoped Uncle Jem would still think it was worthwhile.

He saw Matthew standing in the courtyard, hands in his

pockets, and brightened up. Matthew had come to say good-bye, after all. It did feel worthwhile to have stayed, after all, to have made a friend like this.

"Are you expelled?" Matthew asked, which James thought was slightly obtuse.

"Yes?" he said, indicating his father and his trunk.

"I thought you were," said Matthew, nodding vigorously so his much-brushed hair went tumbling every which way. "So I had to act. But I wanted to make absolutely certain. You see, James, the thing is—"

"Isn't that Alastair Carstairs?" asked Father, perking up.

Alastair did not meet James's eyes as he slunk toward him. He definitely did not respond to Father's beaming smile. He seemed very interested in the flagstones of the courtyard.

"I just wanted to say . . . sorry for everything," he mumbled. "Good luck."

"Oh," said James. "Thanks."

"No hard feelings, old sport," said Matthew. "As a bit of a jolly prank, I put all your belongings in the south wing. I don't know why I did that! Boyish high spirits, I suppose."

"You did *what?*" Alastair gave Matthew a harried look, and departed at speed.

Matthew turned to James's father and dramatically clasped his hand.

"Oh, Mr. Herondale!" he said. "Please take me with you!"

"It's Matthew, isn't it?" Father asked. He tried to disengage his hand. Matthew clung to it with extreme determination.

James smiled. He could have told Father about Matthew's determination.

"You see," Matthew proceeded, "I am also expelled from Shadowhunter Academy."

"You got expelled?" James asked. "When? Why?"

"In about four minutes," Matthew said. "Because I broke my solemn word, and exploded the south wing of the Academy."

James and his father both looked at the south wing. It stood, looking as if it would stand for another century.

"I hoped it would not come to this, but it has. I gave Christopher certain materials that I knew he could turn into explosives. I measured them very carefully, I made sure they were slow acting, and I made Thomas swear to bring Christopher away. I have left a note explaining that it was all my fault, but I do not wish to explain this to Mother. Please take me with you to the London Institute, so I can be taught how to be a Shadowhunter with James!"

"Charlotte will cut off my head," said Father.

He sounded tempted, though. Matthew was sparkling wickedly up at him, and Father enjoyed wickedness. Besides which, he was no more immune to The Smile than anyone else.

"Father, please," James said in a quiet voice.

"Mr. Herondale, please!" said Matthew. "We cannot be parted." James braced himself for the explanation about truth and beauty, but instead Matthew said, with devastating simplicity: "We are going to be *parabatai*."

James stared.

Father said: "Oh, I see."

Matthew nodded encouragingly, and smiled encouragingly.

"Then nobody should come between you," said Father.

"Nobody." Matthew shook his head as he said "nobody," then nodded again. He looked seraphic. "Exactly."

"Very well," said Father. "Everybody get into the carriage."

"Father, you did not steal Uncle Gabriel's carriage again," said James.

"This is your time of trouble. He would want me to have it, and he would have given it to me if I asked him, which as it happens I did not," said Father.

He helped James and Matthew up, then swung himself up to sit on James's other side. He grasped the reins and they were off.

"When the south wing collapses, there could be flying debris," Father remarked. "Any one of us could be injured." He sounded very cheerful about this. "Best to stop on our way home and see the Silent Brothers."

"That seems excessi—" Matthew began, but James elbowed him. Matthew would learn how Father was about the Silent Brothers soon enough.

Anyway, James did not feel Matthew had a right to characterize anyone else's behavior as excessive, now that he had blown up the Academy.

"I was thinking we could split our training time between the London Institute and my house," Matthew went on. "The Consul's house. Where people cannot insult you, and can get used to seeing you."

Matthew had really meant it about being trained together, James thought. He had worked it all out. And if James was in Idris more often, he could perhaps see Grace more often too.

"I'd like that," said James. "I know you'd like to see more of your father."

Matthew smiled. Behind them, the Academy exploded. The carriage jolted slightly with the force of the impact.

"We don't . . . have to be *parabatai*," Matthew said, his

voice quiet under the sound of the blast. "I said it to make your father take me with you, so I could execute my new plan, but we don't . . . have to. I mean, unless you . . . maybe want to be."

James had thought he wanted a friend like himself, a *parabatai* who was shy and quiet and would enter in on James's feelings about the terror of parties. Instead here was Matthew, who was the life and soul of every party, who made dreadful hairbrush decisions, who was unexpectedly and terribly kind. Who had tried to be his friend and kept trying, even though James did not know what trying to be a friend looked like. Who could see James, even when he was a shadow.

"Yes," James said simply.

"What?" said Matthew, who always knew what to say.

"I'd like that," said James. He curled his hands, one around his father's coat sleeve, and one around Matthew's. He held on to them, all the way home.

Shadowhunter Academy, 2008

"So James found a *parabatai* and everything worked out great," Simon said. "That's awesome."

James was Tessa Gray's son, Simon had realized, a long way into the story. It was strange to think of that: It seemed to bring that lost boy very close, he and his friend. Simon liked the sound of James. He'd liked Tessa, too.

And though he was starting to get the feeling, even without his memories, that he hadn't always liked Jace Herondale—he liked him now.

Catarina rolled her eyes so hard Simon thought he could

hear them roll, like tiny, exasperated bowling balls.

"No, Simon. The Academy drove James Herondale out for being different, and all the people who loved him could do was follow him out. The people who drove them out did have to rebuild part of their precious Academy, mind you."

"Uh," said Simon. "Sorry, is the message I'm meant to be learning 'get out, get out as fast as you can'?"

"Maybe," Catarina said. "Maybe the message is to trust your friends. Maybe the message is not that people in the past did badly but that now we must all strive to do better. Maybe the message is you have to work these things out for yourself. You think all lessons have easy conclusions? Don't be a child, Daylighter. You're not immortal anymore. You don't have much time to waste."

Simon took that as the dismissal it was, scooping up his books. "Thanks for the story, Ms. Loss."

He ran down the stairs and out of the Academy, but he was too late, as he'd known he would be.

He was barely out of the door when he saw the dregs, filthy and tired, arm in arm, lurching up from the training grounds. Marisol was in front, her arm looped with George's. It looked as if someone had tried to pull out all her hair.

"Where were you, Lewis?" she called. "We could have used you cheering for us as we won!"

Some way behind them were the elites. Jon was looking very unhappy, which filled Simon with a deep sense of peace.

Trust your friends, Catarina had said.

Simon might speak up for mundies in class, but it mattered more that George and Marisol and Sunil spoke up too. Simon didn't want to change things by being the special one, the exceptional mundane, the former Daylighter and former hero. They had all chosen to come try to be heroes. His fellow dregs could win without him.

There was one more motive Catarina might have had that she had not announced, Simon thought.

She had heard this story from her dead friend Ragnor Fell.

Catarina had listened to her friend's stories, the way James Herondale had listened to his father's stories. Being able to tell the stories over again, having someone to listen and learn, meant her friend was not lost.

Maybe he could write to Clary, Simon thought, as well as Isabelle. Maybe he could trust her to love him despite how often he might fail her. Maybe he was ready to be told stories about himself and about her. He didn't want to lose his friend.

Simon was writing his letter to Clary when George came in, toweling his hair. He had taken his life in his hands and risked the showers in one of the dregs' bathroom.

"Hey," Simon said.

"Hey, where were you while the game was happening?" George asked. "I thought you were never coming back and I'd have to be pals with Jon Cartwright. Then I thought about being pals with Jon, was overwhelmed with despair, and decided to find one of the frogs I know are living in here, give it little frog glasses, and call it Simon 2.0."

Simon shrugged, not sure how much he was supposed to tell. "Catarina kept me after class."

"Careful, or someone might start rumors about you two," said

George. "Not that I would judge. She's obviously . . . ceruleanly charming."

"She was telling me a long story about Shadowhunters being jerks and about *parabatai*. What do you think about the whole *parabatai* thing, anyway? The *parabatai* rune is like a friendship bracelet you can never take back."

"I think it sounds nice," said George. "I'd like that, to have someone who would always watch my back. Someone who I could count on at the times when this scary world gets the scariest."

"Makes it sound like there's someone you'd ask."

"I'd ask you, Si," said George, with an awkward little smile. "But I know you wouldn't ask me. I know who you would ask. And that's okay. I've still got Frog Simon," he added thoughtfully. "Though I'm not sure he's exactly Shadowhunter material."

Simon laughed at the joke, as George had meant him to, smoothing over the awkward moment.

"How were the showers?"

"I have one word for you, Si," said George. "A sad, sad word. Gritty. I had to shower, though. I was gross. Our victory was amazing but hard-won. Why are Shadowhunters so bendy, Simon? Why?"

George kept complaining about Jon Cartwright's enthusiastic if unskilled attempts at playing baseball, but Simon was not listening.

I know who you would ask.

A flash of memory came to Simon, as it did sometimes, cutting like a knife. *I love you,* he'd told Clary. He'd said it believing he was going to die. He'd wanted those to be his last words before he died, the truest words he could speak.

He'd been thinking all this time about his two possible lives, but he didn't have two possible lives. He had a real life, with real memories and a real best friend. He had his childhood as it had actually been, holding hands with Clary as they crossed the street, and the last year as it had actually been, with Jace saving his life and with him saving Isabelle's and with Clary there, Clary, always Clary.

The other life, the so-called normal life without his best friend, was a fake. It was like a giant woven tapestry portraying his life, scenes shown in threads that were all the colors of the rainbow, except it had one color—one of the brightest colors—ripped out.

Simon liked George, he liked all his friends at the Academy, but he was not James Herondale. He had already had friends before he came here.

Friends to live and die for, to have entangled with every memory. The other Shadowhunters, especially Clary, were a part of him. She was the color that had been ripped out, the bright thread woven through his first memories to his last. Something was missing from the pattern of Simon's life, without Clary, and it would never be right again, unless she was restored.

My best friend, Simon thought. Another thing worth living in this world for, worth being a Shadowhunter for. Maybe she wouldn't want to be his *parabatai.* God knew Simon was no prize. But if he got through this school, if he managed to become a Shadowhunter, he would have all the memories of his best friend back.

He could try for the bond between Jace and Alec, between James Herondale and Matthew Fairchild. He could ask if she would perform the ritual and speak the words that told the world what was between you, and that it was unbreakable.

He could at least ask Clary.

The Evil We Love

By Cassandra Clare and Robin Wasserman

It seemed suddenly very important to have space between him and Michael. As much space as possible.

"You're what?"

He hadn't meant to shout.

—The Evil We Love

There were, Simon Lewis thought, so many ways to destroy a letter. You could shred it into confetti. You could light it on fire. You could feed it to a dog—or a Hydra demon. You could, with the help of your friendly neighborhood warlock, Portal it to Hawaii and drop it into the mouth of a volcano. And given all the letter-destroying options available, Simon thought, maybe the fact that Isabelle Lightwood had returned *his* letter intact was of significance. Maybe it was actually a good sign.

Or at least a not-entirely-terrible sign.

That, at least, was what Simon had been telling himself for the last few months.

But even he had to admit that when the letter in question was a sort-of-maybe love letter, a letter that included heart-felt, humiliating phrases like "you're amazing" and "I know I am that guy you loved"—and when said letter was returned unopened, "RETURN TO SENDER" scrawled across it in red lipstick—"not-entirely-terrible" might be overly optimistic.

At least she had referred to him as "sender." Simon was pretty sure that Isabelle had devised some other choice names for him, none quite so friendly. A demon had sucked out all of his memories, but his observational faculties were intact— and he'd observed that Isabelle Lightwood wasn't the kind of girl who liked to be rejected. Simon, in defiance of all laws of nature and common sense, had rejected her twice.

He'd tried to explain himself in the letter, apologize for pushing her away. He'd confessed how much he wanted to fight his way back to the person he once was. *Her* Simon. Or at least, a Simon worthy of her.

Izzy—I don't know why you would wait for me, but if you do, I promise to make myself worth that wait, he'd written. *Or I'll try. I can promise I am going to try.*

One month to the day after he sent it, the letter came back unread.

As the dorm room door creaked open, Simon hastily shoved the letter back into his desk drawer, careful to avoid the cobwebs and pockets of mold that coated every piece of furniture no matter how diligently he cleaned. He didn't move hastily enough.

"Not the letter *again?*" Simon's roommate at the Academy, George Lovelace, groaned. He flung himself down on his bed, sweeping an arm melodramatically across his forehead. "Oh, Isabelle, my darling, if I stare at this letter long enough, maybe I'll telepathically woo you back to my weeping bosom."

"I don't have a bosom," Simon said, with as much dignity as he could muster. "And I'm pretty sure if I did, it wouldn't be weeping."

"Heaving, then? That's what bosoms do, isn't it?"

"I haven't spent much time around them," Simon admitted. Not much that he could remember, at least. There had been that aborted attempt at groping Sophie Hillyer back in the ninth grade, but her mother busted him before he could even find the clasp on her bra, much less master it. There had, presumably, been Isabelle. But Simon tried very hard these days not to think about that. The clasp on Isabelle's bra; his hands on Isabelle's body; the taste of—

Simon shook his head violently, almost hard enough to clear it. "Can we stop talking about *bosoms*? Like, forever?"

"Didn't mean to interrupt your very important moping-about-Izzy time."

"I'm not moping," Simon lied.

"Excellent." George grinned triumphantly, and Simon realized he'd fallen into some kind of trap. "So then you'll come out to the training field with me, help break in the new daggers. We're sparring, mundies versus elites—losers have to eat extra helpings of soup for a week."

"Oh yeah, Shadowhunters really know how to party." His heart wasn't in the sarcasm. The truth was, his fellow students *did* know how to party, even if their idea of fun usually involved pointy weapons. With exams behind them and only one more week before the end-of-year party and summer vacation, Shadowhunter Academy felt more like camp than school. Simon couldn't believe he'd been here the whole school year; he couldn't believe he'd *survived* the year. He'd learned Latin, runic writing, and a smattering of Chthonian; he'd fought tiny demons in the woods, endured a full moon night with a new-born werewolf, ridden (and nearly been trampled by) a horse, eaten his weight in soup, and in all that time, he'd been neither expelled nor exsanguinated. He'd even bulked up enough to trade in his ladies'-size gear for a men's size, albeit the smallest one available. Against all odds, the Academy had come to feel like home. A slimy, moldy, dungeonlike home without work-ing toilets, maybe, but home nonetheless. He and George had even named the rats that lived behind their walls. Every night, they left Jon Cartwright Jr., III, and IV a piece of stale bread to nibble, in hopes they'd prefer the crumbs to human feet.

This last week was a time for celebration, late-night carous-ing, and petty wagering over dagger fights. But Simon couldn't quite find the will for fun. Maybe it was the looming shadow of summer vacation—the prospect of going home to a place that didn't feel much like home anymore.

Or maybe it was, as it always was, Isabelle.

"Definitely you'll have much more fun here, sulking," George said as he changed into his gear. "Silly of me to suggest otherwise."

Simon sighed. "You wouldn't understand."

George had a movie-star face, a Scottish accent, a sun-kissed tan, and the kind of muscles that made girls—even the Shadow-hunter Academy girls, who until they met Simon had apparently never encountered a human male without a six-pack—giggle and swoon. Girl trouble, particularly the brand involving humil-iation and rejection, was beyond his comprehension.

"Just to be clear," George said, in the rich brogue that even Simon couldn't help but find charming, "you don't remember anything about dating this girl? You don't remember being in love with her, you don't remember what it was like when the two of you—"

"That's right," Simon cut him off.

"Or even *if* the two of you—"

"Again, correct," Simon said quickly. He hated to admit it, but this was one of the things about demon amnesia that bothered him the most. What kind of seventeen-year-old guy doesn't know whether or not he's a virgin?

"Because you're apparently running low on brain cells, you *tell* this gorgeous creature that you've forgotten all about her, reject her publicly, and yet when you pledge your love to her in some goopy romantic letter, you're surprised when she's not having it. Then you spend the next two months mooning over her. Is that about right?"

Simon dropped his head into his hands. "Okay, so when you put it that way, it makes no sense."

"Oh, I've *seen* Isabelle Lightwood—it makes all the sense in the world." George grinned. "I just wanted to get my facts straight."

He bounded out the door before Simon could clarify that it wasn't about how Isabelle looked—although it was true that she looked, to Simon, like the most beautiful girl in the world. But it wasn't about her curtain of silky black hair or the bottomless dark brown of her eyes or the deadly liquid grace with which she swung her electrum whip. He couldn't have explained what it *was* about, since George was right, he didn't remember anything about her or what the two of them had been like as a couple. He still had some trouble believing they ever *were* a couple.

He just knew, on a level beneath reason and memory, that some part of him belonged with Isabelle. Maybe even belonged *to* Isabelle. Whether he could remember why, or not.

He'd written Clary a letter too, telling her how much he wanted to remember their friendship—asking for her help. Unlike Isabelle, she'd written back, telling him the story of how they first met. It was the first of many letters, all of them adding episodes to the epic, lifelong story of Clary and Simon's Excellent Adventure. The more Simon read, the more he remembered, and sometimes he even wrote back with stories of his own. It felt safe, somehow, corresponding by letter; there was no chance that Clary could expect anything of him, and no chance that he would fail her, see the pain in her eyes when she realized all over again that *her* Simon was gone. Letter by letter, Simon's memories of Clary were beginning to knit themselves together.

Isabelle was different. It felt like his memories of Isabelle were buried inside a black hole—something dangerous and ravenous, threatening to consume him if he got too close.

Simon had come to the Academy, in part, to escape his painful and confusing double vision of the past, the cognitive dissonance between the life he remembered and the one he'd actually lived. It was like that cheesy old joke his father had loved. "Doctor, my arm hurts when I move like this," Simon would say, setting him up. His father would answer in an atrocious German accent, his version of "doctor voice": "Then . . . *don't move like that.*"

As long as Simon didn't think about the past, the past couldn't hurt him. But, increasingly, he couldn't help himself. There was too much pleasure in the pain.

✳ ✳ ✳

Classes may have been over for the year, but the Academy faculty was still finding new ways to torture them.

"What do you think it is this time?" Julie Beauvale asked as they settled onto the uncomfortable wooden benches in the main hall. The entire student body, Shadowhunters and mundanes alike, had been summoned first thing Monday morning for an all-school meeting.

"Maybe they finally decided to kick out all the dregs," Jon Cartwright said. "Better late than never."

Simon was too tired and too uncaffeinated to think up a clever retort. So he simply said, "Suck it, Cartwright."

George snorted.

Over the last several months of classes, training, and demon-hunting disasters, their class had grown pretty close—especially the handful of students who were around Simon's age. George was George, of course; Beatriz Mendoza was surprisingly sweet for a Shadowhunter; and even Julie had turned out to be slightly less snotty than she pretended to be. Jon Cartwright, on the other hand . . . The moment they met, Simon had decided that if looks matched personalities, Jon Cartwright would look like a horse's ass. Unfortunately, there was no justice in the world, and he looked instead like a walking Ken doll. Sometimes first impressions were misleading; sometimes they peered straight through to a person's inner soul. Simon was as sure now as he'd ever been: Jon's inner soul was a horse's ass.

Jon gave Simon a patronizing pat on the shoulder. "I'm going to miss your witty repartee this summer, Lewis."

"I'm going to hope you get eaten by a spider demon this summer, Cartwright."

George slipped an arm around both of them, grinning maniacally and humming "Can You Feel the Love Tonight?"

George had, perhaps, embraced the spirit of celebration a little too enthusiastically of late.

Up at the front of the hall, Dean Penhallow cleared her throat loudly, looking pointedly in their direction. "If we could have some silence, please?"

The room continued chattering, Dean Penhallow continued clearing her throat and asking nervously for order, and things could have gone on like that all morning had Delaney Scarsbury, their training master, not climbed up on a chair. "We'll have silence, or we'll have one hundred push-ups," he boomed. The room hushed immediately.

"I suppose you've all been wondering how you would keep busy now that exams are past?" Dean Penhallow said, her voice rising at the end of her sentence. The dean had a way of turning almost everything into a question. "I think you'll all recognize this week's guest speaker?"

An intimidating barrel-chested man in gray robes strode onto the makeshift stage. The room gasped.

Simon gasped too, but it wasn't the appearance of the Inquisitor that had blown his mind. It was the girl trailing after him, glaring fiercely at his robes like she hoped to set them on fire with her mind. A girl with a curtain of silky black hair and bottomless brown eyes: the Inquisitor's daughter. Known to friends, family, and humiliatingly rejected ex-boyfriends as Isabelle Lightwood.

George elbowed him. "You seeing what I'm seeing?" he whispered. "You want a tissue?"

Simon couldn't help remembering the last time Izzy had

shown up at the Academy, for the express purpose of warning every girl in school away from him. He'd been horrified. Right about now, he couldn't imagine anything better.

But Isabelle didn't look inclined to say anything to the class. She simply sat beside her father, arms crossed, glowering.

"She's even prettier when she's angry," Jon whispered.

In a miraculous triumph of restraint, Simon didn't spear him in the eye with a pen.

"You've nearly completed your first year at the Academy," Robert Lightwood told the assembled students, somehow making it sound less like a congratulations than it did like a threat. "My daughter tells me that one of the mundanes' great heroes has a saying, 'With great power comes substantial responsibility.'"

Simon gaped. There was only one way Isabelle Lightwood, as far from a comics nerd as a person could get, would know a line—even a mangled one—from Spider-Man. She'd been quoting Simon.

That had to mean something . . . right?

He tried to catch her eye.

He failed.

"You've learned a lot about power this year," Robert Lightwood continued. "This week I'm going to talk to you about responsibility. And what happens when power runs unchecked, or is freely given to the wrong person. I'm going to talk to you about the Circle."

At those words, a hush fell across the room. The Academy faculty, like most Shadowhunters, were very careful to avoid the subject of the Circle—the group of rogue Shadowhunters that Valentine Morgenstern had led in the Uprising.

The students knew about Valentine—*everyone* knew about Valentine—but they learned quickly not to ask too many questions about him. Over the last year, Simon had come to understand that the Shadowhunters preferred to believe their choices were perfect, their laws infallible. They didn't like to think about the time they'd been nearly destroyed by a group of their own.

It explained, at least, why the dean was hosting this session, rather than their history teacher, Catarina Loss. The warlock seemed to tolerate most Shadowhunters—*barely*. Simon suspected that when it came to former members of the Circle, "barely" was too much to hope for.

Robert cleared his throat. "I'd like all of you to ask yourselves what you would have done, were you a student here in Valentine Morgenstern's day. Would you have joined the Circle? Would you have stood by Valentine's side at the Uprising? Raise your hand, if you think it's possible."

Simon was unsurprised to see not a single hand in the air. He'd played this game back in mundane school, every time his history class covered World War II. Simon knew no one ever thought they would be a Nazi.

Simon also knew that, statistically, most of them were wrong.

"Now I'd like you to raise your hand if you think you're an exemplary Shadowhunter, one who would do anything to serve the Clave," Robert said.

Unsurprisingly, many more hands shot up this time, Jon Cartwright's the highest.

Robert smiled mirthlessly. "It was the most eager and loyal of us who were first to join Valentine's ranks," he told them.

"It was those of us most dedicated to the Shadowhunter cause who found ourselves the easiest prey."

There was a rustling in the crowd.

"Yes," Robert said. "I say *us*, because I was among Valentine's disciples. I was in the Circle."

The rustling burst into a storm. Some of the students looked unsurprised, but many of them looked as if a nuclear bomb had just gone off inside their brains. Clary had told Simon that Robert Lightwood used to be a member of the Circle, but it was obviously hard for some people to reconcile that with the position of the Inquisitor, which this tall, fearsome man now held.

"The *Inquisitor*?" Julie breathed, eyes wide. "How could they let him . . . ?"

Beatriz looked stunned.

"My father always said there was something off about him," Jon murmured.

"This week, I will teach you about the misuses of power, about great evil and how it can take many forms. My able daughter, Isabelle Lightwood, will be assisting with some of the classwork." Here he gestured to Isabelle, who glanced briefly at the crowd, her impossibly fierce glare somehow growing even fiercer. "Most of all, I will teach you about the Circle, how it began and why. If you listen well, some of you might even learn something."

Simon wasn't listening at all. Simon was staring at Isabelle, willing her to look at him. Isabelle studiously stared at her feet. And Robert Lightwood, Inquisitor of the Clave, arbiter of all things lawful, began to tell the story of Valentine Morgenstern and those who had once loved him.

1984

Robert Lightwood stretched out on the quad, trying not to think about how he'd spent this week the year before. The days after exams and before the summer break were, traditionally, a bacchic release of pent-up energy, faculty looking the other way as students pushed the Academy rules to their limits. A year ago, he and Michael Wayland had snuck off campus and taken a boldly illicit midnight skinny-dip in Lake Lyn. Even with their lips firmly sealed shut, the water had taken its hallucinogenic effect, turning the sky electric. They had lain on their backs side by side, imagining falling stars carving neon tracks across the clouds and dreaming themselves into a stranger world.

That was a year ago, when Robert had still imagined himself young, free to waste his time with childish delights. Before he had understood that, young or not, he had responsibilities.

That was a year ago, before Valentine.

The members of the Circle had co-opted this quiet, shady corner of the quad, where they would be safe from prying eyes—and where they, in turn, would be spared the sight of their classmates having their pointless, meaningless fun. Robert reminded himself that he was lucky to be huddled here in the shade, listening to Valentine Morgenstern declaim.

It was a special privilege, he reminded himself, to be a member of Valentine's coterie, privy to his revolutionary ideas. A year ago, when Valentine had inexplicably befriended him, he'd felt nothing but intense gratitude and a desire to hang on Valentine's every word.

Valentine said the Clave was corrupt and lazy, that these

days it cared more about maintaining the status quo and fascistically suppressing dissent than it did carrying out its noble mission.

Valentine said the Shadowhunters should stop cowering in the darkness and walk proudly through the mundane world they lived and died to protect.

Valentine said the Accords were useless and the Mortal Cup was built to be used and the new generation was the hope of the future and the Academy classes were a waste of time.

Valentine made Robert's brain buzz and his heart sing; he made Robert feel like a warrior for justice. Like he was a *part* of something, something extraordinary—like he and the others had been chosen, not just by Valentine, but by the hand of destiny, to change the world.

And yet, very occasionally, Valentine also made Robert feel uneasy.

Valentine wanted the Circle's unquestioning loyalty. He wanted their belief in him, their conviction in the cause, to suffuse their souls. And Robert wanted desperately to give that to him. He didn't want to question Valentine's logic or intent; he didn't want to worry that he believed too little in the things that Valentine said. Or that he believed too much. Today, showered in sunlight, the infinite possibility of summer opening up before him, he didn't want to worry at all. So, as Valentine's words washed over him, Robert let his focus drift, just for a moment. Better to tune out than to doubt. Just for now, his friends could do his listening for him, fill him in later. Wasn't that what friends were for?

There were eight of them today, the Circle's innermost circle, all sitting in hushed silence as Valentine ranted about the

Clave's kindness to Downworlders: Jocelyn Fairchild, Maryse Trueblood, Lucian and Amatis Graymark, Hodge Starkweather, and, of course, Michael, Robert, and Stephen. Though Stephen Herondale was the most recent addition to the crowd—and the most recent addition to the Academy, arriving from the London Institute at the beginning of the year—he was also the most devoted to the cause, and to Valentine. He'd arrived at the Academy dressed like a mundane: studded leather jacket, tight acid-washed jeans, blond hair gelled into preposterous spikes like the mundane rock stars who postered his dorm room walls. Only a month later, Stephen had adopted not only Valentine's simple, all-black aesthetic but also his mannerisms, so that the only major difference between them was Valentine's shock of white-blond hair and Stephen's blue eyes. By first frost, he'd sworn off all things mundane and destroyed his beloved Sex Pistols poster in a sacrificial bonfire.

"Herondales do nothing halfway," Stephen said whenever Robert teased him about it, but Robert suspected that something lay beneath the lighthearted tone. Something darker—something hungry. Valentine, he had noticed, had a knack for picking out disciples, homing in on those students with some kind of lack, some inner emptiness that Valentine could fill. Unlike the rest of their gang of misfits, Stephen was ostensibly whole: a handsome, graceful, supremely skilled Shadowhunter with a distinguished pedigree and the respect of everyone on campus. It made Robert wonder . . . what was it that only Valentine could see?

His thoughts had wandered so far astray that when Maryse gasped and said, in a hushed voice, "Won't that be dangerous?" he wasn't sure what she was talking about. Nonetheless, he squeezed her hand reassuringly, as this was what boyfriends were meant to do. Maryse was lying with her head in his lap, her silky black hair splayed across his jeans. He smoothed it away from her face, a boyfriend's prerogative.

It had been nearly a year, but Robert still found it difficult to believe that this girl—this fierce, graceful, bold girl with a mind like a razor blade—had chosen *him* as her own. She glided through the Academy like a queen, granting favor, indulging her fawning subjects. Maryse wasn't the most beautiful girl in their class, and certainly not the sweetest or the most charming. She didn't care for things like sweetness or charm. But when it came to the battlefield, no one was more ready to charge the enemy, and certainly no one was better with a whip. Maryse was more than a girl, she was a *force*. The other girls worshipped her; the guys *wanted* her—but only Robert had her.

It had changed everything.

Sometimes, Robert felt like his entire life was an act. That it was only a matter of time before his fellow students saw through him, and realized what he really was, beneath all that brawn and bluster: Cowardly. Weak. Worthless. Having Maryse by his side was like wearing a suit of armor. No one like *her* would choose someone worthless. Everyone knew that. Sometimes, Robert even believed it himself.

He loved the way she made him feel when they were in public: strong and safe. And he loved even more the way she made him feel when they were alone together, when she pressed her lips to the nape of his neck and traced her tongue down the arc of his spine. He loved the curve of her hip and the whisper of her hair; he loved the gleam in her eye when she strode into combat. He loved the taste of her. So why was it that whenever she said, "I love you," he felt like such a liar for saying it back? Why was it that he occasionally—maybe more than occasionally—found his thoughts straying to other girls, to how *they* might taste?

How could he love the way Maryse made him feel . . . and still be so uncertain that what he felt was love?

He'd taken to surreptitiously watching the other couples around him, trying to figure out whether they felt the same way, whether their declarations of love masked the same confusion and doubt. But the way Amatis's head nestled comfortably against Stephen's shoulder, the way Jocelyn carelessly threaded her fingers through Valentine's, even the way Maryse idly played with his jeans' fraying seams, as if his clothing, his body, were her property . . . all of them seemed so certain of themselves. Robert was certain only of how good he'd gotten at faking it.

"We should glory in the danger, if it means a chance to take down a filthy, rogue Downworlder," Valentine said, glowering. "Even if this wolf pack doesn't have a lead on the monster that—" He swallowed, hard, and Robert knew what he was thinking, because it seemed like these days, it was all Valentine was ever thinking, the fury of it radiating off him as if the thought were written in fire, *the monster that killed my father.* "Even if it doesn't, we'll be doing the Clave a favor."

Ragnor Fell, the green-skinned warlock who'd taught at the Academy for nearly a century, paused halfway across the quad and peered over at them, almost as if he could hear their discussion. Robert assured himself that was impossible. Still, he didn't like the way the warlock's horns angled toward them, as if marking his target.

Michael cleared his throat. "Maybe we shouldn't talk like that about, uh, Downworlders out here."

Valentine snorted. "I hope the old goat does hear me. It's a disgrace, them letting him teach here. The only place a Downworlder has at the Academy is on the dissection table."

Michael and Robert exchanged a glance. As always, Robert knew exactly what his *parabatai* was thinking—and Robert was thinking the same. Valentine, when they first met him, had cut a dashing figure with his blinding white hair and blazing black eyes. His features were smooth and sharp at once, like sculpted ice, but beneath the intimidating veneer was a surprisingly kind boy roused to anger only by injustice. Valentine had always been intense, yes, but it was an intensity bent toward doing what he believed was right, what was *good*. When Valentine said he wanted to correct the injustices and inequities imposed on them by the Clave, Robert believed him, and still did. And while Michael may have had a bizarre soft spot for Downworlders, Robert didn't like them any more than Valentine did; he couldn't imagine why, in this day and age, the Clave was still allowing warlocks to meddle in Shadowhunter affairs.

But there was a difference between clear-eyed intensity and irrational anger. Robert had been waiting a long time now for Valentine's grief-fueled rage to simmer down. Instead, it had sparked an inferno.

"So you won't tell us where you got your intel from," Lucian said, the only one other than Jocelyn who could question Valentine with impunity, "but you want us to sneak off campus and hunt down these werewolves ourselves? If you're so sure the Clave would want them taken care of, why not leave it to them?"

"The Clave is useless," Valentine hissed. "You know that

better than anyone, Lucian. But if none of you are willing to risk yourselves for this—if you'd rather stay here and go to a *party* . . ." His mouth curled as if even speaking the word repelled him. "I'll go myself."

Hodge pushed his glasses up on his nose and leaped to his feet. "I'll go with you, Valentine," he said, too loud. It was Hodge's way—always a little too loud or too quiet, always misreading the room. There was a reason he preferred books to people. "I'm always at your side."

"Sit down," Valentine snapped. "I don't need *you* getting in the way."

"But—"

"What good does your loyalty do me when it comes with a big mouth and two left feet?"

Hodge paled and dropped back to the ground, eyes blinking furiously behind thick lenses.

Jocelyn pressed a hand to Valentine's shoulder—ever so gently, and only for a moment, but it was enough.

"I only mean, Hodge, that your particular skills are wasted on the battlefield," Valentine said, more kindly. The shift in tone was abrupt, but sincere. When Valentine favored you with his warmest smile, he was impossible to resist. "And I couldn't forgive myself if you were injured. I can't . . . I can't lose anyone else."

They were all silent then, for a moment, thinking of how quickly it had happened, the dean pulling Valentine off the training field to deliver the news, the way he'd taken it, silent and steady, like a Shadowhunter should. The way he'd looked when he returned to campus after the funeral, his hollow eyes, his sallow skin, his face aging years in a week. Their parents were all warriors, and they knew: What Valentine had lost, any of them could lose. To be a Shadowhunter was to live in the shadow of death.

They couldn't bring his father back, but if they could help him avenge the loss, surely they owed him that much.

Robert, at least, owed him everything.

"Of course we'll come with you," Robert said firmly. "Whatever you need."

"Agreed," Michael said. Where Robert went, he would always follow.

Valentine nodded. "Stephen? Lucian?"

Robert caught Amatis rolling her eyes. Valentine never treated the women with anything less than respect, but when it came to battle, he preferred to fight with men by his side.

Stephen nodded. Lucian, who was Valentine's *parabatai* and the one he relied on most, shifted uncomfortably. "I promised Céline I would tutor her tonight," he admitted. "I could cancel it, of course, but—"

Valentine waved him off, laughing, and the others followed suit.

"Tutoring? Is that what they're calling it these days?" Stephen teased. "Seems like she's already aced her O levels in wrapping you around her little finger."

Lucian blushed. "Nothing's happening there, trust me," he said, and it was presumably the truth. Céline, younger than the rest of the Circle, with the fragile, delicately pretty features of a porcelain doll, had been trailing their group like a lost puppy. It was obvious to anyone with eyes that she'd fallen hard for Stephen, but he was a lost cause, pledged to Amatis for life. She'd picked Lucian as her consolation prize, but it was just as obvious that Lucian had no romantic interest in anyone but Jocelyn Fairchild. Obvious, that is, to everyone except Jocelyn.

"We don't need you for this one," Valentine told Lucian. "Stay and *enjoy* yourself."

"I should be with you," Lucian said, the merriment faded from his voice. He sounded pained at the thought of Valentine venturing into dangerous territory without him, and Robert understood. *Parabatai* didn't always fight side by side—but knowing your *parabatai* was in danger, without you there to support and protect him? It caused an almost physical pain. And Lucian and Valentine's *parabatai* bond was even more intense than most. Robert could almost feel the current of power flowing between them, the strength and love they passed back and forth with every glance. "Where you go, I go."

"It's already decided, my friend," Valentine said, and that simply, it was. Lucian would stay on campus with the others. Valentine, Stephen, Michael, and Robert would slip away from campus after dark and venture into Brocelind Forest in pursuit of a werewolf encampment that, supposedly, could lead them to Valentine's father's killer. They'd make up the rest as they went along.

As the others hurried off to the dining hall for lunch, Maryse grabbed Robert's hand and pulled him close.

"You'll be careful out there, yes?" she said sternly. Maryse said everything sternly—it was one of the things he liked best about her.

She pressed her lithe body against his, kissed his neck, and he felt, in that moment, a passing sense of supreme confidence, that this was where he belonged . . . at least, until she whispered, "Come home to me in one piece."

Come home to me. As if he belonged to her. As if, in her mind, they were already married, with a house and children and a lifetime of togetherness, as if the future was already decided.

It was the appeal of Maryse, as it was the appeal of Valentine, the ease with which they could be so sure of what should be, and what was to come. Robert continued hoping that one day it would rub off on him. In the meantime, the less certain he was, the more certain he acted—there was no need for anyone to know the truth.

Robert Lightwood wasn't much of a teacher. He gave them a neatly sanitized account of the early days of the Circle, laying out Valentine's revolutionary principles as if they were a list of ingredients for baking a particularly bland cake. Simon, fruitlessly devoting most of his energy to telepathic communication with Isabelle, was barely listening. He found himself cursing the fact that Shadowhunters were so haughty about the whole we-don't-do-magic thing. If he were a warlock, he'd probably be able to command Isabelle's attention with the flick of a finger. Or, if he were still a vampire, he could have used his vampy powers to enthrall her—but that was something Simon preferred not to think about, because it raised some unsettling questions about how he'd managed to enthrall her in the first place.

What he did hear of Robert's tale didn't much interest him. Simon had never liked history much, at least as it was relayed to him in school. It sounded too much like a brochure, everything neatly laid out and painfully obvious in retrospect. Every war had its bullet-pointed causes; every megalomaniac dictator was so cartoonishly evil you wondered how stupid the people of the past had to be, not to notice. Simon didn't remember much of his own history-making experiences, but he remembered enough to know it wasn't so clear when it was happening. History, the way teachers liked it, was a racetrack, a straight shot from start to finish line; life itself was more of a maze.

Maybe the telepathy worked after all. Because when the speech ended and the students were given permission to disperse, Isabelle hopped off the stage and strolled right up to Simon. She gave him a sharp nod hello.

"Isabelle, I, uh, maybe we could—"

She flashed him a brilliant smile that, for just a moment, made him think all his worrying had been for nothing. Then she said, "Aren't you going to introduce me to your friends? Especially the handsome ones?"

Simon turned to see half the class crowding in behind him, eager for a brush with the famous Isabelle Lightwood. At the front of the pack were George and Jon, the latter practically drooling.

Jon elbowed past Simon and thrust out a hand. "Jon Cartwright, at your service," he said in a voice that oozed charm like a blister oozed pus.

Isabelle took his hand—and instead of jujitsuing him to the ground with a humiliating thump or slicing his hand off at the wrist with her electrum whip, she let him turn her hand over and bring it to his lips. Then she *curtsied*. She *winked*. Worst of all, she *giggled*.

Simon thought he might puke.

Unendurable minutes of torment passed: George blushing and making goofy attempts at jokes, Julie struck speechless,

Marisol pretending to be above it all, Beatriz engaging in wan but polite small talk about mutual acquaintances, Sunil bouncing in the back of the crowd, trying to make himself seen, and through it all, Jon smirking and Isabelle beaming and batting her eyes in a display that could only be meant to make Simon's stomach churn.

At least, he desperately hoped it was meant for that. Because the other option—the possibility that Isabelle was smiling at Jon simply because she wanted to, and that she accepted his invitation to squeeze his rock-hard biceps because she wanted to feel his muscles contract beneath her delicate grip—was unthinkable.

"So what do you people do around here for fun?" she asked finally, then narrowed her eyes flirtatiously at Jon. "And don't say 'me.'"

Am I already dead? Simon thought hopelessly. *Is this hell?*

"Neither the circumstances nor the population here have proven themselves conducive to fun," Jon said pompously, as if the bluster in his voice could disguise the fire in his cheeks.

"That all changes tonight," Isabelle said, then turned on her spiky heel and strode away.

George shook his head, letting out an appreciative whistle. "Simon, your girlfriend—"

"*Ex*-girlfriend," Jon put in.

"She's magnificent," Julie breathed, and from the looks on the others' faces, she was speaking for the group.

Simon rolled his eyes and hurried after Isabelle—reaching out to grab her shoulder, then thinking better of it at the last moment. Grabbing Isabelle Lightwood from behind was probably an invitation to amputation.

"Isabelle," he said sharply. She sped up. So did he, wondering where she was headed. "Isabelle," he said again. They burrowed deeper into the school, the air thick with damp and mold, the stone floor increasingly slick beneath their feet. They hit a fork, corridors branching off to the left and right, and she paused before choosing the one on the left.

"We don't go down this one, generally," Simon said.

Nothing.

"Mostly because of the elephant-size slug that lives at the end of it." This was not an exaggeration. Rumor had it that some disgruntled faculty member—a warlock who'd been fired when the tide turned against Downworlders—had left it behind as a parting gift.

Isabelle kept walking, slower now, picking her way carefully over seeping puddles of slime. Something skittered loudly overhead. She didn't flinch—but she did look up, and Simon caught her fingers playing across the coiled whip.

"Also because of the rats," he added. He and George had gone on an expedition down this corridor in search of the supposed slug . . . they gave up after the third rat dropped from the ceiling and somehow found its way down George's pants.

Isabelle breathed a heavy sigh.

"Come on, Izzy, hold up."

Somehow, he'd stumbled on the magic words. She spun around to face him. "Don't call me that," she hissed.

"What?"

"My friends call me Izzy," she said. "You lost that right."

"Izzy—Isabelle, I mean. If you'd read my letter—"

"No. You don't call me Izzy, you don't send me letters, you don't follow me into dark corridors and try to save me from rats."

"Trust me, we see a rat, it's every man for himself."

Isabelle looked like she wanted to feed him to the giant slug. "My point, Simon Lewis, is that you and I are strangers now, just like you wanted it."

"If that's true, then what are you doing here?"

Isabelle looked incredulous. "It's one thing for Jace to believe the world revolves around him, but come on. I know you love fantasy, Simon, but the suspension of disbelief can only go so far."

"This is my school, Isabelle," Simon said. "And you're my—"

She just stared at him, as if defying him to come up with a noun that would justify the possessive.

This wasn't going the way he'd planned.

"Okay, then, why are you here? And why are you being so nice to all my, uh, friends?"

"Because my father's *forcing* me to be here," she said. "Because I guess he thinks some delightful father-daughter bonding time in a slime-covered pit will make me forget that he's a deadbeat adulterer who ditched his family. And I'm being nice to your friends because I'm a nice person."

Now it was Simon who looked incredulous.

"Okay, I'm not," she admitted. "But I've never actually been to school, you know. I figured if I have to be here, I might as well make the best of it. See what I'm missing. Is that enough information for you?"

"I get that you're mad at me, but—"

She shook her head. "You *don't* get it. I'm not mad at you. I'm not anything at you, Simon. You asked me to accept that you were a different person now, someone who I don't know. So I've accepted that. I loved someone—he's gone now. You're nobody I know, and, as far as I can tell, nobody I need to know. I'll only be here a few days, and then we never need to see each other again. How about we don't make it harder than it has to be?"

He couldn't quite catch his breath.

I loved someone, she'd said, and it was the closest she—or any girl—had ever come to saying *I love you* to Simon.

Except that it wasn't close at all, was it?

It was a world away.

"Okay." It was the only word he could force out, but she was already walking on down the corridor. She didn't need his permission to be a stranger; she didn't need anything from him. "You're going the wrong way!" he called after her. He didn't know where she wanted to go, but there seemed little chance she wanted to go slug-ward.

"They're all wrong," she called back, without turning around.

He tried to sense some subtext in her words, a glimmer of pain. Something that would give the lie to her claim, betray the feelings she still harbored for him—prove this was as hard and confusing for her as it was for him.

But the suspension of disbelief could only go so far.

Isabelle had said she wanted to make the best of her time at the Academy, and she'd proposed they not make it any harder than it needed to be. Unfortunately, Simon soon discovered, these two things were mutually exclusive. Because Isabelle's version of making the best of things involved Isabelle stretched out like a cat on one of the student lounge's musty leather couches, surrounded by sycophants, Isabelle partaking in George's illicit supply of scotch and inviting the others to do so as well, so that soon all of Simon's friends and enemies were drunk and giddy and in much too good a mood for his liking. Making the best of things apparently meant encouraging Julie to flirt with George and teaching Marisol how to smash statuary with a whip and, worst of all, agreeing to "maybe" be Jon Cartwright's date for the end-of-year party later in the week.

Simon wasn't sure whether any of this was harder than it needed to be—who knew what qualified as *needed to be?*—but it was excruciating.

"So, when does the real fun start?" Isabelle finally said.

Jon waggled his eyebrows. "Just say the word."

Isabelle laughed and touched his shoulder.

Simon wondered whether the Academy would expel him for murdering Jon Cartwright in his sleep.

"Not that kind of fun. I mean, when do we sneak off campus? Go party in Alicante? Go swimming in Lake Lyn? Go . . ." She trailed off, finally noticing that the others were gaping at her like she was speaking in tongues. "Are you telling me you don't do *any* of that?"

"We're not here to have fun," Beatriz said, somewhat stiffly. "We're here to learn to be Shadowhunters. There are rules for a reason."

Isabelle rolled her eyes. "Haven't you ever heard that rules are meant to be broken? Students are *supposed* to get into a little trouble at the Academy—at least the best students are. Why do you think the rules are so strict? So that only the best can get around them. Think of it like extra credit."

"How would you know?" Beatriz asked. Simon was surprised by her tone. Usually, she was the quietest among them, always willing to go with the flow. But there was an edge in her voice now, something that reminded him that, gentle as she seemed, she was a born warrior. "It's not like you went here."

"I come from a long line of Academy graduates," Isabelle said. "I know what I need to know."

"We're not all interested in following in your *father's* footsteps," Beatriz said, then stood up and walked out of the room.

There was silence in her wake, everyone tensely waiting for Isabelle to react.

Her smile didn't waver, but Simon could feel the heat radiating from her and understood it was taking a great deal of energy for her not to explode—or collapse. He didn't know which it would be; he didn't know how she felt about her father once being one of Valentine's men. He didn't know anything about her, not really. He admitted that.

But he still wanted to scoop her into his arms and hold her until the storm passed.

"No one has ever accused my father of being fun," Isabelle said flatly. "But I assume *my* reputation precedes me. If you meet me here at midnight tomorrow, I'll show you what you've been missing." She took Jon's hand in her own and allowed him to pull her off the couch. "Now. Will you show me to my room? This place is simply impossible to navigate."

"My pleasure," Jon said, winking at Simon.

Then they were gone.

Together.

The next morning the hall echoed with yawning and the groan of hangovers in (fruitless) search of grease and coffee. As Robert Lightwood launched into his second lecture, some tedious disquisition on the nature of evil and a point-by-point analysis of Valentine's critique of the Accords, Simon had to keep pinching himself awake. Robert Lightwood was possibly the only person on the planet who could make the story of the Circle drop-dead boring. It didn't help that Simon had stayed up till dawn, tossing and turning on the lumpy mattress, trying to drive nightmare images of Isabelle and Jon out of his head.

There was something going on with her, Simon was sure of it. Maybe it wasn't about him—maybe it was about her father or some residual homeschooling issues or just some girl thing he couldn't fathom, but she wasn't acting like herself.

She's not your girlfriend, he kept reminding himself. Even if something was wrong, it was no longer his job to fix it. *She can do what she wants.*

And if what she wanted was Jon Cartwright, then obviously she wasn't worth losing a night of sleep over in the first place.

By sunrise he'd almost managed to convince himself of this. But there she was again, up onstage beside her father, her fierce and fiercely intelligent gaze evoking all those annoying *feelings* again.

They weren't memories, exactly. Simon couldn't have named a single movie they watched together; he didn't know any of Isabelle's favorite foods or inside jokes; he didn't know what it felt like to kiss her or twine his fingers with hers. What he felt whenever he looked at her was deeper than that, dwelling in some nether region of his mind. He felt like he *knew* her, inside and out. He felt like he had Superman vision and could x-ray her soul. He felt sorrow and loss and joy and confusion; he felt a cavemanlike urge to slaughter a wild boar and lay it at her feet; he felt the need to do something extraordinary and the belief that, in her presence, he could.

He felt something he'd never felt before—but he had a sinking sensation that he recognized it anyway.

He was pretty sure he felt like he was in love.

1984

Valentine made it easy for them. He'd induced permission from the dean for an "educational" camping trip in Brocelind Forest—two days and nights free to do as they pleased, as long as it resulted in a few scribbled pages on the curative powers of wild herbs.

By all rights, with his uncomfortable questions and rebellious theories, Valentine should have been the black sheep of Shadowhunter Academy. Ragnor Fell certainly treated him like a slimy creature who'd crawled out from under a rock and should be hastily returned there. But the rest of the faculty seemed blinded by Valentine's personal magnetism, unable or unwilling to see through to the disrespect that lay beneath. He was endlessly dodging deadlines and ducking out of classes, excusing himself with nothing more than the flash of a smile. Another student might have been grateful for the latitude, but it only made Valentine loathe his teachers more—every loophole the faculty opened for him was only more evidence of weakness.

He had no qualms about enjoying its consequences.

The werewolf pack, according to Valentine's intel, was holed up in the old Silverhood manor, a decrepit ruin at the heart of the forest. The last Silverhood had died in battle two generations before, and was used as a name to spook young Shadowhunter children. The death of a soldier was one thing: regrettable, but the natural order of things. The death of a line was a tragedy.

Maybe they were all secretly apprehensive about it, this illicit mission that seemed to cross an invisible line. Never before had they struck against Downworlders without the express permission and oversight of their elders; they had broken rules, but never before had they strayed so close to breaking the Law.

Maybe they just wanted to spend a few more hours like normal teenagers, before they went so far they couldn't turn back.

For whatever reason, the four of them made their way through the woods with a deliberate lack of speed, setting up camp for the night a half mile from the Silverhood estate. They would, Valentine decided, spend the next day staking out the werewolf encampment, gauging its strengths and weaknesses, charting the rhythms of the pack, and attack at nightfall, once the pack had dispersed to hunt. But that was tomorrow's problem. That night, they sat around a campfire, roasted sausages over leaping flames, reminisced about their pasts, and rhapsodized about their futures, which still seemed impossibly far away.

"I'll marry Jocelyn, of course," Valentine said, "and we'll raise our children in the new era. They'll never be warped by the corrupt laws of a weak, sniveling Clave."

"Sure, because by that time, we'll run the world," Stephen said lightly. Valentine's grim smile made it seem less like a joke than a promise.

"Can't you just see it?" Michael said. "Daddy Valentine, knee deep in diapers. A busload of kids."

"However many Jocelyn wants." Valentine's expression softened, as it always did when he said her name. They'd only been together a couple of months—since his father died—but no one questioned that they were together for good. The way he looked at her . . . like she was a different species than the rest of them, a *higher* species. "Can't you see it?" Valentine had confided once, early on, when Robert asked him how he could be so sure of love, so soon. "There's more of the Angel in her than in the rest of us. There's greatness in her. She shines like Raziel himself."

"You just want to flood the gene pool," Michael said. "I imagine you think the world would be better off if every Shadowhunter had a little Morgenstern in them."

Valentine grinned. "I'm told false modesty doesn't suit me, so . . . no comment."

"While we're on the subject," Stephen said, a blush rising in his cheeks. "I've asked Amatis. And she said yes."

"Asked what?" Robert said.

Michael and Valentine only laughed, as Stephen's cheeks took fire. "To marry me," he admitted. "What do you think?"

The question was ostensibly directed to all of them, but his gaze was fixed on Valentine, who hesitated an impossibly long time before answering.

"Amatis?" he said finally, furrowing his brow as if he'd have to give the matter some serious thought.

Stephen caught his breath, and in that moment, Robert almost thought it was possible that he needed Valentine's approval—that despite proposing to Amatis, despite loving her so deeply and desperately that he nearly vibrated with emotion whenever she came near, despite writing her that abominable love song Robert had once found crumpled under his bed, Stephen would cast her aside if Valentine commanded it.

In that moment, Robert almost thought it was possible that Valentine *would command* it, just to see what happened.

Then Valentine's face relaxed into a wide smile, and he threw an arm around Stephen, saying, "It's about time. I don't know what you were waiting for, you idiot. When you're lucky enough to have a Graymark by your side, you do whatever you can to make sure it's forever. I should know."

Then everyone was laughing and toasting and plotting bachelor party schemes and teasing Stephen about his short-lived attempts at songwriting, and it was Robert who felt like the idiot, imagining even for a second that Stephen's love for Amatis could waver, or that Valentine had anything but their best interests at heart.

These were his friends, the best he would ever have, or anyone could ever have.

These were his comrades in arms, and nights like these, bursts of joy beneath starry skies, were their reward for the special obligation they'd taken upon themselves.

To imagine otherwise was only a symptom of Robert's secret weakness, his inveterate lack of conviction, and he resolved not to let himself do so again.

"And you, old man?" Valentine asked Robert. "As if I even have to ask. We all know Maryse does what she wants."

"And inexplicably, she seems to want you," Stephen added.

Michael, who had fallen unusually silent, caught Robert's eye. Only Michael knew how little Robert liked to think about the future, especially this part of it. How much he dreaded being forced into marriage, parenting, responsibility. If it were up to Robert, he would stay at the Academy forever. It made little sense. Because of what had happened when he was a kid, he was a couple of years older than his friends—he should have been chafing at the restrictions of youth. But maybe—because of what had happened—part of him would always feel cheated and want that time back. He'd spent so long wanting the life he had now. He wasn't ready to let go of it quite yet.

"Well, this old man is exhausted," Robert said, dodging the question. "I think my tent is calling."

As they extinguished the fire and tidied up the site, Michael shot him a grateful smile, having been spared his own interrogation. The only one of them still single, Michael disliked this line of conversation even more than Robert did. It was one of the many things they had in common: They both enjoyed each other's company more than that of any girl. Marriage seemed like such a misguided concept, Robert sometimes thought. How could he care for any wife more than he did for his *parabatai*, the other half of his soul? Why should he possibly be expected to?

He couldn't sleep.

When he emerged from the tent into the silent predawn, Michael was sitting by the ashes of the campfire. He turned toward Robert without surprise, almost as if he'd been waiting for his *parabatai* to join him. Maybe he had. Robert didn't know whether it was an effect of the bonding ritual or simply the definition of a best friend, but he and Michael lived and breathed in similar rhythms. Before they were roommates, they'd often run into each other in the Academy corridors, sleeplessly roaming the night.

"Walk?" Michael suggested.

Robert nodded.

They traipsed wordlessly through the woods, letting the sounds of the sleeping forest wash over them. Screeches of night birds, skitters of insects, the hush of wind through fluttering leaves, the soft crunch of grass and twigs beneath their feet. There were dangers lurking here, they both knew that well enough. Many of the Academy's training missions took place in Brocelind Forest, its dense trees a useful refuge for werewolves, vampires, and even the occasional demons, though most of those were unleashed by the Academy itself, an ultimate test for particularly promising students. This night the forest felt safe. Or maybe it was simply that Robert felt invincible.

As they walked, he thought not of the mission to come but of Michael, who had been his first true friend.

He'd had friends when he was young, he supposed. The kids growing up in Alicante all knew each other, and he had vague memories of exploring the Glass City with small bands of children, their faces interchangeable, their loyalties nonexistent. As he discovered for himself the year he turned twelve and got his first Mark.

This was, for most Shadowhunter children, a proud day, one they looked forward to and fantasized about the way mundane children inexplicably fixated on birthdays. In some families, the first rune was applied in a quick, businesslike fashion, the child Marked and sent on his way; in others, there was great festivity, presents, balloons, a celebratory feast.

And, of course, in a very small number of families, the first rune was the last rune, the touch of the stele burning the child's skin, sending him into shock or madness, a fever so intense that only cutting through the Mark would save the life. Those children would never be Shadowhunters; those families would never be the same.

No one ever thought it would happen to them.

At twelve Robert had been scrawny but sure-footed, quick for his age, strong for his size, sure of the Shadowhunting glory that awaited him. As his extended family looked on, his father carefully traced the Voyance rune across Robert's hand.

The stele's tip carved its graceful lines across his pale skin. The completed Mark blazed bright, so bright Robert shut his eyes from the glare of it.

That was the last thing he remembered.

The last he remembered clearly, at least.

After that there was everything he'd tried so hard to forget.

There was pain.

There was the pain that seared through him like a lightning strike and the pain that ebbed and flowed like a tide. There was the pain in his body, lines of agony radiating from the Mark, burrowing from his flesh to his organs to his bones—and then, so much worse, there was the pain in his mind, or maybe it was his soul, an ineffable sensation of *hurt*, as if some creature had burrowed into the depths of his brain and gotten hungrier with the firing of every neuron and synapse. It hurt to think, it hurt to feel, it hurt to remember—but it felt necessary to do these things, because, even in the heart of this agony, some dim part of Robert stayed alert enough to know that if he didn't hang on, didn't feel the hurt, he would slip away forever.

Later he would use all these words and more to try to describe the pain, but none of them captured the experience. What had happened, what he had felt, that was beyond words.

There were other torments to endure, through that eternity he lay in bed, insensible to all around him, imprisoned by his Mark. There were visions. He saw demons, taunting and torturing him, and worse, he saw the faces of those he loved, telling him he was unworthy, telling him he was better off dead. He saw charred, barren plains and a wall of fire, the hell dimension awaiting him if he let his mind slip away, and so, through it all, somehow, he held on.

He lost all sense of himself and the world around him, lost his words and his name—but he held on. Until finally, one month later, the pain abated. The visions faded. Robert awoke.

He learned—once he'd recovered himself enough to understand and care—that he'd been semiconscious for several weeks while a battle had been raging around him, members of the Clave warring with his parents over his treatment as two Silent Brothers did their best to keep him alive. They had all wanted to strip him of the Mark, his parents told him, the Silent Brothers warning daily that this was the only way to ensure his survival and spare him further pain. Let him live out his life as a mundane: This was the conventional treatment for Shadowhunters who couldn't bear Marks.

"We couldn't let them do that to you," his mother told him.

"You're a Lightwood. You were born to this life," his father told him. "This life and no other."

What they didn't say, and didn't need to: *We would rather see you dead than mundane.*

Things were different between them, after that. Robert was grateful to his parents for believing in him—he too would rather be dead. But it changed something, knowing his parents' love for him had a limit. And something must have changed for them, too, discovering that a part of their son couldn't handle the Shadowhunter life, being forced to bear that shame.

Now Robert could no longer remember what his family had been like before the Mark. He remembered only the years since, the coldness that lived between them. They acted their parts: loving father, doting mother, dutiful son. But it was in their presence that Robert felt most alone.

He was, in those months spent recovering, frequently alone. The kids he'd thought of as his friends wanted nothing to do with him. When forced into his presence, they shied away, as if he were contagious.

There was nothing wrong with him, the Silent Brothers said. Having survived the ordeal with the Mark intact, there was no risk of future danger. His body had teetered on the edge of rejection, but his will had turned the tide. When the Silent Brothers examined him for the last time, one of them spoke somberly inside his head, with a message for Robert alone.

You will be tempted to think this ordeal marks you as weak. Instead, remember it as proof of your strength.

But Robert was twelve years old. His former friends were tracing themselves with runes, shipping off to the Academy, doing everything normal Shadowhunters were supposed to do—while Robert hid away in his bedroom, abandoned by his friends, cold-shouldered by his family, and afraid of his own stele. In the face of so much evidence for weakness, even a Silent Brother couldn't make him feel strong.

In this way, nearly a year passed, and Robert began to imagine this would be the shape of the rest of his life. He would be a Shadowhunter in name only; a Shadowhunter afraid of the Marks. Sometimes, in the dark of night, he wished his will hadn't been so strong, that he'd let himself be lost. It would have to be better than the life he'd returned to.

Then he met Michael Wayland, and everything changed.

They hadn't known each other very well, before. Michael was a strange kid, allowed to tag along with the others, but never quite accepted. He was prone to distraction and strange flights of fancy, pausing in the middle of a sparring session to consider where Sensors had come from, and who had thought to invent them.

Michael had shown up at the Lightwoods' manor one day asking if Robert might like to go for a horseback ride. They'd spent several hours galloping through the countryside, and once it was over, Michael said, "See you tomorrow," as if it were a foregone conclusion. He kept coming back. "Because you're interesting," Michael said, when Robert finally asked him why.

That was another thing about Michael. He always said exactly what was in his head, no matter how tactless or peculiar.

"My mother made me promise not to ask about what happened to you," he added.

"Why?"

"Because it would be rude. What do you think? Would it be rude?"

Robert shrugged. No one ever asked him about it or referred to it, not even his parents. It had never occurred to him to wonder why, or whether this was preferable. It was simply the way things were.

"I don't mind being rude," Michael said. "Will you tell me? What it was like?"

Strange, that it could be that simple. Strange, that Robert could be burning to tell someone without even realizing it.

That all he needed was someone to ask. The floodgates opened. Robert talked and talked, and when he trailed off, afraid he was going too far, Michael would jump in with another question.

"Why do you think it happened to *you?*" Michael asked. "Do you think it was genetic? Or, like, some part of you just isn't meant to be a Shadowhunter?"

It was, of course, Robert's greatest, most secret fear—but to hear it tossed off so casually like this defused it of all its power.

"Maybe?" Robert said, and instead of shunning him, Michael's eyes lit up with a scientist's curiosity.

He grinned. "We should find out."

They made it their mission: They probed libraries, pored over ancient texts, asked questions that no adult wanted to hear. There was very little written record of Shadowhunters who'd experienced what Robert had—this kind of thing was meant to be a shameful family secret, never spoken of again. Not that Michael cared how many feathers he ruffled or which traditions he overturned. He wasn't particularly brave, but he seemed to have no fear.

Their mission failed. There was no rational explanation for why Robert had reacted so strongly to the Mark, but by the end of that year, it didn't matter. Michael had turned a nightmare into a puzzle—and had turned himself into Robert's best friend.

They performed the *parabatai* ritual before leaving for the Academy, swearing the oath without hesitation. By then they were fifteen years old, a physically unlikely pairing: Robert had finally hit his growth spurt, and loomed over his peers, his muscles thick, his shadow of a beard growing in thicker every day. Michael was slim and wiry, his unruly curls and dreamy expression making him look younger than his age.

"Entreat me not to leave thee,
Or return from following after thee—
For whither thou goest, I will go,
And where thou lodgest, I will lodge.
Thy people shall be my people, and thy God my God.
Where thou diest, will I die, and there will I be buried.
The Angel do so to me, and more also,
If aught but death part thee and me."

Robert recited the words, but they were unnecessary. Their bond had been cemented the day he turned fourteen, when he finally got up the nerve to Mark himself again. Michael was the only one he told, and as he held the stele over his skin, it was Michael's steady gaze that gave him the courage to bear down.

Unthinkable that they had only one last year together before they'd be expected to part. Their *parabatai* bond would remain after the Academy, of course. They'd always be best friends; they'd always charge into battle side by side. But it wouldn't be the same. They'd each marry, move into houses of their own, refocus their attention and their love. They would always have a claim on each other's souls. But after next year, they would no longer be the most important person in each other's lives. This, Robert knew, was simply how life worked. This was growing up. He just couldn't imagine it, and he didn't want to.

As if listening in on Robert's thoughts, Michael echoed the question he'd dodged earlier. "What really is going on with you and Maryse?" he asked. "Do you think it's for real? Like, for good?"

There was no need to put on a show for Michael. "I don't know," he said honestly. "I don't even know what that would feel like. She's perfect for me. I love spending time with her, I love . . . *you know*, with her. But does that mean I love her? It should, but . . ."

"Something's missing?"

"Not between us, though," Robert said. "It's like there's something missing in me. I see how Stephen looks at Amatis, how Valentine looks at Jocelyn—"

"How *Lucian* looks at Jocelyn," Michael added with a wry grin. They both liked Lucian, despite his irritating tendency to act like Valentine's favor had given him insight beyond his years. But after all these years of watching him pine away for Jocelyn, it was hard to take him entirely seriously. The same went for Jocelyn, who somehow managed to remain oblivious. Robert didn't understand how you could be the center of someone's world without even realizing it.

"I don't know," he admitted, wondering if any girl would ever be the center of his world. "Sometimes I worry there's something wrong with me."

Michael clapped a hand to his shoulder and fixed him with an intense gaze. "There's *nothing* wrong with you, Robert. I wish you could finally see that."

Robert shook off the hand, along with the weight of the moment. "How about you?" he said with forced gaiety. "It's been, what, three dates with Eliza Rosewain?"

"Four," Michael admitted.

He'd sworn Robert to secrecy about her, saying he didn't want the other guys to know until he was sure it was real. Robert suspected he didn't want *Valentine* to know, as Eliza was a particular thorn in Valentine's side. She asked nearly as many disrespectful questions as he did, and harbored a similar disdain for the current policies of the Clave, but she wanted nothing to do with the Circle or its goals. Eliza thought that a new, united front with mundanes and Downworlders was the key to the future. She argued—loudly, and to the disgust of most of the faculty and students—that the Shadowhunters should be addressing the problems of the mundane world. She could often be found in the quad, shoving unwanted leaflets in students' faces, ranting about nuclear testing, Middle East oil tyrants, some trouble no one understood in South Africa, some disease no one wanted to acknowledge in America . . . Robert had heard every lecture in full, because Michael always insisted on staying to listen.

"She's very odd," Michael said. "I like it."

"Oh." It was a surprise, a not entirely pleasant one. Michael never liked *anyone*. Until this moment, Robert hadn't realized how much he had counted on that. "Then you should go for it," he said, hoping he sounded sincere.

"Really?" Michael looked rather surprised himself.

"Yes. Definitely." Robert reminded himself: *The less certain you feel, the more certain you act.* "She's perfect for you."

"Oh." Michael stopped walking and settled under the shadow of a tree. Robert dropped to the ground beside him. "Can I ask you something, Robert?"

"Anything."

"Have you ever been in love? For real?"

"You know I haven't. Don't you think I would have mentioned it?"

"But how can you know for sure, if you don't know what it would feel like? Maybe you have without even realizing it. Maybe you're holding out for something you already have."

There was a part of Robert that hoped this was the case, that what he felt for Maryse *was* the kind of eternal, soulmate love that everyone talked about. Maybe his expectations were simply too high. "I guess I don't know for sure," he admitted. "What about you? Do you think you know what it would feel like?"

"Love?" Michael smiled down at his hands. "Love, real love, is being seen. Being *known*. Knowing the ugliest part of someone, and loving them anyway. And . . . I guess I think two people in love become something else, something more than the sum of their parts, you know? That it must be like you're creating a new world that exists just for the two of you. You're gods of your own pocket universe." He laughed a little then, as if he felt foolish. "That must sound ridiculous."

"No," Robert said, the truth dawning over him. Michael didn't talk like someone who was guessing—he talked like someone who *knew*. Was it possible that after four dates with Eliza, he'd actually fallen in love? Was it possible that his *parabatai*'s entire world had changed, and Robert hadn't even noticed? "It sounds . . . nice."

Michael turned his head up to face Robert, his face crinkled with an unusual uncertainty. "Robert, there's something I've been meaning to tell you . . . needing to tell you, maybe."

"Anything."

It wasn't like Michael to hesitate. They told each other everything; they always had.

"I . . ."

He stopped, then shook his head.

"What is it?" Robert pressed.

"No, it's nothing. Forget it."

Robert's stomach cramped. Is this what it would be like now that Michael was in love? Would there be a new distance between them, important things left unsaid? He felt like Michael was leaving him behind, crossing the border into a land where his *parabatai* couldn't follow—and though he knew he shouldn't blame Michael, he couldn't help himself.

Simon was dreaming he was back in Brooklyn, playing a gig with Rilo Kiley to a club full of screaming fans, when suddenly his mother wandered onto the stage in her bathrobe and said, in a flawless Scottish accent, "You're going to miss all the fun."

Simon blinked himself awake, confused, for a moment, why he was in a dungeon that smelled of dung rather than his Brooklyn bedroom—then, once he got his bearings, confused all over again about why he was being awoken in the middle of the night by a wild-eyed Scotsman.

"Is there a fire?" Simon asked. "There better be a fire. Or a demon attack. And I'm not talking about some puny lower-level demon, mind you. You want to wake me up in the middle of a dream about rock superstardom, it better be a Greater Demon."

"It's Isabelle," George said.

Simon leaped out of bed—or gallantly tried to, at least. He got a bit tangled in his sheets, so it was more like he tumbled-twisted-*thudded* out of bed, but eventually he made it to his feet, ready to charge into action. "What happened to Isabelle?"

"Why would anything have happened to Isabelle?"

"You said—" Simon rubbed his eyes, sighing. "Let's start over again. You're waking me up because . . . ?"

"We're meeting Isabelle. Having an adventure. Ring a bell?"

"Oh." Simon had done his best to forget about this. He

climbed back into bed. "You can tell me about it in the morning."

"You're not coming?" George asked, as if Simon had said he was going to spend the rest of the night doing extra calisthenics with Delaney Scarsbury, just for fun.

"You guessed it." Simon tugged the blanket over his head and pretended to be asleep.

"But you're going to miss all the fun."

"That is precisely my intention," Simon said, and squeezed his eyes shut until he was asleep for real.

This time he was dreaming of a VIP room backstage at the club, filled with champagne and coffee, a gaggle of groupies trying to break down the door so that—in the dream, Simon somehow knew this was their intent—they could tear off his clothes and ravish him. They pounded at the door, screaming his name, *Simon! Simon! Simon—*

Simon opened his eyes to creeping tendrils of gray, pre-dawn light, a rhythmic pounding at his door, and a girl screaming his name.

"Simon! Simon, wake up!" It was Beatriz, and she didn't sound much in the mood for ravishing.

Sleepily, he padded to the door and let her in. Female students were most definitely not allowed in male students' rooms after curfew, and it was unlike Beatriz to break a rule like that, so he gathered it must be something important. (If the pounding and shouting hadn't already tipped him off.)

"What's wrong?"

"What's wrong? What's wrong is it's nearly five a.m. and Julie and the others are still off somewhere with your stupid girlfriend and what do you think is going to happen if they don't come back before the morning lecture starts and who knows what could have happened to them out there?"

"Beatriz, breathe," Simon said. "Anyway, she's not my girlfriend."

"Is that all you have to say for yourself?" She was nearly vibrating with fury. "She talked them into sneaking out—for all I know, they drank their weight of Lake Lyn and they've all gone *mad*. They could be *dead* for all we know. Don't you care?"

"Of course I care," Simon said, noting that he was alone in the room. George also had not returned. His brain, muddled with sleep, was functioning below optimal speeds. "Next year I'm bringing a coffeemaker," he mumbled.

"Simon!" She clapped her hands sharply, inches from face. "Focus!"

"Don't you think you're being a little alarmist about this?" Simon asked, though Beatriz was one of the most levelheaded girls he'd ever met. If she was alarmed, there was probably a good reason—but he couldn't see what it might be. "They're with Isabelle. Isabelle Lightwood—she's not going to let anything bad happen."

"Oh, they're with *Isabelle*." Her voice dripped with sarcasm. "I feel oh so relieved."

"Come on, Beatriz. You don't know her."

"I know what I see," Beatriz said.

"And what's that?"

"An entitled rich girl who doesn't have to follow the rules, and doesn't have to worry about consequences. What does she care if Julie and Jon get kicked out of here?"

"What do *I* care if Julie and Jon get kicked out?" Simon muttered, too loudly.

"You care about George," Beatriz pointed out. "And Marisol and Sunil. They're all out there somewhere, and they trust Isabelle as much as you seem to. But I'm telling you, Simon, it doesn't seem right to me. What she said about the Academy wanting us to screw up and get into trouble. More like *she* wants us to get in trouble. Or she wants *something*. I don't know what it is. But I don't like it."

Something about what she said rang true more than he would have liked—but Simon wouldn't let himself go there. It felt disloyal, and he'd been disloyal enough. This week was his chance to prove himself to Isabelle, show her that they belonged in each other's lives. He wasn't going to screw that up by doubting her, even if she wasn't here to see it.

"I trust Isabelle," Simon told Beatriz. "Everyone will be fine, and I'm sure they'll be back before anyone knows they were gone. You should stop worrying about it."

"That's it? That's all you're going to do?"

"What do *you* want to do?"

"I don't know. Something!"

"Well, I am doing something," Simon said. "I'm going to go back to bed. I'm going to dream of coffee and a shiny new Fender Stratocaster and if George still isn't back by morning, I'm going to tell Dean Penhallow that he's sick, so he won't get in trouble. And *then* I'll start worrying."

Beatriz snorted. "Thanks for nothing."

"You're welcome!" Simon called. But he waited until the door had slammed shut behind her to do it.

Simon was right.

When Robert Lightwood began his lecture that morning,

every member of the student body was there to hear it, including a very bleary-eyed George.

"How was it?" Simon whispered when his roommate slid into the seat beside him.

"Bloody amazing," George murmured. When Simon pressed him for details, George only shook his head and pressed his finger to his lips.

"Seriously? Just tell me."

"I'm sworn to secrecy," George whispered. "But it's only going to get better. You want in, come along with me tonight."

Robert Lightwood cleared his throat loudly. "I'd like to begin today's lecture, assuming that's all right with the peanut gallery."

George looked around wildly. "They're serving peanuts today? I'm starving."

Simon sighed. George yawned.

Robert began again.

1984

The pack was small, only five wolves. In their deceptively human form: two men, one even bigger than Robert, with muscles the size of his head, and another stooped and aged with scraggly hair spurting from his nose and ears as if his inner wolf were gradually encroaching. One child in blond pigtails. The girl's young mother, her glossy lips and undulating curves prompting thoughts Robert knew better than to say aloud, at least where Valentine could hear. And finally, one sinewy woman with a deep tan and deeper frown who seemed to be in charge.

It was disgusting, Valentine said, werewolves stinking up a distinguished Shadowhunter mansion. And although the manor was decrepit and long abandoned—vines snaking up its walls, weeds sprouting from its foundation, a once noble estate reduced to rust and rubble—Robert saw his point. The house had a lineage, had been home to a line of intrepid warriors, men and women who risked and eventually gave their lives to the cause of humanity, to saving the world from demons. And here were these creatures, infected by their demonic strain— these rogue creatures who'd violated the Accords and killed with abandon, taking refuge in the home of their enemy? The Clave refused to deal with it, Valentine said. They wanted more evidence—not because they weren't sure that these wolves were filthy, violent criminals, but because they didn't want to deal with Downworlder complaints. They didn't want to have to explain themselves; they didn't have the nerve to say: *We knew they were guilty, and so we dealt with it.*

They were, in other words, weak.

Useless.

Valentine said they should be proud to do the job the Clave was unwilling to get done, that they were serving their people, even as they skirted the Law, and with his words, Robert felt that pride bloom. Let the other Academy students have their parties and their petty school melodramas. Let them think growing up meant graduating, marrying, attending meetings. *This* was growing up, just like Valentine said. Seeing an injustice and doing something about it, no matter the risk. No matter the consequences.

The wolves had a keen sense of smell and sharp instincts, even in their human bodies, so the Shadowhunters were careful. They crept around the decaying mansion, peered in windows, waited, watched. Planned. Five werewolves and four young Shadowhunters—those were odds even Valentine didn't want to play. So they were patient, and they were careful.

They waited until dark.

It was disconcerting to watch the wolves in human form, impersonating a normal human family, the younger man washing dishes while the elder one made himself a pot of tea, the child sitting cross-legged on the floor racing her model cars. Robert reminded himself that these trespassers were claiming a home and a life they didn't deserve—that they'd killed innocents and may even have helped slaughter Valentine's father.

Still, he was relieved when the moon rose and they reverted to monstrous form. Robert and the others clung to the shadows while three members of the pack sprouted fur and fangs, leaping through a broken window and into the night. They went out to hunt—leaving, as Valentine suspected they would, their most vulnerable behind. The old man and the child. These were odds more to Valentine's liking.

It wasn't much of a fight.

By the time the two remaining werewolves registered attack, they were surrounded. They didn't even have time to transform. It was over in minutes, Stephen knocking the older one unconscious with a blow to the head, the child cowering in a corner, inches from the tip of Michael's sword.

"We'll take them both for interrogation," Valentine said.

Michael shook his head. "Not the kid."

"They're both criminals," Valentine argued. "Every member of the pack is culpable for—"

"She's a little kid!" Michael said, turning to his *parabatai* for support. "Tell him. We're not dragging some child into the woods to throw her at the mercy of the Clave."

He had a point . . . but then, so did Valentine. Robert said nothing.

"We're *not* taking the child," Michael said, and the look on his face suggested he was willing to back up his words with action.

Stephen and Robert tensed, waiting for the explosion. Valentine didn't take well to being challenged; he had very little experience with it. But he only sighed, and offered up a charmingly rueful smile. "Of course not. Don't know what I was thinking. Just the old man, then. Unless you've got some objection to that as well?"

No one had any objections, and the unconscious old man was skin and bones, his weight barely noticeable on Robert's broad shoulders. They locked the child up in a closet, then carried the old man deep into the woods, back to the campsite.

They tied him to a tree.

The rope was woven with silver filament—when the old man woke up, he would wake to pain. It probably wouldn't be enough to bind him in wolf form, not if he was determined to escape. But it would slow him down. Their silver daggers would do the rest.

"You two, patrol a half-mile perimeter," Valentine told Michael and Stephen. "We don't want any of its grubby little friends catching its stench. Robert and I will guard the prisoner."

Stephen nodded sharply, eager as ever to do as Valentine willed.

"And when he wakes up?" Michael asked.

"When *it* wakes up, Robert and I will question it on the

subject of its crimes, and what it knows about the crimes of its fellows," Valentine said. "Once we've secured its confession, we'll deliver it to the Clave for its punishment. Does that satisfy you, Michael?"

He didn't sound like he much cared about the answer, and Michael didn't give him one.

"So now we wait?" Robert asked, once they were alone.

Valentine smiled.

When he wanted it to, Valentine's smile could worm its way into the most well-fortified heart, melt it from the inside out.

This one wasn't designed for heat. This was a cold smile, and it chilled Robert to the core.

"I'm tired of waiting," Valentine said, and drew out a dagger. Moonlight glinted off the pure silver.

Before Robert could say anything, Valentine pressed the flat side of the blade against the old man's bare chest. There was a sizzle of flesh, then a howl, as the prisoner woke to agony.

"I wouldn't," Valentine said calmly, as the old man's features began to take on a wolfish cast, fur sprouting across his naked body. "I'm going to hurt you, yes. But change back into a wolf, and I promise, I will kill you."

The transformation stopped as abruptly as it had begun.

The old man issued a series of racking coughs that shook his skinny body from head to toe. He was skinny, so skinny that ribs protruded from pale flesh. There were hollows beneath his eyes and only a few sorry strands of gray hair crossing his liver-spotted skull. It had never occurred to Robert that a werewolf could go bald. Under other circumstances, the thought of it might have amused him.

But there was nothing amusing about the sound the man

made as Valentine traced the dagger's tip from jutting collarbone to belly button.

"Valentine, he's just an old man," Robert said hesitantly. "Maybe we should—"

"Listen to your friend," the old man said in a pleading, warbling voice. "I could be your own grandfather."

Valentine struck him across the face with the hilt of the dagger.

"It's not any kind of man," he told Robert. "It's a monster. And it's been doing things it shouldn't be doing, isn't that true?"

The werewolf, apparently concluding that playing aged and weak wouldn't get him out of this one, drew himself up straight and bared sharp teeth. His voice, when he spoke, had lost its tremble. "Who are you, *Shadowhunter*, to tell me what I should and shouldn't be doing?"

"So you admit it, then," Robert said eagerly. "You've violated the Accords."

If he confessed this easily, they could be done with this whole sordid affair, turn the prisoner in to the Clave, go home.

"I don't give my accord to killers and weaklings," the werewolf spat.

"Fortunately, I don't need your accord," Valentine said. "I need only information. You tell me what I need to know, and we'll let you go."

This wasn't what they'd discussed, but Robert held his tongue.

"Two months ago, a pack of werewolves killed a Shadowhunter at the western edge of these woods. Where can I find them?"

"And exactly how would I know that?"

Valentine's icy smile returned. "You better hope that you do, because otherwise you'll be of no use to me."

"Well then, on second thought, maybe I have heard tell of this dead Shadowhunter you're talking about." The wolf barked a laugh. "Wish I could have been there to see him die. To taste of his sweet flesh. It's the fear that gives the meat its taste, you know. Best of all when they cry first, a little salty with the sweet. And rumor has it your doomed Shadowhunter wept buckets. Cowardly, that one was."

"Robert, hold its mouth open." Valentine's voice was steady, but Robert knew Valentine well enough to sense the fury roiling beneath.

"Maybe we should take a moment to—"

"*Hold its mouth open.*"

Robert gripped the man's feeble jaws and pried them open.

Valentine pressed the flat side of the dagger to the man's tongue and held it there as the man's shriek turned into a howl, as his scrawny muscles bulged and fur bloomed across his flesh, as the tongue bubbled and blistered, and then, just as the fully transformed wolf snapped its bindings, Valentine sliced off its tongue. As its mouth gushed blood, Valentine slashed a sharp line across the wolf's midsection. The cut was sure and deep, and the wolf dropped to the ground, intestines spilling from its wound.

Valentine leaped upon the writhing creature, stabbing and slicing, tearing through its hide, flaying flesh to pearly bone, even as the creature flailed and spasmed helplessly beneath him, even as the fight drained out of it, even as its gaze went flat, even as its broken body reclaimed human form, lay still on bloody earth, an old man's face bled pale and turned lifelessly to the night sky.

"That's enough," Robert kept saying, quietly, uselessly. "Valentine, that's enough."

But he did nothing to stop it.

And when his friends returned from their patrol to find Valentine and Robert standing over the disemboweled corpse, he didn't counter Valentine's version of events: The werewolf had slipped free of its bonds and tried to escape. They had endured a fierce battle, killed in self-defense.

The outline of this story was, technically, true.

Stephen clapped Valentine on the back, commiserating with him that he'd lost the potential lead to his father's killer. Michael locked eyes with Robert, his question clear as if he'd spoken it aloud. *What really happened?*

What did you let happen?

Robert looked away.

Isabelle was avoiding him. Beatriz was fuming at him. Everyone else was buzzing with too much excitement about the previous night's adventure and the secret one to come. Julie and Marisol only echoed George's cryptic promise—that something *good* was on the horizon, and if Simon wanted to know about it, he would have to join them.

"I don't think Isabelle would want me there," he told Sunil as they picked warily through the steamed heap of vaguely vegetable-shaped objects that passed for lunch.

Sunil shook his head and grinned. The smile fit his face poorly; Sunil with a grin was like a Klingon in a tutu. He was an unusually somber boy who seemed to consider good cheer as a sign of unseriousness, and treated people accordingly. "She told us to convince you to show up. She said 'whatever it takes.' So, you tell me, Simon." The unsettling smile grew. "What's it going to take?"

"You don't even know her," Simon pointed out. "Why are you suddenly so willing to do whatever she tells you to do?"

"We are talking about the same girl here, yes? Isabelle Lightwood?"

"Yes."

Sunil shook his head in wonder. "And you even have to ask?"

So that was the new order: the cult of Isabelle Lightwood. Simon had to admit, he could completely understand how a roomful of otherwise rational people could fall completely under her spell and give themselves to her entirely.

But why would she want them to?

He decided he was going to have to see this for himself. Simply to understand what was going on and make sure it was all on the up-and-up.

Not at all because he desperately wanted to be near her. Or impress her. Or please her.

Come to think of it, maybe Simon understood the cult of Isabelle better than he wanted to admit.

Maybe he'd been its charter member.

"You intend to do *what*?" On the last word, Simon's voice jumped two octaves above normal.

Jon Cartwright snickered. "Simmer down, Mom. You heard her."

Simon looked around the lounge at his friends (and Jon).

Over the past year, he'd come to know them inside and out, or at least, he thought that he did. Julie bit her nails bloody when she was nervous. Marisol slept with a sword under her pillow, just in case. George talked in his sleep, usually about sheep-shearing techniques. Sunil had four pet rabbits that he talked about constantly, always worried that little Ringo was getting picked on by his bigger, fluffier brothers. Jon had covered one wall of his room with his little cousin's finger paintings, and wrote her a letter every week. They'd all pledged themselves to the Shadowhunter cause; they'd gone through hell to prove themselves to their instructors and one another. They'd almost finished out the year without a single fatal injury or vampire bite . . . and now *this*?

"Ha-ha, very funny," Simon said, hoping he was doing an acceptable job of keeping the desperation out of his tone. "Nice joke on me, get me back for wussing out last night. Utterly hilarious. What's next? You want to convince me they're making another crap *Last Airbender* movie? You want to see me freak out, there are easier ways."

Isabelle rolled her eyes. "No one wants to see you freak out, Simon. Frankly, I could take or leave seeing you at all."

"So this is serious," Simon said. "You're seriously, not at all jokingly, actually, for real planning to *summon a demon?* Here, in the middle of the Shadowhunter Academy? In the middle of the end-of-year party? Because you think it will be . . . *fun?*"

"We're obviously not going to summon it in the middle of the party," Isabelle said. "That would be rather foolish."

"Oh, of course," Simon drawled. "*That* would be foolish."

"We're going to summon it here in the lounge," Isabelle clarified. "Then *bring* it to the party."

"Then kill it, of course," Julie put in.

"Of course," Simon echoed. He wondered if maybe he was having a stroke.

"You're making it sound like a bigger deal than it is," George said.

"Yeah, it's just an imp demon," Sunil said. "No biggie."

"Uh-huh." Simon groaned. "Totally. No biggie."

"Imagine the look on everyone's faces when they see what we can do!" Marisol was nearly glowing at the thought of it.

Beatriz wasn't there. If she had been, maybe she could have talked some reason into them. Or helped Simon tie them up and stuff them in the closet until the end of the semester had safely passed and Isabelle was back in New York where she belonged.

"What if something goes wrong?" Simon pointed out. "You've never faced off against a demon in combat conditions, not without the teachers watching your back. You don't know—"

"Neither do you," Isabelle snapped. "At least, you don't remember, isn't that right?"

Simon said nothing.

"Whereas *I* took down my first imp when I was six years old," Isabelle said. "Like I told your friends, it's no big deal. And *they* trust me."

I trust you—that's what he was meant to say. He knew she was waiting for it. They all were.

He couldn't.

"I can't talk you out of this?" he asked instead.

Isabelle shrugged. "You can keep trying, but you'd be wasting all our time."

"Then I'll have to find another way to stop you," Simon said.

"You gonna tell on us?" Jon sneered. "You gonna go be a crybaby and tattle to your favorite warlock?" He snorted. "Once a teacher's pet, always a teacher's pet."

"Shut up, Jon." Isabelle whacked him softly on the arm. Simon probably should have been pleased, but whacking still required touching, and he preferred that Isabelle and Jon never come into physical contact of any sort. "You could try to tell on us, Simon. But I'll deny it. And then who will they believe— someone like me, or someone like you? Some mundane."

She said "mundane" exactly like Jon always did. Like it was a synonym for "nothing."

"This isn't you, Isabelle. This isn't what you're like." He wasn't sure whether he was trying to convince her or himself.

"You don't know what I'm like, remember?"

"I know enough."

"Then you know that you should trust me. But if you don't, go ahead. Tell," she said. "Then everyone will know what *you're* like. What kind of friend you are."

He tried.

He knew it was the right thing to do.

At least, he thought it was the right thing to do.

The next morning, before the lecture, he went to Catarina Loss's office—Jon was right, she was his favorite warlock and his favorite faculty member, and the only one he would trust with something like this.

She welcomed him in, offered him a seat and a mug of something whose steam was an alarming shade of blue. He passed.

"So, Daylighter, I take it you have something to tell me?"

Catarina intimidated him somewhat less than she had at the beginning of the year—which was a bit like saying Jar Jar

Binks was "somewhat less" annoying in *Star Wars: Episode* II than he'd been in *Star Wars: Episode I.*

"It's possible I know something that . . ." Simon cleared his throat. "I mean, if something were happening that . . ."

He hadn't let himself think through what would happen once the words were out. What would happen to his friends? What would happen to Isabelle, their ringleader? She couldn't exactly get expelled from an Academy where she wasn't enrolled . . . but Simon had learned enough about the Clave by now to know there were far worse punishments than getting expelled. Was summoning a minor demon to use as a party trick a violation of the Law? Was he about to ruin Isabelle's life?

Catarina Loss wasn't a Shadowhunter; she had her own secrets from the Clave. Maybe she'd be willing to keep one more, if it meant helping Simon and protecting Isabelle from punishment?

As his mind spun through dark possibilities, the office door swung open and Dean Penhallow poked her blond head in. "Catarina, Robert Lightwood was hoping to chat with you before his session—oh, sorry! Didn't realize you were in the middle of something?"

"Join us," Catarina said. "Simon was just about to tell me something interesting."

The dean stepped into the office, furrowing her brow at Simon. "You look so serious," she told him. "Go ahead, spit it out. You'll feel better. It's like throwing up."

"What's like throwing up?" he asked, confused.

"You know, when you're feeling ill? Sometimes it just helps to get everything out."

Somehow, Simon didn't think vomiting up his confession

straight to the dean would make him feel any better.

Hadn't Isabelle proven herself enough—not just to him, but to the Clave, to everyone? She had, after all, pretty much saved the world. How much more evidence would anyone need that she was one of the good guys?

How much evidence did *he* need?

Simon stood up and said the first thing that popped into his mind. "I just wanted to tell you that we all really enjoyed that beet stew they served for dinner. You should serve that again."

Dean Penhallow gave him an odd look. "Those weren't beets, Simon."

This didn't surprise him, as the stew had had an oddly grainy consistency and a taste reminiscent of dung.

"Well . . . whatever it was, it was delicious," he said quickly. "I better get going. I don't want to miss the beginning of Inquisitor Lightwood's final lecture. They've been so interesting."

"Indeed," Catarina said dryly. "They've been almost as delicious as the stew."

1984

For most of his time at the Academy, Robert had watched Valentine from a distance. Even though Robert was older, he looked up to Valentine, who was everything Robert wanted to be. Valentine excelled at his training without visible effort. He could best anyone with any weapon. He was careless with his affection, or at least seemed to be, and he was beloved. Not many people noticed how few he truly loved back. But Robert noticed, because when you're watching from the sidelines, invisible, it's easy to see clearly.

It never occurred to him that Valentine was watching him, too.

Not until the day, toward the beginning of this year, that Valentine caught him alone in one of the Academy's dark, underground corridors and said quietly, "I know your secret."

Robert's secret, that he told nobody, not even Michael: He was still afraid of the Marks.

Every time he drew a rune on himself, he had to hold his breath, force his fingers not to tremble. He always hesitated. In class, it was barely noticeable. In battle, it could be the split-second difference between life and death, and Robert knew it. Which made him hesitate even more, at everything. He was strong, smart, talented; he was a *Lightwood*. He should have been among the best. But he couldn't let himself go and act on instinct. He couldn't stop his mind from racing toward potential consequences. He couldn't stop being afraid—and he knew, eventually, it would be the end of him.

"I can help you," Valentine said then. "I can teach you what to do with the fear." As if it were as simple as that—and under Valentine's careful instruction, it was.

Valentine had taught him to retreat to a place in his mind that the fear couldn't touch. To separate himself from the Robert Lightwood who knew how to be afraid—and then to tame that weaker, loathed version of himself. "Your weakness makes you furious, as it should," Valentine had told him. "Use the fury to master it—and then everything else."

In a way Valentine had saved Robert's life. Or at least, the only part of his life that mattered.

He owed Valentine everything.

He at least owed Valentine the truth.

"You don't agree with what I did," Valentine said quietly as the sun crept above the horizon. Michael and Stephen were still asleep. Robert had passed the hours of darkness staring at the sky, sifting through what had happened, and what he should do next.

"You think I was out of control," Valentine added.

"That wasn't self-defense," Robert said. "That was torture. Murder."

Robert was seated on one of the logs around the remains of their campfire. Valentine lowered himself beside him.

"You heard the things it said. You understand why it had to be silenced," Valentine said. "It had to be taught its lesson, and the Clave couldn't have mustered the will. I know the others wouldn't understand. Not even Lucian. But you . . . we understand each other, you and I. You're the only one I can really trust. I need you to keep this to yourself."

"If you're so sure you did the right thing, then why keep it a secret?"

Valentine laughed gently. "Always so skeptical, Robert. It's what we all love most about you." His smile faded. "Some of the others are starting to have doubts. About the cause, about me—" He waved away Robert's denials before they could be voiced. "Don't think I can't tell. Everyone wants to be loyal when it's easy. But when things get difficult . . ." He shook his head. "I can't count on everyone I would like to count on. But I believe I can count on you."

"Of course you can."

"Then you'll keep what passed this night a secret from the others," Valentine said. "Even from Michael."

Much later—too late—it would occur to Robert that Valentine probably had some version of this conversation with each member of the Circle. Secrets bound people together, and Valentine was smart enough to know it.

"He's my *parabatai*," Robert pointed out. "I don't keep secrets from him."

Valentine's eyebrows shot sky-high. "And you think he keeps no secrets from you?"

Robert remembered the night before, whatever it was Michael had been trying so hard not to say. That was one secret—who knew how many more there were?

"You know Michael better than anyone," Valentine said. "And yet, I imagine there are things I know about him that might surprise you. . . ."

A silence hung between them as Robert considered it.

Valentine didn't lie, or issue empty boasts. If he said he knew something about Michael, something secret, then it was true.

And it was temptation, dangling here before Robert.

He needed only to ask.

He wanted to know; he didn't want to know.

"We all have competing loyalties," Valentine said, before Robert could give in to temptation. "The Clave would like to make these things simple, but it's just another example of their obtuseness. I love Lucian, my *parabatai*. I love Jocelyn. If those two loves were ever to come into conflict . . ."

He didn't have to complete the thought. Robert knew what Valentine knew, and understood that Valentine loved his *parabatai* enough to allow it. Just as Lucian loved Valentine enough never to act on it.

Maybe some secrets were a mercy.

He held out his hand to Valentine. "You have my word. My oath. Michael will never know about this."

As soon as the words were out, he wondered if he'd made a mistake. But there was no going back.

"I know your secret too, Robert," Valentine said.

At this, an echo of the first words Valentine had ever said to him, Robert felt the ghost of a smile.

"I think we covered that," Robert reminded him.

"You're a coward," Valentine said.

Robert flinched. "How can you say that after everything we've been through? You know I would never shy away from a battle or—"

Valentine shook his head, silencing him. "Oh, I don't mean physically. We've taken care of that, haven't we? When it comes to taking on physical risk, you're the bravest there is. Overcompensating, perhaps?"

"I don't know what you're talking about," Robert said stiffly—afraid he knew all too well.

"You're not afraid of death or injury, Robert. You're afraid of *yourself* and your own weakness. You lack faith—you lack *loyalty*—because you lack the strength of your own convictions. And it's my own fault for expecting more. After all, how can you be expected to believe in anything or anyone if you don't believe in yourself?"

Robert felt suddenly transparent, and didn't much like it.

"I once tried to teach you to master your fear and your weakness," Valentine said. "I see now that was a mistake."

Robert hung his head, waiting for Valentine to cast him out of the Circle. Exile him from his friends and his duty. Ruin his life.

Ironic that it was his own cowardice that had made his worst fears come true.

But Valentine surprised him. "I've given the matter some thought, and I have a proposition for you," Valentine said.

"What is it?" He was afraid to hope.

"Give up," Valentine said. "Stop trying to pretend away your cowardice, your doubt. Stop trying to ignite some unshakable passion in yourself. If you can't find the courage of your convictions, why not simply accept the courage of mine?"

"I don't understand."

"My proposition is this," Valentine said. "Stop worrying so much about whether or not you're sure. Let me be sure for you. Rely on my certainty, on *my* passion. Let yourself be weak, and lean on me, because we both know I can be strong. Accept that you're doing the right thing because *I* know it to be the right thing."

"If only it were that easy," Robert said, and couldn't deny a stab of longing.

Valentine looked mildly amused, as if Robert had betrayed a childlike misunderstanding of the nature of things. "It's only as hard as you make it," he said gently. "It's as easy as you let it be."

Isabelle brushed past Simon on his way out of the lecture.

"Nine p.m., Jon's room," she whispered in his ear.

"What?" It was like she was informing him of the exact time and place of his death—which, if he was forced to imagine what she might be doing in Jon Cartwright's dorm room, would be imminent.

"Demon o'clock. You know, in case you're still determined

to ruin our fun." She gave him a wicked grin. "Or join it."

There was an implied dare on her face, a certainty that he wouldn't have the nerve to do either. Simon was reminded that though he might have forgotten ever knowing Isabelle, she'd forgotten nothing about him. In fact, it could be argued that she knew him better than he knew himself.

Not anymore, he told himself. A year at the Academy, a year of study and battle and caffeine withdrawal had changed him. It had to.

The question was: Changed him into what?

She'd given him the wrong time.

Of course she had. By the time Simon burst into Jon Cartwright's room, they were nearly ready to complete the ritual.

"You can't do this," Simon told them. "All of you, stop and think."

"Why?" Isabelle said. "Just give us one good reason. Persuade us, Simon."

He wasn't good at speeches. And she knew it.

Simon found himself suddenly furious. This was *his* school; these were *his* friends. Isabelle didn't care what happened here. Maybe there was no deeper story, no hidden pain. Maybe she was exactly what she seemed, and no more: a frivolous person who cared only for herself.

Something at his core revolted against this thought, but he silenced it. This wasn't about his nonrelationship with his nongirlfriend. He couldn't let it be about that.

"It's not just that it's against the rules," Simon said. How were you supposed to explain something that seemed so obvious? It was like trying to persuade someone that one plus one equaled two: It just *did*. "It's not just that you could get expelled or even taken before the Clave. It's *wrong*. Someone could get hurt."

"Someone's always getting hurt," George pointed out, ruefully rubbing his elbow, which, just a couple of days before, Julie had nearly sliced off with a broadsword.

"Because there's no other way to learn," Simon said, exasperated. "Because it's the best of all bad options. This? This is the opposite of necessary. Is this the kind of Shadowhunter you want to be? The kind that toys with the forces of darkness because you think you can handle it? Have you never seen a movie? Read a comic book? That's always how it starts—just a little temptation, just a little taste of evil, and then *bam*, your lightsaber turns red and you're breathing through a big black mask and slicing off your son's hand just to be mean."

They looked at him blankly.

"Forget it."

It was funny, Shadowhunters knew more than mundanes about almost everything. They knew more about demons, about weapons, about the currents of power and magic that shaped the world. But they didn't understand temptation. They didn't understand how easy it was to make one small, terrible choice after another until you'd slid down the slippery slope into the pit of hell. *Dura lex*—the Law is hard. So hard that the Shadowhunters had to pretend it was possible to be perfect. It was the one thing Simon had taken from Robert's lectures about the Circle. Once Shadowhunters started to slide, they didn't stop. "The point is, this is a no-win situation. Either your stupid imp gets out of control and eats a bunch of students— or it *doesn't*, and so you decide next time you can summon a bigger demon. And that one eats you. That is the definition of a lose-lose situation."

"He makes a fair point," Julie said.

"Not as dumb as he looks," Jon admitted.

George cleared his throat. "Maybe—"

"Maybe we should get on with things," Isabelle said, and tossed her silky black hair and blinked her large, bottomless eyes and smiled her irresistible smile—and as if she'd cast some witchy spell over the room, everyone forgot Simon existed and busied themselves with the work of raising a demon.

He'd done everything he could do here. There was only one option left.

He ran away.

1984

Michael let a week pass before he asked the question Robert had been dreading. Maybe he was waiting for Robert to bring it up himself. Maybe he'd tried to convince himself he didn't need to know the truth, that he loved Robert enough not to care—but apparently he had failed.

"Walk with me?" Michael said, and Robert agreed to take one last stroll through Brocelind Forest, even though he'd hoped to stay away from the woods until the next semester. By then, maybe, the memory of what happened there would have faded. The shadows wouldn't seem so ominous, the ground so soaked in blood.

Things had been strange between them this week, quiet and stiff. Robert was keeping his secret about what they'd done to the werewolf, and mulling over Valentine's suggestion, that he be Robert's conscience and Robert's strength, that it would be easier that way. Michael was . . .

Well, Robert couldn't guess what Michael was thinking—about Valentine, about Eliza, about Robert himself. And that's what made things so strange. They were *parabatai*; they were two halves of the same self. Robert wasn't supposed to have to *guess*. Before, he'd always known.

"Okay, so what's the real story?" Michael asked, once they were deep enough in the woods that the sounds of campus had long since faded away. The sun was still in the sky, but here in the trees, the shadows were long and the dark was rising. "What did Valentine do to that werewolf?"

Robert couldn't look at his *parabatai*. He shrugged. "Exactly what I told you."

"You've never lied to me before," Michael said. There was sadness in his voice, and something else, something worse—there was a hint of finality in it, like they were about to say good-bye.

Robert swallowed. Michael was right: Before this, Robert had never lied.

"And I suppose you've never lied to me?" he charged Michael. His *parabatai* had a secret, he knew that now. Valentine said so.

There was a long pause. Then Michael spoke. "I lie to you every day, Robert."

It was like a kick in the stomach.

That wasn't just a secret, that wasn't just a *girl*. That was . . . Robert didn't even know what it was.

Unfathomable.

He stopped and turned to Michael, incredulous. "If you're trying to shock me into telling you something—"

"I'm not trying to shock you. I'm just . . . I'm trying to tell you the truth. Finally. I know you're keeping something from me, something important."

"I'm *not*," Robert insisted.

"You are," Michael said, "and it hurts. And if that hurts *me*, then I can only imagine—" He stopped, took a deep breath, forced himself on. "I couldn't bear it, if I've been hurting you like that all these years. Even if I didn't realize it. Even if *you* didn't realize it."

"Michael, you're not making any sense."

They reached a fallen log, thick with moss. Michael sank onto it, looking suddenly weary. Like he'd aged a hundred years in the last minute. Robert dropped beside him and put a hand on his friend's shoulder. "What is it?" He knocked softly at Michael's head, trying to smile, to tell himself this was just Michael being Michael. Weird, but inconsequential. "What's going on in that nuthouse you call a brain?"

Michael lowered his head.

He looked so vulnerable like that, the nape of his neck bare and exposed, Robert couldn't bear it.

"I'm in love," Michael whispered.

Robert burst into laughter, relief gushing through him. "Is that all? Don't you think I figured that out, idiot? I told you, Eliza's great—"

Then Michael said something else.

Something that Robert must have misheard.

"What?" he said, though he didn't want to.

This time, Michael lifted his head, met Robert's eyes, and spoke clearly. "I'm in love with *you*."

Robert was on his feet before he'd even processed the words.

It seemed suddenly very important to have space between him and Michael. As much space as possible.

"You're what?"

He hadn't meant to shout.

"That's not funny," Robert added, trying to modulate his voice.

"It's not a joke. I'm in—"

"Don't you say that again. You will *never* say that again."

Michael paled. "I know you probably . . . I know you don't feel the same way, that you couldn't . . ."

All at once, with a force that nearly swept him off his feet, Robert was flooded by a rush of memories: Michael's hand on his shoulder. Michael's arms around him in an embrace. Michael wrestling with him. Michael gently adjusting his grip on a sword. Michael lying in bed a few feet away from him, night after night. Michael stripping down, taking his hand, pulling him into Lake Lyn. Michael, chest bare, hair soaked, eyes shining, lying in the grass beside him.

Robert wanted to throw up.

"Nothing has to change," Michael said, and Robert would have laughed, if it wouldn't so surely have led to puking. "I'm still the same person. I'm not asking anything of you. I'm just being honest. I just needed you to know."

This is what Robert knew: That Michael was the best friend he'd ever had, and probably the purest soul he'd ever know. That he should sit beside Michael, promise him that this was okay, that nothing needed to change, that the oath they'd sworn to each other was true, and forever. That there was nothing to fear in Michael's—Robert's stomach turned at the word—*love*. That Robert was arrow straight, that it was *Maryse's* touch that made his body come alive, the memory of *Maryse's* bare chest that made his pulse race—and that Michael's confession didn't call any of this into doubt. He knew he should say something reassuring to Michael, something like, "I can't love you that way, but I will love you forever."

But he also knew what people would think.

What they would think about Michael . . . what they would assume about Robert.

People would talk, they would gossip, they would *suspect* things. *Parabatai* couldn't date each other, of course. And couldn't . . . anything else. But Michael and Robert were so *close*; Michael and Robert were so *in sync*; surely people would want to know if Michael and Robert were *the same*.

Surely people would *wonder*.

He couldn't take it. He'd worked too hard to become the man he was, the Shadowhunter he was. He couldn't stand to have people looking at him like that again, like he was different.

And he couldn't stand to have Michael looking at him like *this*.

Because what if he started wondering too?

"You'll never say that again," Robert said coldly. "And if you insist on it, that will be the last thing you ever say to me. Do you understand me?"

Michael just gaped at him, eyes wide and uncomprehending.

"And you will never speak of it to anyone else, either. I won't have people thinking that about us. About *you*."

Michael murmured something unintelligible.

"What?" Robert said sharply.

"I said, what will they think?"

"They'll think you're disgusting," Robert said.

"Like you do?"

A voice at the back of Robert's mind said, *Stop.*

It said, *This is your last chance.*

But it said so very quietly.

It wasn't sure.

"Yes," Robert said, and he said it firmly enough that there would be no question that he meant it. "I think you're disgusting. I swore an oath to you, and I will honor it. But make no mistake: Nothing between us will ever be the same. In fact, from now on, nothing is between us, period."

Michael didn't argue. He didn't say anything. He simply turned, fled into the trees, and left Robert alone.

What he'd said, what he'd done . . . it was unforgivable. Robert knew that. He told himself: It was Michael's fault, Michael's decision.

He told himself: He was only doing what he needed to do to survive.

But he saw the truth now. Valentine was right. Robert wasn't capable of absolute love or loyalty. He'd thought Michael was the exception, the proof that he could be certain of someone— could be *steady*, no matter what.

Now that was gone.

Enough, Robert thought. Enough struggling, enough doubting his own choices, enough falling prey to his own weakness and lack of faith. He would accept Valentine's offer. He would let Valentine choose for him, let Valentine *believe* for him. He would do whatever he needed to hang on to Valentine, and to the Circle, and to its cause.

It was all he had left.

✳ ✳ ✳

Simon ran through the dingy corridors, skidded across slimy floors, and raced down dented stairways, the whole way cursing the Academy for being such a labyrinthine fortress with no cell reception. His feet pounded against worn stone, his lungs heaved, and though the journey seemed endless, only a few minutes passed before he threw himself into Catarina Loss's office.

She was always there, day or night, and that night was no different.

Well, slightly different: That night she wasn't alone.

She stood behind her desk with her arms crossed, flanked by Robert Lightwood and Dean Penhallow, the three of them looking so somber it was almost like they were waiting for him. He didn't let himself hesitate or think of the consequences.

Or think of Izzy.

"There's a group of students trying to raise a demon," Simon panted. "We have to stop them."

No one seemed surprised.

There was a soft throat clearing—Simon turned to discover Julie Beauvale creeping out from behind the door he'd flung open in her face.

"What are you doing here?"

"Same thing you are," Julie said. Then she blushed and gave him an embarrassed little shrug. "I guess you made a good case."

"But how did you get here before me?"

"I took the east stairwell, obviously. Then that corridor behind the weapons room—"

"But doesn't that dead-end at the dining hall?"

"Only if you—"

"Perhaps we can table this fascinating cartographic discussion until later," Catarina Loss said mildly. "I think we have more important business at hand."

"Like teaching your idiot students a lesson," Robert Lightwood growled, and stormed out of the office. Catarina and the dean strode after him.

Simon exchanged a nervous glance with Julie. "You, uh, think we're supposed to follow them?"

"Probably," she said, then sighed. "We might as well let them expel all of us in one shot."

They traipsed after their teachers, letting themselves fall more and more behind.

As they neared Jon's room, Robert's shouts were audible from halfway down the corridor. They couldn't quite make out his words through the thick door, but the volume and cadence made the situation quite clear.

Simon and Julie eased the door open and slipped inside.

George, Jon, and the others were lined up against the wall, faces pale, eyes wide, all of them looking steeled for a firing squad. While Isabelle was standing by her father's side . . . *beaming?*

"Failures, all of you!" Robert Lightwood boomed. "You lot are supposed to be the best and brightest this school has to offer, and this is what you have to show for yourselves? I *warned* you about the dangers of charisma. I *told* you of the need to stand up for what's right, even if it hurts the ones you love most. And *all of you* failed to listen."

Isabelle coughed pointedly.

"All of you except two," Robert allowed, jerking his head at Simon and Julie. "Well done. Isabelle was right about you."

Simon was reeling.

"It was all a stupid *test*?" Jon yelped.

"A rather clever test, if you ask me?" Dean Penhallow said.

Catarina looked as if she had some things to say on the subject of foolish Shadowhunters playing cat-and-mouse games with their own, but as usual, she bit her tongue.

"What percentage of our grades will this be?" Sunil asked.

With that, there was a lot of yelling. Quite a bit of ranting about sacred responsibilities and carelessness and how unpleasant a night in the dungeons of the Silent City could be. Robert thundered like Zeus, Dean Penhallow did her best not to sound like a babysitter scolding her charges for stealing an extra cookie, while Catarina Loss put in the occasional sarcastic remark about what happened to Shadowhunters who thought it would be fun to slum it in warlock territory. At one point, she interrupted Robert Lightwood's tirade to add a pointed comment about Darth Vader—and a sly look at Simon that made him wonder, not for the first time, just how closely she was watching him, and why.

Through it all, Isabelle watched Simon, something unexpected in her gaze. Something almost like . . . pride.

"In conclusion, next time, you'll listen when your elders talk," Robert Lightwood shouted.

"Why would anyone listen to anything you had to say about doing the right thing?" Isabelle snapped.

Robert's face went red. He turned to her slowly, fixing her with the kind of icy Inquisitor glare that would have left anyone else whimpering in a fetal ball. Isabelle didn't flinch.

"Now that this sordid business is concluded, I'd ask you all to give me and my dutiful daughter here some privacy. I believe we have some things to settle," Robert said.

"But this is my room," Jon whined.

Robert didn't need to speak, just turned that Inquisitor glare on him; Jon flinched.

He fled, along with everyone else, and Simon was about to follow suit when Isabelle's fingers snatched for his wrist.

"He stays," she told her father.

"He most certainly does not."

"Simon stays with me, or I leave with him," Isabelle said. "Those are your choices."

"Er, I'm happy to go—" Simon began, "happy" being his polite substitute for "desperate."

"*You stay*," Isabelle commanded.

Robert sighed. "Fine. You stay."

That ended the discussion. Simon dropped down onto the edge of Jon's bed, trying to wish himself invisible.

"It's obvious to me that you don't want to be here," Robert told his daughter.

"What gave it away? The fact that I told you a million times that I didn't want to come? That I didn't want to play your stupid game? That I thought it was cruel and manipulative and a total waste of time?"

"Yes," Robert said. "That."

"And yet you made me come with you anyway."

"Yes," he said.

"Look, if you thought enforced bonding time was going to fix anything or make up for what you—"

Robert sighed heavily. "I've told you before, what happened between your mother and me has nothing to do with you."

"It has *everything* to do with me!"

"Isabelle . . ." Robert glanced at Simon, then lowered his

voice. "I would really prefer to do this without an audience."

"Too bad."

Simon tried even harder to fade into the background, hoping maybe if he tried hard enough, his skin would take on the same pattern as Jon Cartwright's surprisingly flowered sheets.

"You and I, we've never talked about my time in the Circle, or why I followed Valentine," Robert said. "I hoped you kids would never have to know that part of me."

"I heard your lecture, just like everyone else," she said sullenly.

"We both know that the story tailored for public consumption is never the whole truth." Robert frowned. "What I didn't tell those students—what I've never told anyone—is that unlike most of the Circle, I wasn't what you'd call a true believer. The others, they thought they were Raziel's sword in human form. You should have seen your mother, blazing with righteousness."

"So now it's all Mom's fault? Nice, Dad. Really nice. Am I supposed to think you're some awesome guy for seeing through Valentine but going along with him anyway? Because your girlfriend *said so*?"

He shook his head. "You're missing my point. *I* was the most to blame. Your mother, the others, they thought they were doing what was right. They loved Valentine. They loved the cause. They *believed*. I could never muster that faith . . . but I went along anyway. Not because I thought it was right. Because it was *easy*. Because Valentine seemed so sure. Substituting his certainty for my own seemed like the path of least resistance."

"Why are you telling me this?" Some of the venom had drained from her voice.

"I didn't understand then, what it would mean to be truly certain of something," Robert said. "I didn't know how it felt to love something, or someone, beyond all reservation. Unconditionally. I thought maybe, with my *parabatai*, but then—" He swallowed whatever he'd been about to say. Simon wondered how it could be worse than what he'd already confessed to. "Eventually, I assumed I just didn't have it in me. That I wasn't built for that kind of love."

"If you're about to tell me that you found it with your *mistress* . . ." Isabelle shuddered.

"Isabelle." Robert took his daughter's hands in his own. "I'm telling you that I found it with Alec. With you. With . . ." He looked down. "With Max. Having you kids, Isabelle—it changed everything."

"Is that why you spent years treating Alec like he had the plague? Is that how you show your kids that you love them?" At that, if possible, Robert looked even *more* ashamed of himself. "Loving someone doesn't mean you're never going to make mistakes," he said. "I've made more than my share. I know that. And some of them I will never have the chance to make up for. But I'm trying my best with your brother. He knows how much I love him. How proud I am of him. I need you to know it too. You kids, you're the one thing I'm certain of, the one thing I'll always be certain of. Not the Clave. Not, unfortunately, my marriage. *You*. And if I have to, I'll spend the rest of my life trying to prove to you that you can be certain of me."

It was a lame party, the kind that even Simon had to admit might have been livened up by a demon or two. The decorations—a few sad streamers, a couple of underinflated helium balloons, and a hand-drawn poster that (mis)spelled out "*CONGRATULATONS*"—looked as if they'd been grudgingly thrown together at the last minute by a bunch of fifth graders in detention. The refreshment table was crowded with whatever food had been left over at the end of the semester, including stale croissants, a casserole dish filled with orange Jell-O, a vat of stew, and several plates heaped with unidentifiable meat products. As electricity didn't work in Idris and no one had thought to hire a band, there was no music, but a handful of faculty members had taken it upon themselves to improvise a barbershop quartet. (This, in Simon's mind, didn't qualify as music.) Isabelle's posse of demon summoners had been let off with a stern warning, and even allowed to attend the party, but none of them seemed much in the mood for revelry—or, understandably, for Simon.

He was lingering alone by the punch bowl—which smelled enough like fish to preclude him actually pouring himself any punch—when Isabelle joined him.

"Avoiding your friends?" she asked.

"Friends?" He laughed. "I think you mean 'people who hate my guts.' Yeah, I tend to avoid those."

"They don't hate you. They're embarrassed, because you were right and they were stupid. They'll get over it."

"Maybe." It didn't seem likely, but then, not much that had happened this year fell into the category of "likely."

"So, I guess, thanks for sticking around for that whole thing with my dad," Isabelle said.

"You didn't exactly give me much of a choice," he pointed out.

Isabelle laughed, almost fondly. "You really have no idea how a social encounter is supposed to work, do you? I say 'thank you'; you say 'you're welcome.'"

"Like, if I said, thank you for fooling all my friends into thinking you were a wild-and-crazy demon summoner so that they could get in trouble with the dean, you would say . . . ?"

"You're welcome for teaching them all a valuable lesson." She grinned. "One that, apparently, you didn't need to learn."

"Yeah. About that." Even though it had all been a test—even though, apparently, Isabelle had *wanted* him to report her, he still felt guilty. "I'm sorry I didn't figure out what you were doing. Trust you."

"It was a game, Simon. You weren't supposed to trust me."

"But *I* shouldn't have fallen for it. Of all people—"

"You can't be expected to know me." There was an impossible gentleness in Isabelle's voice. "I do understand that, Simon. I know things have been . . . difficult between us, but I'm not deluded. I may not like reality, but I can't deny it."

There were so many things he wanted to say to her.

And yet, right at this high-pressure moment, his mind was blank.

The uncomfortable silence sat heavily between them. Isabelle shifted her weight. "Well, if that's all, then . . ."

"Back to your date with Jon?" Simon couldn't help himself. "Or . . . was that just part of the game?"

He hoped she wouldn't catch the pathetic note of hope in his voice.

"That was a different game, Simon. Keep up. Did it ever occur to you I just enjoy torturing you?" There was that wicked smile again, and Simon felt like it had the power to light him on fire; he felt like he was already burning.

"So, you and he, you never—"

"Jon's not exactly my type."

The next silence was slightly more comfortable. The kind of silence, Simon thought, where you gazed googly-eyed at someone until the tension could only be broken with a kiss.

Just lean in, he told himself, because even though he couldn't actually *remember* ever making the first move on a girl like this, he'd obviously done so in the past. Which meant he had it in him. Somewhere. *Stop being such a coward and freaking LEAN IN.*

He was still mustering up his courage when the moment passed. She stepped back. "So . . . what was in that letter, anyway?"

He had it memorized. He could recite it to her right now, tell her that she was amazing, that even if his brain didn't remember loving her, his soul was permanently molded to fit hers, like some kind of Isabelle-shaped cookie cutter had stamped his heart. But writing something down was different from saying it out loud—in public, no less.

He shrugged. "I don't really remember. Just apologizing for yelling at you that time. And that other time. I guess."

"Oh."

Did she look disappointed? Relieved? Irritated? Simon searched her face for clues, but it was impervious.

"Well . . . apology accepted. And stop staring at me like I have a bug on my nose."

"Sorry. Again."

"And . . . I guess . . . *I'm* sorry I returned it without reading it."

Simon couldn't remember whether she'd ever apologized to him before. She didn't seem the type to apologize to anyone.

"If you wrote me another one sometime, I might even read it," she said, with studied indifference.

"School's over for the semester, remember? This weekend I go back to Brooklyn." It seemed unimaginable.

"They don't have mailboxes in Brooklyn?"

"I guess I could send you a postcard of the Brooklyn Bridge," Simon allowed—then took a deep breath, and went for it. "Or I could hand deliver one. To the Institute, I mean. If you wanted me to. Sometime. Or something."

"Sometime. Something . . ." Isabelle mulled it over, letting him twist in the wind for a few endless, agonizing seconds. Then her smile widened so far that Simon thought he might actually self-combust. "I guess it's a date."

Pale Kings and Princes

By Cassandra Clare and Robin Wasserman

This morning Mayhew ceded the classroom to a girl a
few years older than Simon. Her white-blond hair fell
in ringlets around her shoulders, her blue-green eyes
sparkled, and her mouth was set in a grim line that
suggested she'd rather be anywhere else. Professor Mayhew
stood beside her, but Simon noticed the way he kept his
distance and was careful not to turn his back on her.
Mayhew was afraid.

—Pale Kings and Princes

What I Did on My Summer Vacation
By Simon Lewis

This summer, I lived in Brooklyn. Every morning I ran
through the park. One morning, I met a nixie who lived in
the dog pond. She had—

Simon Lewis paused to consult his Chthonian/English dictionary for the word for "blond"—there was no entry. Apparently words relating to hair color were a nonissue for creatures of the demon dimensions. Much like, he'd discovered, words relating to family, friendship, or watching TV. He chewed his eraser, sighed, then bent over the page again. Five hundred words on how he spent his summer were due to his

Chthonian teacher by morning, and after an hour of work he had written approximately . . . thirty.

She had hair. And—
—an enormous rack.

"Just trying to help," Simon's roommate, George Lovelace, said, reaching over Simon's shoulder to scrawl in an ending to the sentence.

"And failing miserably," Simon said, but he couldn't suppress a grin.

He'd missed George this summer, more than he had expected to. He'd missed all of it more than he'd expected—not just his new friends, but Shadowhunter Academy itself, the predictable rhythms of the day, all the things he'd spent months complaining about. The slime, the dank, the morning calisthenics, the chittering of creatures trapped in the walls . . . he'd even missed the soup. Simon had spent most of his first year at the Academy worrying that he was out of place—that, any minute, someone important would realize they'd made a terrible mistake and send him back home.

It wasn't until he was back in Brooklyn, trying to sleep beneath Batman sheets with his mother snoring in the next room, that he realized home wasn't home anymore.

Home, unexpectedly, inexplicably, was Shadowhunter Academy.

Park Slope wasn't quite the same as he remembered, not with the werewolf cubs frolicking in the Prospect Park dog run, the warlock selling artisanal cheese and love potions at the Grand Army farmers' market, the vampires lounging on the banks of the Gowanus, flicking cigarette butts at strolling hipsters. Simon had to keep reminding himself that they'd been there all along—Park Slope hadn't changed; Simon had. Simon was the one who now had the Sight. Simon was the one who flinched at flickering shadows and, when Eric had the misfortune of sneaking up behind him, instinctively yanked his old friend off his feet and slammed him to the ground with an effortless judo flip.

"Dude," Eric gasped, goggling up at him from the parched August grass, "stand down, soldier."

Eric, of course, thought he'd spent the year at military school—as did the rest of the guys, as did Simon's mother and sister. Lying to almost everyone he loved: That was another thing different about his Brooklyn life now, and maybe the thing that made him most eager for escape. It was one thing to lie about where he'd been all year, to make up half-assed stories about demerits and drill sergeants, most of them cribbed from bad eighties movies. It was another thing altogether to lie about who he was. He had to pretend to be the guy they remembered, the Simon Lewis who thought demons and warlocks were confined to the pages of comic books, the one whose closest brush with death involved aspirating a chocolate-covered almond. But he wasn't that Simon anymore, not even close. Maybe he wasn't a Shadowhunter, not yet—but he wasn't exactly a mundane anymore either, and he was tired of pretending to be.

The only person he didn't have to pretend with was Clary, and as the weeks passed, he'd spent more and more time with her, exploring the city and listening to stories of the boy he used to be. Simon still couldn't quite remember what they'd been to each other in that other life, the one he'd been magicked into forgetting—but the past seemed to matter less and less.

"You know, I'm not the person I used to be either," Clary had said to him one day, as they nursed their fourth coffee at Java Jones. Simon was doing his best to turn his blood into caffeine, in preparation for September. The Academy was a coffee-free zone. "Sometimes, that old Clary feels just as far away from me as the old Simon must from you."

"Do you miss her?" Simon asked, but he meant: *Do you miss* him? The old Simon. The other Simon. The better, braver Simon, who he was always worried he no longer had it in himself to be.

Clary had shaken her head, fiery red curls bouncing at her shoulders, green eyes glinting with certainty. "And I don't miss you anymore, either," she'd said, with that uncanny knack to know what was going on in his head. "Because I have you back. At least, I hope . . ."

He'd squeezed her hand. It was answer enough for both of them.

"Speaking of what you did on your summer vacation," George said now, flopping back on his sagging mattress, "are you ever going to tell me?"

"Tell you what?" Simon leaned back in his chair—then, at the ominous sound of cracking wood, abruptly leaned forward again. As second-years, Simon and George had been offered the opportunity to claim a room aboveground, but they'd both decided to stay in the dungeon. Simon had gotten rather attached to the gloomy damp—and he'd discovered there were certain advantages to being far from the prying eyes of the faculty. Not to mention the judgmental glares of the elite-track students. While the Shadowhunter kids in his

class had, for the most part, come around to the slim possibility that their mundane peers could have something to offer,
there was a whole new class now, and Simon didn't relish
teaching them the lesson all over again. Still, as his desk chair
decided whether or not to split in half and something furry
and gray scampered past his feet, he wondered if it was too
late to change his mind.

"Simon. Mate. Toss me a bone here. Do you know how I
spent *my* summer vacation?"

"Shearing sheep?" George had sent him a handful of post-
cards over the last two months. The front of each of them had
borne a photograph of the idyllic Scottish countryside. And on
the back, a series of messages circling a single theme:

Bored.
So bored.
Kill me now.
Too late, already dead.

"Shearing sheep," George confirmed. "Feeding sheep.
Herding sheep. Mucking about in sheep muck. While you
were . . . who-knows-what-ing with a certain raven-haired
superwarrior. You're not going to let me live vicariously?"

Simon sighed. George had restrained himself for four and
a half days. Simon supposed that was more than he could have
asked for.

"What makes you think I was doing anything with Isabelle
Lightwood?"

"Oh, I don't know, maybe because last I saw you, you
wouldn't shut up about her?" George affected an American

accent—poorly. "What should I do on my date with Isabelle? What should I say on my date with Isabelle? What should I wear on my date with Isabelle? Oh, George, you bronze Scottish love god, tell me what to do with Isabelle."

"I don't recall those words coming out of my mouth."

"I was paraphrasing your body language," George said. "Now spill."

Simon shrugged. "It didn't work out."

"Didn't work out?" George's eyebrows nearly rocketed off his forehead. *"Didn't work out?"*

"Didn't work out," Simon confirmed.

"You're telling me that your epic love story with the hottest Shadowhunter of her generation that spanned multiple dimensions and several incidences of saving the world is over with a shrug and a"—his voice flattened again to an American accent—"'didn't work out.'"

"Yeah. That's what I'm telling you." Simon tried to sound casual about it, but he must have failed, because George got up and gently slugged his roommate's shoulder.

"Sorry, mate," George said quietly.

Simon sighed again. "Yeah."

How I Spent My Summer Vacation
By Simon Lewis

I screwed up my chances with the most amazing girl in the world.

Not once, not twice, but three times.

She took me on a date to her favorite nightclub, where I stood around like an idiot clod all night and once literally tripped over my own two feet. Then I dropped her off at the Institute and shook her hand good night.

Yes, you read that right: Shook. Her. Hand.

Then I took her on date number two, to my favorite movie theater, where I made her sit through a <u>Star Wars: The Clone Wars</u> marathon and didn't notice when she fell asleep, then I accidentally insulted her taste because how was I supposed to know she once dated some warlock with a tail and not that I wanted to know that anyway and then: Zoom in on yet another good-night handshake.

Date number three, another of my genius ideas: double date with Clary and Jace. Which maybe would have been fine, except for how Clary and Jace are more in love than any people in love in the history of love, and how I'm pretty sure they were playing footsie under the table, because there was that one time when Jace started rubbing his foot against my leg by accident. (I think by accident?) (It better have been by accident.) And then we got attacked by demons, because Clary and Jace are apparently some kind of demon magnet, and I got knocked down in about thirty seconds and just kind of lay around in a corner while the rest of them saved the day and Isabelle did her amazing warrior goddess thing. Because she's an amazing warrior goddess—and I'm a weenie.

After that they all went off on some super-awesome cross-country road trip to chase down the demons that sent the other demons after us, and they wouldn't let me come. (See above re: my weenie-ness.) Then when they came back, Isabelle didn't call me, probably because what kind of warrior goddess wants to date a cowering-in-the-corner

weenie? And I didn't call her, for the same reason . . . and
also because I thought maybe she'd call me.
Which she didn't.
The End

Simon decided to ask his Chthonian teacher for an extension.

The second-year curriculum, it turned out, was much the same as the first—with one exception. This year, as the months ticked down toward Ascension day, the Shadowhunter Academy students were expected to learn current events. Although judging from what they'd learned so far, Simon thought, their current events class could just as easily be titled Why Faeries Suck.

Every day Shadowhunter and mundane second-years crowded into one of the classrooms that had been locked down the year before. (Something about a demonic beetle infestation.) Each squeezed into a rusty chair-desk combo that seemed designed for students half their size, and listened as Professor Freeman Mayhew explained the Cold Peace.

Freeman Mayhew was a scrawny, bald man with a graying Hitler mustache, and though he started most of his sentences with "Back when *I* was fighting demons . . ." it was difficult to imagine him fighting so much as a cold. Mayhew believed it was his responsibility to persuade his students that faeries were shrewd, untrustworthy, coldhearted, and—not that the "lily-livered politicians" running the Clave would admit it any time soon—worthy of extinction.

The students quickly realized that disagreeing—or even

interrupting to ask a question—drove up Mayhew's blood pressure, an angry red blotch blooming across his skull as he snapped, "Were you there? I don't *think* so!"

This morning Mayhew ceded the classroom to a girl a few years older than Simon. Her white-blond hair fell in ringlets around her shoulders, her blue-green eyes sparkled, and her mouth was set in a grim line that suggested she'd rather be anywhere else. Professor Mayhew stood beside her, but Simon noticed the way he kept his distance and was careful not to turn his back on her. Mayhew was afraid.

"Go on," the professor said gruffly. "Tell them your name."

The girl kept her eyes on the floor and mumbled something.

"Louder," Mayhew snapped.

Now the girl lifted her head and faced the class full on, and when she spoke, her voice was loud and clear. "Helen Blackthorn," she said. "Daughter of Andrew and Eleanor Blackthorn."

Simon gave her a closer look. Helen Blackthorn was a name he knew well from the stories Clary told him about the Dark War. The Blackthorns had all lost quite a bit in that fight, but he thought Helen and her brother Mark had lost most of all.

"Liar!" Mayhew shouted. "Try again."

"If I can lie, shouldn't that prove something to you?" she asked, but it was clear she already knew the answer.

"You know the conditions of your presence here," he snapped. "Tell them the truth or go home."

"That's not my home," Helen said quietly but firmly.

After the Dark War, she had been exiled—not that anyone officially used that term—to Wrangel Island, an Arctic outpost that was the hub of the world's protective wards. It was also, Simon had heard, a desolate frozen wasteland. *Officially*, Helen and her girlfriend, Aline Penhallow, were studying the wards, which had to be rebuilt after the Dark War. Unofficially, Helen was being punished for the accident of her birth. The Clave had decided that despite her bravery in the Dark War, despite her impeccable history, despite the fact that her younger siblings were orphans and had no one to care for them but an uncle they barely knew, she couldn't be trusted in their midst. The Clave thought that even though her skin could bear the angelic runes, she wasn't a real Shadowhunter.

Simon thought they were all idiots.

It didn't matter that she had no weapons, was clad in a pale yellow shirt and jeans, and had no visible runes. It was clear, simply from her posture and the control she exerted over herself, transforming rage into dignity, that Helen Blackthorn *was* a Shadowhunter. A warrior.

"Last chance," Mayhew grumbled.

"Helen Blackthorn," the girl said again, and tucked her hair back, revealing delicate pale ears, each of which tapered to an elfin point. "Daughter of Andrew Blackthorn the Shadowhunter and the Lady Nerissa. Of the Seelie Court."

At that Julie Beauvale stood up and, without a word, walked out of the classroom.

Simon felt for her, or tried to. During the final hours of the Dark War, a faerie had murdered Julie's sister right in front of her. But that wasn't Helen's fault. Helen was only half-faerie, and it wasn't the half that counted.

Not that anyone in the Clave—or the classroom—seemed to believe it. The students buzzed, faerie slurs bouncing between them. At the front of the classroom, Helen stood very still, hands clasped behind her back.

"Oh, shut up," Mayhew said loudly. Simon wondered, not for the first time, why the man had become a teacher when it seemed the only thing he loathed more than young people was the obligation to teach them. "I don't expect any of you to respect this . . . *person*. But she's here to offer you a cautionary tale. You will listen."

Helen cleared her throat. "My father and his brother were once students here, just like you." She spoke softly, with flat affect, as if she were talking about strangers. "And perhaps like you, they didn't realize how dangerous the Fair Folk could be. Which almost destroyed them."

It was my father, Andrew's, second year at the Academy—Helen continued—and Arthur's first. Normally, only second-years would be sent on a mission to the land of the fey, but everyone knew Arthur and Andrew fought best side by side. This was long before the Cold Peace, obviously, when the fey were bound by the Accords. But it didn't stop them from breaking the rules where they thought they could get away with it. A Shadowhunter child had been taken. Ten students from the Academy, accompanied by one of their teachers, were sent to get her back.

The mission was a success—or would have been, if a clever faerie hadn't snared my father's hand in a berry thornbush. Without thinking, he sucked the blood from a small wound—and, with it, took in a bit of the juice.

Drinking something in Faerie bound him to the Queen's whim, and the Queen bade him stay. Arthur insisted on staying with him—that's how much the brothers cared for each other.

The Academy teacher quickly made a bargain with the Queen: Their imprisonment would last only one day.

The Academy teachers have, of course, always been rather clever. But the fey were more so. What passed as one day in the world lasted much longer in Faerie.

It lasted for years.

My father and my uncle had always been quiet, bookish boys. They served bravely on the battlefield, but they preferred the library. They weren't prepared for what happened to them next.

What happened to them next was they encountered the Lady Nerissa, of the Seelie Court, the faerie who would become my mother, a faerie whose beauty was surpassed only by her cruelty.

My father never spoke to me of what happened to him at Nerissa's hands, nor did my uncle. But upon their return, they both made full reports to the Inquisitor. I've been . . . *invited* to read these reports in full and relay the details to you.

The details are these: For seven long years Nerissa made of my father her plaything. She bound him to her, not with chains but with dark faerie magic. As her servants held him down, she latched a silver choker around his neck. It was enchanted. It made my father see her not as she was, a monster, but as a miracle. It deceived his eyes and his heart, and turned his hatred of his captor into love. Or, rather, the curdled faerie version of love. A claustrophobic worship. He would do anything for her. He did, over those seven years, do everything for her.

And then there was Arthur, his brother, younger than Andrew and young for his age. Kind, they say. Soft.

Lady Nerissa had no use for Arthur, except as a toy, a tool, something with which to torture my father and affirm his loyalty.

Nerissa forced my father to live all those years in love; she forced Arthur to live in pain.

Arthur was burned alive, many times over, as a faerie fire ate away his flesh and bone but would not kill.

Arthur was whipped, a chain of thorns slashing wounds in his back that would never heal.

Arthur was chained to the ground, cuffs binding his wrists and ankles as if he were a wild beast, and forced to watch his worst nightmares play out before his eyes, faerie glamours impersonating the people he loved most dying excruciating deaths before his eyes.

Arthur was left to believe his brother had abandoned him, had chosen faerie love over flesh and blood, and that was the worst torture of all.

Arthur was broken. It took only a year. The faeries spent the next six stomping and giggling over the rubble of his soul.

And yet.

Arthur was a Shadowhunter, and these should never be underestimated. One day, half-mad with pain and sorrow, he had a vision of his future, of thousands of days of agony, decades, centuries passing in Faerie as he aged into a wizened, broken creature, finally returned to his world to discover that only one day had passed. That everyone he knew was young and whole. That they would pray for his death, so they wouldn't have to live with what had become of him. Faerie was a land beyond time; they could steal his entire life here—they could give him *ten* lifetimes of torture and pain—and still stay true to their word.

The terror of this fate was more powerful than pain, and it gave him the strength he needed to break free of his bonds. He was forced to fight against his own brother, who'd been enchanted into believing he should protect Lady Nerissa at all costs. Arthur knocked my father to the ground and used Lady Nerissa's own dagger to slice her open from neck to sternum. With that same dagger, he cut the enchanted silver from my father's throat. And together, both of them finally free, they escaped Faerie and returned to the world. Both of them still bearing their scars.

After they made their report to the Inquisitor, they left Idris, and left each other. These brothers, once as close as *parabatai*, couldn't stand each other's sight. Each was a reminder of what the other had endured and lost. Neither could forgive the other for where they had failed, and where they had succeeded.

Perhaps they would have reconciled, eventually.

But Arthur went to London, while my father returned home to Los Angeles, where he quickly fell in love with one of the Shadowhunters training at the L.A. Institute. She loved him too and helped him forget those nightmare years. They married. They were happy—and then, one day, their doorbell rang. My mother would have been painting, or developing photographs in her darkroom. My father would have been buried in his books. One of them would have answered the door and discovered two baskets on their doorstep, each of them bearing a sleeping toddler. My brother Mark and me. My father, in his bewitched state, never realized the Lady Nerissa had borne two children.

My father and his wife, Eleanor, raised us like we were full-blooded Shadowhunters. Like we were their own. Like we weren't half-blooded monsters who'd been slipped into their midst by their enemy. Like we weren't constant reminders of destruction and torture, of the long nightmare my father had labored so long to forget. They did their best to love us. Maybe they even *did* love us, as much as anyone could. But I'm assured that Andrew and Eleanor Blackthorn were the best of Shadowhunters. So they would have been smart enough to know, deep down, that we could never truly be trusted.

Trust a faerie at your own risk, because they care for nothing but themselves. They sow nothing but destruction. And their preferred weapon is human love.

This is the lesson I've been asked to teach you. And so I have.

"What the hell was *that*?" Simon exploded as soon as they were dismissed from class.

"I know!" George sagged against the corridor's stone wall—then quickly reconsidered as something green and sluggish wriggled out from behind his shoulder. "I mean, I knew faeries were little bastards, but who knew they were *evil*?"

"I did," Julie said, her face paler than usual. She'd been waiting for them outside the classroom—or, rather, waiting for Jon Cartwright, with whom she now seemed to be somewhat of an item. Julie was even prettier than Jon and almost as big a snob, but still, Simon had thought she had slightly better taste.

Jon put his arm around her, and she curled herself against his muscled torso.

They make it look so easy, Simon thought in wonder. But then, that was the thing about Shadowhunters—they made everything look so easy.

It was slightly disgusting.

"I can't believe they tortured that poor guy for *seven* years," George said.

"And how about his brother!" Beatriz Mendoza exclaimed. "That's even worse."

George looked incredulous. "You think being forced to fall in love with a sexy faerie princess is *worse* than getting burned alive a couple hundred times?"

"I think—"

Simon cleared his throat. "Uh, I actually meant, what the hell was that with Helen Blackthorn, trotting her in here like some kind of circus freak, making her tell us that horrible story about her own mother?" As soon as Helen finished her story, Professor Mayhew had pretty much ordered her out of the room. She'd looked like she wanted to decapitate him—but instead, she'd lowered her head and obeyed. He'd never seen a Shadowhunter behave like that, like she was . . . tamed. It felt sickeningly wrong.

"'Mother' is a bit of a technicality in this situation, don't you think?" George asked.

"You think that means this was *fun* for her?" Simon said, incredulous.

"I think a lot of things aren't fun," Julie said coldly. "I think watching your sister get sliced in half isn't so fun, either. So you'll excuse me if I don't care much about this halfling thing or her so-called feelings." Her voice shook on the last word, and very abruptly she slid out from under Jon's arm and raced off down the hallway.

Jon glared at Simon. "Nice, Lewis. Really nice." He took off after Julie, leaving Simon, Beatriz, and George to stand around awkwardly in their hushed wake.

After a tense moment George scratched his stubbled chin. "Mayhew *was* pretty harsh back there. Acting like she was some kind of criminal. You could tell he was just waiting for her to stab him with a piece of chalk or something."

"She's fey," Beatriz pointed out. "You can't just let your guard down with them."

"Half-fey," Simon said.

"But don't you think that's enough? The Clave must have

thought so," Beatriz said. "Why else send her into exile?"

Simon snorted. "Yeah, because the Clave is always right."

"Her brother rides with the Wild Hunt," Beatriz argued. "How much more faerie can you get?"

"That's not his fault," Simon protested. Clary had told him the whole story of Mark Blackthorn's capture—the way the faeries had snatched up him during the massacre at the Los Angeles Institute. The way the Clave refused to bother trying to get him back. "He's there against his will."

Beatriz was starting to look somewhat cross. "You don't know that. No one can know that."

"Where is this even coming from?" Simon asked. "You've never bought into any of that anti-Downworlder crap." Simon might not have remembered his vampire days very well, but he made it his business not to befriend anyone inclined to stake first, ask questions later.

"I'm *not* anti-Downworlder," Beatriz insisted, full of self-righteousness. "I don't have any problem with werewolves or vampires. Or warlocks, obviously. But the fey are different. Whatever the Clave is doing with them, or to them, it's for *our* benefit. It's to protect us. Don't you think it's possible they know a little more about it than you do?"

Simon rolled his eyes. "Spoken like a true Shadowhunter."

Beatriz gave him an odd look. "Simon—do you realize that you almost always say 'Shadowhunter' like it's an insult?"

That stopped him. Beatriz rarely spoke to anyone sharply like that, especially not him. "I . . ."

"If you think it's so terrible, being a Shadowhunter, I don't know what you're doing here." She took off down the corridor toward her room—which was, like the rest of the second-year elite rooms, high up in one of the turrets with a nice southern exposure and a meadow view.

George and Simon turned the other way, toward the dungeons.

"Not making many friends today," George said cheerfully, softly slugging his roommate. It was George-speak for *don't worry, it'll blow over*.

They clomped down the corridor side by side. A summer cleaning had done nothing to address the dripping ceilings or puddles of suspicious-smelling slime that cluttered the path to the dungeons—or maybe the Academy's janitorial ministrations just didn't extend to dregs' quarters. Either way, by this point Simon and George could have made it down the hallway blindfolded; they sidestepped puddles and ducked spurting pipes by habit.

"I didn't mean to upset anyone," Simon said. "I just don't think it's right."

"Trust me, mate, you made that perfectly clear. And obviously I agree with you."

"You do?" Simon felt a rush of relief.

"Of course I do," George said. "You don't fence off a whole herd just because one sheep's nibbling at the wrong grass, right?"

"Er . . . right."

"I just don't know why you're getting so worked up about it." George wasn't the type to get worked up about much of anything, or at least, not the type to admit it. He claimed apathy was a family credo. "Is it the vampire thing? You know no one thinks about you that way."

"No, it's not that," Simon said. He knew that these days,

his friends barely gave a thought to his vampire past—they considered it irrelevant. Sometimes Simon wasn't so sure. He'd been *dead* . . . how could that be irrelevant?

But that had nothing to do with this.

This simply wasn't right, the way Professor Mayhew ordered Helen around like a trained dog, or the way the others talked about the Fair Folk—as if, because *some* faeries had betrayed the Shadowhunters, *all* Faeries were guilty, now and forevermore.

Maybe that was it: the question of guilt handed down through bloodlines, the sins of the fathers visited on not just their sons but their friends, neighbors, and random acquaintances who happened to have similarly shaped ears. You couldn't just indict an entire people—or in this case, Downworlder species—because you didn't like how a few of them behaved. He'd spent enough time in Hebrew school to know how that kind of thing ended. Fortunately, before he could formulate an explanation for George that didn't name-check Hitler, Professor Catarina Loss materialized before them.

Materialized, literally, in a rather theatrical puff of smoke. Warlock prerogative, Simon supposed, although showing off wasn't Catarina's style. Usually she blended in with the rest of the Academy faculty, making it easy to forget she was a warlock (at least, if you overlooked the blue skin). But he'd noticed that whenever another Downworlder was on campus, Catarina went out of her way to play up her warlockiness.

Not that Helen was a Downworlder, Simon reminded himself.

On the other hand, Simon wasn't a Downworlder either— or hadn't been for more than a year now—and Catarina still insisted on calling him Daylighter. According to her, once a Downworlder, always, in some tiny, subconscious, embedded-in-the-soul part, a Downworlder. She always sounded so certain of this, as if she knew something he didn't. After talking to her, Simon often found himself tonguing his canine teeth, just to make sure he hadn't sprouted fangs.

"Might I speak with you for a moment, Daylighter?" she said. "Privately?"

George, who'd been a bit nervous around Catarina ever since she had, very briefly, turned him into a sheep, had clearly been waiting for an excuse to run away. He took it.

Simon found himself surprisingly glad to be alone with Catarina; *she*, at least, was certain to be on his side. "Professor Loss, you won't believe what just happened in class with Professor Mayhew—"

"How was your summer, Daylighter?" She gave him a thin smile. "Pleasant, I trust? Not too much sun?"

In all the time he'd known Catarina Loss, she'd never bothered with small talk. It seemed an odd time to start. "You did know Helen Blackthorn was here, right?" Simon said.

She nodded. "I know most everything that goes on around here. I thought you'd figured that out."

"Then I'm guessing you know how Professor Mayhew was treating her."

"Like something less than human, I would imagine?"

"Exactly!" Simon exclaimed. "Like something scraped off the bottom of his shoe."

"In my experience, that's how Professor Mayhew treats most people."

Simon shook his head. "If you'd seen it . . . this was worse.

Maybe I should tell Dean Penhallow?" The idea seized him only as it was coming out of his mouth, but he liked the sound of it. "She can, I don't know . . ." It wasn't like she could give him a detention. "*Something.*"

Catarina pursed her lips. "You must do what you think is right, Daylighter. But I can tell you that Dean Penhallow has little authority on the subject of Helen Blackthorn's treatment here."

"But she's the dean. She should—oh." Slowly but surely, the pieces slotted into place. Dean Penhallow was cousin to *Aline* Penhallow. Helen's girlfriend. Aline's mother, Jia, the Consul, was supposedly biased on the subject of Helen, and had recused herself from determining her treatment. If even the Consul couldn't intercede on Helen's behalf, then presumably the dean had even less hope of doing so. It seemed hideously unfair to Simon, that the people who cared most for Helen were the ones least involved in deciding her fate. "Why would Helen even come here?" Simon wondered. "I know Wrangel Island must suck, but could it be any worse than getting paraded around here, where everyone seems to hate her?"

"You can ask her yourself," Catarina said. "That's why I wanted to speak with you. Helen asked me to send you over to her cabin after your classes end today. She has something for you."

"She does? What?"

"You'll have to ask that for yourself too. You'll find her lodgings at the edge of the western quad."

"She's staying on campus?" Simon said, surprised. He couldn't understand why Helen would come here in the first place, but it was even harder to imagine her wanting to stay. "She must have friends in Alicante she could stay with."

"I'm sure she does, even now," Catarina said, something kind and sad in her voice, as if she were, very, very gently, letting down a child. "But, Simon, you're presuming she had a choice."

Simon hesitated at the door of the cabin, willing himself to knock. It was his least favorite thing, meeting someone he'd known in his before life, as he'd come to think of it. There was always the fear they would expect something of him he couldn't deliver, or assume he knew something he'd forgotten. There was, too often, a gleam of hope in their eyes that was extinguished as soon as he opened his mouth.

At least, he told himself, he'd barely known Helen. She couldn't be expecting much from him. Unless there was something he didn't know.

And there must be *something* he didn't know. . . . Why else would she have summoned him?

Only one way to find out, Simon thought, and knocked at the door.

Helen had changed into a bright polka-dotted sundress and looked much younger than she had in the classroom. Also much happier. Her smile widened substantially when she saw who was at the door.

"Simon! I'm so glad. Come on in, sit down, would you like something to eat or drink? Maybe a cup of coffee?"

Simon settled himself on the small living room's only couch. It was uncomfortable and threadbare, embroidered with a faded flower pattern that looked like something his grandmother might have owned. He wondered who usually lived here, or whether the Academy simply maintained the ramshackle cabin for visiting faculty. Though he couldn't imagine there were many visiting faculty members who wanted to live in a broken-down hut on the edge of the woods that looked like somewhere Hansel and Gretel's witch might have lived before she discovered candy-based architecture.

"No, thanks, I'm fine—" Simon stopped as her last word registered with him. "Did you say *coffee*?"

Half a week into the new school year, Simon was already in serious caffeine withdrawal. Before he could tell her *yes, please, a bucketful*, Helen had already placed a steaming mug in his hands. "I thought so," she said.

Simon swallowed greedily, caffeine buzzing through his system. He didn't know how anyone was supposed to be human—much less, in the Shadowhunter case, superhuman—without a daily dose. "Where did you get this?"

"Magnus magicked me up a nonelectric coffeemaker," Helen said, grinning. "Kind of a parting gift before we left for Wrangel Island. Now I can't live without it. "

"How is it there?" Simon asked. "On the island?"

Helen hesitated, and he wondered if he'd made a mistake. Was it rude to ask someone how they were enjoying their exile in a Siberian-like wilderness?

"Cold," she said finally. "Lonely."

"Oh." What could he say to that? "Sorry" didn't quite seem to cover it, and she didn't look like she wanted his pity.

"But we're together, at least. Aline and I. That's something. That's everything, I suppose. I still can't believe she agreed to marry me."

"You're getting married?" Simon exclaimed. "That's amazing!"

"It is, isn't it?" Helen smiled. "It's hard to believe how much light you can find in the darkness, when you have someone who loves you."

"Did she come with you?" Simon asked, looking around the small cabin. There was only one other room, the bedroom, he assumed, its door closed. He couldn't remember meeting Aline, but from everything Clary had told him, he was curious.

"No," Helen said sharply. "That wasn't part of the deal."

"What deal?"

Instead of answering, she abruptly changed the subject. "So, did you enjoy my lecture this morning?"

Now it was Simon who hesitated, unsure how to answer. He didn't want to suggest he'd found her lecture dull—but it seemed equally wrong to suggest he'd enjoyed hearing her terrible story or seeing Professor Mayhew humiliate her. "I was surprised you'd want to give the lecture," he said finally. "It can't be easy, telling that story."

Helen gave him a wry smile. "'Want' is a strong word." She got up to pour him another cup of coffee, then began bustling with a stack of dishes in the tiny kitchenette. Simon got the feeling she was just trying to keep her hands busy. And maybe avoid meeting his eye. "I made a deal with them. The Clave." She ran her hands nervously through her blond hair, and Simon caught a brief glimpse of her pointed ears. "They said if I came to the Academy for a couple days, let them parade me around like some kind of half-faerie show pony, then Aline and I could come back."

"For good?"

She laughed bitterly. "For one day and one night, to be married."

Simon thought, suddenly, of what Beatriz had asked him

earlier that day. Why he was trying so hard to become a Shadow-hunter.

Sometimes he couldn't quite remember.

"They didn't even want to let us come back at all," Helen said bitterly. "They wanted us to have the wedding on Wrangel Island. If you can even call that a wedding, in a frozen hellhole without anyone you love there with you. I guess I should feel lucky I got this much out of them."

Less lucky than disgusted, or maybe enraged, Simon thought, but it didn't seem like it would be helpful to say so out loud. "I'm surprised they care so much about one lecture," he said instead. "I mean, not that it wasn't educational, but Professor Mayhew could have just told us the story himself."

Helen turned away from her kitchen busywork and met Simon's gaze. "They don't care about the lecture. This isn't about your education. It's about humiliating me. That's all." She gave herself a little shake, then smiled too brightly, her eyes shining. "Forget about all that. You came here to get something from me—here it is." Helen slipped an envelope from her pocket and handed it to Simon.

Curious, he tore it open and pulled out a small piece of thick ivory stationery, inscribed with a familiar hand.

Simon stopped breathing.

Dear Simon, Izzy wrote.

I know I've developed a habit of ambushing you at school.

This was true. Isabelle had popped up more than once when he'd least expected her. Every time she showed up on campus, they fought; every time, he was sorry to see her go.

I promised myself I'm not going to do that anymore. But there's something I'd like to talk to you about. So this is me, giving you advance warning. If it's okay for me to come for a visit, you can let Helen know, and she'll get word to me. If it's not okay, you can tell her that, too. Whatever.—Isabelle

Simon read the brief note several times, trying to intuit the tone behind the words. Affectionate? Eager? Businesslike?

Until this week he'd been only an e-mail or a phone call away—why wait until he was back at the Academy to reach out? Why reach out at all?

Maybe because it would be easier to reject him for good when he was safely on another continent?

But in that case, why Portal all the way to Idris to do it face-to-face?

"Maybe you need some time to think about it?" Helen said finally.

He'd forgotten she was there. "No!" Simon blurted out. "I mean, no, I don't need time to think about it, but yes, yes, she can come visit. Of course. Please, tell her."

Stop babbling, he ordered himself. Bad enough he turned into a driveling fool every time Isabelle was in the room with him these days—was he now going to start doing so at the sound of her name?

Helen laughed. "See, I told you so," she said loudly.

"Er, you told me what?" Simon asked.

"You heard him, come out!" Helen called, even louder, and the bedroom door creaked open.

Isabelle Lightwood didn't have it in her to look sheepish. But her face was doing its best. "Surprise?"

When Simon had regained his power of speech, there was only one word available in his brain. "Isabelle."

Whatever crackled and sizzled between them was apparently so palpable that Helen could sense it too, because she swiftly slid past Isabelle into the bedroom and shut the door.

Leaving the two of them alone.

"Hi, Simon."

"Hi, Izzy."

"You're, uh, probably wondering what I'm doing here." It wasn't like her to sound so uncertain.

Simon nodded.

"You never called me," she said. "I saved you from getting decapitated by an Eidolon demon, and you didn't even *call*."

"You never called me, either," Simon pointed out. "And . . . uh . . . also, I kind of felt like I should have been able to save myself."

Isabelle sighed. "I thought you might be thinking that."

"Because I *should* have, Izzy."

"Because you're an *idiot*, Simon." She brightened. "But this is your lucky day, because I've decided I'm not giving up yet. This is too important to give up just because of a bad date."

"Three bad dates," he pointed out. "Like, *really* bad dates."

"The worst," she agreed.

"The *worst*? Jace told me you once went out with a merman who made you have dinner in the river," Simon said. "Surely our dates weren't as bad as—"

"The *worst*," she confirmed, and broke into laughter. Simon thought his heart would burst at the sound of it—there was something so carefree, so joyous in the music of her laugh, it was almost like a promise. That if they could navigate a path through all the awkwardness and pain and burden of expectations, if they could find their way back to each other, something that pure and joyful awaited them.

"I don't want to give up either," Simon said, and the smile she rewarded him with was even better than the laughter.

Isabelle settled beside him on the small couch. Simon was suddenly extremely conscious of the inches separating their thighs. Was he supposed to make a move *right now*?

"I decided New York was too crowded," she said.

"With demons?"

"With memories," Isabelle clarified.

"Too many memories is not exactly my problem."

Isabelle elbowed him. Even that made a spark. "You know what I mean."

He elbowed her back.

To touch her like that, so casually, like it was no big deal . . .

To have her back, so close, so willing . . .

She wanted him.

He wanted her.

It should have been that easy.

Simon cleared his throat and, without knowing why, rose to his feet. Then, like that wasn't enough distance, retreated safely to the other side of the room. "So what do we do now?" he asked.

She looked thrown, but only for a moment. Then she barreled ahead. "We're going on another date," she said. Not a request; a command. "In Alicante. Neutral territory."

"When?"

"I was thinking . . . now."

It wasn't what he expected—but then, why not? Classes were over for the day, and second-year students were allowed off campus. There was no reason *not* to go out with Isabelle immediately. Except that he'd had no time to prepare, no time to come up with a game plan, no time to obsess over his hair and his "casually rumpled" look, no time to brainstorm a list of discussion topics in case conversation flagged . . . but then, none of those things had saved their previous three dates from disaster. Maybe it was time to experiment with spontaneity.

Especially since it didn't seem like Isabelle was giving him much of a choice.

"Now it is," Simon agreed. "Should we invite Helen?"

"On our *date?*"

Idiot. He gave himself a mental slap upside the head.

"Helen, you want to crash our romantic date?" Isabelle called.

Helen emerged from the bedroom. "Nothing I would love more than being an awkward third wheel," she said. "But I'm not actually allowed to leave."

"Excuse me?" Isabelle's fingers played at the electrum whip wrapped around her left wrist. Simon couldn't blame her for wanting to strike something. Or someone. "Please tell me you're kidding."

"Catarina laid a circle of protection around the cabin," Helen said. "It won't stop you from coming and going, but I'm told it will be rather effective if I try to leave before I'm summoned."

"Catarina wouldn't do that!" Simon protested, but Helen put out a hand to quiet him.

"They didn't give her much of a choice," Helen said, "and I asked her to just go along. It was part of the deal."

"That is *unacceptable*," Isabelle said with barely concealed fury. "Forget the date, we're staying here with you."

She was lit up with a beautiful glow of righteous rage, and

Simon wanted suddenly, desperately, to sweep her in his arms and kiss her until the end of the world.

"You will most certainly *not* forget the date," Helen said. "You're not staying here a single second longer. No argument."

There was, in fact, plenty more argument, but Helen finally convinced them that being stuck there with them, knowing she'd ruined their day, would be even worse than being stuck there alone. "Now please, and I say this with love, get the hell out."

She gave Izzy a hug, and then embraced Simon in turn. "Don't screw this up," she whispered in his ear, then pushed them both out the door and closed it behind them.

There were two white horses neighing by the front path, as if they were waiting for Isabelle. Simon supposed they were; animals in Idris behaved differently from how they did back home, almost as if they could understand what their humans wanted and, if you asked nicely enough, were willing to deliver.

"So, where exactly are we going on this date?" Simon asked. It hadn't occurred to him that they would ride into Alicante, but of course, this was Idris. No cars. No trains. Nothing but medieval or magical transportation, and he supposed a horse was better than a vampire motorcycle. Marginally.

Isabelle grinned and swung herself up onto the saddle as easily as if she were mounting a bike. Simon, on the other hand, clumsily heaved himself onto his horse with enough grunting and sweating that he was afraid she'd take one look and call the whole thing off.

"We're going shopping," Isabelle informed him. "It's time you get yourself a sword."

✳ ✳ ✳

"It doesn't actually have to be a sword," Isabelle said as they stepped into Diana's Arrow. The ride to Alicante had been like something out of a dream, or at least a cheesy romance novel. The two of them astride white stallions, galloping across the countryside, charging across emerald meadows and through a forest the color of flames. Isabelle's hair streamed behind her like a river of ink, and Simon had even managed not to fall off his horse—never a foregone conclusion. Best of all, between the rush of wind and the thunder of hoofbeats, it had been too loud for conversation. In motion, things felt easy between them—natural. Simon could almost forget that this was one of the most important moments of his life and anything he said or did could screw it up forever. Now, back at ground level, the weight settled back on his shoulders. It was hard to think of anything clever to say with his brain echoing the same four words over and over again.

Don't. Screw. This. Up.

"They have everything here," Izzy continued, presumably trying to fill the dull silence Simon's nerves left in their wake. "Daggers, axes, throwing stars—oh, and bows, of course. All kinds of bows. It's awesome."

"Yeah," Simon said weakly. "Awesome."

He had, in his year at the Academy, learned to fight almost as well as any beginning Shadowhunter, and had a proficiency with every weapon she'd named. But he'd discovered that knowing how to use a weapon was very different from *wanting* to. In his pre-Shadowhunter life, Simon had delivered many passionate rants on the subject of gun control, and would have loved nothing more than for every weapon in the city to be dumped into the East River. Not that a gun was the same as a sword, and not that he didn't love the feel of unleashing an arrow from his bow and watching it fly swiftly and surely into the heart of his target. But the way Isabelle loved her whip, the way Clary talked about her sword, like it was a member of the family . . . the Shadowhunter passion for deadly weapons still took some getting used to.

Diana's Arrow, a weapons shop on Flintlock Street at the heart of Alicante, was full of more deadly objects than Simon had ever seen in one place—and that included the Academy weapons room, which could have supplied an army. But while the Academy arsenal was more like a storage closet, swords and daggers and arrows piled in haphazard stacks and crowded onto dangerously rickety shelves, Diana's Arrow reminded Simon of a fancy jewelry store. The weapons were on proud display, shining blades fanned across velvet cases, the better to show off their metallic gleam.

"So, what kind of thing are you looking for?" The guy behind the counter had a spiky Mohawk and a faded Arcade Fire T-shirt and looked more suited to a comic-book counter than this one. Simon assumed this probably wasn't Diana.

"How about a bow?" Izzy said. "Something really spectacular. Fit for a champion."

"Maybe not *that* spectacular," Simon said quickly. "Maybe something a little more . . . unobtrusive."

"People often underestimate the importance of good battle style," Isabelle said. "You want to intimidate the enemy before you even make a move."

"You don't think my intimidating wardrobe will do the job there?" Simon gestured at his own T-shirt, which featured an anime cat spewing green puke.

Isabelle gave him what sounded like a pity laugh, then turned back to not-Diana. "What have you got in daggers?" she asked. "Anything gold plated?"

"I'm not really a gold-plated kind of guy," Simon said. "Or, uh, a dagger kind of guy."

"We have some nice swords," the guy said.

"You do look hot with a sword," Isabelle said. "As I recall."

"Maybe?" Simon tried to sound encouraging, but she must have heard the skepticism in his voice.

She turned on him. "It's like you don't even *want* a weapon."

"Well . . ."

"So what are we doing here?" Isabelle snapped.

"You suggested it?"

Isabelle looked like she wanted to stomp her foot—or stomp his face. "Excuse me for trying to help you behave like a respectable Shadowhunter. Forget it. We can go."

"No!" he said quickly. "That's not what I meant."

With Isabelle, it was never what he meant. Simon had always considered himself a man of words, as opposed to a man of deeds. Or of swords, for that matter. His mother liked to say he could talk her into almost anything. All he could do with Isabelle, it seemed, was talk himself out of a girlfriend.

"I'll, ah, just give the two of you some space to look around," the shopkeeper said, backing quickly away from the awkward. He disappeared into the back.

"I'm sorry," Simon said. "Let's stay, please. Of course I want your help picking something out."

She sighed. "No, I'm sorry. Choosing your first weapon is a really personal thing. I get it. Take your time, look around. I'll shut up."

"I don't want you to shut up," he said.

But she shook her head and zipped her lips shut. Then raised three fingers in the air—Scout's honor. Which didn't seem like a Shadowhunter thing, and Simon wondered who had taught her to do that.

He wondered if it had been him.

Sometimes he hated before-Simon and all the things he'd shared with Isabelle, things today-Simon could never understand. It was weird and headache inducing, competing with yourself.

They browsed the store, taking in the options: polearms, athames, seraph blades, elaborately carved crossbows, chakhrams, throwing knives, a full display case of golden whips, over which Isabelle nearly began to drool.

The silence was oppressive. Simon had never had a *good* date—at least not that he could recall—but he was pretty sure they tended to involve some talking.

"Poor Helen," he said, testing the heft and balance of a medieval-looking broadsword. At least this was one subject they were sure to agree on.

"I hate what they're doing to her," Isabelle said. She was stroking a deadly-looking silver *kindjal* as if it were a puppy. "How was it, in class? Was it as bad as I imagine?"

"Worse," Simon admitted. "The look on her face, when she was telling the story of her parents . . ."

Isabelle's grip tightened around the *kindjal*. "Why can't they see how hideous it is to treat her like this? She's *not a faerie*."

"Well, that's not really the point, is it?"

Isabelle laid the *kindjal* down carefully in its velvet case. "What do you mean?"

"Whether or not she's a faerie. It's beside the point."

She fixed Simon with a fiery gaze. "Helen Blackthorn is a *Shadowhunter*," she spit out. "Mark Blackthorn is a *Shadowhunter*. If we can't agree on that, we have a problem."

"Of course we agree on that." It made him love her all the more, seeing how angry she got on behalf of her friends. Why couldn't he just *say* that to her? Why was everything so hard? "They're as much Shadowhunters as you are. I just mean that even if they weren't, if we were talking about some actual faerie, it still wouldn't be right to treat her like she's the enemy, because of what she was, right?"

"Well . . ."

Simon was astonished. "What do you mean, 'well . . .'?"

"I mean that maybe any faerie *is* potentially an enemy, Simon. Look what they did to us. Look how much misery they caused."

"They didn't *all* cause that misery—but they're all paying for it."

Isabelle sighed. "Look, I don't like the Cold Peace any more than you do. And you're right, not all faeries are the enemy. Obviously. Not all of them betrayed us, and it's not fair that they should all be punished for that. You think I don't know that?"

"Good," Simon said.

"But—"

"I really don't see how there can be a 'but,'" Simon cut in.

"*But* it's not as simple as you're trying to make it. The Seelie Queen *did* betray us. A legion of faeries *did* join Sebastian in the Dark War. A lot of good Shadowhunters got killed. You've got to see why that would leave people angry. And afraid."

Stop talking, Simon told himself. His mother had once told him you should never discuss religion or politics on a date. He was never quite sure which one of those categories Clave policies fell into, but either way, this was like trying to defend J. J. Abrams to a hard-core Trekkie: hopeless.

But inexplicably, and despite the sincere wishes of his brain, Simon's mouth kept moving. "I don't care how angry or scared you get, it's not right to punish all the faeries for a few faeries' mistakes. Or to discriminate against people—"

"I'm not saying anyone should discriminate—"

"Actually, that's exactly what you're saying."

"Oh, great, Simon. So the Seelie Queen and her minions screw us over and enable the death of hundreds of Shadowhunters, not to mention the ones they slaughtered themselves, and *I'm* the terrible person?"

"I didn't say you were a terrible person."

"You're thinking it," she said.

"Would you stop telling me what I think?" he barked, more harshly than he'd intended.

Her mouth snapped shut.

She took a deep breath.

He counted to ten.

Each waited the other out.

When Isabelle spoke again, she sounded calmer—but also, somehow, angrier. "I told you, Simon. I don't like the Cold Peace. I hate it, for your information. Not just for what it's doing to Helen and Aline. Because it's wrong. But . . . it's not like I have a better idea. This isn't about who you or I want to trust; this is about who the *Clave* can trust. You can't sign accords with leaders who refuse to be bound by their promises. You simply can't.

If the Clave wanted revenge"—Isabelle looked pointedly around the store, gaze resting on each weapons display in turn—"trust me, they could take it. The Cold Peace isn't just about the Fair Folk. It's about us. I may not like it, but I understand it. Better than you do, at least. If you'd been there, if you knew—"

"I was there," Simon said quietly. "Remember?"

"Of course I do. But you *don't*. So it's not the same. You're not . . ."

"The same," he finished for her.

"That's not what I meant, I just—"

"Trust me, Izzy. I get it. I'm not him. I'll never be him."

Isabelle made a noise halfway between a hiss and a yowl. "Would you drop it already with this old Simon/new Simon inferiority complex? It's getting old. Why don't you get a little creative and find a new excuse?"

"New excuse for what?" he asked, genuinely confused.

"For you not to be with me!" she yelled. "Because you're obviously looking for one. Try harder."

She stomped out of the store, slamming the door shut behind her. It dinged as it closed and not-Diana emerged from the back. "Oh, it's still just you," he said, sounding distinctly disappointed. "Have you decided?"

Simon could give up right now; he could stop trying, stop fighting, just let her go. That would be the easiest of decisions. All he'd have to do would be to let it happen.

"I decided a long time ago," Simon said, and ran out of the shop.

He needed to find Isabelle.

It wasn't much of a challenge. She was sitting on a small bench across the street, head in her hands.

Simon sat down beside her. "I'm sorry," he said quietly.

She shook her head without lifting it from her hands. "I can't believe I was dumb enough to think this would work."

"It still can," he said with an embarrassing tinge of desperation. "I still want it to, if you—"

"No, not you and me, idiot." She finally looked up at him. Mercifully, her eyes were dry. In fact, she didn't look sad at all—she looked furious. "This stupid weapons-shopping idea. Last time I take dating advice from *Jace.*"

"You let *Jace* plan our date?" Simon said, incredulous.

"Well, it's not like either of us was doing a very good job of it. He took Clary here to buy a sword, and it was this whole disgustingly sexy thing, and I just thought, maybe . . ."

Simon laughed in relief. "I hate to break it to you, but you're not dating Jace."

"Um, yeah. Disgusting."

"No, I mean, you're not dating a guy who's anything *like* Jace."

"I wasn't aware I was dating anyone at all," she said, frost in her voice. His heart caught in his throat like it was snagged on barbed wire. But then, ever so slightly, she melted. "Kidding. Mostly."

"Relieved," he said. "Mostly."

Isabelle sighed. "I'm sorry this was such a disaster."

"It's not all your fault."

"Well, obviously it's not all my fault," she said. "Not even mostly my fault."

"Uh . . . I thought we'd moved into the apologies portion of the day."

"Right. Sorry."

He grinned. "See, now you're talking."

"So, what now? Back to the Academy?"

"Are you kidding?" Simon stood up and extended a hand to her. Miracle of miracles, she took it. "We're not giving up until we get this right. But we're not going to get there pretending to be Jace and Clary. That's our whole problem, isn't it? Trying to be people we're not? I can't be some kind of cool, hipster nightclub hopper."

"I don't think there's any such thing as a 'nightclub hopper,'" Isabelle said wryly.

"This proves my point. And you're never going to be some kind of gamer who wants to stay up all night debating Naruto plot points and battling D&D orcs."

"Now you're just making up words."

"And neither of us is ever going to be Jace and Clary—"

"Thank God," they said, in sync, then exchanged a grin.

"So what are you suggesting?" Izzy asked.

"Something new," Simon said, mind racing to come up with an actual concrete, useful idea. He knew he was onto something, he just wasn't sure what. "Not your world, not my world. A new world, for just the two of us."

"Please tell me you don't want us to Portal to some other dimension. Because that didn't work out so well the last time."

Simon grinned, an idea dawning. "Maybe we can find a spot slightly closer to home. . . ."

As the sun dipped beneath the horizon, the clouds overhead blushed cotton-candy pink. Their reflections gleamed on the crystalline waters of Lake Lyn. The horses whinnied, the birds chirped, and Simon and Isabelle crunched their peanut brittle and popcorn. This, Simon thought, was the sound of happiness.

"You still haven't told me how you found this place," Isabelle said. "It's perfect."

Simon didn't want to admit that it was Jon Cartwright who'd told him about the isolated inlet on the edge of Lake Lyn, its hanging willows and rainbow of wildflowers making it the perfect spot for a romantic picnic. (Even when the picnic consisted of peanut brittle, popcorn, and the handful of other random teeth-decaying, artery-clogging snacks they'd grabbed on their way out of Alicante.) Simon, who had long ago grown tired of hearing about Jon's romantic exploits, had done his best to tune the jerk out. But apparently a few details had lodged in his subconscious. Enough, at least, to find the place.

Jon Cartwright was a blowhard and a buffoon—Simon would maintain this to his dying day.

But it turned out the guy had good taste in romantic date spots.

"Just stumbled on it," Simon mumbled. "Good luck, I guess."

Isabelle gazed out at the impossibly smooth water. "This place reminds me of Luke's farm," she said softly.

"Me too," he said. In that other life, the one he barely remembered, he and Clary had spent many long, happy days at Luke's summer house upstate, splashing in the lake, lying in the grass, naming the clouds.

Isabelle turned to him. Simon's jacket was spread out between them as an improvised picnic blanket. It was a small jacket—not very much distance for him to cross, if he wanted to reach her.

He'd never wanted anything more.

"I think about it a lot," Izzy said. "The farm, the lake."

"Why?"

Her voice softened. "Because that was where I almost lost you—where I was sure I would lose you. But I got you back."

Simon didn't know what to say.

"It doesn't even matter," she said, harder now. "Not like you even know what I'm talking about."

"I know what happened there." Namely, Simon had summoned the Angel Raziel—and the Angel had actually shown up.

He wished he could remember it; he would like to know how that felt, talking to an angel.

"Clary told you," she said flatly.

"Yeah." Isabelle was a little sensitive on the subject of Clary. She definitely didn't need to hear about all the time he'd had with Clary this summer, the long hours spent lying in Central Park, side by side, swapping stories of their past—Simon telling her what he remembered; Clary telling him what actually happened.

"But she wasn't even there," Isabelle said.

"She knows the important stuff."

Isabelle shook her head. She reached across the picnic blanket and rested a hand on Simon's knee. He worked very hard to hear her over the sudden buzzing in his ears. "If she wasn't there, she can't know how brave you were," Isabelle said. "She can't know how scared I was for you. *That's* the important stuff."

There was silence between them, then. But finally, it wasn't the awkward kind. It was the good kind, the kind where Simon could hear what Isabelle was saying without her having to say it, and where he could answer her in kind.

"What's it like?" she asked him. "Not remembering. Being a blank slate."

Her hand was still warm on his knee.

She'd never asked him that before. "It's not quite a blank slate," he explained, or tried to. "It's more like . . . double vision. Like I'm remembering two different things at the same time. Sometimes one seems more real, sometimes the other does. Sometimes everything is blurry. That's when I usually take some Advil, and a nap."

"But you're starting to remember things."

"Some things," he allowed. "Jordan. I remember a lot about Jordan. Caring about him. Losing—" Simon swallowed hard. "Losing him. I remember my mom freaking out about me being a vampire. And some stuff before Clary's mom got kidnapped. The two of us being friends, before all of this started. Normal Brooklyn stuff." He stopped talking as he realized her face was clouding over.

"Of course you remember *Clary*."

"It's not like that," he said.

"Like what?"

Simon didn't think about it. He just did it.

He took her hand.

She let him.

He wasn't sure how to explain this—it was still all jumbled in his head—but he had to try. "It's not like the things I remember are more important than the things I can't remember. Sometimes it seems like it's random. But sometimes . . . I don't know, sometimes it feels like the most important things are going to be the hardest to get back. Picture all these memories buried, like dinosaur bones, and me trying to dig them up. Some of them are just lying right beneath the surface, but the important ones, those are miles down."

"And you're saying that's where I am? Miles beneath the surface?"

He held on to her tightly. "You're basically down there at the molten center of the earth."

"You are *so weird.*"

"I try my best."

She threaded her fingers through his. "I'm jealous, you know. Sometimes. That you can forget."

"Are you kidding?" Simon couldn't even begin to understand that one. "Everything you have, all the people in your life—no one would *want* that taken away."

Isabelle looked back out at the lake, blinking hard. "Sometimes people get taken away from you whether you want it or not. And sometimes that hurts so much, it might be easier to forget."

She didn't have to say his name. Simon said it for her. "Max."

"You remember him?"

Simon had never realized what a sad sound it was, hope.

He shook his head. "I wish I did, though."

"Clary told you about him," she said. Not a question. "And what happened to him."

He nodded, but her gaze was still fixed on the water.

"He died in Idris, you know. I like being here sometimes. I feel closer to him here. Other times I wish this place would evaporate. That no one could ever come here again."

"I'm sorry," Simon said, thinking they had to be the lamest, most useless words in the English language. "I wish I could say something that would help."

She faced him; she whispered, "You did."

"What?"

"After Max. You . . . said something. You helped."

"Izzy . . ."

"Yes?"

This was it, this was The Moment—the moment talking gave way to gazing, which would inevitably give way to kissing. All he had to do was lean slightly forward and give himself over to it.

He leaned back. "Maybe we should start heading back to campus."

She made that angry cat noise again, then lobbed a chunk of peanut brittle at him. "What is *wrong* with you?" she exclaimed. "Because I know there's nothing wrong with me. You would be insane not to want to kiss me, and if this is some stupid playing-hard-to-get thing, you're wasting your time, because trust me, I know when a guy wants to kiss me. And you, Simon Lewis, want to kiss me. So what is happening here?"

"I don't know," he admitted, and ridiculous as this was, it was also wholly true.

"Is it the stupid memory thing? Are you seriously still afraid that you can't live up to some amazing forgotten version of yourself? Do you want me to tell you all the ways you weren't amazing? For one, you snored."

"Did not."

"Like a Drevak demon."

"This is slander," Simon said, outraged.

She snorted. "My point, Simon, is that you're supposed to be past all of this. I thought you figured out that no one is expecting you to be anyone other than who you are. That I just need you to be you. I only want you. This Simon. Isn't that why we're here? Because you finally got that through your thick head?"

"I guess."

"So what are you afraid of? It's obviously something."

"How do you know?" he asked, curious how she could be so certain, when he still had no clue himself.

She smiled, and it was the kind of smile you give to someone who can make you want to throttle them and kiss them all at the same time. "Because I know *you.*"

He thought about gathering her up in his arms, about how it would feel—and that's when he realized what he was afraid of.

It was that feeling, the hugeness of it, like staring into the sun. Like *falling* into the sun.

"Losing myself," he said.

"What?"

"That's what I'm afraid of. Losing myself, in this. In you. I've spent this whole year trying to find myself, to figure out who I am, and now there's you, there's us, there's this all-consuming, terrifying black hole of a feeling, and if I give into it . . . I feel like I'm standing on the edge of the Grand Canyon, you know? Like, here's something bigger, deeper than the human mind is built to fathom. And I'm just supposed to . . . jump in?"

He waited nervously for her reaction, suspecting that girls probably didn't like it much when you admitted you were afraid of them. Girls like Izzy probably didn't like it when you admitted you were afraid of anything. Nothing scared her; she deserved someone just as brave.

"Is that all?" Her face lit up. "Simon, don't you think I'm scared of that too? You're not the only one on that ledge. If we jump, we jump together. We fall *together.*"

Simon had spent so long trying to gather together the pieces of himself, to fit the puzzle back together. But the final piece, the most important piece, had been right in front of him the whole time. Losing himself to Izzy—could it be that this was the only way to really find himself?

Could it be that this, here, was home?

Enough bad metaphors, he told himself. *Enough delaying.*

Enough being afraid.

He stopped thinking about the person he used to be or the relationship they used to have; he stopped thinking about whether he was screwing things up or why he wanted to; he stopped thinking about demon amnesia and Shadowhunter Ascension and the Fair Folk and the Dark War and politics and homework and the unregulated traffic of deadly sharp objects.

He stopped thinking about what could happen, and what could go wrong.

He took her in his arms and kissed her—kissed her the way he'd been longing to kiss her since he first laid eyes on her, kissed her not like a romance novel hero or a Shadowhunter warrior or some imaginary character from the past, but like Simon Lewis kissing the girl he loved more than anything in the world. It *was* like falling into the sun, falling together, hearts blazing with pale fire, and Simon knew he would never stop falling, knew that now that he'd grabbed hold of her again, he would never let go.

The marriage of true minds admits no impediments—but the make-out sessions of teenagers all too often do. Especially when one of the teenagers was a student at Shadowhunter Academy, with both homework and a curfew. And when the other was a demon-fighting warrior with a stakeout in the morning.

If Simon had had his way, he would have spent the next week, or possibly the next eternity, entangled with Izzy on the grass, listening to the lake lap against the shore, losing himself in the touch of her fingers and the taste of her lips. Instead, he spent a memorable two hours doing so, then galloped at breakneck speed back to Shadowhunter Academy and spent another hour kissing her good-bye, before letting her leap into the Portal with a promise to return as soon as she could.

He had to wait until the next day to thank Helen Blackthorn for her help. He caught her just as she was packing up to leave.

"I see the date went well," she said as soon as she opened the door.

"How could you tell?"

Helen smiled. "You're practically radioactive."

Simon thanked her for relaying Izzy's message and handed her a small bag of cookies he'd cadged from the dining hall. They were the only thing at the Academy that actually tasted good. "Consider this a small down payment on what I owe you," he said.

"You don't owe me anything. But if you really want to pay me back, come to the wedding—you can be Izzy's plus one."

"I wouldn't miss it," Simon promised. "So when's the big day?"

"First of October," she said, but there was a quavering note in her voice. "Probably."

"Maybe sooner?"

"Maybe not at all," she admitted.

"What? You and Aline aren't breaking up!" Simon caught himself, remembering that he was talking to someone he barely knew. He couldn't exactly command her to have a happy ending just because he'd suddenly fallen in love with love. "I'm sorry, it's none of my business, but . . . why would you come all this way and take all their crap if you didn't want to marry her?"

"Oh, I want to marry her. More than anything. It's just, being back here has made me wonder if I'm being selfish."

"How could marrying Aline be selfish?" Simon asked.

"Look at my life!" Helen exploded, the day's—or maybe the year's—worth of pent-up fury blasting out of her. "They look at me like I'm some kind of freak show—and those are the kind ones, the ones who don't look at me like I'm the enemy. Aline is already stuck on that godforsaken island because of me. Is she supposed to suffer like that for the rest of her life? Just because she made the mistake of falling in love with me? What kind of person does that make me?"

"You can't possibly think any of this is *your* fault." He didn't know her very well, but none of this sounded right to him. Not like something she would say or believe.

"Professor Mayhew told me that if I really loved her, I would leave her," Helen admitted. "Instead of dragging her into this nightmare with me. That holding on to her is just proof I'm more faerie than I think."

"Professor Mayhew is a troll," Simon said, and wondered what it would take to get Catarina Loss to turn him into one for real. Or maybe a toad or a lizard. Something that would more befit the reptilian nature of his soul. "If you really loved Aline, you would do everything you can to hold on to her. Which is exactly what you're doing. Besides, you're assuming that if you tried to break up with her for her own good, she'd let you. From what I've heard about Aline, that's not likely."

"No," Helen said fondly. "She'd fight me tooth and nail."

"Then why not fast-forward to the inevitable? Accept that you're stuck with her. The love of your life. Poor you."

Helen sighed. "Isabelle told me what you said about the fey, Simon. About how you think it's wrong to discriminate against them. That faeries can be good, just as much as anyone else."

He didn't understand where she was going with this, but he wasn't sorry to have the chance to confirm it. "She was right, I do think that."

"Isabelle believes that too, you know," Helen said. "She's been doing her best to convince me."

"What do you mean?" Simon asked, confused. "Why would *you* need convincing."

Helen kneaded her fingers together. "You know, I didn't want to come here to tell a bunch of kids the story of my mother and father—I didn't do that voluntarily. But I also didn't make it up. That's what happened. That's who my mother was, and that's what half of me is."

"No, Helen, that's not—"

"Do you know the poem 'La Belle Dame Sans Merci'?"

Simon shook his head. The only poetry he knew was by Dr. Seuss or Bob Dylan.

"It's Keats," she said, and recited a few stanzas for him by memory.

She took me to her elfin grot,
And there she wept, and sigh'd fill sore,
And there I shut her wild wild eyes
With kisses four.

And there she lullèd me asleep,
And there I dream'd—Ah! woe betide!
The latest dream I ever dream'd
On the cold hill's side.

I saw pale kings and princes too,
Pale warriors, death-pale were they all;
They cried—"La Belle Dame sans Merci
Hath thee in thrall!"

"Keats wrote about *faeries*?" Simon asked. If they'd covered this in English class, he might have paid closer attention.

"My father used to recite that poem all the time," Helen said. "It was his way of telling me and Mark the story of where we came from."

"He recited you a poem about an evil faerie queen luring men to their deaths as a way of telling you about your mother? Repeatedly?" Simon asked, incredulous. "No offense, but that's kind of . . . harsh."

"My father loved us despite where we came from," Helen said in the way of someone trying to convince herself. "But it always felt like he kept some part of himself in reserve. Like he was waiting to see her in me. It was different with Mark, because Mark was a boy. But girls take after their mothers, right?"

"I'm not really sure that's scientifically accurate logic," Simon said.

"That's what Mark said. He always told me the faeries had no claim on us or our nature. And I tried to believe him, but then, after he was taken . . . after the Inquisitor told me the story of my birth mother . . . I wonder . . ." Helen was looking past Simon, past the walls of her domestic prison cell, lost in her own fears. "What if I'm luring Aline to that cold hill's side? What if that need to destroy, to use love as a weapon, is just hibernating in me somewhere, and I don't even know it? A gift from my mother."

"Look, I don't know anything about faeries," Simon said. "Not really. I don't know what the deal was with your mother, or what it means for you to be half one thing and half another. But I know your blood doesn't define you. What defines you is the choices you make. If I've learned anything this year, it's that. And I also know that loving someone—even when it's scary, even when there are consequences—is never the wrong thing to do. Loving someone is the opposite of hurting her."

Helen smiled at him, her eyes brimming with unshed tears. "For both our sakes, Simon, I really hope that you're right."

In the Land under the Hill, in the Time Before . . .

Once upon a time, there was a beautiful lady of the Seelie Court who lost her heart to the son of an angel.

Once upon a time, there were two boys come to the land of Faerie, brothers noble and bold. One brother caught a glimpse of the fair lady and, thunderstruck by her beauty, pledged himself to her. Pledged himself to stay. This was the boy Andrew. His brother, the boy Arthur, would not leave his side.

And so the boys stayed beneath the hill, and Andrew loved the lady, and Arthur despised her.

And so the lady kept her boy close to her side, kept this beautiful creature who swore his fealty to her, and when her sister lay claim to the other, the lady let him be taken away, for he was nothing.

She gave Andrew a silver chain to wear around his neck, a token of her love, and she taught him the ways of the Fair Folk. She danced with him in revels beneath starry skies. She fed him moonshine and showed him how to give way to the wild.

Some nights they heard Arthur's screams, and she told him it was an animal in pain, and pain was in an animal's nature.

She did not lie, for she could not lie.

Humans are animals.

Pain is their nature.

For seven years they lived in joy. She owned his heart, and he hers, and somewhere, beyond, Arthur screamed and screamed. Andrew didn't know; the lady didn't care; and so they were happy.

Until the day one brother discovered the truth of the other.

The lady thought her lover would go mad with the grief of it and the guilt. And so, because she loved the boy, she wove him a story of deceitful truths, the story he would want to believe. That he had been ensorcelled to love her; that he had never betrayed his brother; that he was only a slave; that these seven years of love had been a lie.

The lady set the useless brother free and allowed him to believe he had freed himself.

The lady subjected herself to the useless brother's attack and allowed him to believe he had killed her.

The lady let her lover renounce her and run away.

And the lady beheld the secret fruits of their union and kissed them and tried to love them. But they were only a piece of her boy. She wanted all of him or none of him.

As she had given him his story, she gave him his children.

She had nothing left to live for, then, and so lived no longer.

This is the story she left behind, the story her lover will never know; this is the story her daughter will never know.

This is how a faerie loves: with her whole body and soul. This is how a faerie loves: with destruction.

I love you, she told him, night after night, for seven years. Faeries cannot lie, and he knew that.

I love you, he told her, night after night, for seven years. Humans can lie, and so she let him believe he lied to her, and she let his brother and his children believe it, and she died hoping they would believe it forever.

This is how a faerie loves: with a gift.

Bitter of Tongue

By Cassandra Clare and Sarah Rees Brennan

There were more horses joining the roan, more and more of the Wild Hunt. Simon saw Kieran, a white silent presence. The faerie on the roan turned his horse toward the place where Simon and Isabelle stood, and Simon saw the roan sniff the air like a dog.

—Bitter of Tongue

The sun was shining, the birds were singing, and it was a beautiful day at Shadowhunter Academy.

Well, Simon was pretty sure the sun was shining. There was a faint luminescence to the air in his and George's underground chamber, casting a pleasant glow upon the green slime that coated their walls.

And all right, he could not hear the birds from his subterranean room, but George did come back from the showers singing.

"Good morning, Si! I saw a rat in the bathroom, but he was taking a nice nap and we didn't bother each other."

"Or the rat was dead of a very infectious disease, which has now been introduced to our water system," Simon suggested. "We may be drinking plague-rat water for weeks."

"Nobody likes a Gloomy Gus," George scolded him. "Nobody likes a Sullen Si. Nobody is here for a Moody Mildred. No one fancies—"

"I have gathered the general tenor of your discourse, George," said Simon. "I object strongly to being referred to as a Moody Mildred. Especially as I really feel like I'm a Mildly Good-Humored Mildred right now. I see you're looking forward to your big day?"

"Have a shower, Si," George urged. "Start the day refreshed. Maybe style your hair a little. It wouldn't kill you."

Simon shook his head. "There's a dead rat in the bathroom, George. I am not going in the bathroom, George."

"He's not dead," George said. "He's just sleeping. I'm certain of it."

"Senseless optimism is how plagues get started," Simon said. "Ask the medieval peasants of Europe. Oh, wait, you can't."

"Were they a jolly bunch?" George asked skeptically.

"I'm sure they were much jollier before all the plague," said Simon.

He felt he was making really good points, and that he was backed up by history. He pulled off the shirt he'd slept in, which read LET'S FIGHT! and below in tiny letters OUR ENEMY OFF WITH CUNNING ARGUMENTS. George whipped Simon's back with his wet towel, which made Simon yelp.

Simon grinned as he pulled his gear out of their wardrobe. They were getting started right after breakfast, so he might as well change into gear straight off. Plus, every day wearing gear made for men was a victory.

He and George went up to breakfast in good humor with all the world.

"You know, this porridge isn't at all bad," Simon said, digging in. George nodded enthusiastically, his mouth full.

Beatriz looked sad for them, and possibly sad that boys were so stupid in general. "This isn't porridge," she told them. "These are scrambled eggs."

"Oh no," George whispered faintly, his mouth still full, his voice terribly sad. "Oh no."

Simon dropped his spoon and stared into the depths of his bowl with horror.

"If they are scrambled eggs . . . ?" he asked. "And I'm not arguing with you, Beatriz, I'm just asking what I feel is a very reasonable question . . . if they are scrambled eggs, why are they gray?"

Beatriz shrugged and continued eating, carefully avoiding the lumps. "Who can say?"

That could be made into a sad song, Simon supposed. *If they are eggs, why are they gray? Who can say, who can say?* He found himself still thinking of song lyrics sometimes, even though he was out of the band.

Admittedly, "Why Are the Eggs So Gray?" might not be a big hit, even on the hipster circuit.

Julie plopped her bowl down on the table beside Beatriz.

"The eggs are gray," she announced. "I don't know how they do this. Surely at this point, it would actually make sense for them not to mess up the food sometimes. Every time, every day, for over a year? Is the Academy cursed?"

"I have been thinking it might be," George said earnestly. "I hear an eldritch rattling sometimes, like ghosts shaking their terrible chains. Honestly, I was hoping the Academy *was* cursed, since otherwise it's probably creatures in the pipes." George shuddered. "Creatures."

Julie sat down. George and Simon exchanged a private pleased look. They had been keeping track of how often Julie chose to sit with the three of them, rather than with Jon Cartwright. Currently they were winning, sixty percent to forty.

Julie choosing to sit with them seemed like a good sign, since this was George's big day.

Now that they were Shadowhunter trainees in their second year, and in the words of Scarsbury "no longer totally hopeless and liable to cut off your own stupid heads," they were given their own slightly more important missions. Every mission had an appointed team leader, and the team leader got double points if the mission was a success. Julie, Beatriz, Simon, and Jon had already been team leaders, and they had killed it: everyone's mission accomplished, demons slain, people saved, Downworlders breaking the Law penalized severely but fairly. In some ways it was a pity that Jon's mission had gone so well, as he had bragged about it for weeks, but they couldn't help it. They were just too good, Simon thought, even as he slapped the wooden table so as not to jinx himself. There was no way for them to fail.

"Feeling nervous, team leader?" asked Julie. Simon had to admit she could sometimes be an unsettling companion.

"No," said George, and under Julie's gimlet eye: "Maybe. Yes. You know, an appropriate amount of nervous, but in a cool, collected, and good-under-pressure way."

"Don't go all to pieces," said Julie. "I want a perfect score."

An awkward silence followed. Simon comforted himself by looking over at Jon's table. When Julie abandoned him, Jon had to eat all alone. Unless Marisol decided she wanted to sit with him and torment him. Which, Simon noted, she was doing today. Little devil. Marisol was hilarious.

Jon made urgent gestures for help, but Julie had her back turned to him and did not see.

"I'm not saying this to scare you, George," she said. "That's a side benefit, obviously. This is an important mission. You know faeries are the worst kind of Downworlder. Faeries crossing over into the mundane realm and tricking the poor things into eating faerie fruit is no joke. Mundanes can wither away and die after eating that fruit, you know. It's murder, and it's murder we can hardly ever get them for, because by the time the mundanes die, the faeries are long gone. You're taking this seriously, right?"

"Yes, Julie," said George. "I actually do know murder is bad, Julie."

Julie's whole face pursed up in that alarming way it did sometimes. "Remember it was you who almost screwed up my mission."

"I hesitated slightly to tackle that vampire child," George admitted.

"Precisely," said Julie. "No more hesitation. As our team leader, you have to act on your own initiative. I'm not saying you're bad, George. I am saying you need to learn."

"I'm not sure anybody needs this kind of motivational speech," Beatriz said. "It would freak anyone out. And it's too easy to freak George out as it is."

George, who had been looking touched at Beatriz's gallant defense, stopped looking touched.

"I just think they should do a repeat team leader occasionally," Julie grumbled, letting them know where all this hostility was coming from. She stabbed her gray eggs wistfully. "I was so good."

Simon raised his eyebrows. "You had a horsewhip and threatened to beat me about the head and face if I didn't do what you said."

Julie pointed her spoon at him. "Exactly. And you did what I said. That's leadership, that is. What's more, I *didn't* beat you about the head and face. Kind but firm, that's me."

Julie discussed her own greatness at some length. Simon got up to get another glass of juice.

"What kind of juice do you think this is?" Catarina Loss asked, joining him in the line.

"Fruit," said Simon. "Just fruit. That's all they would tell me. I found it suspicious as well."

"I like fruit," Catarina said, but she did not sound sure about that. "I know you're excused from my class this afternoon. What are you up to this morning?"

"A mission to stop faeries from slipping over their borders and engaging in illicit trade," Simon said. "George is team leader."

"George is team leader?" Catarina asked. "Hm."

"Why is everyone so down on George today?" Simon demanded. "What's wrong with George? There's nothing wrong with George. It is not possible to find fault with George. He's a perfect Scottish angel. He always shares the snacks that his mother sends him, and he's better-looking than Jace. There, I said it. I'm not taking it back."

"I see you're in a good mood," said Catarina. "All right then. Go on, have a good time. Take care of my favorite student."

"Right," said Simon. "Wait, who's that?"

Catarina gestured him away from her with her indeterminate juice. "Get lost, Daylighter."

Everyone else was excited to go on another mission. Simon

was looking forward to it as well, and pleased for George's sake. But Simon was mostly excited because after the mission, he had somewhere else to be.

The Fair Folk had been seen last on a moor in Devon. Simon was a bit excited to Portal there and hoped there would be time to see red postboxes and drink lager at an English pub.

Instead, the moor turned out to be a huge stretch of uneven field, rocks, and hills in the distance, no red postboxes or quaint pubs in sight. They were immediately given horses by the contact with the Sight who was waiting for them.

Lots of fields, lots of horses. Simon was not sure why they had bothered to leave the Academy, because this was an identical experience.

The first words George said as they were riding on the moor were: "I think it would be a good idea to split up."

"Like in . . . a horror movie?" Simon asked.

Julie, Beatriz, and Jon gave him looks of irritated incomprehension. Marisol's uncertain expression suggested she agreed with Simon, but she did not speak up and Simon didn't want to be the one mutinying against his friend's leadership. They would cover more moor if they split up. Maybe it was a great idea. More moor! How could it go wrong?

"I'll be partners with Jon," Marisol said instantly, a glint in her dark eyes. "I wish to continue our conversation from breakfast. I have many more things to say to him on the subject of video games."

"I don't want to hear any more about video games, Marisol!" snapped Jon, a Shadowhunter in a nightmare of torrential mundane information.

Marisol smiled. "I know."

Marisol had only just turned fifteen. Simon was not sure how she had worked out that telling Jon every detail about the mundane world would be such effective psychological terrorism. Her evil had only grown in the year and change Simon had known her. Simon had to respect that.

"And Si and I will be together," George said easily.

"Um," said Simon.

Neither he nor George was a Shadowhunter yet, and though Catarina helped them see through glamours, no mundane . . . er, non-Shadowhunter . . . was as securely protected from faerie glamour as one of the Nephilim. But Simon didn't want to question George's authority or suggest he didn't want to be partners. He was also scared of being partnered with Julie, and beaten about the head and face.

"Great," Simon finished weakly. "Maybe we can split up but also stay . . . within hearing range of each other?"

"You want to split up but stay together?" Jon asked. "Do you not know what words mean?"

"Do you know what the words 'World of Warcraft' mean?" asked Marisol menacingly.

"Yes, I do," said Jon. "All put together in that way, no, I do not, and I do not wish to."

He urged his horse onward across the moor. Marisol followed in pursuit. Simon stared at the back of Jon's head and worried he would go too far.

Except that they were meant to be splitting up. This was all right.

George gazed around at the remaining members of the team and appeared to come to a decision. "We'll stay within hearing range of each other, and comb over the moors, and see if we can see the Fair Folk in any of the places they were reported lurking. Are you with me, team?"

"I'm with you to the end, if it doesn't take too long! You know I'm going to Helen Blackthorn and Aline Penhallow's wedding," said Simon.

"Ugh, hate weddings," said George sympathetically. "You have to wear a monkey suit and go sit around for ages while everybody secretly hates each other over some fight about the flower arrangements. Plus, bagpipes. I mean, I don't know how Shadowhunter weddings go. Are there flowers? Are there bagpipes?"

"Can't talk right now," said Beatriz. "Picturing Jace Herondale in a tuxedo. In my head, he looks like a beautiful spy."

"James Bond," George contributed. "James Blond? I still don't like monkey suits. But it doesn't seem like you mind, Si."

Simon lifted a hand from the reins to point proudly to himself, a maneuver that would've had him falling off his horse a year ago. "This monkey is going as Isabelle Lightwood's date."

Just saying the words suffused Simon with a sense of wellbeing. In such a wonderful world, how could anything go wrong?

He looked around at his team: the whole lot of them, wearing long-sleeved gear against the autumn chill, figures in black with bows strapped to their backs and their breath white plumes in the cold air, riding fast horses through the moors on a mission to protect humankind. His three friends by his side, and Jon and Marisol in the distance. George, so proud to be team leader. Marisol, scornful city kid, riding her horse with easy grace. Even Beatriz and Julie, even Jon, born

Shadowhunters all, looked a little different to Simon, now that they were well into their second year at the Academy. Scarsbury had honed them, Catarina had lectured them, and even their fellow Academy students had changed them. Now the born Shadowhunters rode with mundanes and performed missions with them as a unit, and the so-called dregs could keep up.

The moor was rolling fields, tree line to their left all quivering leaves as if the trees were dancing in the slight breeze. The sunlight was pale and clear, shining on their heads and their black clothes alike. Simon found himself thinking, with affection and pride, that they looked like they might make real Shadowhunters after all.

He noticed that by silent mutual agreement, Beatriz and Julie were coaxing their mounts on faster. Simon squinted up into the distance, where he could just about still make out Jon and Marisol, and then squinted at Beatriz's and Julie's backs. He felt again that pang of uneasiness.

"Why are they all racing ahead?" Simon asked. "Um, not to tell you your job, but, brave team leader, maybe command them not to go too far."

"Ah, give them a minute," George said. "You know she kind of likes you."

"What?" said Simon.

"Not that she's going to do anything about it," said George. "Nobody who likes you is going to do anything about it. On account of, nobody would enjoy having Isabelle Lightwood cut their head off."

"Likes me?" Simon echoed. "Something about the way you're talking suggests multiple people. Who like *me*."

George shrugged. "Apparently you're the type who grows on people. Don't ask me. I thought girls liked abs."

"I could have abs," Simon told him. "I watched in the mirror once and I think I found an ab. I'm telling you, all this training is doing my body good."

It wasn't like Simon thought he was a hideous creature or anything. He'd now seen several demons who had tentacles coming out of their eyes, and he was fairly sure it did not revolt people merely to look upon him.

But he wasn't Jace, who made girls' heads spin around as if they were possessed. It made no sense that out of all the students in the Academy, Beatriz might like *him*.

George rolled his eyes. George did not truly understand the slow development of actual physical fitness. He'd probably been born with abs. Some were born with abs, some achieved abs, and some—like Simon—had abs thrust upon them by cruel instructors.

"Yes, Si, you're a real killer."

"Feel this arm," said Simon. "Rock hard! I don't mean to brag, but it's all bone. All bone."

"Si," said George. "I don't need to feel it. I believe in you, because that's what bros do. And I'm happy for your mysterious popularity with the ladies, because that's how bros are. But seriously, watch out for Jon, because I think he's going to shank you one of these days. He does not get your indefinable but undeniable allure. He's got abs to the chin and he thought he had the ladies of the Academy locked down."

Simon rode on, somewhat dazed.

He'd been thinking that Isabelle's affection for him was a stunning and inexplicable occurrence, like a lightning strike.

(Gorgeous and courageous lightning whom he was lucky to be struck by!) Given current evidence, however, he was starting to believe it was time to reevaluate.

He had been reliably informed that he'd dated Maia, the leader of the New York werewolf pack, though he'd received the impression that he had well and truly messed that one up. He'd heard rumors about a vampire queen who might have been interested. He'd even gathered, strange as it seemed, that there was a brief period of time when he and Clary had gone out. And now possibly Beatriz liked him.

"Seriously, George, tell me the truth," said Simon. "Am I beautiful?"

George burst out laughing, his horse wheeling back a few easy paces in the sunlight.

And Julie shouted: "Faerie!" and pointed. Simon looked toward a hooded and cloaked figure with a basket of fruit over one arm, emerging as if innocently from the mist behind a tree.

"After it!" roared George, and his horse charged for the figure, Simon plunging after him.

Marisol, far ahead, shouted: "Trap!" and then gave a scream of pain.

Simon looked desperately toward the trees. The faerie, he saw, had reinforcements. They had been warned the Fair Folk were all more wary and desperate in the aftermath of the Cold Peace. They should have listened better and thought harder. They should have planned for this.

Simon, George, Julie, and Beatriz were all riding hard, but they were too far from her. Marisol was swaying in her saddle, blood pouring down her arm: elfshot.

"Marisol!" Jon Cartwright shouted. "*Marisol*, to me!"

She pulled the horse toward his. Jon stood on his horse and leaped onto hers, bow already in hand and firing arrows into the trees, standing on the horse's back and thus shielding Marisol like a strange bow-shooting acrobat. Simon knew he'd never be able to do anything like that, ever, unless he Ascended.

Julie and Beatriz turned their horses toward the trees where the concealed faeries were firing.

"They have Marisol," George panted. "We can still get the fruit seller."

"No, George," Simon began, but George had already wheeled his horse toward the hooded figure, now disappearing behind the tree and the mist.

There was a spear of sunlight shooting between the trunk and the branch of the tree, a dazzling white line between the crooked arc of tree limbs. It seemed to refract in Simon's eyes, becoming broad and fair, like the path of moonlight on the sea. The hooded figure was slipping away, half-disappeared into the dazzle, and George's horse was inches from danger, George's hand reaching for the edge of the figure's cloak, George heedless of the course he had placed himself upon.

"*No, George!*" Simon shouted. "We are not going to trespass into Faerie!"

He forced his own horse into George's path, making George pull up, but he was so hell-bent on stopping George that he did not take into consideration his mount, now terrified and fleeing and urged to speed.

Until the white dazzling light filled Simon's vision. He remembered suddenly the feeling of falling away into Faerie, soaked to the skin, in a pool filled with water: remembered Jace being kind to him, and how much he had resented that, how he'd thought: *Don't show me up any further*, and his chest had burned with resentment.

Now he was tumbling into Faerie with the scream of a terrified horse in his ears, leaves blinding him and twigs scraping at his face and his arms. He tried to shield his eyes and found himself thrown on rock and bones, with darkness rushing at him. He would have been very grateful if Jace had been there.

Simon woke in Faerieland. His whole skull was throbbing, in the way your thumb did when you hit it with a hammer. He hoped nobody had hit his head with a hammer.

He woke in a gently swaying bed, slightly prickly under his cheek. He opened his eyes and saw that he was not exactly in a bed, but lying amid twigs and moss, scattered across a swaying surface constructed of wooden laths. There were strange stripes of darkness in front of his vision, obscuring his view of the vista beyond.

Faerieland almost looked like the moors in Devon, yet it was entirely different. The mists in the distance were faintly purple, like storm clouds clinging to the earth, and there was movement in the cloud suggesting odd and menacing shapes. The leaves on the trees were green and yellow and red like the trees of the mundane world, but they shone too brightly, like jewels, and when the wind rustled through them Simon could almost make out words, as if they were whispering together. This was nature run riot, alchemized into magic and strangeness.

And Simon was, he realized, in a cage. A big wooden cage. The stripes of darkness across his vision were his cage bars.

The thing that outraged him most was how familiar it felt. He remembered being trapped like this before. *More than once.*

"Shadowhunters, vampires, and now faeries, all longing to throw me in prison," Simon said aloud. "Why exactly was I so anxious to get back all these memories? Why is it always me? Why am I always the chump in the cage?"

His own voice made his aching head hurt.

"You are in my cage now," said a voice.

Simon sat up hastily, though it made his head throb fiercely and all of Faerieland reel drunkenly around him. He saw, on the other side of his cage, the hooded and cloaked figure whom George had tried so desperately to capture on the moors. Simon swallowed. He could not see the face beneath the hood.

There was a whirl in the air, like a shadow whipping over the sun. A new faerie dropped out of the clear blue sky, the leaves of the forest floor crunching under his bare feet. Sunlight washed his fair hair into radiance, and a long knife glittered in his hand.

The hooded and cloaked faerie dropped his hood and bowed his head in sudden deference. Unhooded, Simon saw, he had large ears, tinted purple, as if he had an eggplant stuck to each side of his face, and wisps of long white hair that curled over his eggplant ear like cloud.

"What has happened, and why are your tricks interfering with the work of your betters, Hefeydd? A horse from the mundane world ran into the path of the Wild Hunt," the new faerie said. "I do hope the steed was not of immense emotional significance, because the hounds have it now."

Simon's heart bled for that poor horse. He wondered if he, too, was about to be fed to the hounds.

"I am so sorry to have disturbed the Wild Hunt," the cloaked faerie said, bowing his white head even further.

"You should be," answered the faerie of the Wild Hunt. "Those who cross the path of the Hunt always regret it."

"This is a Shadowhunter," continued the other anxiously. "Or at least one of the children they hope to change. They were lying in wait for me in the mortal world, and this one pursued me even into Faerie, so he is my rightful prey. I had no wish to disturb the Wild Hunt and bear no fault!"

Simon felt this was an inaccurate and hurtful summary of the situation.

"Is it so? Come now, I am in a merry mood," said the Wild Hunt faerie. "Give me your regrets and words with your captive— as you know, I have some little interest in Shadowhunters—and I will not bring back my lord Gwyn your tongue."

"Never was a fairer bargain made," said the cloaked faerie in some haste, and ran off as though afraid the Wild Hunt faerie might change his mind, almost tripping over his own cloak.

As far as Simon was concerned, this was out of the faerie frying pan and into the faerie fire.

The new faerie looked like a boy of sixteen, not much older than Marisol and younger than Simon, but Simon knew that how faeries looked was no indicator of their age. He had mismatched eyes, one amber as the beads found in the dark heart of trees, and one the vivid blue-green of sea shallows when sunlight strikes through. The jarring contrast of his eyes and the light of Faerie, filtered green through wickedly whispering leaves and touched with false gold, made his thin, dirt-streaked face wear a sinister aspect.

He looked like a threat. And he was coming closer.

"What does a faerie of the Wild Hunt want with me?" Simon croaked.

"I am no faerie," said the boy with eerie eyes, pointed ears, and leaves in his wild hair. "I am Mark Blackthorn of the Los Angeles Institute. It doesn't matter what they say or what they do to me. I still remember who I am. I am Mark Blackthorn."

He looked at Simon with wild hunger in his thin face. His thin fingers clutched the bars of the cage.

"Are you here to save me?" he demanded. "Have the Shadowhunters come for me at last?"

Oh no. This was Helen Blackthorn's brother, the one who was half-faerie like her, the one who had believed his family dead and been taken by the Wild Hunt and never returned. This was very awkward.

This was worse than that. This was horrific.

"No," said Simon, because hope seemed the cruelest blow he could deal Mark Blackthorn. "It's just like the other faerie said. I wandered here by accident and I was captured. I'm Simon Lewis. I . . . know your name, and I know what happened to you. I'm sorry."

"Do you know when the Shadowhunters are coming for me?" Mark asked with heartbreaking eagerness. "I—sent them a message, during the war. I understand the Cold Peace must make all dealings with faerie difficult, but they must know I am loyal and would be valuable to them. They must be coming, but it has been . . . it has been weeks and weeks. Tell me, when?"

Simon stared at Mark, dry-mouthed. It had not been weeks and weeks since the Shadowhunters had abandoned him here. It had been a year and more.

"They're not coming," he whispered. "I was not there, but my friends were. They told me what happened. The Clave took a vote. The Shadowhunters do not want you back."

"Oh," said Mark, a single soft sound that was familiar to Simon: It was the kind of sound creatures made when they died.

He turned away from Simon, his back arched in a spasm of pain that looked physical. Simon saw, on his bare lean arms, the old marks of a whip. Even though Simon could not see his face, Mark covered it for a moment, as if he could not even bear to look upon Faerieland.

Then he turned and snapped: "What about the children?"

"What?" Simon asked blankly.

"Helen, Julian, Livia, Tiberius, Drusilla, Octavian. And Emma," said Mark. "You see? I have not forgotten. Every night, no matter what has happened during the day, no matter if I am torn and bloodied or so bone-tired I wish I were dead, I look up at the stars and I give each star a brother's name or a sister's face. I will not sleep until I remember every one. The stars will burn out before I forget."

Mark's family, the Blackthorns. They were all younger than Mark but Helen; Simon knew that. And Emma Carstairs lived with the younger Blackthorn kids in the Los Angeles Institute, the little girl with blond hair who had been orphaned in the war and who wrote to Clary a lot.

Simon wished he knew more about them. Clary had talked about Emma. Magnus had spoken passionately this summer, several times, about the Cold Peace and had given the Blackthorns as an example of the horrors that the Clave's decision to punish faeries had visited on those of faerie blood. Simon had listened to Magnus and felt sorry for the Blackthorns, but they had seemed like just another tragedy of the war: something terrible but distant, and ultimately easy to forget. Simon had felt he had so much to remember himself. He had wanted to go to the Academy and become a Shadowhunter, to learn more about his own life and remember everything he had lost, to become someone stronger and better.

Except that you did not become someone stronger and better by only thinking about yourself.

He did not know what they were doing to Mark in Faerie, to make his family slip away from him.

"Helen's well," he said awkwardly. "I saw her recently. She came and lectured at the Academy. I'm sorry. I had a demon take—a lot of memories from me, not so long ago. I know what it's like, not to remember."

"Fortunate are the ones who know the name of their heart. They are the ones whose hearts are never truly lost. They can always call their heart back home," Mark said, his voice almost a chant. "Do you remember the name of your heart, Simon Lewis?"

"I think so," Simon whispered.

"How are they?" Mark asked in a low, worn voice. He sounded very tired.

"Helen's getting married," Simon offered. It was the only good thing, he felt, that he had to offer Mark. "To Aline Penhallow. I think—they really love each other."

He almost said he was going to their wedding, but even that felt cruel. Mark could not go to his own sister's wedding. He had not been invited. He had not even been told.

Mark did not seem angry or hurt. He smiled, softly as a child being told a bedtime story, and leaned his face against the bars of Simon's cage.

"Sweet Helen," he said. "My father used to tell stories about

Helen of Troy. She was born out of an egg, and the most beautiful woman in the world. Being born out of an egg is very unusual for humans."

"I've heard that," said Simon.

"She was very unhappy in love," Mark continued. "Beauty can be like that. Beauty cannot be trusted. Beauty can slip through your fingers like water and burn on your tongue like poison. Beauty can be the shining wall that keeps you from all you love."

"Um," said Simon. "Totally."

"I am glad that my beautiful Helen will be happier than the last beautiful Helen," said Mark. "I am glad she will be given beauty for beauty, love for love, and no false coin. Tell her that her brother Mark sends her felicitations on her wedding day."

"If I make it there, I will."

"Aline will be able to help her with the children, too," Mark said.

He was paying very little attention to Simon, his face still wearing that fixed and faraway expression, as if he were listening to a story or recalling a memory. Simon feared that stories and memory were becoming much the same to Mark Blackthorn: longed-for, beautiful, and unreal.

"Ty needs special attention," Mark went on. "I remember my parents talking about it." His mouth twisted. "I mean my father and the woman who sang me to sleep every night though I was not of her blood, the Shadowhunter I am no longer allowed to call my mother. Songs are not blood. Blood is all that matters to Shadowhunters and faeries alike. The songs matter only to me."

Blood is all that matters to Shadowhunters.

Simon could not remember the context, but he could remember the constant refrain, from people he loved now but had not loved then. *Mundane, mundane, mundane.* And later, *vampire. Downworlder.*

He remembered that the first prison he had ever been inside was a Shadowhunter prison.

He wished he could tell Mark Blackthorn that anything he said was wrong.

"I'm so sorry," he said.

He was sorry for not listening, and sorry for not caring more. He'd thought he was the voice of reason in the Academy, and had not realized how complacent he'd grown, how easy it was to hear his friends sneer at people who were—after all—not like him anymore, and let them get away with it.

He wished he knew how to say any of this to Mark Blackthorn, but he doubted Mark would care.

"If you are sorry, speak," said Mark. "How is Ty? There is nothing wrong with Ty, but he is different, and the Clave hates all that is different. They will try to punish him, for being who he is. They would punish a star for burning. My father was there to stand between him and our cruel world, but my father is gone and I am gone too. I might as well be dead, for all the good I am to my brothers and sisters. Livvy would walk over hot coals and hissing serpents for Ty, but she is as young as he is. She cannot do and be everything to him. Is Helen having difficulties with Tiberius? Is Tiberius happy?"

"I don't know," Simon said helplessly. "I think so."

All he knew was that there were a bunch of Blackthorn kids: faceless, nameless victims of the war.

"And there's Tavvy," said Mark.

His voice grew stronger as he kept talking, and he used nick-names for his brothers and sisters rather than the full names he had worked so laboriously to remember. Simon supposed Mark was not usually allowed even to speak of his mortal life or his Nephilim family. He didn't want to think about what the Wild Hunt might do to Mark, if he tried.

"He is so little," said Mark. "He won't remember Dad, or M—or his mother. He's the littlest thing. They let me hold him, the day he was born, and his head fit into the palm of my hand. I can still feel its weight there, even when I cannot grasp his name. I held him and I knew I had to support his head: that he was mine to support and protect. Forever. Oh, but forever lasts such a short time in the mortal world. He will not remem-ber me either. Maybe Drusilla will forget as well." Mark shook his head. "I do not think so, though. Dru learns everything by heart, and she has the sweetest heart of us all. I hope her memo-ries of me stay sweet."

Clary must have told Simon every one of the Blackthorns' names, and talked a little bit about how each of them was doing. She must have let fall some scrap of information, which Simon had discarded as useless and which would be better than treasure to Mark.

Simon stared at him helplessly.

"Just tell me if Aline is helping with the younger ones," said Mark, his voice growing sharper. "Helen cannot do it all by her-self, and Julian will not be able to help her!" His voice softened again. "Julian," he said. "Jules. My artist, my dreamer. Hold him up to the light and he would shine a dozen different colors. All he cares about is his art and his Emma. He will try to help Helen, of course, but he is still so young. They are so young and so easily lost. I know what I am saying, Shadowhunter. In the land under the hill we prey on the tender and new-hearted. And they never grow old, with us. They never have the chance."

"Oh, Mark Blackthorn, what are they doing to you?" Simon whispered.

He could not keep the pity out of his voice, and he saw it sting Mark: the slow flush that rose to his thin cheeks, and the way he lifted his chin, holding his head high.

Mark said: "Nothing I cannot bear."

Simon was silent. He did not remember everything, but he remembered how much he had been changed. People could bear so much, but Simon did not know how much of the original you was left when the world had twisted you into a whole different shape.

"I remember you," Mark said suddenly. "We met when you were on your way to Hell. You were not human then."

"No," said Simon awkwardly. "I don't remember much about it."

"There was a boy with you," Mark continued. "Hair like a halo and eyes like hellfire, a Nephilim among Nephilim. I'd heard stories about him. I—admired him. He pressed a witchlight into my hand, and it meant—it meant a lot to me. Then."

Simon could not remember, but he knew who that must have been.

"Jace."

Mark nodded, almost absentmindedly. "He said, 'Show them what a Shadowhunter is made of; show them you aren't afraid.' I thought I was showing them, the Fair Folk and the Shadowhunters both. I could not do what he asked me. I was afraid, but I did not let it stop me. I got a message back to the

Shadowhunters and I told them the Fair Folk were betraying them and allying with their enemy. I made sure they knew and could protect the City of Glass. I warned them, and the Hunters could have killed me for it, but I thought if I died I would die knowing my brothers and sisters were saved, and that everyone would know I was a true Shadowhunter."

"You did," said Simon. "You got the message back. Idris was protected, and your brothers and sisters were saved."

"What a hero I am," Mark murmured. "I proved my loyalty. And the Shadowhunters left me here to rot."

His face twisted. In the depths of Simon's heart, fear twined with pity.

"I tried to be a Shadowhunter, even in the depths of Faerie, and what good did it do me? 'Show them what a Shadowhunter is made of!' What is a Shadowhunter made of, if they desert their own, if they throw away a child's heart like rubbish left on the side of the road? Tell me, Simon Lewis, if that is what Shadowhunters are, why would I wish to be one?"

"Because that's not all they are," Simon said.

"And what are faeries made of? I hear Shadowhunters say they are all evil now, barely more than demons set upon the earth to do wicked mischief." Mark grinned, something wild and fey in the grin, like sunlight glittering through a spider-web. "And we do love mischief, Simon Lewis, and sometimes wickedness. But it is not all bad, to ride the winds, run upon the waves, and dance upon the mountains, and it is all I have left. At least the Wild Hunt wants me. Maybe I should show Shadowhunters what a faerie is made of instead."

"Maybe," said Simon. "There's more to both sides than the worst."

Mark smiled, a faint terrible smile. "Where has the best gone? I try to remember my father's stories, about Jonathan Shadowhunter, about all the golden heroes who have served as shields for humanity. But my father is dead. His voice fades away with the north wind, and the Law he held sacred is something written in the sand by a child. We laugh and point, that anyone should be so foolish as to think it would last. All that is good, and true, is lost."

Simon had never thought there was much of a silver lining about his memory loss. It occurred to him now that he had been shown some small accidental mercy. All his memories had been stripped away at once.

While Mark's memories were being torn at and worn away, sliding from him one by one, in the cold dark under the hill where nothing gold lasted.

"I wish I could remember," Simon said, "when we first met."

"You weren't human then," said Mark bitterly. "But you're human now. And you look like more of a Shadowhunter than I do."

Simon opened his mouth and found all words wanting. He did not know what to say: It was true, as everything Mark said was true. When he'd first seen Mark, he'd thought *faerie*, and felt instinctively uneasy. Shadowhunter Academy must have been rubbing off on him even more than he'd thought.

And the environment Mark was in had changed him, too, changed him already almost past reclaiming. There was an eerie quality to him that went beyond the fine bones and delicately pointed ears of faerie. Helen had possessed those too, but ultimately she had moved like a fighter, stood tall like a Shadowhunter, spoken as the Clave and the people of the

Institutes spoke. Mark spoke like a poem and walked like a dance. Simon wondered, even if Mark found his way back, if he could possibly fit into the Shadowhunter world now.

He wondered if Mark had forgotten how to lie.

"What do you think I am, apprentice Shadowhunter?" Mark asked. "What do you think I should do?"

"Show them what Mark Blackthorn is made of," said Simon. "Show them all."

"Helen, Julian, Livia, Tiberius, Drusilla, Octavian. And Emma," Mark whispered, his voice low and reverent, one Simon recognized from the synagogue, from the voice of mothers calling their children, from all the times and places he had heard people call on what they held most sacred. "My brothers and sisters are Shadowhunters, and in their name I will help you. I will."

He turned and shouted: "Hefeydd!"

Hefeydd of the purple ears sidled back into view, back from among the trees.

"This Shadowhunter is my kinsman," said Mark, with some difficulty. "Do you dare to insist you have a claim on a kinsman of the Wild Hunt?"

That was ridiculous. Simon was not even a Shadowhunter yet, Hefeydd was never going to believe— Only here was Mark, Simon realized. A faerie, to all appearances, and a faerie somewhat to be feared. Even Simon had not known if he could lie.

"Of course I would not insist," Hefeydd said, bowing. "That is—"

Simon was watching the sky. He had not even realized he was doing so, that he had been scanning the skies since someone had dropped from them, until now.

Now that Simon was watching, he could see what was happening more clearly: not someone falling from the sky, but a wild sky-bound horse charging for the earth and letting fall its rider. This horse was white as a cloud or mist given proud and shining shape, and the rider who hurtled toward the ground was in dazzling white as well. He had cobalt hair, the dark blue of evening before it became the black of night, and one gleaming-jet and one gleaming-silver eye.

"The prince," whispered Hefeydd.

"Mark of the Hunt," said the new faerie. "Gwyn sent you to find out why the Hunt had been so disturbed. He did not suggest you delay the Hunt yourself by tarrying a year and a day. Are you running away?"

The question was asked with emotion behind it, though Simon could not tell if it was suspicion or something else. He could tell that the question was more serious, perhaps, than the asker had meant it to be.

Mark gestured to himself. "No, Kieran. As you see. Hefeydd has caught himself a Shadowhunter, and I was a little curious."

"Why?" asked Kieran. "The Nephilim are behind you, and looking behind causes nothing but broken spells and wasted pain. Look forward, to the wild wind and to the Hunt. And to my back, because I am like to be before you in any hunt."

Mark smiled, in the way you did with a friend you were used to teasing. "I can recall several hunts in which that has not been the case. But I see you hope for better luck in the future, while I rely on skill."

Kieran laughed. Simon felt a leap of hope—if this faerie was Mark's friend, then the rescue mission was still on. He had moved unconsciously closer to Mark, his hand closing on one of the bars of his cage. Kieran's eye was drawn to the movement, and for an instant he glared at Simon with eyes gone perfectly cold: shark-black, mirror-shard eyes.

Simon knew, with absolute bone-deep certainty and with no idea why, that Kieran did not like Shadowhunters and did not wish Simon any good.

"Leave Hefeydd with his toy," said Kieran. "Come away."

"He told me something interesting," Mark informed Kieran in a brittle voice. "He said the Clave voted against coming for me. My people, the people I was raised among and taught by and trusted, agreed to leave me here. Can you believe that?"

"Can you be surprised? His kind has always liked cruelty full as much as justice. His kind have nothing to do with you any longer," Kieran said, voice caressing and persuasive, laying a hand on Mark's neck. "You are Mark of the Wild Hunt. You ride on the air, a hundred dizzy wheeling miles above them all. They will never hurt you again, save that you let them. Do not let them. Come away."

Mark hesitated, and Simon found himself doubting. Kieran was right, after all. Mark Blackthorn owed the Shadowhunters nothing.

"Mark," Kieran said, a thread of steel in his voice. "You know there are those in the Hunt who would seize any reason to punish you."

Simon could not tell if Kieran's words were a warning or a threat.

A smile crossed Mark's face, dark as a shadow. "Better than you," he said. "But I thank you for your care. I will go with you and explain myself to Gwyn." He turned to look at Simon, his bicolored eyes unreadable, sea glass and bronze. "I will come back. Do not harm him," he told Hefeydd. "Give him water."

He nodded toward Hefeydd, slight emphasis in the gesture, and nodded toward Simon. Simon nodded in return.

Kieran, whom Hefeydd had called a prince, kept his grip on Mark and turned him so that he was facing away from Simon. He whispered something to Mark that Simon could not hear, and Simon could not tell if the tight grasp of Kieran's hand was affection, anxiety, or a wish to imprison.

Simon had no doubt that if Kieran had his way, Mark would not come back.

Mark whistled, and Kieran made the same sound. On the wind, as a shadow and a cloud, came a dark and a light horse swooping down for their riders. Mark leaped into the air and was gone in a flicker of darkness, with a cry of joy and challenge.

Hefeydd chuckled, the low sound creeping through the undergrowth.

"Oh, I will give you water with pleasure," he said, and came over with a cup fashioned out of bark, filled to the brim with water that seemed to shine with light.

Simon reached out through the bars and accepted the drink, but fumbled it and spilled half the water. Hefeydd cursed and caught the cup, holding it to Simon's lips and smiling a darkly encouraging smile.

"There is still some left," he whispered. "You can drink. Drink."

Except Simon was Academy trained. He had no intention of accepting food or drink from faeries, and he was sure Mark had not meant him to. Mark had been nodding at the key dangling from one of the long sleeves of Hefeydd's cloak.

Simon pretended to drink as Hefeydd smiled. He slipped

the key into his gear, and when Hefeydd trotted away he waited, and counted the minutes until he thought the coast was clear. He slid his hand through the bars, slipped the key into the lock, and swung the cage door slowly open.

Then he heard a sound, and froze.

Stepping out of the whispering green trees, wearing a red velvet jacket and a long black lace dress that turned into transparent cobwebs around the knees, in boots and red gloves that Simon thought he might remember, graceful as a gazelle and intent as a tiger, was Isabelle Lightwood.

"Simon!" she exclaimed. "What do you think you're doing?"

Simon drank her in with his eyes, better than water from any land. She had come for him. The others must have fled back to the Academy and said that Simon was lost in Faerie, and Isabelle had gone charging into Faerieland to find him. First out of anybody, when she was meant to be getting ready to attend a wedding. But she was Isabelle, and that meant she was always ready to fight and defend.

Simon recalled feeling conflicted when she had rescued him from a vampire last year. Right now he could not imagine why.

He knew her better now, he thought, knew her all over again, and knew why she would always come.

"Er, I was escaping my terrible captivity," said Simon. Then he took a step back from the cage door, met Isabelle's eyes, and grinned. "But, you know . . . not if you don't want me to."

Isabelle's eyes, which had been hard with worry and purpose, were suddenly glittering like jet.

"What are you saying, Simon?"

Simon spread his hands. "I'm just saying, if you came all

the way here to rescue me, I don't wish to appear ungrateful."

"Oh no?"

"No, I'm the grateful type," Simon said firmly. "So here I am, humbly awaiting rescue. I hope you can see your way clear to saving me."

"I think I could possibly be persuaded," Isabelle said. "Given an incentive."

"Oh, please," Simon said. "I languished in prison, praying that someone brave and strong and babelicious would swoop in and save me. Save me!"

"Brave and strong *and* babelicious? You don't ask for much, Lewis."

"That's what I need," Simon said, with growing conviction. "I need a hero. I'm holding out for a hero, in fact, until the morning light. And she's gotta be sure, and it's gotta be soon— because I have been kidnapped by evil faeries—and she's gotta be larger than life."

Isabelle did look larger than life, like a girl on a big screen with her lip gloss glittering like starlight and music playing to accompany every swish of her hair.

She opened the cage door and stepped inside, twigs crackling under her boots, and crossed the floor of the cage to slide her arms around Simon's neck. Simon drew her face to his and kissed her lips. He felt the luxurious give of her ruby mouth, the slide of her tall strong beautiful body against his. Isabelle's kiss was like rich wine laid out for him alone, like a challenge offered and a promise kept.

He felt, curving against his mouth, her smile.

"Why, Lord Montgomery," Isabelle murmured. "It's been such a long time. I was worried I'd never see you again."

Simon wished he had braved the showers in the Academy this morning. What did dead rats matter, in the face of true love?

There was a rush of blood in his ears, and the sound of a tiny creak: the cage door swinging shut again.

Simon and Isabelle pulled abruptly apart. Isabelle looked ready to spring, like a tiger in lace. Hefeydd did not look particularly worried.

"Two Shadowhunters for the price of one, and a new bird for my cage," Hefeydd said. "And such a pretty bird."

"You think your cage can hold this bird?" Isabelle demanded. "You're dreaming. I got in, and I can get out."

"Not without your stele and your bag of tricks," Hefeydd said. "Throw them all through the bars of the cage, or I shoot your lover with elfshot and you watch him die before your eyes."

Isabelle looked at Simon and, stone-faced, began to strip off her weapons and shove them through the cage bars. Simon was now, perhaps unsettlingly, aware of the placement of many of Isabelle's weapons, and he noted that she had skipped the knife on the inside of her left boot. Oh, and the long knife in the sheath at her back.

Isabelle had many, many knives.

"It will not be so long until you need water to live, pretty bird," said Hefeydd. "I can wait."

He shimmered away. Isabelle collapsed at the bottom of the cage as if her strings had been cut.

Simon stared at her in horror. "Isabelle—"

"I am so humiliated," said Isabelle, her face in her hands. "I didn't even hear him coming. I have brought shame upon the Lightwood name. Utter shame. Total, total humiliation."

"I'm really flattered, if that helps."

"I got distracted making out with a boy, and then locked up by a goblin," Isabelle moaned. "You don't understand! You don't remember, but I was never like this before you. No boy ever meant anything to me. I had poise. I had purpose. I didn't get dumb crushes, because I was never dumb. I was pure battle skill in a bustier. Nobody could shatter my sheer demon-hunting sangfroid. I was cool before I met you! And now I spend my time chasing after a guy with demon amnesia and losing my head in enemy territory! Now I'm a chump."

Simon reached out for one of Isabelle's hands, and after a moment Isabelle let him peel the hand off her face and link her fingers with his. "We can be two chumps in a cage together."

"You're definitely a chump," Isabelle snapped. "Remember, you're still a mundane."

"How could I forget?"

"Did it never occur to you that I might be a faerie wearing a strong glamour, sent to deceive you?"

Do you remember the name of your heart?

"No," said Simon. "I'm a chump, but I'm not that much of a chump. I don't remember everything about our past, but I remember enough. I haven't learned everything about you now that we have another chance, but I have learned enough. I know you when I see you, Isabelle."

Isabelle looked at him for a long moment, and then smiled her lovely defiant smile.

"We're two chumps going to a wedding," she said. "I hope you noticed that I let him think I busted my way into this cage myself. Of course, I secured the key before I ever stepped into the cage." She pulled the key out of the front of her dress and held it up, glittering in the light of Faerie. "I may be a chump, but I'm not an idiot."

She leaped to her feet, her lace skirts swaying around her like a bell, and let them out of the cage. She picked up her weapons and stele from where they were lying in the dirt, and once her weapons were secured, she took Simon's hand.

They were only a few steps into the faerie forest when a shadow swooped down and upon them. Isabelle went for her knives, but it was only Mark.

"You have not escaped yet?" Mark demanded, looking harried. "And you stopped to acquire a paramour?"

Isabelle stopped dead. She, unlike Simon, recognized him right away. "Mark Blackthorn?" she asked.

"Isabelle Lightwood," Mark noted, mimicking her tone of voice.

"We met earlier," said Simon. "He helped me get that key."

"Oh now," said Mark, tilting his head in a birdlike movement. "It was no uneven bargain. You gave me some very interesting information about the Shadowhunters, and the great loyalty they have shown one of their own."

Isabelle's back straightened as it did at any challenge, black hair flying like a flag as she took a step toward him. "You have been done a terrible wrong," she said. "I know you are a true Shadowhunter."

Mark took a step back. "Do you?" he asked softly.

"For what it's worth, I disagree with the Clave's decision."

"That's the Clave, isn't it? I mean, I like Jia Penhallow okay, and it's not that I . . . dislike your dad," Simon, who did not actually like Robert Lightwood, said awkwardly. "But the Clave, basically assholes, am I right? We all know that."

Isabelle held her hand out, palm down, and rocked it back and forth in a gesture that said *You've got a point but I refuse to agree with it out loud.*

Mark laughed. "Yeah," he said, and he sounded a little more sane, a little more human, as if the laugh had grounded him somehow. There was an accent to his words that made Simon think not *faerie* but: *L.A. boy.* "Basically assholes."

There was a rustle in the trees, a rising of the wind. Simon thought he could hear laughter and calling voices, hoofbeats upon the cloud and the currents of the air, the baying of hounds. The sounds of a hunt, the Hunt, the most remorseless hunt in this or any world. Faint, but not far enough away, and coming closer.

"Come with us," said Isabelle suddenly. "Whatever price there is to be paid, I will pay it."

Mark gave her a look that was equal parts admiring and disdainful. He shook his fair head, leaves quivering and light lancing through the bright locks.

"What do you think would happen if I did? I would go home . . . home . . . and the Wild Hunt would follow me there. Do you imagine I have not dreamed of running home a thousand times? Every time, I see gentle Julian pierced with the spears of the Wild Hunt. I see little Dru and baby Tavvy ridden down. I see my Ty, ripped apart by their hounds. I cannot go until there is some way to go to them without bringing destruction down on them. I will not go. You go, and go fast."

Simon pulled Isabelle backward, toward the trees. She resisted, her eyes still on Mark, but she let him draw her away into concealing leaves as more faerie horses hurtled down, lightning amid the trees, shadows against the sun.

"What trouble are you causing now, Shadowhunter?" asked a faerie on a roan horse, laughing as the steed whirled. "What is this word of more of your kind?"

"No word," said Mark.

There were more horses joining the roan, more and more of the Wild Hunt. Simon saw Kieran, a white silent presence. The faerie on the roan turned his horse toward the place where Simon and Isabelle stood, and Simon saw the roan sniff the air like a dog.

The rider pointed. "Why do I spy Shadowhunters, then, in our land and answerable to us? Should I ask them what they are about?"

He rode forward, but he did not make it far. He was wearing a cloak embroidered with silver, showing the constellations, the silver enchanted to move as though time were sped up and planets spun fast enough for the eye to see. His horse stopped short, its rider almost falling, when his beautiful silvery cloak was suddenly pinned to a tree by a well-placed arrow.

Mark lowered his bow. "I see nothing," he said, pronouncing the lie with a certain satisfaction. "And nothing should go—now."

"Oh, boy, you will pay for this," hissed the rider on the roan.

The horses and the riders shrieked like pterodactyls, circling him, but Mark Blackthorn of the Los Angeles Institute stood his ground.

"Run!" he shouted. "Get home safe! Tell the Clave that I have saved more Shadowhunter lives, that I will be a Shadowhunter and be damned to them, that I will be a faerie and curse them! And tell my family that I love them, I love them, and I will never forget. One day I will go home."

Simon and Isabelle ran.

George threw himself on Simon the instant he and Isabelle appeared in the grounds of the Academy, his arms strangling-tight. Beatriz and, to Simon's amazement, even Julie flew at him only a second behind George, and both of them mercilessly pummeled his arms.

"Ow," said Simon.

"We're so glad you're alive!" said Beatriz, punching him again.

"Why must you hurt me with your love?" asked Simon. "Ow."

He disentangled himself from their grip, touched but also mildly bruised, then looked around for another familiar face. He felt a cold touch of fear.

"Is Marisol all right?" he demanded.

Beatriz snorted. "Oh, she's better than all right. She's in the infirmary with Jon waiting on her hand and foot. Because you mundanes can't be healed with runes and she is milking that for all it's worth. I'm not sure which has Jon more terrified, the thought of how fragile mundanes are, or the fact that she keeps threatening to explain X-ray machines to him."

Simon was very impressed that even elfshot could not slow down Marisol and all her evil.

"We thought *you* might be dead," said Julie. "The Fair Folk will do anything to vent their spite against Shadowhunters, those evil, treacherous snakes. They could have done anything to you."

"And it would have been my fault," George said, pale-faced. "You were trying to stop me."

"It would have been the faeries' fault," said Julie. "But you were careless. You have to remember what they are, less human than sharks."

George was nodding humbly. Beatriz looked as if she was in full agreement.

"You know what?" said Simon. "I've had enough."

They all stared at him in blank incredulity. But Isabelle glanced at him and smiled. He thought he finally understood the fire that burned in Magnus, what made him keep talking when the Clave would not listen.

"I know you all think I'm always criticizing the Nephilim," Simon went on. "I know you believe I don't think enough of— the sacred traditions of the Angel, and the fact that you are ready to lay down your lives, any day, to protect humans. I know you think it doesn't matter to me, but it does matter. It means a lot. But I don't have the luxury of only seeing things from one perspective. You all notice when I put down Shadowhunters, but none of you check yourselves when you talk about Downworlders. I *was* a Downworlder. Today I was saved by someone the Clave decided to condemn as a Downworlder, even though he was brave as any Shadowhunter, even though he was loyal. It seems like you want me to just accept that the Nephilim are great and nothing needs to change, but I won't accept anything."

He took a deep breath. He felt as if all the comfort of the morning had been stripped away. But maybe that was for the best. Maybe he'd been getting too comfortable.

"I wouldn't want to be a Shadowhunter if I thought I was

going to be a Shadowhunter like your father or your father's father before him. And I wouldn't like any of you as much as I do if I thought you were going to be Shadowhunters like all the Shadowhunters before you. I want all of us to be better. I haven't figured out how to change everything yet, but I want everything to change. And I'm sorry if it upsets you, but I'm going to keep complaining."

"Later," said Isabelle. "He's going to keep complaining later, because we're going to a wedding right now."

Everyone looked mildly stunned that their emotional reunion had turned into a speech on Downworlder rights. Simon thought Julie might beat him about the head and face, but instead she patted him on the back.

"All right," she said. "We'll listen to your tedious whining later. Please try to keep it brief."

She walked off with Beatriz. Simon squinted after her, and noticed that Isabelle was squinting after as well, a look of faint suspicion on her face.

Simon had a moment of doubt. George had meant Beatriz when he was talking about a girl liking Simon, right?

Surely not Julie. It couldn't be Julie.

No, surely not. Simon was pretty certain he was just getting a pass on account of the narrow escape in Faerie.

George hung back. "I really am so sorry, Si," he told Simon. "I lost my head. I—I maybe wasn't quite ready to lead a team. But I'm going to be ready one day. I'm going to do what you said. I'm going to become a better Shadowhunter than any Shadowhunters before us. You won't have to pay for my mistakes again."

"George," Simon said. "It's fine."

None of them was perfect. None of them could be.

George's sunny face still looked under a cloud, unhappy as he almost never did. "I'm not going to fail again."

"I believe in you," said Simon, and grinned at him, until finally George grinned back. "Because that's what bros do."

Once he arrived in Idris, Simon found himself plunged into a state of wedding chaos. Wedding chaos seemed to be very different from normal kinds of chaos. There were, in fact, many flowers. Simon had a sheaf of lilies shoved upon him and he stood holding it, afraid to move in case the flowers spilled and he was responsible for ruining the whole wedding.

Many wedding guests were running about, but there was only one group that was all kids and no adults. Simon clutched his lilies and focused his attention on the Blackthorns.

If he had not met Mark Blackthorn, he was pretty sure he would've thought of them as a riot of anonymous kids.

Now, though, he knew they were someone's family: someone's heart's desire.

Helen, Julian, Livia, Tiberius, Drusilla, Octavian. And Emma.

Willow-slim, silver-fair Helen, Simon already knew. She was in one of the many rooms he was forbidden to go into, having mysterious bridal things done to her.

Julian was the next oldest, and he was the calm center of a bustling Blackthorn crowd. He had a kid in his arms, who was a little big for Julian to carry but was clinging tenaciously to Julian's neck like an octopus in unfamiliar surroundings. The kid must be Tavvy.

All the Blackthorns were dressed up for the wedding, but already a little grubby around the edges, in that mysterious way kids got. Simon wasn't sure how. They were all, aside from Tavvy, a little too old to be playing in the dirt.

"I'll get Dru all cleaned up," volunteered Emma, who was tall for fourteen, with a crown of blond hair that made her stand out among the dark-haired Blackthorns like a daffodil in a bed of pansies.

"No, don't bother," said Julian. "I know you want to spend some quality time with Clary. You've only been talking about it for, oh, fifteen thousand years, give or take."

Emma shoved him playfully. She was taller than he was: Simon remembered being fourteen and shorter than all the girls too.

All the girls except one, he recalled slowly, the real picture of his fourteenth year sliding over the false one, where the most important person in his life had been clumsily photoshopped out. Clary had always been tiny. No matter how short or awkward Simon had felt, he had always towered over her and felt it was his right to protect her.

He wondered if Julian wished Emma were shorter than he was. From the look on Julian's face as he regarded Emma, there was not one thing about her he would change. *His art and his Emma*, Mark had said, as if they were the two essential facts about Julian. His love of beauty and his wish to create it, and his best friend in all the world. They were going to be *parabatai*, Simon was pretty sure. That was nice.

Emma sped away on a quest to find Clary, with one last grin for Julian.

Only, Mark had been wrong. Art and Emma were clearly not all that occupied Julian's thoughts. Simon watched as he held on to Tavvy and stooped over a small girl with a round beseeching face and a cloud of brown hair.

"I lost my flower crown and I can't find it," whispered the girl.

Julian smiled down at her. "That's what happens when you lose things, Dru."

"But if I'm not wearing a flower crown like Livvy, Helen will think I'm careless and I don't mind my things and I don't like her as much as Livvy does. Livvy still has her flower crown."

The other girl in the group, taller than Dru and in that coltish stage where her arms and legs were thin as sticks and too long for the rest of her body, was indeed wearing a flower crown on her light brown hair. She was sticking close to the side of a boy who had headphones on in the midst of the chaos of the wedding, and winter-gray eyes fixed on some distant private sight.

Livvy would walk over hot coals and hissing serpents for Ty, Mark had said. Simon remembered the infinite tenderness with which Mark had said: *my Ty.*

"Helen knows you better than that," Julian said.

"Yes, but . . ." Drusilla tugged at his sleeve so he would bend down and she could say, in an agonized whisper: "She's been gone such a long time. Maybe she doesn't remember . . . everything about me."

Julian turned his face away, so none of his siblings could see his expression. Only Simon saw the flash of pain, and he knew he wasn't meant to. He knew he wouldn't have seen it, if he hadn't seen Mark Blackthorn, if he hadn't been paying attention.

"Dru, Helen has known you since you were born. She does remember everything."

"But just in case," said Drusilla. "She's going away again really soon. I want her to think I'm good."

"She knows you're good," Julian told her. "The best. But we'll find your flower crown, all right?"

The younger kids did not know Helen in the same way Julian did, as a sibling who was there all the time. They could not rely on someone who was so far away.

Julian was their father, Simon thought with a dawning of horror. There was nobody else.

Even though the Blackthorns had family who wanted to be there for them, wanted it desperately. The Clave had ripped a family apart, and Simon did not know what effects that would have in the future or how the wounds the Clave had inflicted would heal.

He thought, again, as if he were still speaking to his friends at the Academy: *We have to be better than this. Shadowhunters have to be better than this. We have to figure out what kind of Shadowhunters we want to be, and show them.*

Maybe Mark had not known Julian as well as he thought. Or maybe Mark's little brother, with no choice, had changed quietly and profoundly.

They all had to change. But Julian was so young.

"Hey," said Simon. "Can I help?"

The two brothers did not look much alike, but Julian flushed and lifted his chin in the same way Mark had: as if no matter what, he was too proud to admit he might be hurting.

"No," he said, and gave Simon a bright warm smile that was actually very convincing. "I'm fine. I have this."

It seemed true, until Julian Blackthorn had gone out of Simon's reach, and then Simon noticed again that Julian was carrying a kid who was too big for him to carry, with another kid holding on to his shirt. Simon could actually see how much there was on those thin young shoulders.

✳ ✳ ✳

Simon did not fully understand the traditions of the Shadow-hunter people.

There was a lot in the Law about whom you could and could not marry: If you married a mundane who did not Ascend, you got your Marks stripped and were out on your ear. You could marry a Downworlder in a mundane or a Downworlder ceremony, and you wouldn't be out on your ear but everyone would be embarrassed, some people would act like your marriage did not count, and your terribly traditional Nephilim great-aunt Nerinda would start referring to you as the shame of the family. Plus with the Cold Peace functioning as it was, any Shadowhunter wanting to marry a faerie was probably out of luck.

But Helen Blackthorn was a Shadowhunter, by their own Law, no matter how many people might despise or distrust her for her faerie blood. And Shadowhunters had not actually built it into their precious Law that Shadowhunters could not marry someone of the same sex. Possibly this was just because it hadn't occurred to anyone even as an option way back when.

So Helen and Aline actually could be married, in a full Shadowhunter ceremony, in the eyes of both their families and their world. Even if they were exiled again right afterward, they got this much.

In a Shadowhunter wedding, Simon had been told, you dressed in gold and placed the wedding rune over each other's hearts and arms. There was a tradition a little like giving away the bride, for both parties in a marriage. The bride and groom (or in this case, the bride and bride) would each choose the most significant person to them from their family—sometimes a father, but sometimes a mother, or a *parabatai* or a sibling or chosen friend, or their own child or an elder who symbolized the whole family—and the chosen one, or *suggenes*, would give the bride or groom to their beloved, and welcome the beloved to their own family.

This was not always possible in Shadowhunter weddings, on account of sometimes your whole family and all your friends had been eaten by snake demons. You never knew with Shadowhunters. But Simon thought it was kind of beautiful that Jia Penhallow, Consul and most important member of the Clave, was standing as *suggenes* to give her daughter Aline to the tainted, scandalous Blackthorns, and to receive Helen into the bosom of her family.

Aline'd had some nerve suggesting it. Jia'd had some nerve agreeing to it. But Simon supposed that the Clave had already effectively exiled Jia's daughter: What more could they do to her? And how better to politely spit in their eye than to say: Helen, the faerie girl you spat on and sent away, is now as good as the Consul's daughter.

What is a Shadowhunter made of, if they desert their own, if they throw away a child's heart like rubbish left on the side of the road?

Julian was the one standing to give Helen away. He stood in his gold-inscribed clothes, his sister on his arm, and his sea-in-the-sunlight eyes shone as if he was happy as any kid could be. As though he had not a care in the world.

Helen and Aline were both dressed in golden gowns, golden thread glittering like starlight in Aline's black hair. They were both so happy, their faces outshone their gowns. They stood at the center of the ceremony, twin suns, and for a moment all the world seemed to spin and turn on them.

Helen and Aline drew the marriage runes over each other's

hearts with steady hands. When Aline drew Helen's bright head down to her own for a kiss, there was applause all throughout the hall.

"Thank you for letting us come," whispered Helen after the ceremony was over, embracing her new mother-in-law.

Jia Penhallow folded her daughter-in-law in her arms and said, in a voice considerably louder than a whisper: "I am sorry I must let you be sent away again."

Simon did not tell Julian Blackthorn about meeting Mark, any more than he had told Mark that Helen was not there to care for the Blackthorn children. It seemed hideous cruelty, to load another burden on shoulders already burdened almost past bearing. It seemed better to lie, as faeries could not.

But when he went to Helen and Aline to congratulate them, he stepped up and kissed Helen on the cheek, so he could whisper to her: "Your brother Mark sends you his love, and his happiness for your love."

Helen stared at him, sudden tears in her eyes but her smile even more radiant than before.

Everything is going to change for the Shadowhunters, Simon thought. *For all of us. It has to.*

Simon had special permission to stay the night in Idris, so he would not have to leave the wedding celebrations early.

There was going to be dancing later, but for now people were standing about in groups talking. Helen and Aline were sitting on the floor, in the center of the Blackthorns, like two golden flowers who had sprung up from the ground and bloomed. Tiberius was describing to Helen, in a serious voice, how he and Julian had prepared for the wedding.

"We went through any potential scenario that might occur," he told her. "As if we were reconstructing a crime scene, but in reverse. So I know exactly what to do, no matter what happens."

"That must have been a lot of work," Helen said. Tiberius nodded. "Thanks, Ty. I really appreciate it."

Ty looked pleased. Dru, wearing her flower crown and beaming ear to ear, tugged at Helen's golden skirts for her attention. Simon thought he had rarely seen any group of people who all seemed so happy.

He tried not to think of what Mark would have given to be here.

"You want to go for a walk down the river with me and Izzy?" Clary asked, nudging him.

"What, no Jace?"

"Ah, I see him all the time," said Clary, with the comfort of familiar and trusted love. "Not like my best friend."

Jace—who was sitting talking with Alec, Alec who once again had not addressed a single word to Simon—made an obscene gesture to Simon as he left with Isabelle and Clary on either arm. Simon was not actually fooled that Jace was angry. Jace had hugged him when he saw him, and more and more Simon was coming to believe that he and Jace had not had a relationship in which they hugged before.

But apparently they were huggers now.

Simon, Isabelle, and Clary went walking down by the river. The waters looked like black crystal in the moonlight, and in the distance the demon towers gleamed like columns of moonlight itself. Simon walked a little more slowly than the girls, not used as they were to the strangeness and magic of this city, a city most of the world did not know existed, the shining heart of a secret and hidden land.

Simon was used to the Academy now. He would no doubt get used to all of Idris in time.

So much had changed, and Simon had changed too. But in the end, he had not lost what was most precious to him. He had been given back the name of his heart.

Isabelle and Clary looked back at him, walking so close that Isabelle's waterfall of raven hair mingled with Clary's fiery sunset of curls. Simon smiled and knew how lucky he was, lucky compared to Mark Blackthorn, who was locked away from what he loved best, lucky compared to a billion other people who did not know what it was they loved best of all.

"Are you coming, Simon?" Isabelle called out.

"Yes," Simon called back. "I'm coming."

He was lucky to know them, and lucky to know what they were to him, what he was to them: beloved, remembered, and not lost.

The Fiery Trial

By Cassandra Clare and Maureen Johnson

He turned his head back down to tell Clary to look at the statue,
but Clary was gone. He spun around, a full rotation.
She was nowhere in sight.

—The Fiery Trial

Simon was starting to wonder about the fires. The fires didn't like him. The fires moved around.

That seemed paranoid.

Outside, the trees were bare and the grass was brown. Inside, even the mold had retreated to its winter quarters between the stones in the basement walls. Shadowhunters didn't believe much in central heating. The Academy had fireplaces, never too close together, and never near enough to anyone. No matter where Simon sat, they were at the far end of the room, crackling away. The elites tended to get into rooms first, and they took the fireside seats. But even when they didn't—even when everyone entered at once—Simon ended up farthest from the fire. When you're cold, a crackling fire starts to sound like gentle, mocking laughter. Simon tried to dismiss this thought from his head, because clearly the fires were not laughing at him.

Because *that* was paranoid.

There were several fireplaces in the cafeteria, but George and Simon had stopped trying to get seats near them. Simon had enough to worry about. He was looking at his plate. He had also told himself to stop doing this. Stop thinking about the food. Just eat the food. But he couldn't help himself. Every night he teased it apart. Tonight looked to be some kind of stir-fry, but it appeared to have bread in it. There were peppers. There was something red.

It was pizza. Someone had stir-fried a pizza.

"No," he said out loud.

"What?"

His roommate, George Lovelace, was already shoveling down his dinner. Simon just shook his head. These things didn't bother George in the same way. Back home in Brooklyn, if Simon had heard that someone had stir-fried a pizza he would not have been upset. He would have assumed that some hipster restaurant had decided to deconstruct the pizza, because that is what hipster restaurants in Brooklyn do. Simon would have laughed, and maybe at some point it would have become popular, and then there would be trucks that sold stir-fried pizza, and then he would have eaten it. Because that is how Brooklyn works and because pizza. Best guess in this situation? Maybe someone dropped the pizza, or it broke up in the middle of cooking and for some reason the only conceivable solution was to put it in a pan and wing it.

The problem wasn't the pizza, not really. The problem was that the pizza made him think of home. Any New Yorker confronted with bad pizza will mentally return home for at least a few moments. Simon was born and raised a New Yorker in the same way the elites were born and raised Shadowhunters. It was a part of him—the hum and the throb of the city. It could be as rough as the Academy. He knew to look down for rats on the subway tracks or near the edges of public squares. He was trained instinctively to swerve to avoid getting splashed with dirty snow slush by cabs. He didn't even need to look down to step over puddles left by dogs.

Obviously, there were better parts than that. He missed coming over the Brooklyn Bridge at night and seeing the sweep of it all—the city lit up for the night; the grand, man-made mountains; the river surging underneath. He missed the feeling of being around so many people doing and making amazing things. He missed the constant feeling of the whole thing being a magnificent show. And he missed his family and friends. It was the holiday season now, and he should have been at home. His mother would have already taken out the menorah that he had painted at the do-it-yourself clay workshop when he was a kid. It was bright, decorated in thick, messy strokes of blue, white, and silver paint. He and his sister were in charge of making potato pancakes together. They'd all sit on the sofa and exchange gifts. And everyone he cared about was just a short walk away, a subway stop at the most.

"You've got that look again," George said.

"Sorry," Simon said.

"Don't be sorry. It's okay to be miserable. It's the holidays, and we're here."

This was what was so great about George—he always got

it, and he never judged. There were many downsides to Shadowhunter Academy, but George made up for most of them. Simon had had good friends before. George was like having a brother. They shared a room. They shared their misery and their small triumphs and their terrible meals. And in the competitive atmosphere of the Academy, George always had his back. He never reveled in doing something better than Simon (and being built like one of the lesser Greek gods, George often did excel at physical things). Simon felt his spirits buoy again. Just that George knew what he was thinking—just having his friend there—it was everything.

"What's she doing here?" George asked, nodding his head at someone behind Simon.

Dean Penhallow had appeared at the far end of the room (near the laughing fireplace). She didn't usually come to dinner in the cafeteria. She never came near the place.

"Your attention, please," she said. "We have some wonderful news to share with all students at the Academy. Julie Beauvale. Beatriz Mendoza. Please join me."

Julie and Beatriz stood at the same time and looked at each other with a smile. Simon had seen that kind of smile before, that kind of synchronized movement. That was Jace and Alec all over. The pair made their way through the room. Chairs scraped as people made way, and there was the lightest murmur. The fire laughed and laughed and popped and laughed. When they reached the end of the room, the dean put an arm around each, and they all faced the school body.

"I am pleased to announce that Julie and Beatriz have decided to become *parabatai*."

A sudden rush of applause. Several people stood, mostly in

the elite track, and hooted and called out. This was allowed for a few moments, and then the dean raised her hand.

"As you all know, the *parabatai* ceremony is a serious commitment, a bond broken only by death. I know this news will cause many of you to consider whether you will find a *parabatai*. Not all Shadowhunters have a *parabatai*, or even want one. In fact, most of you will not. That is very important to remember. If you feel, as Julie and Beatriz do, that you have found your *parabatai*, or if you want to speak to someone about any part of the ceremony or what it means, you can speak to any of us. We are all here to help you make this most important of decisions. But again, congratulations to Julie and Beatriz. In their honor, there is a cake this evening."

As she spoke, the lurking evil that was the Academy cooks were bringing out a large, uneven cake.

"You may now resume your meal, and please do have some cake."

"Where did *that* come from?" George asked. "Those two? *Parabatai?*"

Simon shook his head. Shadowhunter families twined around each other like climbing vines. It was easier to find your lifetime partner when you started from birth. Many at the Academy were strangers. Julie and Beatriz, in the elite track, had more connections to each other, but Simon had never gotten the idea that they were that close.

"Well, that was a surprise," George said in a low voice. "You all right?"

It had hit Simon like a bit of a blow. He had thought of asking Clary to be his *parabatai*. But *parabatai* were like Alec and Jace, training together as Shadowhunters since they were kids.

Sure, Simon and Clary had known each other that long, but not in the throwing-knives-and-killing-demons way (except in video games, which, unfortunately, did not count). Simon started to move the idea of *parabatai* into the mental category of things he probably would not have. He was training all the time. He hadn't seen her. He was . . .

. . . very good at making up excuses.

He'd chickened out. He had seen his birthday coming, like a giant countdown clock. Every day he told himself it was too late. Clary had come the day before his birthday, bringing him a *Sandman Omnibus* as a gift. By then, he told himself, the countdown was over. The buzzer went off in his mind. He was nineteen.

He'd tried to put it out of his mind. But now, looking at these two newly announced *parabatai*, he delivered himself a mental kick.

"It's not for everyone, Si," George said. "Come on. Eat up, and we'll go back and you can tell me more about *Firefly*."

In the evenings, Simon had been expanding George's cultural education by explaining the plot of every episode of *Firefly*, one by one. This had become a pleasant ritual, but it, too, had a countdown. There was only one more episode to go.

Before they could do this, the dean made her way past their table and stopped.

"Simon Lewis, if you would please come with me for a moment?"

People from other tables glanced over. George looked down and poked at his pizza-fry.

"Sure?" Simon said. "Am I in trouble?"

"No," she said, her voice flat. "No trouble."

Simon pushed back his chair and stood.

"I'll see you back at the room, yeah?" George said. "I'll bring you some cake."

"Sure," Simon said.

Many people watched him go, because that is what happens when the dean gets you in the middle of dinner. Most of the elites, though, had clustered around Julie and Beatriz. There were laughs and squeals and everyone was talking very loudly. Simon worked his way around them to get to the dean.

"This way," she said.

Simon tried to pause by the fire just for a second, but the dean was already moving toward the door that teachers used to enter and leave the cafeteria. The teachers didn't eat with them all the time. There was clearly some other place, some other dining room somewhere in the Academy. Catarina Loss was the only one who came regularly, and Simon got the impression that she did so because she would rather brave the terrible student food than sit around with a bunch of Shadowhunters in a private room.

Simon had never been in the hall that the dean led him down. It was more dimly lit than the halls the students used. There were tapestries on the stone walls that were certainly as threadbare as the ones in the rest of the school, but they also looked more valuable. The colors were brighter and the gold threading had the glint of real gold. There were weapons along these walls. The student weapons were all in the weapons room, and those had some kind of safety to keep them in place. If you wanted a sword, you needed to undo several straps to get it down. These were placed in simple holders, making them easy to snatch at a second's notice.

The noise of the cafeteria shrank away within the first few steps, and then there was quiet all around. The hall was a series of closed doorways, and the silence crowded him in.

"Where are we going?" Simon asked.

"To the reception room," the dean said.

Simon looked out of the windows as they passed. Here, the glass was a quilt of tiny panes, held together by lead piping. Each diamond of glass was old and warped, and the overall effect was like a cheap kaleidoscope, one that showed only dark and a very lightly falling snow. It was the kind of snow that didn't amount to anything on the ground. It would just dust the dead grass. The technical term for that level, he decided, was an "annoyance" of snow.

They reached a turn in the hall. The dean opened the first door after the turn and revealed a small but grand room, with furnishings that were not in the slightest bit broken or thread-bare. Every chair in the room had legs of the same length, and the sofas were long and comfortable-looking with no visible sags or stuffing. Everything was upholstered in a lush, grape-purple velvet. There was a low table made of cherrywood, and on it was a massive and elaborate silver tea set with china cups. And sitting around the table on the fine-quality chairs and sofas were Magnus Bane, Jem Carstairs, Catarina Loss, and Clary, her red hair bright against her light blue sweater. Magnus and Catarina were together at the end (near the fire— of course it was, as in all other rooms, at the far end). Clary looked up at Simon, and though she smiled as soon as she saw him, her expression suggested that her invitation to this little party had also been recent and not well explained.

"Simon," Jem said. "So good to see you. Please have a seat."

Simon had only had a few encounters with Jem Carstairs, who was apparently as old as his wife, Tessa Gray. They both looked amazingly fit for 150 years. Tessa even looked pretty hot. (Maybe Jem looked hot too? As Simon had thought once before, he probably wasn't the greatest judge of male attractiveness.) Was it weird to think people who were twice as old as your grandparents were good-looking?

"I'll leave you to it," the dean said, and again there was something missing in her tone. It was like she had just said, "I'll just give you this dead snake." She closed the door.

"We're having tea," Magnus said. He was measuring out spoonfuls of loose tea leaves into the strainer of a tiny teapot. "One for each cup. One for the pot."

He set the tiny tea canister aside and picked up one of the large silver pots and poured steaming water through the strainer into the teapot. Catarina was watching him do this with a strange fascination.

Jem looked at ease in a white sweater and dark jeans. His black hair had a single, dramatic streak of silver in it that stood out against his brown skin. "How are you finding the training?" he asked, leaning forward.

"I don't bruise as much anymore," Simon said, shrugging.

"That's excellent," Jem said. "It means you're finding your feet and deflecting more blows."

"Really?" Simon said. "I thought it was because I was dead inside."

Magnus dropped the lid back onto the tiny tea canister very suddenly, making a loud clanking noise.

"I'm very sorry to interrupt your dinner," Jem said. He had a formal way of speaking that was the only thing about him that really showed his age.

"Never be sorry about that," Simon muttered.

"I take it the food in the Academy isn't its best feature."

"I'm not sure it has a 'best' feature," Simon replied.

Jem smiled, his face lighting up. "We have cakes here, and scones. I think these are of a slightly higher quality than you are currently used to."

He indicated a china plate full of small cakes and scones that looked very edible. Simon didn't hesitate. He grabbed the closest scone and shoved it into his mouth. It was a bit dry, but it was better than anything he'd had in a while. He knew crumbs were falling out of his mouth and onto his dark T-shirt, but he found himself not caring.

"Okay, Magnus," Clary said. "You said you would explain why you brought me here when Simon got here. Not that I'm not happy to see you, but you're making me nervous."

Simon nodded and chewed to show he agreed and backed Clary up 100 percent, as best friends were supposed to do. At least he hoped he was communicating that.

Magnus pulled himself up. When a very tall warlock with cat eyes pulls himself up to attention, it changes the mood in the room. There was suddenly a real air of purpose, with an undercurrent of strange energy. Catarina sank back into the sofa, dropping into Magnus's shadow. It wasn't like Catarina to be so silent. Catarina was the blue-tinted voice of reason and minor rebellion in the hallowed halls of the Academy.

"I've been asked to bring you both a message," Magnus said, twisting one of the many rings that adorned his long fingers.

"Emma Carstairs and Julian Blackthorn are to become *parabatai*. The ceremony requires two witnesses, and they have asked for you to be those witnesses."

Clary raised an eyebrow and looked over to Simon.

"Of course," she said. "Emma's a sweetheart. Definitely. I'm in."

Simon was midreach for another scone. He drew back his arm.

"Definitely," he said. "Me too. But why couldn't they just send us a letter?"

Magnus paused for a moment and looked at Catarina, then turned to Simon with a wink.

"Why send a letter when you can send something truly magnificent?"

It was a very Magnus thing to say, but it rang a little hollow. Something about Magnus seemed a little hollow. His voice, maybe.

"The ceremony will be performed in the Silent City tomorrow," Jem said. "We have already arranged permission for you to attend."

"Tomorrow?" Clary said. "And we're just being asked now?"

Magnus shrugged elegantly, indicating that sometimes things like this just happened.

"What do we have to do?" Simon asked. "Is it complicated?"

"Not at all," Jem said. "The position of the witness is largely symbolic, much like a wedding. You have nothing you have to say. It's just a matter of standing with them. Emma chose Clary—"

"I can understand that," Simon said. "But Julian wouldn't choose me. We hardly know each other. Why not Jace?"

"Because Julian isn't particularly close to him, either," said Jem, "and Emma made the suggestion that you and Clary, as best friends, would be meaningful witnesses for them. Julian agreed."

Simon nodded as if he understood, though he wasn't sure he did, really. He remembered having spoken to Julian at Helen and Aline's wedding, not long ago. He remembered thinking what a weight he had on his slight shoulders, and how much he seemed to hold contained, hidden and within. Perhaps it was simply that there was no one else Julian cared for enough to stand as his witness? No one he looked up to? That was incredibly sad, if so.

"In any case," said Magnus, "you are to stand with them as they go through the Fiery Trial."

"The what?" Simon asked.

"That is the true name of the ceremony," Jem said. "The two *parabatai* stand inside rings of fire."

"Tea's ready," Magnus said suddenly. "Never let it sit for more than five minutes. Time to drink up."

He poured two cups from the small pot.

"There's only two cups," Clary said. "What about you?"

"The pot is small. I'll make another one. These are for the two of you. Drink up."

The two cups were presented. Clary shrugged and sipped. Simon did the same. It was, to be fair, exceptional tea. Maybe this was why English people got so excited about it. There was a wonderful clarity to the flavor. It warmed his body as it went down. The room was no longer cold.

"This really is good," Simon said. "I don't really do tea, but I like this. I mean, they give us tea here, but one time I had a cup that had a bone in it, and that was one of the best cups I had."

Clary laughed. "So what are we supposed to wear?" she said. "As witnesses, I mean."

"For the ceremony, formal gear. For the dinner afterward, regular clothing. Something nice."

"Wedding stuff," Catarina finally said. "It's a lot like a wedding but . . ."

". . . without the romance and flowers."

That was Jem.

Magnus was now eying them intently, his cat eyes glistening in the dark. The room had gotten very dark indeed. Simon gave Clary a look that was supposed to mean: *This is weird.* She responded with a very clear look of response that said: *Superweird.*

Simon drank his tea down in a few large gulps and returned the cup to the table.

"It's funny," he said. "There was just another *parabatai* announcement at dinner. Two students from the elite track."

"That's not uncommon for this time of year," Jem said. "As the year draws to a close, people reflect, they make decisions."

The room suddenly got warmer. Had the fire gotten higher? Had it sneaked closer? It was definitely crackling loudly, but now it didn't sound like laughter—it sounded like breaking glass. The fire was speaking to them.

Simon caught himself. The fire was *speaking?* What was wrong with him? He looked around the room fuzzily, and heard Clary make an odd, surprised sound, as if she'd seen something she hadn't expected.

"I think it's time to begin," said Jem. "Magnus?"

Simon could hear Magnus sigh as he stood up. Magnus was

really tall. This, Simon had always known. Now he looked like he might hit the ceiling. He opened a door that Simon hadn't noticed was there.

"Come through here," Magnus said. "There are some things you need to see."

Clary got up and went over to the door. Simon followed. Catarina caught his eye as he went. Everything was unsaid in this room. She didn't quite approve of what was happening. Neither did Magnus.

Whatever was on the other side of the doorway was utterly dark, and Clary hesitated for a second.

"It's fine," Magnus said. "It's just a bit cold in there. Sorry."

Clary went in, and Simon followed a step behind. They were in a shadowy space, definitely cold. He turned, but could no longer see the door. It was just him and Clary. Clary's hair shone bright red in the dark.

"We're outside," Clary said.

Sure enough. Simon blinked. His thoughts were a little slow and stretched. Of course they were outside.

"They maybe could have said we were going outside," Simon said, shivering. "No one here believes in coats."

"Turn around," Clary said.

Simon turned. The door they had just come through—in fact, the entire building they had just come from—was gone. They were simply outdoors, surrounded by just a few trees. The sky above was a purple-gray parchment that seemed to be lit by a low haze of lights on the horizon, just out of sight. There was a web of brick paths all around, dotted with fenced-off areas of trees and urns that probably contained flowers in better weather and now stood as reminders of the season.

It was familiar, and yet, it was like nowhere Simon had ever been.

"We're in Central Park," Clary said. "I think . . ."

"What? We . . ."

But as soon as he said it, it became clear. The low metal fences that marked off the brick paths. But there were no benches, no trash cans, no people. There was no view of the skyline in any direction.

"Okay . . . ," said Simon. "This is weird. Did Magnus just completely screw up? Can that happen? You guys just came from New York. Did he just open up the same Portal?"

"Maybe?" Clary said.

Simon took a deep breath of the New York air. It was bitterly cold and burned the inside of his nose, waking him up.

"They'll realize in a second," Clary said, shivering in the cold. "Magnus doesn't make mistakes."

"So maybe it wasn't a mistake. Maybe we just got a free trip to New York. Or, I did. I'm going to assume that we go wherever we want until they come and get us. You know they have their ways. Might as well take advantage!"

This unexpected and utterly sudden trip home had completely reinvigorated Simon.

"Pizza," he said. "Oh my God. They stir-fried pizza tonight. It was the worst. Maybe coffee. Maybe there's time to get to Forbidden Planet? I just . . ."

He patted his pockets. Money. He had no money.

"You?" he asked.

Clary shook her head.

"In my bag. Back there."

That didn't matter. It was enough to be home. The

suddenness of it only made it more wonderful. Now that he looked more carefully, Simon could see clearly the outlines of the skyscrapers that lined the south end of the park. They looked like the blocks he used to play with as a kid—just a series of rectangles of various sizes set side to side. Some had the faint glow of signs above them, but he couldn't read the writing. He could, however, see the colors of the signs with an unusual clarity. One sign was a pink rose, a bright bloom. The next was the color of electricity. It wasn't just the colors that were sharp. He could smell everything in the air. The metallic tang of the cold. The sea funk of the East River, blocks away. Even the jutting bits of bedrock that reached up and made the many tiny mountains of Central Park seemed to have an odor. There was no garbage, though, and no smells of food or traffic. This was elemental New York. This was the island itself.

"I feel a little weird," Simon said. "Maybe I should have finished dinner. And now that I've just said that, I know there must be something wrong with me."

"You need to eat," Clary said, giving him a light punch. "You're turning into a big muscle man."

"You noticed?"

"It's hard *not* to notice, Superman. You're like the after photo on some commercial for home workout equipment."

Simon blushed and looked away. It wasn't snowing anymore. It was just dark and open, with many trees around. There was a bright bitterness to the cold.

"Where do you think we are?" Clary said. "I'm guessing about . . . midway?"

Simon knew it was possible to walk for some time in Central Park without really having a sense of where you are. The paths wind. The trees create a canopy. The land goes up and down in sharp inclines and declines.

"Over there," he said, pointing at a low pattern of shadows. "It opens up over there. It's the entrance to something. Let's go that way and look."

Clary rubbed her hands together and huddled against the cold. Simon wished he had a coat to offer her, almost more than he wished he had a coat to offer himself. Still, being cold in New York was better than being cold in the Academy. He had to admit, though, that Idris was more temperate. New York weather went to more extremes. This was the kind of cold that would give you frostbite if you stayed out in it too long. They probably needed to figure out where they were and get out of the park and into a building—any building. A store, a coffee shop, whatever they could find.

They walked toward the opening, which revealed itself to be a collection of elaborately carved stone plinths. There were several of these, in sets. Eventually they led to an equally elaborately carved staircase that bent on its way down to a wide terrace with a massive fountain. There was a lake just beyond, covered in ice.

"Bethesda Terrace," Simon said, nodding. "That's where we are. That's in the Seventies, right?"

"Seventy-Second," Clary said. "I've drawn it before."

The terrace was just a large, ornamental area inside of the park and not really somewhere to be on a cold night—but it seemed to be the only place to be. If they walked toward it, at least they would know where they were, as opposed to wandering around in the trees and looping paths. They walked down the stairs together. Strangely, the fountain was going tonight.

It was often turned off in the winter, and certainly when it was freezing cold. But the water flowed freely, and there was no ice on the water in the fountain base. The lights were on and all focused on the statue of the angel that stood in the middle of the fountain on top of two layered tiers and four tiny cherubs.

"Maybe Magnus did mess up," she said.

Clary walked right up to the low edge of the fountain, sat down, and wrapped her arms around herself. Simon stared at the fountain. Funny, he thought, how they hadn't noticed any lights a few minutes ago as they approached. Maybe they'd just come on. The angel of the Bethesda Fountain was one of the most famous statues in all of Central Park—wings extended, water pouring off her outstretched hands.

He turned his head back down to tell Clary to look at the statue, but Clary was gone. He spun around, a full rotation. She was nowhere in sight.

"Clary?" he called.

There were no real places to conceal yourself on the terrace, and he'd looked away for only a moment. He walked halfway around the base of the fountain, calling her name several times. He looked up at the statue again. Same statue, looking down benevolently, water still dripping from her hands.

Except the statue was facing him. And he'd walked to the other side. He should have been looking at the back of it. He took a few more steps. While he never saw anything move, with every step the statue was still facing him directly, her stone expression soft and blank and angelic.

Something clicked in Simon's head.

"Pretty sure this isn't real," he said. "Pretty sure."

The evidence now seemed ridiculously obvious. The

geography of the park was subtly wrong. For a moment he considered the bright, glowing sky, which was now filled with bleached-white clouds the size of entire states. They slid along the firmament, as if watching his progress in an embarrassed drive-by fashion. He was certain he could smell the Atlantic Ocean, and the rocks and stones.

"Magnus!" Simon screamed. "Are you kidding me? Magnus! Jem! Catarina!"

No Magnus. No Jem. No Catarina. No Clary.

"Okay," Simon said to himself. "You have been in worse situations than this. This is just weird. That's all. Just weird. Just very, very weird. Weird's okay. Weird's normal.

"I am in some kind of dream. Something has happened. And I'm going to figure this out. What would I do if this were D and D?"

It was as good a question as any, except the answer had to do with rolling a D20, so maybe it wasn't actually that helpful.

"Is this a trap? Why would they send us to a trap? It must be a game. It's a puzzle. If she was in trouble, I'd know."

That was interesting. He had the sudden and complete knowledge that if Clary were hurt, he would absolutely know it. He didn't feel any hurt. He did feel an absence, a pull to locate her.

As this thought occurred to him, a very unusual thing happened—namely, the great stone angel of Bethesda Fountain flapped her wings and flew straight up into the night sky. As she flew, the base of the fountain remained connected to her feet and pulled up the fountain like it was a plant. The massive reservoir of the fountain became unmoored and started to pull toward the sky. The bricks and mortar tore, and a root network of pipes was revealed, and a raw hole in the earth that rapidly filled with water. The ice on the lake cracked all at once, and the entire terrace started to flood. Simon backed up toward the steps as the water spilled out. He retreated slowly, step by step, until the water evened. The lake now incorporated the terrace, eight steps high. The fountain and the angel were gone.

"That," Simon said, "was weirder than normal."

As he spoke, a sound seemed to tear the night in two. It was a chord, a pure, thundering harmonic that rattled the tympanic bones in his head and physically shook him to his knees. The clouds scattered, as if in fear, and the moon shone clear and full above him. It was a bright yellow, so bright he could barely look at it. He had to shield his eyes and look down.

There was a rowboat. This was not so mysterious—it had come loose from the boathouse, not far away. All of the boats were floating freely, excited to be out on their own for the evening. But this boat had come all the way over and bumped up next to where he was standing.

Also, unlike all of the other rowboats, this one was shaped like a swan.

"I take it I'm supposed to get in," he said, flinching, in case the sky decided to make any more terrifying noises. There was no reply from the sky, so Simon grabbed the neck of the swan with both hands and carefully stepped inside and sat in the middle. The water couldn't be very deep. He would certainly be able to stand in it if the boat capsized. But still—freezing night, flying fountain, magic boat, and missing Clary. No reason to add "falling into cold water" to the mix.

As soon as he was in it, the little swan boat bobbed off, as if it knew it had somewhere to be. It drifted into the lake, avoiding the other loose boats. Simon huddled in, wrapping his arms around himself as he took his cold, gentle journey on the lake. The surface was utterly smooth, reflecting the moon and clouds. Simon hadn't ever done this before. The whole "boating in Central Park" thing seemed like it was meant for tourists. But in his recollection, the lake was fairly small and wide. He was surprised when it narrowed very suddenly and made itself into a channel under a thick canopy of trees. Once under the trees, there was absolutely no light at all for several minutes. Then everything lit up at once—rows of superbright bulbs lined the sides of the channel, and in front of him was a low tunnel with the words TUNNEL OF LOVE written around the arch in lights. Bright pink hearts bookended the word.

"You're joking," Simon said for what felt like the millionth time.

The air was now thick with the smell of popcorn and sea air, and there were sounds of fairground rides. The swan boat bumped, as if moving onto a track that would take it into the tunnel ride. Simon glided in. The light behind him faded, and the tunnel had a soft, blue glow. Some nondescript, classical-lite music played, full of violins. The boat settled into the track. The walls were painted in old-fashioned scenes of lovers—people sitting on porch swings kissing, women lounging on a depiction of a crescent moon, sweethearts leaning over an ice cream soda to kiss. The water was lit from underneath and glowed green, reflecting off the ceiling. Simon looked over the side of the boat to get a sense of how deep it was, or if there was something under him, but it looked shallow, like any normal water ride.

"This is a weird place to meet," said a voice.

Simon turned to see that he was now sharing his little swan

with Jace. Jace was standing at the front of the boat, leaning against the swan's head. Being Jace, his balance was perfect, so the boat didn't rock to the side.

"Okay," Simon said, "this is really taking a turn I didn't expect."

Jace shrugged and looked around at the tunnel.

"I suppose these things had a use at one time," he said. "It was probably risqué to take this ride. You'd get a whole four minutes of unsupervised *necking*."

The word "necking" was bad. Hearing Jace say it was a new kind of bad.

"So," Jace said, "do you want to talk or should I?"

"Talk about what?"

Jace indicated the tunnel around them, as if this was very obvious.

"I'm not going to kiss you," Simon said. "Ever."

"I've never heard anyone say that before," Jace mused. "It was a unique experience."

"Sorry." Simon didn't feel even a little guilty. "If I *was* into guys, I don't think you'd make the top ten."

Jace released the swan's head and came to sit down by Simon's side. "I remember how we met. Do you?"

"You're playing a game of *what do you remember* with me?" Simon asked. "That's classy."

"It's not a game. I saw you. You didn't see me. But I saw. I saw it all."

"This is fun," Simon said. "You and me and the tunnel of what the hell are you talking about."

"You need to try to remember this," Jace said. "This is important. You need to remember how we met."

Whatever this was—a dream, some kind of altered state—it was veering in a very odd direction.

"How is it everything is about you?" Simon said.

"This isn't about me at all. This is about what I saw. This is about what you know. You can get there. You need to get this one back. You need this memory."

"You're asking me to remember somewhere I *didn't see you*?"

"Exactly. Why wouldn't you have seen me?"

"Because you were glamoured," Simon said.

"But someone did see me."

That had to be Clary. Obvious choice. But . . .

Now there was something rocking in the back of Simon's mind. He had been somewhere with Clary, and Jace was there . . . except Jace wasn't there.

That was both in his memory and in the present. Jace was gone. The boat trundled on, turning a corner and plunging back into the dark. There was a short decline and a burst of fog, then the *ooOoOOOoOOoo* of a cartoon ghost and the mocked-up entryway of some kind of Gothic mansion. The ride had gone from lovers' lane to haunted mansion. Simon rode along, through tableaux of the mansion's rooms. In the library, ghosts dangled from wires and a skeleton popped out of a grandfather clock.

This fantasy, or whatever it was, seemed to be tapping into his memories of going to the Haunted Mansion at Disney World when he was a kid. And yet, as they moved from room to room, things looked more familiar—the cracking stone walls, the threadbare tapestries . . . the Haunted Mansion was turning into the Academy. There was a ghostly version of the cafeteria and the classrooms.

"Over here, Simon."

It was Maia, waving from what looked like an elegant, wood-paneled office. There was a sign on the wall behind her, some kind of verse of poetry. Simon only caught a line of it: *"as old and as true as the sky."* Maia wore an elegant suit, her hair clipped back, and gold bangle bracelets on her wrists. She looked sadly at Simon. "Are you really going to leave us?" she said. "Leave being a Downworlder? Become one of them?"

"Maia," Simon said, a lump in his throat. He remembered only bits and pieces of his friendship with her—more than friendship, maybe? How brave she was, and how she'd been his friend when he'd desperately needed one.

"Please," she said. "Don't go."

The boat moved swiftly past, to another room, a completely standard apartment living room, with some cheap furniture. It was Jordan's apartment. Jordan stepped out of the bedroom doorway. There was a wound in his chest; his shirt was black with blood.

"Hey, roomie," he said.

Simon's heart felt like it stopped in his chest. He tried to speak, but before he could say a word, everything plunged into darkness. He felt the boat slide off its track with a soft bump, as if he had come to the end of the ride. Everything rushed forward. The tunnel opened out, and the boat lurched forward suddenly and began to speed up, as if carried on a current. Simon gripped the bench he sat on to hold himself steady.

He had been dumped out on a massive body of water, a river, very wide. Next to him the New York skyline was dark—the buildings eerily not illuminated—but he could make out their shapes. Not far up on the left side, he could see the silhouette of the Empire State Building. Ahead of him, maybe a mile or so up, there was a bridge spanning the river he was on. He could even make out the shadowy outline of an old-fashioned Pepsi-Cola sign on the right bank. That, he knew. That sign was near the base of the 59th Street Bridge to Queens.

"The East River," he said to himself, casting a glance around.

The East River was not somewhere to be at night, in the cold, in a small rowboat shaped like a swan. The East River was dangerous, fast, and deep.

He felt something bump the back of his tiny swan and turned, expecting a trash barge or a freighter. Instead it was another swan-shaped boat. This one contained a young girl, maybe thirteen or fourteen, in a tattered prom dress. She had long blond hair drawn up in uneven pigtails, giving the impression of constant lopsidedness. She pulled her swan to the side of Simon's and, seemingly without a care in the world, pulled up her skirt and stepped from one boat to the other. Simon instinctively reached one hand out to help her and one hand to steady himself. He was sure that the transfer would cause their little swan to topple, and while it did sway uncertainly as the weight distribution changed, somehow they stayed upright. The girl dropped herself next to Simon on the bench. The swan was designed for people to cozy up to each other, so she was pressed against his side.

"Hi!" she said happily. "You're back!"

"I . . . am?"

There was something wrong with the girl's face. She was too pale. There were deep circles all the way around her eyes, and her lips were faintly gray. Simon wasn't sure who she was, but he got a very uneasy feeling.

"It's been forever!" she said. "But you're back. I knew you'd come back for me."

"Who are you?"

She fun-punched him in the arm, like he'd told a great joke.

"Shut up," she said. "You're so funny. That's why I love you."

"You love me?"

"Shut up!" she said again. "You know I love you. It's always been you and me. You and me forever."

"I'm sorry," Simon said. "I don't remember."

The girl looked around at the churning river and dark buildings as if this was all very wonderful and exactly where she wanted to be.

"It was all worth it," she said. "You're worth it."

"Thanks?"

"I mean, they killed me for you. They dumped me in a trash can. But I don't hold it against you."

The chill was now inside of Simon as well as out.

"But you're looking for her, aren't you? She's so annoying."

"Clary?" Simon asked.

The girl waved her hand as if blowing away a cloud of unwanted cigarette smoke.

"You could be with me. Be my king. Be with Queen Maureen. Queen Maureen, queen of death! Queen of the night! I ruled over all of this!"

She swept her hand toward the skyline. While it seemed unlikely that this very young girl could have ruled over New York, there was something about the story that rang true. He knew this. It was his fault. He didn't do anything exactly, but he could feel guilt—terrible, crushing guilt and responsibility.

"What if you could save me?" she asked, leaning into him. "Would you?"

"I . . ."

"What if you had to pick?" Maureen said, smiling at the thought. "We could play a game. You could pick. Me or her. I mean, you are the reason I died, so . . . you should pick me. Save me."

The clouds, ever watchful when something interesting was going on, crowded back in. The wind kicked up and the river took on a heavy wake, rocking the boat from side to side.

"She's in the water, you know," Maureen said. "The water in the fountain that comes from the lake. The water in the lake that comes from the river. The water in the river that comes from the sea. She's in the water, in the water, in the water. . . ."

There was a tremendous pang in Simon's chest, like someone had punched him right in the sternum. Just off to the side of the boat, something appeared, something like stone and seaweed. No. A face, and a crown of hair. It was Clary, floating on her back, eyes closed, hair leading the way. He reached out to her, but the water was going too fast and she was pulled upriver.

"You could make it all better!" Maureen shouted, jumping up. The boat rocked. "Who are you going to save, Daylighter?"

With that she dove off the other side of the boat. Simon grasped the long neck of the swan to hold his balance and scanned the waters. Clary had already floated twenty or more feet away, and Maureen was floating in the same manner, now quiet and seemingly asleep, at about half the distance.

There was not a lot of time to think. He wasn't the strongest swimmer, and the undertow of the river would probably pull him down. The cold would render him numb and probably kill him first.

And he had two people to save.

"This isn't real," he said to himself. But the pain in his chest said otherwise. The pain was calling to him. He was also sure that, real or not, when he jumped in the river, it was going to hurt as much or more as anything he'd ever felt. The river was real *enough*.

What was real? What did he have to do? Was he supposed to swim *past* a young girl and leave her? If he ever made it that far.

"Hard choices," said a voice behind him.

He didn't have to turn to know it was Jace, balanced elegantly on the tail of the wooden swan.

"That's what it's all about. Hard choices. They never get easier."

"You're not helping," Simon said, kicking off his shoes.

"So you're going in?" Jace looked at the water and cringed. "Even I'd think twice about that. And I'm amazing."

"Why do you have to get involved in everything?" Simon asked.

"I go where Clary goes."

The two bodies drifted on.

"So do I," Simon said. And he jumped off the right side of the boat, holding his nose. No diving. No need for theatrics. Jumping was enough, and at least it would keep him upright.

The pain of the water was even worse than he thought. It was like jumping through glass. The icy cold crackled all over his body, forcing all the air from his lungs. He reached for the boat but it drifted off, with Jace at the tail, waving. Simon's clothes were pulling him under, but he had to fight. Hard as it was to move his arms, he stretched out to try to swim. His muscles contracted, unable to function at this temperature.

None of them could survive this. And this did not feel like a dream. Being in this water, which was pulling harder now, pulling him down—this was as good as being dead. But something crackled into his mind, some knowledge that had been well, well pushed away. He had known what it was like to be dead. He had had to claw his way out of the ground. He'd had soil in his eyes and in his mouth. The girl, Maureen, she was dead. Clary was not. He knew this because his own heart was still beating—erratically, but still beating.

Clary.

He reached out again and struggled with the water. One stroke.

Clary.

Two strokes. Two strokes were ridiculous. The water was faster and stronger and his limbs were shaking and so heavy. He started to feel sleepy.

"You can't give up now," said Jace. The boat had circled around and was now on Simon's right side, just out of reach. "Tell me what you know."

Simon was not in the mood to be quizzed. The river and the earth itself were pulling him down.

"Tell me what you know," Jace insisted.

"I . . . I . . ."

Simon couldn't make words.

"Tell me!"

"C . . . C . . . Clar . . ."

"Clary. And what do you know about her?"

Simon definitely couldn't speak anymore. But he knew the

answer. He would go to her. Alive. Dead. Fighting the river. Even if his dead body drifted alongside hers, that would somehow have to be enough. The knowledge caused his body to warm, just a bit. He kicked against the water.

"There you go!" said Jace. "Now you're getting it. Now, you go."

Simon's entire body shuddered violently. His face dipped below the surface for a moment and he took on water, which burned him from the inside. He pushed out again, spat it out.

One stroke. Two. Three. It wasn't as futile now. He was swimming. Four. Five. He counted them off. Six. Seven.

"I know the feeling," Jace said, drifting alongside him. "It's hard to explain. They don't make greeting cards for it."

Eight. Nine.

The city began to light up. Starting at the ground level, the lights appeared, reaching up toward the sky.

"When you realize it," Jace said, "you know that you can do anything, because you have to. Because it's you. You're one."

Ten. Eleven.

No need to count now. Jace and the swan were lagging behind, and now he was alone, swimming on, his body pumping with adrenaline. He turned to look for Maureen, but she was gone. Clary, however, was still clearly visible, floating just ahead. Not floating.

Swimming. Toward him. She was doing exactly what he was doing, forcing her body on, shuddering, pushing through the water.

Simon powered through the last strokes and felt the touch of her hand. He would go—he would go with her. And she was smiling, her lips blue.

And then he felt the ground under him—some surface under the water, something just a foot or two down. Clary reacted at the same moment, and they both grabbed at each other and struggled to their feet. They were standing in the Bethesda Fountain, the angel statue looking down on them, pouring water on their heads.

"Y—you—" Clary said.

Simon didn't try to speak. He embraced her, and they shuddered together before stepping carefully out of the fountain and lying down on the bricks of the terrace, heaving for breath. The moon was wide—too wide and too close.

Mentally, Simon told the moon to stop being so close and bright and that it should just generally shut up with the mooniness. He reached out and took Clary's hand, which was already extended, waiting for his.

When he opened his eyes, he was not outside. He was on something fairly comfortable and plush. Simon reached around and felt a velvety surface under him. He sat up and realized he was on a sofa in the reception room. The tea set was there, in front of him. Magnus and Catarina were standing against the wall, conferring, and Jem sat in the chair between them and watched them both.

"Sit up slowly," he said. "Take a few deep breaths."

"What the hell?" Simon said.

"You drank water from Lake Lyn," Jem said quietly. "The waters produce hallucinations."

"You had us drink water from *Lake Lyn*? Where's Clary?"

"She is fine," Jem said quietly. "Drink some water. You must be thirsty."

A glass was already against Simon's lips. Catarina was holding it.

"Are you joking?" Simon said. "You want me to drink that? After what just happened?"

"It's fine," Catarina said. She took a long sip from the glass and held it back in front of Simon's mouth. He did have a crazy case of cottonmouth, actually. His tongue felt thick. He took the glass and drank it back in one go, then filled it again, and again from a pitcher on the table. Only after the third glass did he feel like he could speak again.

"Doesn't that drive people insane?" he said, not bothering to disguise his anger in any way.

Jem sat calmly, his hands resting on his knees. Simon could see his age now, not in his face but behind his eyes. They were dark mirrors that reflected the passage of uncounted years.

"Had something gone wrong, you would have been with the Silent Brothers within the hour. I may not be a Silent Brother anymore, but I have previously treated those who have consumed the waters. Magnus prepared the tea because he has worked with both of your minds. Catarina, of course, is a nurse. You were always safe. I am sorry. None of us wanted to deceive you. This was done for your benefit."

"Not an explanation," Simon said. "I want to see Clary. I want to know what's going on."

"She's fine," Catarina said. "I'll go check on how she's doing. Don't worry."

She left, and Jem leaned forward in his chair.

"Before Clary comes in, I need to know: What did you *see*?"

"When you drugged me?"

"Simon, this is important. What did you see?"

"I was in New York. I . . . thought I was in New York. Did we go to New York? Did you open a Portal?"

Jem shook his head.

"You were in this room the entire time. Please. Tell me."

"Clary and I were in Central Park, by the Bethesda Fountain. The angel in the fountain flew away and the fountain flooded, and Clary disappeared. Then some boat came and I was on a 'tunnel of love' ride with Jace, and he kept telling me to remember where we met, even though I didn't see him."

"Stop a moment," Jem said. "What does that mean to you?"

"I have no idea. I just know he was saying that I had to remember."

"*Do* you remember?"

"No," Simon snapped. "I barely remember anything. I know I was probably with Clary. Clary could see him."

"Go on," Jem said. "What happened then?"

"I saw Maia, he said. "And I saw Jordan. He was covered in blood. Then this ride dumped me out on the East River, and some kid named Maureen said she died because of me and jumped in. Clary was floating on the water and I . . ."

He shuddered again, and Jem immediately stood and produced a blanket, wrapping it around his shoulders.

"Move closer to the fire," Jem said, guiding him up and to a chair. When Simon had settled a bit and warmed, Jem encouraged him to continue.

"Maureen told me I had to decide which one of them to save. Jace showed up again and gave me some lecture about how all the choices were hard. I jumped in."

"Who did you decide to save?" Jem asked.

"I hadn't . . . decided . . . anything. I knew I had to jump. And I guess I knew Maureen was dead. She said she was dead. But Clary wasn't. I just had to get to Clary. I got all of this energy all of a sudden and I could swim to her. And when I swam to her, I looked up and she was swimming to me."

Jem sat back and tented his fingers together for a moment.

"I want to see Clary," Simon said through chattering teeth. His body was warm—it had probably never been cold, really—but the river water still felt so real.

Catarina reappeared a moment later with Clary, who was also wrapped in a blanket. Jem immediately got up and offered her his chair. Clary's eyes were wide and shining, and she looked to Simon in relief.

"Did it happen to you, too?" she said. "Whatever that was."

"I think we both got it," he replied. "Are you okay?"

"I'm fine. I'm just . . . really cold. I thought I was in the river."

Simon stopped shivering.

"You thought you were in the river?"

"I was trying to swim to you," Clary said. "We were in Central Park, and you got sucked into the ground—like you were being buried alive. And Raphael came, and I was on his motorcycle, and we were flying over the river and I saw you. I jumped off. . . ."

From behind Clary's chair, Catarina nodded.

"I saw something kind of like that," Simon said. "Not exactly, but . . . enough. And I reached you. You were swimming to me. Then we were back . . ."

". . . in Central Park. By the fountain with the angel."

Magnus had joined the group as well and stretched himself out on a sofa. "Bethesda Fountain," he said. "Shadowhunters may have had something to do with building it. I'm just saying."

"What does this all mean?" Simon asked. "What was this about?"

"The two of you are different," Magnus said. "There are things in your backgrounds that mean that . . . things have to be done differently. For a start, both of you have had blocks put on your memories. Clary has an unusual amount of angel blood. And you, Simon, used to be a vampire."

"We know that. But why did you have to drug us to do something symbolic?"

"It wasn't symbolic. The *parabatai* test is the test of fire," Catarina said. "You stand in rings of fire to make your bond. This . . . this is the test of water. The nature of the test requires that you have no knowledge of the test. Mentally preparing for the test can affect the outcome. This test wasn't about Julian and Emma. It's about the two of you. Think about what you both saw, what you both learned. Think about what you felt. Think about when you were both able to swim to each other when you had nothing left, when you should have died."

Simon and Clary stared at each other. The fog began to lift.

"You took the water," Jem said. "And you joined in the same place in your minds. You were able to find each other. You were linked. 'And it came to pass that the soul of Jonathan was knit with the soul of David, and Jonathan loved him as his own soul.'"

"*Parabatai?*" Simon said. "Wait, wait, wait. Are you trying to tell me this is about being *parabatai*? I can't have a *parabatai*. I turned nineteen two months ago."

"Not exactly," Magnus said.

"What do you mean *not exactly*?"

"Simon," Magnus said plainly, "you died. You were dead for nearly half a year. You may have been walking around, but you were not alive, not as a human. That time does not count. By Shadowhunter standards, you are still eighteen. And you have the whole year until your nineteenth birthday to find a *parabatai*." He looked toward Clary. "Clary, as you know, is still within the age limit. There should be time for you to Ascend and then for you two to become *parabatai* immediately—if that's what you want."

"Some people are uniquely suited to be *parabatai*," said Magnus. "Born to it, you might say. People think it's about getting along, about always agreeing, being in sync. It's not. It's about being better together. Fighting better together. Alec and Jace haven't always agreed, but they've always been better together."

"It has been spoken of often to me," Jem said in his soft voice, "how much the two of you were dedicated to each other. The manner in which you have always stood up for each other and put the other first. When a *parabatai* bond is true, when the friendship runs deep and honest, it can be . . . transcendent." There was sadness in his eyes, a sadness so profound it was almost frightening. "We needed to find out if what had been observed about the two of you was true for your sake. You're about to witness the ceremony. That can cause a powerful reaction in true *parabatai*. We had to know for sure that it was true and that you could withstand it. The test told us what we needed to know."

Clary's eyes had gone very wide. "Simon . . . ," she whispered. Her voice was raspy.

"It's a bit of a technicality," Magnus added, "but Shadowhunters have no problems with technicalities. They love a technicality. Look at Jem. Jem is a technicality in the flesh. People don't come back from being Silent Brothers, either, and there he is."

Jem smiled at this, the sadness in his eyes receding.

"*Parabatai*," Clary said again.

And in that moment, something settled over Simon. Something like a blanket on a cold day. Something completely reassuring.

"*Parabatai*," he said.

A long moment settled between them, and in that moment, all was decided. There was no need to discuss it. You do not need to ask if your heart should beat, or if you should breathe. He and Clary were *parabatai*. All of Simon's anger was gone. Now he knew. He had Clary, and she would have him. Forever. Their souls knit.

"How did you know?" Simon asked.

"It's not that hard to see," Magnus replied, and finally some of the usual levity was in his voice. "I'm also literally magic."

"It's pretty obvious," Catarina added.

"Even I knew," said Jem. "And I don't know you very well. There's always something about true *parabatai*. They don't need to speak to communicate. I saw the two of you having entire conversations without saying a word. It was like that with my *parabatai*, Will. I never had to ask Will what he was thinking. In fact, it was usually *better* not to ask Will what he was thinking. . . ."

That got a smile from Magnus and Catarina both.

"But I see it between you. True *parabatai* are linked long before the ceremony takes place."

"So we can . . . we can do the ceremony?" Clary asked.

"You can," Jem said. "Not tonight. There will be some

discussions in the Silent City about it, surely, as this is an unusual case."

"All right," Catarina said. "Now the nurse is taking over. That's enough for tonight. You two need sleep. That water packs a punch. You'll be fine in the morning, but you need to rest. Rest and hydrate. Come on."

Simon went to stand and found that his legs had left him and had been replaced with a wobbly, leg-shaped substance. Catarina caught him up under the shoulder and helped him. Magnus helped Clary to her feet.

"There's a room for you here tonight, Clary," Catarina said. "In the morning we'll have the dress gear brought to you both for Julian and Emma's ceremony."

"Wait," Simon said as he was being ushered out. "Jace kept saying something about how I had to remember how he and I met. What does that mean?"

"That's for you to figure out," Jem said. "The visions caused by Lake Lyn can stir very powerful feelings."

Simon nodded. His body was giving out. He allowed Catarina to help him back to his room.

"What happened to you?" George said as Catarina got him in the door.

"How long have I been gone?" Simon replied, dropping face-first onto his bed. It was a sign of his exhaustion that his terrible, sharp-springed bed felt good. It felt like a hundred down pillows heaped on the back of a bouncy castle.

"Maybe two hours," George said. "You look terrible. What was it?"

"The food," Simon mumbled. "It finally got me."

And then he was asleep.

* * *

He felt surprisingly okay when he woke up. He woke before George, even. He got out of bed quietly and picked up his towel and things to go down to the bathrooms. On the ground outside the door, in a black box, was a set of formal gear. Formal Shadowhunter gear looked much like regular gear—it was just lighter in weight, somehow more deeply black, and cleaner than most gear. No tears. No ichor. Fancy duds. He put the box on his bed and quietly continued to the bathroom. No one was awake yet, so he had the whole moldy place to himself. It turned out if you woke up first, you could actually get a tiny bit of hot water, so he stood under the spray, pretended that it didn't taste of rust, and let his body relax in the warmth. There was just enough light coming through the window high up on the wall that he could get what amounted to an almost even shave.

He walked through the empty halls of the Academy, which were softened by the early morning light. Nothing looked so severe this morning. It was almost cozy. He even found one of the hall fires burning, and he stood beside it to get warm before going outside for some air. He wasn't surprised to find Clary there, already dressed, sitting on the top step, looking out over the mist that floated over the grounds at dawn.

"You woke up early too, huh?" she said.

He sat down next to her.

"Yup. Get up before the kitchen starts cooking. That's the only way to escape it. I'm starving, though."

Clary rummaged around in her bag for a moment and produced a bagel wrapped in several small deli napkins.

"Is that . . . ," Simon said.

"You think I would come from New York empty-handed?

No cream cheese, but, you know, it's something. I know what you need."

Simon held the bagel for a moment.

"It makes sense," she said. "You and me. I feel like it's always been true. It's always what we were. You don't . . . I know you don't remember it all, but it's always been you and me."

"I remember enough," he said. "I feel enough."

He wanted to say more, but the enormity of it all—much of this was best left unsaid. For now, anyway. It was still so fresh in his mind, this feeling. This feeling of *completeness*.

So he ate the bagel. Always eat the bagel.

"Emma and Julian," Simon said between bites. "They're only fourteen."

"Jace and Alec were fifteen."

"Still, it seems . . . I mean, they've been through a lot. The attack on the L.A. Institute."

"I know," Clary said, nodding. "But bad stuff . . . it brings people together sometimes. They've had to grow up fast."

A black horse-drawn carriage appeared on the edge of the road leading to the Academy. As it grew closer, Simon could see a figure in a plain, parchment-colored robe at the reins. When the carriage stopped and the figure turned to them, Simon could see the runes that sealed the man's mouth. When the man spoke, it was not through normal words, but in a voice that landed right inside of Simon's mind.

I am Brother Shadrach. I am here to take you to the ceremony. Please get inside.

"You know," said Simon quietly as they got into the carriage, "there was probably a time when we would have considered this creepy."

"I don't remember that time anymore," replied Clary.

"I guess we're finally even on something we don't remember."

The carriage was simply appointed in black silk, black curtains, black everything, really. But it was well sprung and comfortable, as far as speeding horse carriages go. Brother Shadrach had no fear of speed, and soon the Academy was in the distance and Simon and Clary were looking at each other from across the carriage as they bounced along. Simon tried to talk a few times, but his voice juddered from the impact, the constant *thud thud thud* of the carriage making its way across Brocelind Plain. The roads in Idris were not the smooth highways Simon was used to. They were paved in stone, and there were no rest stops with bathrooms and Starbucks. There was no heat, but each had been provided with a heavy fur blanket. As a vegetarian, Simon didn't really want to use it. As a person without much choice who was freezing, he did.

Simon also had no watch, no phone, nothing to tell the passing time except the rising of the late-autumn sun. He estimated that they rode an hour, maybe more. They entered the calming shade of the Brocelind Forest. The smell of the trees and leaves was almost intoxicating, and the sun came through in slashes and ribbons, illuminating Clary's face and hair, her smile.

His *parabatai*.

They stopped not too far into the forest. The door opened, and Brother Shadrach was there.

We have arrived.

Somehow, it was worse when it stopped. Simon's head and body still felt like they were shaking. Simon looked up and saw that they were near the base of a mountain. It stretched above the trees.

This way.

They followed Brother Shadrach down a barely marked track—a light trail where several feet had passed, leaving just the tiniest scar on the ground, a few inches wide. Through a thicket of trees against the mountainside, there was a doorway, about fifteen feet in height. It was wide at the base and narrower at the top. There was a bas-relief carving of an angel just above the lintel. Brother Shadrach took one of the rings on the door and knocked it hard, just once. The door opened, seemingly of its own accord.

They walked down a narrow passage with smooth marble walls, and descended a staircase made of stone. There were no rails, so he and Clary put their hands on either wall to keep from falling. Brother Shadrach, in his long robe, had no such fear of falling. He seemed to glide down. From there, they were in a larger space, which Simon at first thought was made of stones. After a moment he saw that the walls were mosaicked with bones—some chalky white, some gray, some ashy, and some a disturbing brownish color. Long bones formed arches and columns, and skulls, top side out, formed most of the walls. They were finally left in a room where the bone art was really ambitious—great circling patterns of skulls and bones gave the room shape. Above, smaller bones formed more delicate structures, such as chandeliers, which glowed with witchlights. It was like being shown the end of the world's worst home-decorating show.

You will wait here.

Brother Shadrach exited the chamber, and Simon and Clary were left alone. One thing about the Silent City: It really lived up to its name. Simon had never been anywhere so utterly devoid of sound. Simon worried that if he spoke, the walls of bones would come down on his head and bury them both. They probably wouldn't—that would be a major design flaw—but the sensation was strong.

After several moments the door opened again and Julian appeared alone. Julian Blackthorn may only have been fourteen, but he seemed older, even older than Simon. He had grown quite a bit, and now Simon could look him eye to eye. He had his family's characteristic thick, curling dark-brown hair, and his face had a look of quiet seriousness. It was a seriousness that reminded Simon of the way his mother had looked when his father died, and she'd spent nights awake worrying about how to pay the mortgage and feed her children, how to raise them all by herself. No one wore this kind of expression by choice. The only sign that Julian wasn't an adult was the way his dress gear fit a bit loose, and the way he was just a bit gangly.

"Julian!" Clary said, looking as if she was considering hugging him and then discarding the idea. He seemed too dignified to be squeezed. "Where's Emma?"

"Talking to Brother Zachariah," Julian said. "I mean Jem. She's talking to Jem."

Julian seemed deeply puzzled about this, but also didn't look to be in the mood to be questioned further.

"So," Clary said, "how do you feel?"

Julian simply nodded and looked around.

He hesitated. "I just want to . . . do it. I want to get it done."

This seemed like a slightly odd response. Now that Simon was thinking about his own ceremony with Clary, the prospect seemed amazing. Something to be looked forward to. But Julian had been through a lot. He'd lost his parents, his older brother and sister. It was probably hard to go through something this major without them there.

It was hard to look at Julian and not remember that he had seen Julian's brother Mark not that long ago—Mark, imprisoned and half-mad. That he had decided not to share this fact with Julian, because it would have been unbelievably cruel to do so. Simon still believed his decision had been the right one, but that didn't mean it didn't weigh like a stone in his soul.

"How's L.A.?" he said, and immediately regretted it. How's L.A.? How's that place you live in where you saw your father murdered and your brother taken hostage forever by faeries? How's that?

Julian's mouth curled up at the corner. As if he sensed that Simon was feeling uncomfortable, and he felt sympathetic, but also thought it was funny.

Simon was used to that.

"Hot," Julian said.

Which was fair enough.

"How's your family?" Clary asked.

Julian's face lit up, his eyes glowing like the surface of water. "Everyone is good. Ty's really into detective stuff, Dru's into horror—watching all sorts of mundane movies she's not supposed to. But then she scares herself and has to sleep with the witchlight on. Livvy's gotten really good with the sabre, and Tavvy—"

He broke off as Jem and Emma came down the stairs. Emma's step seemed lighter. There was something about Emma that made Simon think of eternal summers on a beach—her sunbleached hair, her graceful way of moving, her winter tan. Along the inside of one of her arms was a vicious long scar.

She looked at once to Julian, who nodded before starting to pace around the room. Emma immediately wrapped Simon in a hug. Her arms, though smaller than his, wound around him like steel cables. She smelled like sea spray.

"Thank you for being here," she said. "I wanted to write to you but they . . ." She looked at Jem for a moment. "They said they would tell you. Thank you, both of you."

Julian ran his hand along the smooth marble wall. He seemed to have trouble looking over at Emma. Emma went to him, and Jem followed, speaking to them both for a moment. Clary and Simon stood back and watched them. Something about the way Emma and Julian were acting wasn't quite what Simon expected. Sure, they would be nervous but . . .

No, it was something else.

Clary tugged on Simon's sleeve, indicating that he should lean down so she could whisper to him.

"They look so"—Clary broke off her sentence and cocked her head slightly to the side—"young."

There was a hint in her voice that this was not a completely satisfactory statement. Something about this was off. But Simon had no time to figure out what. Jem, Emma, and Julian joined them again.

"I will accompany you into the chamber," Jem said. "Clary will walk with Emma. Simon will walk with Julian. Do you feel ready to continue?"

Both Emma and Julian visibly swallowed hard and got very wide-eyed, but both managed to say yes.

"Then we will proceed. Please follow me."

More corridors, but the bone gave way to more white marble, and then marble that had the appearance of gold. They arrived at a great set of doors, which were opened by Brother Shadrach. The room they led to was the largest yet, with a towering, domed ceiling. There were marbles of all colors—white, black, pink, gold, silver. Every surface was utterly smooth. The room was occupied by a ring of Silent Brothers, maybe twenty in all, who parted to allow them in. The light in the room was dim and came from golden sconces and flickering candlelight. The air was thick with incense.

"Simon Lewis and Julian Blackthorn." Jem's voice resonated—for a moment Simon almost thought he heard it inside his mind, the way he had once heard Brother Zachariah's. It still held a depth to it that seemed richer than human. "Cross to the other side of the circle, where they have made a space for you. When you get there, remain there. You will be told what to do."

Simon looked to Julian, who had turned the color of copier paper. Despite looking like he might faint, Julian walked firmly across the room, and Simon followed. Clary and Emma took their places on the opposite side. Jem joined the circle of Silent Brothers, who all stepped back as one, widening the circle. Now the four of them were at the center.

Suddenly, two rings of white and gold fire appeared out of the floor, the flames rising just a few inches, but burning bright and hot.

Emma Carstairs. Step forward.

The voices rang in Simon's head—it was all of the Brothers speaking as one. Emma looked to Clary, then took a single step into one of the rings. She fixed her eyes on Julian and smiled widely.

Julian Blackthorn. Step forward.

Julian stepped into the other ring. His step was quicker, but he kept his head down.

Witnesses, you will stand on the wings of the angel.

This took Simon a moment to work out. He finally saw that at the top of the circle, carved roughly into the floor, was another figure of an angel with outstretched wings. He took his place on one, and Clary the other. This brought him a little closer to the ring of fire. He felt the heat of it creep pleasantly over his cold feet. From this vantage point, he could see Emma's and Julian's expressions.

What was he seeing? It was something he knew.

We begin the Fiery Trial. Emma Carstairs, Julian Blackthorn, enter the center ring. In this ring, you will be bound.

A central ring appeared, joining the two. A Venn diagram of fire. As soon as Emma and Julian were in it, the center ring burned higher, reaching waist height.

Something flickered between Julian and Emma at that moment. It was so quick that Simon couldn't tell which direction it had come from, but he'd seen it out of the corner of one of his eyes. Some look, something about the way one of them stood, something—but it was a look or a stance or *something* that he had seen before.

The fire flashed higher. It was up to their shoulders now.

You will now recite the oath.

Emma and Julian began speaking as one, their voices both with a small tremble as they recited the ancient Biblical words.

"Whither thou goest, I will go . . ."

Simon was hit with a bolt of anxiety. What had he just seen? Why was it so familiar? Why did it put him on edge? He studied Emma and Julian again, as best as he could over the fire. They looked like two nervous kids about to do something very serious, while standing in a flaming circle.

There it was again. So quick. The direction was obscured by the flickering at the top of the ring. What the hell was it? Maybe this was precisely what witnesses were supposed to do. Maybe they were supposed to watch for this kind of thing. No. Jem said it was a formality. A formality. Maybe he should have asked this question before standing next to the giant ring of fire.

"Where thou diest, I will die, and there will I be buried . . ."

Shadowhunter rituals, always cheery.

"The Angel do so to me, and more also . . ."

Julian tripped on the words "do so to me." He cleared his throat and finished the statement a second after Emma.

Something clicked in Simon's mind. He remembered Jace, suddenly, in his hallucination, saying something about the first time they'd met. And then the memory flashed across his mind like one of those banners trailing off the back of the little planes that flew above the beach off Long Island. . . .

He was sitting with Clary in Java Jones. They were watching Eric read poetry. Simon had decided this was the moment—he was going to tell her. He had to tell her. He had gotten them both coffees and the cups were hot. His fingers were burned. He had to blow on them, which was not a smooth move.

He could feel the burning. The feeling that he had to speak.

Eric was reading some poem that contained the words "nefarious loins." *Nefarious loins, nefarious loins* . . . the words danced in his head. He had to speak.

"There's something I want to talk to you about," he said.

Clary made some remark about his band name, and he had to get her back on point.

"It's about what we were talking about before. About me not having a girlfriend."

"Oh, I don't know. Ask Jaida Jones out. She's nice, and she likes you."

"I don't want to ask Jaida Jones out."

"Why not? You don't like smart girls? Still seeking a *rockin' bod*?"

Was she blind? How could she not see? What exactly did he have to do? He had to keep it together. Also, "seeking a rockin' bod"?

But the more he tried, the more oblivious she seemed. And then she became fixated on a green sofa. It was like that sofa contained everything in the world. Here he was, trying to declare his lifelong love, and Clary had fallen for the furniture. But it was more than that. Something was wrong.

"What is it?" he asked. "What's wrong? Clary, what's wrong?"

"I'll be right back," she said. And with that, she put down the coffee and ran away. He watched her through the window, and somehow he knew that this moment was over, forever. And then he saw . . .

The ring of fire had extinguished. It was over. The oath was made, and Emma and Julian stood before them all. Julian had a rune on his collarbone, and Emma on her upper arm.

Clary was tugging his arm. He looked over at her and blinked a few times.

You okay? her expression said.

His memory had chosen quite a moment to return.

After the ceremony, they returned to Alicante, where they were taken to the Blackthorn manor to change their clothes. Emma and Julian were taken by the staff to rooms on the main floor. Clary and Simon were led up the grand staircase.

"I don't know what I'm supposed to change into," Simon said. "I didn't get a lot of advance notice."

"I brought you a suit from home," Clary said. "I borrowed it."

"Not from Jace."

"From Eric."

"Eric has a suit? Do you promise it wasn't, like, his dead grandfather's?"

"I can't promise anything, but I do think it will fit."

Simon was shown to a small, fussy bedroom on the second floor, overstuffed with furniture and crowded in by flocked wallpaper and the penetrating stares of some long-deceased Blackthorns who had taken up residence in the form of severe portraits. The suit bag was on the bed. Eric did have a suit—a plain black one. A shirt had also been provided, along with a silver-blue tie and some dress shoes. The suit was an inch or two too short. The shirt was too tight—Simon's daily training had made him into one of these people who burst through a dress shirt. The shoes didn't fit at all, so he wore the soft black shoes that were part of the formal gear. The tie fit fine. Ties were good for this.

He sat on the bed for a moment and let himself think about all that had happened. He closed his eyes and fought the urge to sleep. He felt himself wobbling and dropping off when there was a soft knock on the door. He snorted as he came back from the microsleep.

"Sure," he said, which wasn't what he meant to say. "Yeah. I mean, come in."

Clary entered wearing a green dress that perfectly complemented her hair, her skin, every part of her. And Simon had a revelation. If he still felt romantic attraction toward Clary, seeing her at that moment might have caused him to start sweating and stammering. Now he saw someone he loved, who looked beautiful, and was his friend. And that was all.

"Listen," she said, shutting the door, "back at the ceremony, you looked . . . weird. If you don't want to do it . . . The *parabatai* thing. It was a shock and I don't want you to be . . ."

"What? No. No."

Instinctively he reached for her hand. She squeezed it hard.

"Okay," she said. "But something happened in there. I saw it."

"In the hallucination I had, from the lake water, I saw Jace, and he kept telling me to remember how we met," he said. "So I was trying to remember. And then right in the middle of the ceremony, I got the memory back. It just kind of . . . downloaded."

Clary frowned, her nose wrinkling in confusion. "The memory of how you met Jace? Wasn't it at the Institute?"

"Yes and no. The memory was really about us, you and me. We were in the coffee shop, Java Jones. You were naming all of these girls I could date and I was . . . I was trying to tell you that you were the one I liked."

"Yeah," Clary said, looking down.

"And then you ran out. Just like that."

"Jace was there. You couldn't see him."

"That's what I thought." Simon studied her face. "You ran out while I was telling you how I felt. Which is okay. We were never meant to be . . . like that. I think that's what my subconscious, in the annoying form of Jace, wanted me to know. Because I think we are meant to be *together*. *Parabatai* can't like each other like that. That's why it was important for me to remember. I had to remember that I felt like that. I had to know it was different now. Not in a bad way. In the right way."

"Yes," Clary said. She had gotten a little teary-eyed. "In the right way."

Simon nodded once. It was too big to reply to in words. It was everything. It was all the love he saw in Jem's eyes when he talked about Will, and the love in Alec's face when he looked at Jace, even when Jace was being annoying, and a clear memory he had of Jace holding Alec while he was wounded and the desperation in Jace's eyes, that terror that comes only from thinking you might lose someone you can't live without.

It was Emma and Julian, looking at each other.

Someone was calling for them from downstairs. Clary brushed away a tear and got up and smoothed her already smooth dress.

"This *is* like a wedding," she said. "I feel like they're going to tell us we have to go pose for the photographer in a minute."

Clary hooked her arm through his.

"One thing," he said, remembering Maia, and Jordan. "Even when I'm a Shadowhunter, I'm still going to be a little bit a Downworlder. I'm never going to turn my back on them. That's the kind of Nephilim I want to be."

"I wouldn't have expected anything else," Clary said.

Downstairs, the two new *parabatai* were examining each other from across the room. Emma stood on one side, wearing a brown dress covered in twining gold flowers. Julian stood on the other, twitching inside his gray suit.

"You look amazing," Clary said to them both, and they looked down shyly.

At the Accords Hall, Jace was waiting for them on the front step, looking like Jace in a suit. Jace in a suit was unbearable. He gave Clary a look up and down.

"That dress is . . ."

He had to clear his throat. Simon enjoyed his discomfiture. Not much ever threw Jace, but Clary had always been able to throw him like a Wiffle ball on a windy day. His eyes were practically cartoon hearts.

"It's very nice," he said. "So how was the ceremony? What did you think?"

"Definitely more fire than a bar mitzvah," Simon said. "More fire than a barbecue. I'm going to go with Formal Event with the Most Fire."

Jace nodded.

"They were amazing," Clary said. "And . . ."

She looked to Simon.

"We have news," she said.

Jace cocked his head in interest.

"Later," she said, smiling. "I think everyone is waiting for us to sit down."

"Then we need to get Emma and Julian over here."

Emma and Julian were lurking in the corner of the room, heads close, but with an awkward gap between their bodies.

"I'm going to go talk to them," Jace said, nodding at Julian and Emma. "Give them a few words of manly, thoughtful advice."

As soon as Jace walked away, Clary started to speak, but they were immediately joined by Magnus and Alec. Magnus was about to start guest teaching at the Academy, and they wanted to know how bad the food was. Julian's younger brothers and sisters—Ty, Livvy, Drusilla, and Octavian—were clustered together around the table with the appetizers. Simon glanced over his shoulder and saw Jace unloading Jacely advice onto the new *parabatai*. There was the delicious smell of roasting meat. Large platters of it were being placed on the tables now, along with vegetables and potatoes and breads and cheeses. The wine was being poured. It was time to celebrate. It was nice, Simon thought, in the midst of all the terrible things that could happen and sometimes did happen, there was also this. There was a lot of love.

As Simon turned back, he saw Julian hurrying out of the hall. Jace returned, his arm around Emma's shoulders.

"Everything okay?" Clary asked.

"Everything's fine. Julian needed air. This ceremony, it's intense. So many people. You need to eat."

This was to Emma, who smiled, but kept looking over at the door her *parabatai* had just gone through. Then she turned and saw Ty running across the Hall with a tray containing an entire wheel of cheese.

"Oh," she said, "yeah, that's bad. He can actually eat that entire cheese, but then he'll throw up. I'd better get that or this will end badly for Jules."

She ran after Ty.

"They have a lot on their hands," Jace said, watching her go. "Good thing they have each other. They always will. That's what being *parabatai* is about." He smiled at Alec, who grinned back at him in a way that lit up his whole face.

"About that *parabatai* business," Clary said. "We might as well tell you the news. . . ."

Born to Endless Night

By Cassandra Clare and Sarah Rees Brennan

Magnus had left behind a sleeping child and his worn-out love, and he opened the door on a scene of absolute chaos. For a moment it seemed as if there were a thousand people in his rooms, and then Magnus realized the real situation was far worse.

—Born to Endless Night

Every Night & every Morn
Some to Misery are Born
Every Morn and every Night
Some are Born to sweet delight
Some are Born to sweet delight
Some are Born to Endless Night
—"Auguries of Innocence," William Blake

Magnus believed that many old things were creations of enduring beauty. The pyramids. Michelangelo's *David*. Versailles. Magnus himself.

However, just because something was old and imbued with years of tradition did not *make* it a work of art. Not even if you were Nephilim and thought having the blood of the Angel meant your stuff was better than anybody else's.

Shadowhunter Academy was not a creation of enduring beauty. Shadowhunter Academy was a dump.

Magnus did not enjoy the countryside in early spring, before winter had truly ended. The whole landscape was as monochrome as an old movie, without the narrative energy. Dark gray fields rolled under a pale gray sky, and trees were stripped down to gray claws clutching for the rain clouds. The Academy matched its surroundings, squatting in the landscape like a great stone toad.

Magnus had been here a few times before, visiting friends. He had not liked it. He remembered walking long ago under the cold eyes of students who had been trained in the dark, narrow ways of Clave and Covenant, and who were too young to realize the world might be more complicated than that.

At least back then the place had not been falling down. Magnus stared at one of the slender towers that stood at each of the four corners of the Academy. It was not standing up straight; in fact, it looked like a poor relation of the Leaning Tower of Pisa.

Magnus stared at it, concentrated, and snapped his fingers. The tower leaped back into place as if it were a crouching person who had suddenly straightened up. There was a faint series of cries issuing from the tower windows. Magnus had not realized there were people inside. This struck him as unsafe.

Well, the inhabitants of the formerly leaning tower would soon realize he had done them a favor. Magnus eyed the angel in the stained-glass window set above the door. The angel stared down at him, sword blazing and face censorious, as if he disapproved of Magnus's dress sense and was going to ask him to change.

Magnus walked under the judgmental angel and into the stone hall, whistling softly. The hall was empty. It was still very early in the morning, which perhaps explained some of the grayness. Magnus hoped the day would brighten before Alec arrived.

He had left his boyfriend in Alicante, at his father's house. Alec's sister, Isabelle, was staying there too. Magnus had slept uneasily at the Inquisitor's house last night, and said he would leave them to have breakfast alone—just the family. For years he and Robert and Maryse Lightwood had arranged their lives so that they never saw each other unless duty called or large cash payments for Magnus beckoned.

Magnus was fairly sure Robert and Maryse missed those days and wished they would come back. Magnus knew they would never have chosen him for their son, and even if their son had to date a man, they would have preferred not a Downworlder, and certainly not a Downworlder who had been around during the days of Valentine's Circle and seen them at a time in their lives they were not proud of now.

For himself Magnus did not forget. He might love one Shadowhunter, but it was impossible to love them all. He expected many more years politely avoiding and, when necessary, politely tolerating Alec's parents. It was a very small price to pay to be with Alec.

Just now he had escaped Robert Lightwood and had a chance to inspect the rooms Magnus had requested the Academy prepare for them. From the state of the rest of the Academy, Magnus had dark forebodings about these rooms.

He ran lightly up the stairs in that silent, echoing place. He knew where he was going. He had agreed to come and give a series of guest lectures at the request of his old friend Catarina Loss, but he was, after all, the High Warlock of Brooklyn and he had certain standards. He had no intention of leaving his boyfriend for weeks. He had made it clear that he required a suite for himself and for Alec, and that the suite had to include a kitchen. He was not going to eat any of the meals Catarina had described in her letters. If possible, he intended to avoid even seeing any of the meals Catarina had described.

The map Catarina had drawn him was accurate: He found their rooms at the top of the building. The connected attic rooms could, Magnus guessed, possibly count as a suite. And there was a little kitchen, though Magnus feared it had not been updated since the 1950s. There was a dead mouse in the sink.

Maybe someone had left it there to welcome them. Maybe it was a festive gift.

Magnus wandered through the rooms, waving a hand that encouraged the windows and countertops to wash themselves. He snapped his fingers and sent the dead mouse as a present to his cat, Chairman Meow. Maia Roberts, the leader of the New York werewolf pack, was cat-sitting for them. Magnus hoped she would think Chairman Meow was a mighty hunter.

Then he opened the little refrigerator. The heavy door fell off, until Magnus gave it a stern look and it hopped back on. Magnus looked inside the refrigerator, waved his free hand, and saw to his satisfaction that it was now filled with many items from Whole Foods.

Alec would never have to know, and Magnus would send the money to Whole Foods later anyway. He swept through the rooms one more time, adding cushions to the bare, sad wooden chairs and heaping their multicolored blankets from home onto the lopsided canopy bed.

Emergency decorating mission accomplished and feeling

far more cheerful, Magnus descended into the main hall of the Academy, hoping to find Catarina or see Alec coming. There was no sign of activity, so despite his misgivings, Magnus went to check for Catarina in the dining hall.

She was not there, but there were a few scattered Nephilim students having breakfast. Magnus supposed the poor creatures had gotten up early to throw javelins or some other unsavory business.

There was a thin blond girl heaping a gray substance that could have been porridge or eggs onto her plate. Magnus watched with silent horror as she carried it toward a table, acting as if she actually intended to eat it.

Then she noticed Magnus.

"Oh, *hello*," said the blonde, stopping in her tracks as if she had been hit by a beautiful truck.

He gave her his most charming smile. Why not? "Hello."

Magnus had been around the block before blocks were invented. He was familiar with what this look meant. People had undressed him with their eyes before.

He was impressed with the intensity of this particular look. It was rarer for people to rip off his clothes and send them flying to various corners of the room with their eyes.

They were not even particularly exciting clothes. Magnus had decided to dress with quiet dignity, as befitted an educator, and was wearing a black shirt and tailored pants. He was also, for that stylish educator touch, wearing a short robe over the shirt, but the glittering gold thread running through the robe was very subtle.

"You must be Magnus Bane," the blonde said. "I've heard a lot about you from Simon."

"I can't blame him for bragging," said Magnus.

"We're so glad to have you here," continued the blonde. "I'm Julie. I'm practically Simon's best friend. I'm very cool with Downworlders."

"How nice for us Downworlders," Magnus murmured.

"I'm very excited for your lectures. And to spend time together. You, me, and Simon."

"Won't that be a party," said Magnus.

She was trying, at least, and not all Nephilim did. And she mentioned Simon every other breath, despite Simon being a mundane. Besides, the attention was flattering. Magnus turned the smile up another notch.

"I look forward to getting to know you better, Julie."

It was possible he misjudged the smile. Julie reached out a hand as if to take Magnus's, and dropped her tray. She and Magnus looked down at the broken bowl and the sad, gray contents.

"It's better this way," Magnus said with conviction.

He gestured, and the whole mess vanished. Then he gestured to Julie's outstretched hand, and a pot of blueberry yogurt with a small spoon appeared in it.

"Oh!" Julie exclaimed. "Oh, wow, thank you."

"Well, since the alternative was going back and getting more of the Academy food," said Magnus, "I think you owe me big. Possibly you owe me your firstborn. But don't worry, I'm not in the market for anybody's firstborn."

Julie giggled. "Do you want to sit down?"

"Thank you for the offer, but actually, I was looking for someone."

Magnus surveyed the room, which was slowly filling up. He

still did not see Catarina, but at the door he saw Alec, with the air of someone newly arrived and talking to a mundane Indian boy who looked about sixteen.

He caught Alec's eye and smiled.

"There's my someone," he said. "Lovely to meet you, Julie."

"Likewise, Magnus," she assured him.

As Magnus approached Alec, the other boy shook Alec's hand. "I just wanted to say thanks," the boy said, and left, with a nod to Magnus.

"Do you know him?" Magnus asked.

Alec looked mildly dazed. "No," he said. "But he knew all about me. We were talking about—all the ways there are to be a Shadowhunter, you know?"

"Check you out," said Magnus. "My famous boyfriend, inspiration to the masses."

Alec smiled, a little embarrassed but mostly amused. "So, that girl was flirting with you."

"Really?" Magnus asked. "How could you tell?"

Alec gave him a skeptical look.

"Well, it has been known to happen. I've been around for a long time," said Magnus. "I've also been gorgeous for a long time."

"Is that so?" said Alec.

"I'm in high demand. What are you going to do about it?"

He could not, and would not, have teased Alec like this years ago. Alec had been new to love, stumbling through his own terror at who he was and how he felt, and Magnus had been as careful with him as he knew how to be, afraid to hurt Alec and afraid to shatter this feeling between them, new to Magnus as it was to Alec.

It was a recent joy to be able to tease Alec and know he would not hurt him, to see Alec standing in a different way than he used to, easy and casual and confident in his own skin, with none of his *parabatai*'s swagger but with a quiet assurance all his own.

The dimly lit stone dining room, the clatter of students eating and gossiping, faded away, nothing but background to Alec's smile.

"This," said Alec. He reached out and tugged Magnus to him by the front of his robe, leaning back against the door frame and drawing Magnus slowly in for a kiss.

Alec's mouth was soft and sure, the kiss slow, his strong hands holding Magnus close, pressed along the warm line of his body. Behind Magnus's closed eyelids, the morning turned from gray to gold.

Alec was here. Even a hell dimension, as Magnus recalled, had been greatly improved by Alec's presence. Shadowhunter Academy was going to be a snap.

Simon came up late to breakfast and found Julie capable of talking about nothing but Magnus Bane.

"Warlocks are sexy," she said in the tones of one who had had a revelation.

"Ms. Loss is our teacher, and I am trying to eat." Beatriz stared dispiritedly at her plate.

"Vampires are gross and dead, werewolves are gross and hairy, and faeries are treacherous and would sleep with your mom," said Julie. "Warlocks are the sexy Downworlders. Think about it. They *all* have daddy issues. And Magnus Bane is the sexiest of them all. He can be High Warlock of my pants."

"Uh, Magnus has a boyfriend," said Simon.

There was a frightening glint in Julie's eye. "There are some mountains you still want to climb, even though there are 'No Trespassing' signs up."

"I think that's gross," said Simon. "You know, the way you think vampires are."

Julie made a face at him. "You're so sensitive, Simon. Why must you always be so sensitive?"

"You're so terrible, Julie," said Simon. "Why must you always be so terrible?"

Alec had been with Magnus, Julie reported. Simon was thinking more about that than Julie's terribleness, which after all was not anything new. Alec was going to be staying at the Academy for weeks. He usually saw Alec in crowds of people, and it had never seemed the right time to talk to him. It was the right time now. It was time to talk it out, the problem between them that Jace had hinted at so darkly. He didn't want there to be something wrong between him and Alec, who seemed like a good guy from what Simon could remember. Alec was Isabelle's big brother, and Isabelle was—he was almost certain—Simon's girlfriend.

He wanted her to be.

"Should we try to get a little archery practice in before class?" George asked.

"That's jock talk, George," said Simon. "I've asked you not to do that. But sure."

They all got up, pushing their bowls aside, and walked to the front doors of the Academy, heading for the practice grounds.

That was the plan, but none of them made it to the practice grounds that day. None of them made it past the threshold of the Academy. They all stood on the front step, in a horrified cluster.

On the stone of the front step was a bundle, wrapped in a fuzzy yellow blanket. Simon's eyes failed him in a way that had nothing to do with his glasses and everything to do with panic, refusing to register what was actually before him. *It's a bundle of junk*, Simon told himself. Someone had left a parcel of garbage on their doorstep.

Except the bundle was moving, in small incremental movements. Simon watched the fretful stir beneath the blanket, looked at the gleaming eyes peering out from the cocoon of fuzzy yellows, and his mind accepted what he was seeing, even as another shock came. A tiny fist emerged from the blankets, waving as if in protest at everything that was occurring.

The fist was blue, the rich navy of the sea when it was deep and you were on a boat as evening fell. The blue of Captain America's suit.

"It's a baby," Beatriz breathed. "It's a warlock baby."

There was a note pinned to the baby's yellow blanket. Simon saw it at the precise moment that the wind caught it, snatching it off the blanket and whirling it away. Simon grabbed the paper out of the cold grip of the wind and looked at the writing, a hasty scribble on a torn scrap of paper.

The note read: *Who could ever love it?*

"Oh no, the baby's blue," said George. "What are we going to do?"

He frowned as if he had not meant that to rhyme. Then he knelt down, because George was the not-so-secret sweetheart of the group, and awkwardly took the yellow-wrapped bundle in his arms. He stood up, his face ashen, holding the baby.

"What are we going to do?" Beatriz warbled, echoing George. "What are we going to do?"

Julie was plastered up against the door. Simon had personally seen her cut off a very large demon's head with a very small knife, but she appeared as if she would expire with terror if someone asked her to hold the baby.

"I know what to do," said Simon.

He would go find Magnus, he thought. He knew Magnus and Alec had arrived and were awake. He needed to talk to Alec anyway. Magnus had fixed Simon's demon amnesia. Magnus had been around for centuries. He was the most adult adult that Simon knew. A warlock baby abandoned in this fortress of Shadowhunters was a problem Simon had no idea how to fix, and he felt he needed an adult. Simon was already turning to go.

"Should I give the baby mouth to mouth?" George asked.

Simon froze. "No, don't do that. The baby is breathing. The baby's breathing, right?"

They all stood and stared at the little bundle. The baby waved his fist again. If the baby was moving, Simon thought, the baby must be breathing. He was not even going to think about zombie babies at this time.

"Should I get the baby a hot water bottle?" George said.

Simon took a deep breath. "George, don't lose your head," he said. "This baby is not blue because he is cold or because he cannot breathe. Mundane babies are not blue in this way. This baby is blue because he is a warlock, just like Catarina."

"Not just like Ms. Loss," Beatriz said in a high voice. "Ms. Loss is more of a sky blue, whereas this baby is more of a navy blue."

"You seem very knowledgeable," George decided. "You should hold the baby."

"No!" Beatriz squawked.

She and Julie both threw up their hands in surrender. As far as they were concerned, it was clear, George was holding a loaded baby and should not do anything rash.

"Everybody stay where you are," said Simon, trying to keep his voice calm.

Julie perked up. "Oooh, Simon," she said. "Good idea."

Simon fled across the hall and up the stairs, moving at a pace that would have amazed his evil Shadowhunter gym teacher. Scarsbury had never provided him with motivation like this.

He knew that Magnus and Alec had been put in a fancy suite up in the attics. Apparently there was even a separate kitchen. Simon just kept heading up, knowing he would hit the attics at some point.

He reached the attics, heard murmuring and movement behind the door, and flung the door wide open.

Then he stood, arrested on his second threshold of the day.

There was a sheet over Alec and Magnus, but Simon could see enough. He could see Alec's white, rune-scarred shoulders and Magnus's wild black hair spread on the pillow. He could see Alec freeze, then turn his head and give Simon a look of absolute horror.

Magnus's golden cat eyes gleamed from over Alec's pale shoulder. He sounded almost amused as he asked: "Can we help you?"

"Oh my God," Simon said. "Oh wow. Oh wow, I am really sorry."

"Please leave," said Alec in a tight, controlled voice.

"Right!" said Simon. "Of course!" He paused. "I can't leave."

"Believe me," said Alec. "You can."

"There is an abandoned baby on the front steps of the Academy and I think it's a warlock!" Simon blurted out.

"Why do you think the baby is a warlock?" Magnus asked. He was the only one in the room who was composed.

"Um, because the baby is navy blue."

"That is fairly compelling evidence," Magnus admitted. "Could you give us a moment to get dressed?"

"Yes! Of course!" said Simon. "Again, I'm very sorry."

"Go now," Alec suggested.

Simon went.

After a short while Magnus emerged from the attic suite dressed in skintight black clothes and a shimmering gold robe. His hair was still wrecked, going every which way as if Magnus had been caught in a small personal tempest, but Simon was not going to quibble about the hair of his potential savior.

"Really sorry again," said Simon.

Magnus made a lazy gesture. "Seeing your face was not the best moment of my day, Simon, but these things happen. Admittedly, they have never happened to Alec before, and he needs a few more minutes. Show me where the child is."

"Follow me," said Simon.

He ran down the stairs as fast as he had run up them, taking two at a time. He found the tableau at the threshold just as he had left it, Beatriz and Julie the horrified audience to George's terrified and inexpert baby-holding. The bundle was now making a low, plaintive sound.

"What took you so long?" Beatriz hissed.

Julie still looked very shaken, but she managed to say: "Hello, Magnus."

"Hello again, Julie," said Magnus, once again the only calm person in a room. "Let me hold the baby."

"Oh, thank you," George breathed. "Not that I don't like the baby. But I have no idea what to do with it."

George appeared to have bonded in the time it took Simon to run up and down a flight of stairs. He looked mushily down at the baby, clutching the bundle for a moment, and then as he handed the baby over to Magnus, he fumbled and almost dropped the baby on the stone floor.

"By the Angel!" Julie exclaimed, hand pressed to her breast.

Magnus arrested the fumble and caught the child, holding the blanket-wrapped bundle close against his gold-embroidered chest. He held the baby with more expertise than George did, which meant that he supported the baby's head and it appeared as if he might have held a baby once or twice in his life. George had not looked like he was going to win any baby-holding championships.

With a hand glimmering with rings, Magnus drew the blanket back a little, and Simon held his breath. Magnus's eyes traveled over the baby, his impossibly small hands and feet, the wide eyes in his small face, the curls on his head so dark a blue they were almost black. The baby's low constant sound of complaint rose a little, complaining harder, and Magnus smoothed the blanket back into place.

"He's a boy," said Magnus.

"Aw, a boy," said George.

"He's about eight months old, I would say," Magnus continued. "Someone raised him until they could not bear it anymore, and I suppose through the recruitment of mundanes to the Academy, someone thought they knew the place to bring a child they did not want."

"But someone wouldn't leave their child . . . ," George began, and fell silent under Magnus's gaze.

"People would. People do. And the choices people make are different, with warlock children," Magnus said. His voice was quiet.

"So there's no chance anyone is coming back for him," said Beatriz.

Simon took the note he had found folded on the child's blanket and gave it to Magnus. He did not feel, looking into Magnus's face, that he could give it to anyone else. Magnus looked at the note, nodded. *Who could ever love it?* flashed between his fingers, and then he tucked it away into his robe.

There were other students gathering around them, and a rising hubbub of noise and confusion. If Simon had been in New York, he figured people would have been taking pictures of the baby with their phones. He felt a little like an exhibition in a zoo, and he was so grateful Magnus was there.

"What is happening?" asked a voice from the top of the stairs.

Dean Penhallow was standing there, with her strawberry-blond hair loose over her shoulders, clutching around her a black silk robe etched with dragons. Catarina stood at her side, fully dressed in jeans and a white blouse.

"Seems like someone left a baby instead of the milk bottles," she said. "That was careless. Welcome, Magnus."

Magnus gave her a little wave with his free hand and a wry smile.

"What? Why? Why would anyone do such a thing? What are we supposed to do with it?" the dean asked.

Sometimes Simon forgot that Dean Penhallow was really young, young for a teacher, let alone a dean. Other times he was forcefully reminded of that fact. She looked as panicked as Beatriz and Julie had.

"He's much too young to be taught," said Scarsbury, peering down from the crowded staircase. "Perhaps we should contact the Clave."

"If the baby needs a bed," George offered, "Simon and I could keep him in our sock drawer."

Simon gave George an appalled glare. George looked distressed.

Alec Lightwood moved like a shadow through the crowds of students, head and shoulders above most of them but not shoving anyone aside. He moved quietly, persistently, until he was where he wanted to be: at Magnus's side.

When Magnus saw Alec, his whole body relaxed. Simon had not even been aware of the tension running all through Magnus's frame until he saw the moment when ease returned.

"This is the warlock child Simon was talking about," Alec said in a low voice, and nodded toward the baby.

"As you see," said Magnus, "the baby would not be able to pass for a mundane. His mother clearly does not want him. He is in a nest of the Nephilim, and I cannot think, among faeries or Shadowhunters or werewolves, where in the world he could possibly belong."

Magnus's calm and amusement had seemed infinite until a few minutes ago. Now Simon heard his voice fraying, a rope on which too much strain had been put, and which must soon snap.

Alec put a hand on Magnus's upper arm, just above the elbow. He clasped Magnus's arm firmly, almost absently providing silent support. He looked up at Magnus and then looked down, for a long, thoughtful moment, at the baby.

"Can I hold him?" Alec asked.

Surprise flew over Magnus's face but did not linger. "Sure," he said, and put the baby in Alec's arms, held out to receive him.

Maybe it was that Alec had held a baby more recently than Magnus had, and certainly more often than George. Maybe it was that Alec was wearing what seemed to be an incredibly ancient sweater, worn soft with years and faded from dark green to gray, with only traces remaining of the original color.

Whatever the reason, as soon as Alec took the baby, the continuous soft whimpering noise ceased. There was still the buzzing of urgent whispers, up and down the hall, but the small group surrounding the child suddenly found themselves in a pocket of hushed silence.

The baby gazed up at Alec with grave eyes only a shade darker than Alec's own. Alec gazed back at the baby. He looked as surprised as anyone else by the baby's sudden hush.

"So," said Delaney Scarsbury. "Should we contact the Clave and put this matter before them, or what?"

Magnus turned in a whirl of gold and fixed Scarsbury with a look that made him shrink back against the wall.

"I do not intend to leave a warlock child to the tender mercies of the Clave," Magnus declared, his voice extremely cold. "We have this, don't we, Alec?"

Alec was still looking down at the baby. He glanced up when Magnus addressed him, his face briefly dazed, as a man woken from a dream, but his expression set as with a sudden resolve.

"Yeah," he answered. "We do."

Magnus mirrored the move Alec had made before, clasping Alec's upper arm in silent thanks, or a show of support. Alec returned to looking down at the baby.

It felt as if a huge weight had been lifted off Simon's chest. It was not that he had been truly worried that he and George would have to raise the baby in their sock drawer—well, possibly a little worried—but the specter of a huge responsibility had loomed before him. This was a helpless, abandoned little child. Simon knew, all too well, how Downworlders were viewed by Shadowhunters. Simon had had no idea what to do. Magnus had taken the responsibility. He had taken the baby from them, both metaphorically and in actuality. He had not turned a hair as he did it. He had not acted as if it were a big deal at all.

Magnus was a really cool guy.

Simon knew Isabelle had slept over in Alicante, so she and Alec would both be with her father for one night. She was going down to the house where Ragnor Fell had once lived, where there was a working telephone. Catarina had set up another telephone in the Academy she said he could use this once. They had a telephone date. Simon was planning to tell her how cool Magnus and her brother had been.

Magnus thought he might become the first recorded warlock in history to have a heart attack.

He was walking around the practice grounds of Shadowhunter Academy at night because he could not stay in there and breathe stifling air with hundreds of Nephilim any longer.

That poor child. Magnus had hardly been able to look at

him, he was so small and so entirely helpless. He could not do anything but think of how vulnerable the child was, and how deep the misery and pain of his mother must have been. He knew what kind of darkness warlocks were conceived under and born into. Catarina had been brought up by a loving family who had known what she was, and raised her to be who she was. Magnus had been able to pass for human, until he was not.

Magnus knew what happened to warlock children who were born visibly not human, who their mothers and the whole world could not bring themselves to accept. He could not calculate how many children there might have been down all the dark ages of the world, who could have been magical, who could have been immortal, but had never gotten the chance to live at all. Children abandoned as this one had been, or drowned as Magnus himself had almost been, children who never left a bright magical mark in history, who never received or gave love, who were never anything but a whisper fading on the wind, a memory of pain and despair fading into the dark. Nothing else was left of those lost children, not a spell, not a laugh, not a kiss.

Without luck, Magnus would have been among the lost. Without love, Catarina and Ragnor would have been among the lost.

Magnus had no idea what to do with this latest lost child.

He thanked, not for the first time, whatever strange, beautiful fortune had sent him Alec. Alec had been the one who carried the warlock baby up the stairs to the attic, and when Magnus had conjured up a crib, Alec had been the one to place the baby tenderly in it.

Then when the baby had started to scream his little blue

head off, Alec had taken the baby out of the crib and walked the floor with him, patting his back and murmuring to him. Magnus called up supplies and tried to make formula milk. He'd read somewhere that you tested how hot the milk was on yourself, and ended up burning his own wrist.

The baby had cried for hours and hours and hours. Magnus supposed he could not blame the small lost soul.

The baby was finally sleeping now that the sun had set through the tiny attic windows, and the whole day was gone. Alec was half sleeping, leaning against the baby's crib, and Magnus had felt he had to get out. Alec had simply nodded when Magnus said he was stepping out for a breath of air. Possibly Alec had been too exhausted to care what Magnus did.

The moon shone, round as a pearl, turning the stained-glass angel's hair to silver and the bare winter fields into expanses of light. Magnus was tempted to howl at the moon like a werewolf.

He could not think of anywhere he could take the child, anyone he could entrust the child to who would want it, who might love it. He could scarcely think of anywhere in this hostile world where the child might be safe.

He heard the sound of raised voices and rushing footsteps, this late, out in front of the Academy. *Another emergency,* Magnus thought. *It's been one day, and at this rate the Academy is going to kill me.* He went running from the practice grounds to the front of the door, where he saw the very last person he had ever expected to see here in Idris: Lily Chen, the head of the New York vampire clan, with blue streaks in her hair that matched her blue waistcoat and her high heels leaving deep indentations in the dirt.

"Bane," she said. "I need help. Where is he?"

Magnus was too tired to argue with her.

"Follow me," said Magnus, and led the way back up the stairs. Even as he went, he thought to himself that all the noise he had heard outside the Academy could not possibly have been Lily alone.

He thought that, but he did not suspect what was to come.

Magnus had left behind a sleeping child and his worn-out love, and he opened the door on a scene of absolute chaos. For a moment it seemed as if there were a thousand people in his rooms, and then Magnus realized the real situation was far worse.

Every single one of the Lightwood family was there, each one causing enough noise for ten. Robert Lightwood was there, saying something in his booming voice. Maryse Lightwood was holding a bottle and appeared to be waving it around, giving a speech. Isabelle Lightwood was standing on top of a stool for no reason in the world Magnus could see. Jace Herondale was, even more mysteriously, lying flat out on the stone floor, and apparently he'd brought Clary, who looked at Magnus as if she were puzzled by her presence here as well.

Alec was standing in the middle of the room, in the middle of the human storm that was his family, holding the baby protectively to his chest. Magnus could not believe it was possible for his heart to sink further, but it somehow struck him as the greatest disaster in the world that the baby was awake.

Magnus stopped on the threshold, staring at the chaos, feeling entirely uncertain about what to do next.

Lily had no such hesitation.

"LIGHTWOOD!" Lily bellowed, charging in.

"Ah yes, Lily Chen, I believe?" said Robert Lightwood,

turning to her with the dignity of the Inquisitor and no sign of surprise. "I remember you were interim representative for the vampires on the Council for a time. Glad to see you again. What can I do for you?"

Robert was obviously doing his best to show every courtesy to an important vampire leader. Magnus appreciated that, a little.

Lily did not care. "Not you!" she snapped. "Who even are you?"

Thick black brows shot up to the sky.

"I'm the Inquisitor?" said Robert. "I was the head of the New York Institute for over a decade?"

Lily rolled her dark eyes. "Oh, congratulations, do you want a medal? I need *Alexander* Lightwood, obviously," said Lily, and swanned past a staring Robert and Maryse to their son. "Alec! You know that faerie dealer, Mordecai? He's been selling fruit to mundanes at the edge of Central Park. Again! He's at it again! And then Elliott bit a mundane who had partaken."

"Did he reveal his vampire nature to anyone while intoxicated?" Robert asked sharply.

Lily gave him a withering look, as if wondering why he was still here, then returned her attention to Alec. "Elliott performed a dance called the Dance of the Twenty-Eight Veils in Times Square. It is on YouTube. Many commenters described it as the most boring erotic dance ever performed in the history of the world. I have never been so embarrassed in my unlife. I'm thinking of quitting being leader of the clan and becoming a vampire nun."

Magnus noticed Maryse and Robert, who did not have the best relationship and hardly ever spoke to each other, having a brief whispered consultation about what YouTube might be.

"As the current head of the New York Institute," Maryse said, with an attempt at firmness, "if there is illegal Downworlder activity happening, it should be reported to me."

"I do not *talk* to *Nephilim* about *Downworlder business*," Lily said severely.

The Lightwood parents stared at her, and then swung their heads in sync to stare at their son.

Lily waved a dismissive hand in their direction. "Except for Alec, he's a special case. The rest of you Shadowhunters just come in, lay down your precious Law, and chop off people's heads. We Downworlders can handle our business ourselves. You Nephilim can stick to chopping off demons' heads and I will consult with you as soon as the next great evil occurs, instead of the next great annoyance, which will occur probably on Tuesday, and which I, Maia, and Alec will deal with. Thank you. Please stop interrupting me. Alec, can these people even be trusted?"

"They're my parents," said Alec. "I know about the faerie fruit. The fey have been taking more and more chances lately. I already sent a message to Maia. She's got Bat and some other boys prowling the precincts of the park. Bat's friends with Mordecai; he can reason with him. And you keep Elliott away from the park. You know how he is with faerie fruit. You know he bit that mundie on purpose."

"It could have been an accident," Lily muttered.

Alec gave Lily a deeply skeptical look. "Oh, it could have been his seventeenth accident? He has to stop or he's going to lose control under the influence and kill somebody. He didn't kill the man, did he?"

"No," Lily said sullenly. "I stopped Elliott in time. I knew you'd kill him, and then I knew you'd give me your disappointed look." She paused. "You're sure the werewolves have this in hand?"

"Yes," said Alec. "You didn't need to charge to Idris and spill Downworlder business in front of my whole family."

"If they're your family, they know you can handle a little thing like this," Lily said dismissively. She ran two hands through her sleek black hair, fluffing it up. "This is such a relief. Oh," she added, as if she had just noticed. "You're holding a baby."

Lily tended to have laser focus.

After the war with Sebastian, the Shadowhunters had been left dealing with the betrayal of the faeries and the crisis of how many Institutes had fallen and how many Nephilim had been Endarkened and lost in the war, their second war in a year.

They were in no shape to keep a close eye on the Downworlders, but the Downworlders had lost a great deal as well. Old structures that had held their society in place for centuries, like the Praetor Lupus, had been destroyed in the war. The faeries were waiting to revolt. And the werewolf and vampire clans of New York both had brand-new leaders. Both Lily and Maia were young to be leaders, and had succeeded entirely unexpectedly to leadership. Both of them had found themselves, due to inexperience and not lack of trying, in trouble.

Maia had called Magnus and asked if she could come and visit him, to ask his advice on a few things. When she showed up, she'd dragged Lily along with her.

Lily, Maia, and Magnus then sat around Magnus's coffee table shouting at each other for hours.

"You can't just kill someone, Lily!" Maia kept saying.

Lily kept saying: "Explain why."

Alec had been cranky that day, having wrenched his arm almost out of its socket during a fight with a dragon demon. He'd been leaning against the kitchen counter, listening, nursing his arm, and texting Jace messages like Y DO U SAY THINGS R XTINCT WHEN THINGS R NOT XTINCT and Y R U THE WAY THAT U R.

Until he ran out of patience.

"Do you know, Lily," he said in a cold voice, putting down his phone, "that you spend more than half the time you are speaking baiting Magnus and Maia, instead of offering suggestions? And you make them spend about the same amount of time arguing you down. So you're making everything last twice as long. Which means you're wasting everyone's time. That's not a really efficient way for a leader to behave."

Lily was so startled she looked almost blank for a moment, almost truly young, before she hissed: "Nobody asked you, Shadowhunter."

"I am a Shadowhunter," said Alec, still calm. "The issue you're having with the mermaids. The Rio de Janeiro Institute was having the same problem a couple of years ago. I know all about it. Do you want me to tell you? Or do you want to end up with half a dozen tourists on a boat to Staten Island drowned, at least that many Shadowhunters asking you embarrassing questions, and a little voice in your head saying, 'Wow, I wish I'd listened to Alec Lightwood when I had the chance'?"

There was a silence. Maia had put an entire cookie into her mouth as they waited. Lily kept her arms crossed and looked sulky.

"Don't waste my time, Lily," Alec said. "What do you want?"

"I want you to sit down and help me, I suppose," Lily grumbled.

Alec had sat down.

Magnus had not expected the meetings to happen more than a few times, let alone to see a rapport spring up between Alec and Lily. Alec had not been entirely comfortable with vampires, once. But Alec always responded to being relied on, being turned to. Whenever Lily came to him with a problem, at first haughtily and with an air of reluctance and later with demanding confidence, Alec did not rest until he had solved it.

One Thursday evening Magnus had heard the doorbell and walked in from the bedroom to find Alec laying out glasses, and realized that the occasional emergency gatherings had become regular meetings. That Maia and Lily and Alec would unroll a map of New York to pinpoint problem areas and have heated debates in which Lily made very nasty werewolf jokes, and each of them would call the other when they had a problem they did not know how to solve. That Downworlders and Shadowhunters alike would come to New York knowing there was a group with Downworlders and Shadowhunters who had power and would cooperate to solve problems. They would come to consult and find out if the group could help them, too.

On the occasions when Alec had served as acting head of the New York Institute, it had been obvious that he didn't enjoy it very much. Alec had less patience with bureaucracy now than he had before the war. He'd accidentally found his calling, working with Downworlders rather than the Clave. Magnus realized that this was his life now, and he would not have it different.

"I like Alec so much," Lily told Magnus at a party months

later, slightly drunk and with glitter in her hair. "Especially when he gets snippy with me. He reminds me of Raphael."

"How dare you," Magnus had replied. "You are speaking of the man I love."

He was bartending. His tuxedo had a glow-in-the-dark waistcoat, which made bartending in the artful gloom of the party somewhat easier. He'd spoken without thinking, casually, and then stopped, glass in his hand winking turquoise in the party lights. He'd been talking about Raphael easily, casually insulting, as if Raphael were still alive.

Lily had been Raphael's ally and backup for decades. She had been utterly loyal to him.

"Well, I loved Raphael," said Lily. "And Raphael never loved anyone, I know that much. But he was my leader. If I compare anybody to Raphael, it's a compliment. I like Alec. And I like Maia." She regarded Magnus with wide eyes, pupils dilated until they were almost black. "I've never been terribly fond of you. Except Raphael always said you were an idiot, but you could be trusted."

Raphael had loved many people, Magnus knew. He had loved his mortal family. Maybe Lily didn't know about them: Raphael had been so careful about them. Magnus thought Raphael might have loved Lily, though not in the way she had wanted.

He knew Raphael had trusted her. And Raphael had trusted Magnus. They stood together, these two Raphael had trusted, in one of those quietly terrible moments remembering the dead and knowing you would never see them again.

"Do you want another drink?" Magnus asked. "I can be trusted to make you another drink."

"Bring on the party O neg, I'm feeling frisky," Lily told him. She stared off into the distance as Magnus made her drink, her eyes fixed on showers of glitter that fell from the ceiling at intervals, but not seeing them. "I never thought I'd have to lead the clan. I thought Raphael would always be there. If I didn't have the sessions with Alec and Maia, I wouldn't know what to do half the time. A werewolf and a Shadowhunter. Do you think Raphael would be ashamed?"

Magnus slid Lily's drink across the bar to her. "I don't," he told her.

Lily had smiled, a flash of fang beneath her plum-colored lipstick, and, clutching her drink, wandered over to Alec.

Now Lily stood next to Alec, having followed him to Idris, and looked at the baby in his arms.

"Hello, baby," Lily whispered, hovering over the child. She snapped her fangs in the baby's direction.

Jace rolled lightly, off the floor and to his feet. Robert, Maryse, and Isabelle put their hands on their weapons. Lily snapped her teeth again, entirely unaware the Lightwood family was clearly ready to mobilize and tear her into pieces. Alec looked at his family over Lily's head and shook his own head in a small, firm gesture. The baby looked up at Lily's glinting fangs and laughed. Lily clicked her teeth for him again and he laughed again.

"What?" Lily asked, looking up at Alec and sounding shy suddenly. "I always liked children, when I was alive. People said I was good with them." She laughed, a little self-consciously. "It's been a while."

"That's great," said Alec. "You'll be willing to babysit occasionally, then."

"Ha-ha, I'm the head of the New York vampire clan and I'm

much too important," Lily told him. "But I'll see him when I drop by your place."

Magnus wondered how long Alec was envisioning it would be until they found the baby a home. Alec must think that it would take a while, and Magnus feared Alec was right.

He watched Alec, his head bowed over the baby in his arms, leaning toward Lily as they murmured to the baby together. Alec did not seem too upset, he thought. It was Lily who, after a space of baby-whispering, began to look a little uneasy.

"It occurs to me that I might be intruding," Lily said.

"Oh really?" asked Isabelle, her arms crossed. "Do you think?"

"Sorry, Alec," said Lily, pointedly not apologizing to anyone else. "See you in New York. Come back quick or some fool will burn the place down. Good-bye, Magnus, random other Lightwoods. Bye, baby. Good-bye, little baby."

She stood on her tiptoes in high-heeled boots, kissed Alec on the cheek, and sashayed out.

"I do not like that vampire's attitude," said Robert in the silence following Lily's departure.

"Lily's all right," said Alec mildly.

Robert did not say another word against Lily. He was careful with his son, Magnus had observed, painfully careful, but Robert was the one who had made the pain necessary. Robert had been thoughtless with his son in the past. It would be a long time of pain and care until things were right between them.

Both Robert and Alec were trying. That was why Alec had stayed to have breakfast with his father this morning.

Though Magnus was not at all sure what Robert Lightwood

was doing here at the Shadowhunter Academy in the dark of night.

Let alone Maryse, who should be running the New York Institute. Let alone Isabelle and Jace.

Magnus was always pleased to see Clary.

"Hello, biscuit," he said.

Clary sidled over to the doorway and grinned up at him, a thousand gallons of trouble in a pint-size body. "Hi."

"What's—"

Magnus intended to discreetly ask what the hell was going on, but he was interrupted by Jace lying down full length on the floor again. Magnus looked down, somewhat distracted.

"What are you doing?"

"I'm stuffing crevices with bits of material," said Jace. "It was Isabelle's idea."

"I ripped up one of your shirts to do it," Isabelle told him. "Not one of your nice shirts, obviously. One of the shirts that don't suit you and which you shouldn't wear again."

The world blurred briefly in front of Magnus's eyes. "You did what?"

Isabelle stared down at him from the stool where she was standing, her hands on her hips.

"We're childproofing the whole suite. If you could call this a suite. This whole Academy is a baby death trap. After we get finished here, we're going to childproof your loft."

"You're not allowed in our apartment," Magnus told her.

"Alec gave me a set of keys that says different," Isabelle told him.

"I did do that," Alec said. "I did give her keys. Forgive me, Magnus, I love you, I did not know she was going to be like this."

Usually Robert looked slightly uneasy whenever Alec expressed affection to Magnus. This time, however, he was staring fixedly at the warlock baby and did not even seem to hear.

Magnus was starting to feel ever more disturbed by the turns this night was taking.

"Why are you being like this?" Magnus asked Isabelle. "*Why?*"

"Think about it," said Isabelle. "We had to deal with the crevices. The baby could crawl around and get his hand or his foot stuck in a crevice! He could be hurt. You don't want the baby to get hurt, do you?"

"No," said Magnus. "Nor do I intend to tear my whole life into strips and rearrange it because of a baby."

What he said sounded eminently reasonable to him. He was stunned when Robert and Maryse both laughed.

"Oh, I remember thinking that way," Maryse said. "You'll learn, Magnus."

There was something strange in the way Maryse was speaking to him. She sounded fond. Usually she was carefully polite or businesslike. She had never been fond before.

"I expected this," declared Isabelle. "Simon told me all about the baby on the phone. I knew you guys would be stunned and overwhelmed. So I got hold of Mom, and she contacted Jace, and Jace was with Clary, and we all came right away to pitch in."

"It's really good of you," Alec said.

There was an air of surprise about him, which Magnus fully understood, but he seemed touched, which Magnus did not understand at all.

"Oh, it's our pleasure," Maryse told her son. She advanced

on Alec, her hands out. She reminded Magnus of a bird of prey, talons outstretched, overcome by hunger. "What do you say," she said in an alarmingly sweet voice, "you let me hold the baby? I'm the one in the room with the most experience with babies, after all."

"That's not true, Alec," said Robert. "That is not true! I was very involved with all of you when you were young. I'm excellent with babies."

Alec blinked at his father, who had appeared by Alec's side with Shadowhunter speed.

"As I recall," Maryse said, "you *bounce* them."

"Babies love that," Robert claimed. "Babies love bouncing."

"Bouncing will make the baby spit up."

"Bouncing will make the baby spit up *with joy*," said Robert.

Magnus had, for several moments, believed that the only possible explanation was that the whole family was drunk. Now he was coming to a much worse conclusion.

Isabelle had come, in an organizing whirlwind, to childproof the whole suite. She had been able to persuade Jace and Clary to come and childproof too. And Maryse had spoken to her son's partner with affection she had never shown before, and now she wanted to hold the baby.

Maryse was experiencing full-on grandma fever.

The Lightwoods thought he and Alec were keeping the baby.

"I need to sit down," said Magnus in a hollow voice. He held on to the door frame so he did not fall down.

Alec glanced over at him, startled and concerned. His parents took their chance to pounce, hands outstretched for the baby, and Alec retreated a step. Jace sprang up from the floor, having his *parabatai*'s back, and Alec visibly came to a decision and put the baby into his *parabatai*'s arms so he had his hands free to ward his parents off.

"Mom and Dad, maybe don't crowd him," Magnus heard Alec suggesting.

Magnus found, for some reason, that his own focus had slipped to the baby. It was natural concern, he told himself. Anybody would be concerned. Jace, as far as Magnus knew, was not accustomed to children. It was not like the Shadowhunters were always babysitting for the kids down the block.

Jace was holding the baby somewhat awkwardly. His golden head, his hair full of fluff and dirt from lying down on the floor dealing with crevices, was bowed over the baby, staring down into the baby's solemn little face.

The baby was dressed, Magnus saw. He was wearing an orange onesie, and the feet of the onesie were shaped to look like little fox paws. Jace rubbed one of the fox paws with a brown hand, fingers scarred like a warrior's and slim as a musician's, and the baby gave a sudden, vigorous wriggle.

Magnus rushed forward, realizing he had moved only when he was halfway across the room. He also realized that everyone else had lunged forward to catch the baby too.

Except Jace had kept hold of the baby despite the wriggle.

Jace looked flat-out terrified for a minute, then relaxed and looked around at everyone with his usual air of mild superiority.

"He's fine," Jace told them. "He's tough."

He looked toward Robert, clearly remembering Robert's early words, and bounced the baby gingerly. The baby flailed, one small fist bouncing off Jace's cheek.

"That's good," Jace encouraged. "That's right. Maybe a little harder next time. We'll have you punching demons in the face in no time. Do you want to punch demons in the face with me and Alec? Do you? Yes, you do."

"Jace, honey," Maryse cooed. "Give me the baby."

"Want to hold the baby, Clary?" asked Jace in the tone of one offering an enormous treat to his lady love.

"I'm good," said Clary.

The Lightwoods, including Jace, all stared at her with a kind of sad wonder, as if she had just proven herself tragically insane.

Isabelle had leaped down from the stool at the same time they had all rushed forward, ready to catch him. She looked at Magnus now.

"Are you going to kneecap your parents so you can hold the baby?" Magnus asked.

Isabelle laughed lightly. "No, of course not. Soon his formula will be ready. Then . . ." Isabelle's face changed, set with terrifying determination. "I am going to feed the baby. Until then, I can wait, and help you guys come up with the perfect name for him."

"We were talking about that a little as we came in from Alicante," said Maryse, her voice eager.

Robert made another of his lightning-swift, cat-footed, and unsettling moves, this time to Magnus's side. He put a heavy hand on Magnus's shoulder. Magnus eyed Robert's hand and felt deep unease.

"Of course, it's up to you and Alec," Robert assured him.

"Of course," said Maryse, who never agreed with Robert on anything. "And we don't want you to do anything you're not comfortable with. I would never want the little darling to have a name associated with—sadness rather than joy, or for either of you to feel like you have to do this. But we thought since . . . well, warlocks pick their own surnames a little later, so 'Bane' is not part of a family tradition . . . We thought you might consider, in memory but not as a burden . . ."

Isabelle said, her voice clear: "Max Lightwood."

Magnus found himself blinking, partly in perplexity, but partly because of another feeling he found much less easy to define. His vision had blurred again and something in his chest had twisted.

The mistake the Lightwoods had made was ridiculous, and yet Magnus could not help but be stunned by their offer, and how genuine and sincere it had been.

This was a warlock child, and they were all Shadowhunters. Lightwood was an old, proud Shadowhunter name. Max Lightwood had been the Lightwoods' youngest son. It was a name for one of their own.

"Or if you don't like that . . . Michael. Michael's a nice name," Robert offered into the long silence. He cleared his throat after he spoke, and looked out of the attic windows, into the woods surrounding the Academy.

"Or you could hyphenate," Isabelle said, her voice a little too bright. "Lightwood-Bane or Bane-Lightwood?"

Alec moved, reaching out not to take the baby but to touch him. The baby flung a hand up, tiny fingers curling around Alec's finger, as if reaching back. Alec's face, stricken since the mention of his brother's name, was warmed by a sudden faint smile.

"Magnus and I haven't talked about it yet, and we need to," he said quietly. His voice had authority, even when it was quiet. Magnus saw Robert and Maryse nodding along to it, almost unconsciously. "But I was thinking maybe Max as well."

That was when Magnus realized the magnitude of the situation. It was not just a wild conclusion Isabelle had leaped to and improbably convinced everyone else of. It was not just the Lightwoods.

Alec thought that he and Magnus were keeping the baby as well.

Magnus did go and sit down then, on one of the rickety chairs with a cushion from home placed on it. He could not feel his fingers. He thought he might be in shock.

Robert Lightwood followed him.

"I couldn't help but notice that the baby is blue," Robert said. "Alec's eyes are blue. And when you do the"—he made a strange and disturbing gesture, and then made the sound *whoosh, whoosh*—"magic, sometimes there's a blue light."

Magnus stared at him. "I'm failing to see your point."

"If you made the baby for yourself and Alec, you can tell me," said Robert. "I'm a very broad-minded man. Or—I'm trying to be. I'd like to be. I would understand."

"If I made . . . the . . . baby . . . ?" Magnus repeated.

He was not certain where to start. He had imagined Robert Lightwood knew how babies were made.

"Magically," Robert whispered.

"I am going to pretend you never said that to me," said Magnus. "I am going to pretend we never had this conversation."

Robert winked, as if they understood each other. Magnus was speechless.

The Lightwoods continued on their quest to childproof the suite, feed the baby, and all hold the baby at once. Witchlight on every side, filling the whole small space of the attic, blazed and burned in Magnus's vision.

Alec thought they were keeping the baby. He wanted to name him Max.

"I saw Magnus Bane and a sexy vampire lady in the hall," Marisol announced as she passed Simon's table.

Jon Cartwright was carrying her tray, and he almost dropped it. "A vampire," he repeated. "In the *Academy*?"

Marisol looked up into his scandalized face and nodded. "A sexy one."

"They're the worst kind," Jon breathed.

"So you weren't too bad, then, Simon," Julie remarked as Marisol walked on, spinning her tale of an alluring vampiress.

"You know," Simon said, "sometimes I think Marisol goes too far. I know she likes jerking Jon's chain, but nobody is dumb enough to believe in a warlock baby and a vampire on the same day. It's too much. It makes no sense. Jon is going to catch on."

He poked a mysterious lump in his stew. Dinner was very late tonight, and very congealed. Marisol fibbing about vampires must have put the idea in his head: Simon looked back on drinking blood and thought that it could not have been as bad as this.

"You would think she'd had enough excitement for one day," George agreed. "I wonder how the poor little baby is doing. I was thinking, do you think he might change colors like a chameleon? How cool would that be?"

Simon brightened. "So cool."

"Nerds," said Julie.

Simon took that as praise. He did feel that George had really come along under his tutelage. He had even voluntarily bought graphic novels when he was in Scotland over Christmas. Maybe someday the student would become the master.

"This is hard luck for you, Simon," said George. "I know you wanted to talk to Alec."

Simon's brief moment of cheer faded, and he collapsed with his face on the table. "Forget about talking to Alec. When I went to tell them about the baby, I walked in on Alec and Magnus. If Alec didn't like me before, he *definitely* hates me now."

Another old memory flashed in Simon's mind, absolutely unwelcome: Alec's pale, furious face as he looked down at Clary. Maybe Alec hated Clary, too. Maybe once someone crossed him, he never forgot and never forgave, and would always hate them both.

His hideous imaginings were interrupted by a sensation around their dinner table.

"What? Where? When? How? Did Magnus seem like an athletic yet tender lover?" Julie demanded.

"Julie!" said Beatriz.

"Thank you, Beatriz," said Simon.

"Don't say a word, Simon," said Beatriz. "Not until I have acquired a pen and paper so I can write down everything you say. I'm sorry, Simon, but they are famous, and celebrities have to bear with this interest in their love lives. They're like Brangelina."

Beatriz rummaged through her bag until she found a notebook, and then opened it and gazed at Simon with an expectant air.

Julie, Idris born and bred, made a face. "What is Brangelina? It sounds like a demon."

"It does not!" George protested. "I believe in their love."

"They are not like Brangelina," Simon said. "What would you even call them? Algnus? That sounds like a foot disease."

"Obviously you would call them Malec," said Beatriz. "Are you stupid, Simon?"

"I will not be distracted!" said Julie. "Does Magnus have piercings? Of course he does; when would he miss an opportunity to shine?"

"I didn't notice, and even if I had noticed, I wouldn't discuss it," said Simon.

"Oh, because people in the mundane world never obsess about celebrities and their love lives," Beatriz said. "See also, Brangelina. And that boy band George is obsessed with. He has all kinds of theories about their romances."

"What . . . boy band . . . George is obsessed with?" Simon asked slowly.

George looked shifty. "I don't want to talk about it. The band's going through some hard times lately, and it makes me too sad."

Far too many disturbing and upsetting things had happened to Simon today. He decided to stop thinking about George and the boy band.

"I'm the one who grew up a subway ride from Broadway, I know people get too interested in celebrities," he said. "But it's weird for me when you girls obsess over Jace or Magnus. It's weird when Jon trails after Isabelle with his tongue hanging out."

"Is George's crush on Clary weird too?" asked Beatriz.

"Is this Betray George Day, Beatriz?" George demanded. "Si, I may have had certain thoughts about certain pocket-size vixens, but I would never tell you about them! I don't want to make it weird!"

"Pocket-size vixens?" Simon stared. "Congratulations, you made it weird."

George hung his head in shame.

"It's weird for me because everybody acts as if they know famous people, but I really do know these people. They're not images, like posters to hang on the wall. They're not anything like you think they are. They have a right to privacy. It's weird because I see everyone acting like they know who my friends are, when they only know a tiny bit of them, and it's weird to see anyone acting as if they have some sort of claim on my friends and their lives."

Beatriz hesitated, then put her pen down. "Okay," she said. "I can see it's weird for you, but—it does come from everyone admiring what they've done. People act like they know them because they want to know them. And being admired means they have a lot of influence over other people. They can do a lot of good with that. Alec Lightwood is Sunil's inspiration to be a Shadowhunter. And you, Simon. A lot of people follow you because they admire you. There might be some weirdness mixed in with being admired like that, but I think there's more good."

"Oh, it's not the same for me," Simon mumbled. "I mean, I don't even remember. I meant my friends. Including Alec, who is . . . my friend who doesn't like me. They're the special ones."

He couldn't be cool and assured like Magnus or Jace. He didn't know what Beatriz was talking about. Also he felt suddenly paranoid over whether people were wondering if he had piercings.

Simon had no piercings. He used to be a musician in Brooklyn. He probably should have piercings.

Beatriz hesitated another instant, then tore off the page

she'd written on and rolled it into a ball. "You're special too, Simon," she said, and blushed. "Everybody knows that."

Simon looked at her red face and remembered George mentioning someone had a crush on him. He'd thought for a moment it might be Julie, and though it would be both bizarre and bizarrely flattering to have changed the heart of a Shadowhunter ice princess with his manly charms, he supposed Beatriz made more sense. He and Beatriz were really good friends. Beatriz had the best smile in the Academy. Simon would've been thrilled to have an attractive girl he was friends with get a crush on him, back in Brooklyn.

He felt mainly awkward now. He wondered if he was supposed to let Beatriz down easily.

Julie cleared her throat. "And just so you know . . . ," she said, "there have been invasive questions asked about you. Also there was an incident where someone tried to steal one of your used socks and keep it as a trophy."

"Who was the sock person?" Simon demanded. "That's just nasty."

"We never tell them anything," Julie said. "And they may ask once, but they never ask again." Her lip curled back from her teeth. She looked like a snarling blond tiger. "Because you're a real person to us, Simon. And you're our friend."

She reached across the table and touched Simon's hand, then drew it back as if she had been burned. Beatriz snatched Julie's hand as soon as she'd drawn it back and pulled her out of her chair and toward the corner of the room where the food was laid out.

Neither of them needed more food. They had barely touched their stew. Simon watched as they went, and then stood talking to each other in fraught whispers.

"Well, they both seem strangely upset."

George rolled his eyes. "Come on, Si, don't be dense."

"You can't mean . . . ," began Simon. "They can't both—like me?"

There was a long silence.

"Neither of them like you?" Simon said. "You work out. And! You have a Scottish accent."

"Don't rub it in. Maybe girls fear me, because my keen eyes see too deeply into their souls," George said. "Or maybe they're intimidated by my good looks. Or maybe . . . Please don't make me talk about what a lonely bugger I am anymore."

He looked after Julie and Beatriz a little wistfully. Simon could not tell if George was wistful about Julie or Beatriz, or simply wistful about love in general. He'd had no idea his friends were involved in such an emotional tangle.

He was surprised. He felt awkward. And he didn't feel anything else.

He liked Beatriz a lot. Julie was terrible, but Simon thought of Julie telling him about her sister, and he had to admit: Julie was terrible, but he liked her, too. Both of them were beautiful and badass and did not come with a burden of lost memories and tangled emotions.

He wasn't even pleased they liked him. He wasn't even slightly tempted.

He wished, with single-minded intensity, that Isabelle was here—not a letter, not a voice on the phone, but here.

He looked at George's sad face and offered: "Want to talk about when Magnus and Alec go, and we steal their suite and make our own meals in our own little kitchen?"

George sighed. "Could we really, Simon, or is that too beautiful a dream? Every day would be a song. All I want is to make a sandwich, Simon. Just a humble sandwich, with ham, cheese, maybe a little dab of . . . oh my God."

Simon wondered what a dab of "oh my God" would taste like. George had frozen, spoon to his lips, eyes fixed on a point over Simon's shoulder.

Simon turned around in his seat and saw Isabelle framed in the doorway of the Academy dining hall. She was wearing a long dress the color of irises and her arms were spread wide, bracelets gleaming. Time seemed to slow, like a movie, like magic, like she was a genie who could appear in a puff of glittering smoke to grant wishes, and every wish would be her.

"Surprise," said Isabelle. "Miss me?"

Simon jumped to his feet. He might have knocked his bowl clear across the table and into George's lap. He was sorry, but he would make it up to him later.

"Isabelle," he said. "What are you doing here?"

"Congratulations, Simon, that's a very romantic question," Isabelle told him. "Am I meant to take it as 'No, I didn't miss you, and I'm seeing other girls'? If so, don't worry about it. Why worry, when life is short? Specifically, your life, because I am going to cut off your head."

"I'm confused by what you're saying," Simon told her.

Isabelle raised her eyebrows and opened her lips, but before she could speak Simon caught her by the waist and drew her in against him, kissing her surprised mouth. Isabelle's mouth relaxed, curving under his. She flung her arms around his neck and kissed him back, sultry and exuberant at once, a femme fatale and a warrior princess, all the dream girls of all his nerdy fantasies in one. Simon pulled back for a moment to look into Isabelle's night-dark eyes.

"I wasn't aware," said Simon, "that there are any other girls in the world but you."

He was embarrassed as soon as he said it. It was in no way a smooth line. It was pathetically honest, trying to tell Isabelle what he had only just realized himself. But he saw Isabelle's eyes shine like new stars waking in the night, felt her arm around his neck pulling him down for another kiss, and he thought to himself that the line might be a little smooth. After all, it had gotten him a girl, *the* girl. The only girl Simon wanted.

It was midnight before Magnus got all of the Lightwoods out of their suite. Isabelle had left to see Simon some time before, and Clary and Jace could usually be persuaded to go off together, but for a while he thought he was actually going to have to use magic on Maryse and Robert. He shoved them out of the door while they were still giving him helpful baby tips.

As soon as they were gone, Alec stumbled over to the bed and lay flat on his face, instantly asleep. Magnus was left with the baby.

It was possible the baby was stunned by the Lightwoods too. He lay in his crib staring up at the world with wide eyes. The crib was under a window, and he was in a small pool of light, moonshine shimmering on his crumpled blanket and his little fat legs. Magnus crouched down by the crib and watched him, waiting for the next eruption of screaming that meant he needed to be changed and fed. Instead he fell asleep too, his mouth open, a tiny blue rosebud.

Who could ever love it? the baby's mother had written, but the baby did not know that yet. He slept, innocent and serene as any child secure of love. Magnus's mother might have thought the same despairing words.

Alec thought they were keeping him.

Keeping him had not even occurred to Magnus. He had thought he lived life believing a thousand possibilities were open to him, but he had not thought of this possibility as being open to him: family life like mundanes and Nephilim had, love so secure that it could be shared with someone brand-new to the world and helpless.

He tried out the thought now.

Keeping him. Keeping the baby. Having a baby, with Alec.

Hours passed. Magnus hardly noticed, time went by so quietly, as if someone had laid out the carpet of the night to muffle time's footsteps. He did not register anything but that small face, until he felt a soft touch on his shoulder.

Magnus did not get up, but he turned to see Alec looking down at him. The moonlight turned Alec's skin silver and his eyes a darker, deeper blue, infinitely tender.

"If you thought I was asking you to keep the baby," Magnus said, "I wasn't."

Alec's eyes widened. He absorbed this in silence.

"You're . . . still really young," Magnus said. "I'm sorry if sometimes it seems as if I do not remember that. It's strange to me—being immortal means both being young and being old are strange to me. I know I must seem strange to you sometimes."

Alec nodded, thoughtful and not hurt. "You do," he said, and leaned down with one hand gripping the side of the crib, touched Magnus's hair, and gave him a moonlight-soft kiss. "And I never want anything but this. I never want a less strange love."

"But you don't have to be scared I would ever leave you,"

said Magnus. "You don't have to be scared of what will happen to the baby or that I will be hurt because the baby—is a warlock, and was not wanted. You do not have to feel trapped. You do not have to be scared, and you do not have to do this."

Alec knelt down in the shadows and on the bare, dusty boards of the attic, next to the crib and facing Magnus.

"What if I want to?" he asked. "I'm a Shadowhunter. We marry young, and we have children young, because we might die young, because we want to do our duty to the world and have all the love in the world we can. I used to . . . I used to think I could never do that, never have that. I used to feel trapped. I don't feel trapped now. I could never ask you to live in an Institute, and I don't want to. I want to stay in New York, with you, and with Lily and Maia. I want to keep doing what we're doing. I want Jace to run the Institute after my mother, and I want to work with him. I want to be part of the connection between the Institute and Downworlders. For so long I thought I could never have any of the things I wanted, except that I could maybe keep Jace and Isabelle safe. I thought I could have their backs in a fight. Now I have more and more people I care about, and . . . I want everyone I care about—I want people I don't even know, I want all of us—to know we have each other's backs so we do not have to fight alone. I am not trapped. I'm happy. I am exactly where I want to be. I know what I want, and I have the life I want. I'm not scared of any of the things you said."

Magnus took a deep breath. It was better to ask Alec than to keep imagining the wrong thing. "What are you scared of, then?"

"Do you remember Mom suggesting calling the baby Max?"

Magnus nodded, carefully quiet.

He had never even met Alec's little brother, Max. Robert and Maryse Lightwood had always tried to keep their children away from Downworlders, and Max had been too young to disobey.

Alec's voice was soft, both for the baby and with memory. "I was never the cool brother. I remember when Mom used to leave Max with me, when he was really little, just learning how to walk, and I was always scared he would fall down and it would be my fault. I'd constantly try to get him to obey the rules and do what Mom said. Isabelle was so great with him, always making him laugh, and by the Angel, Max wanted to be *just* like Jace. He thought Jace was the coolest, the best Shadowhunter who ever lived, that the sun rose and set on him. Jace gave him a little toy soldier and Max used to take it to bed with him. I was jealous of how much Max loved that toy. I used to give him other things, toys that I thought were better, but he always loved that soldier best. He died holding that toy for comfort. I'm so glad he had it, that he had something he loved to comfort him. It was stupid and petty to be jealous."

Magnus shook his head. Alec gave him a rueful smile, and then bowed his black head, looking at the floor.

"I always thought there would be more time," said Alec. "I thought Max would get older, and he'd train with us more, and I'd help him train. I thought he would come on missions with us, and I'd have his back, the way I always try to have Jace's and Isabelle's backs. He'd know his boring big brother was good for something then. He'd know he could count on me, no matter what. He should have been able to count on me."

"He was able to count on you," Magnus said. "I know that. He knew that. Nobody who has ever met you could doubt it."

"He never even knew that I'm gay," said Alec. "Or that I love you. I wish he could have met you."

"I wish I could have met him," said Magnus. "But he knew you. He loved you. You know that, don't you?"

"I do know that," said Alec. "I just . . . I always wished I could be more for him."

"You always try to be more, for everyone you love," Magnus said. "You don't see how your whole family turns to you, how they rely on you. I rely on you. Even *Lily* relies on you, for God's sake. You love the people you love so much that you want to be an impossible ideal for them. You don't realize that you are more than enough."

Alec shrugged, a little helplessly.

"You asked me what I was scared of. I'm scared he won't like me," Alec said. "I'm scared I'll let him down. But I want to try to be there for him. I want him. Do you?"

"I didn't expect him," said Magnus. "I didn't expect anything like this to come, for me. Even if I thought sometimes about what it might be like if you and I did have a family, I thought it would not be for years. But yes. Yes, I want to try as well."

Alec smiled, his smile so brilliant that Magnus realized how relieved he was, and realized belatedly how worried Alec had been that Magnus would say no.

"It is quick," Alec admitted. "I thought about having a family, but I guess I always thought . . . Well, I guess I never expected anything like this to happen before we got married."

"What?" said Magnus.

Alec just stared up at him. One long, strong archer's hand was dangling into the baby's crib, but Alec was intent on Magnus, his dark blue eyes darker than ever in the shadows, one look from Alec more important than a kiss from anyone else. Magnus saw he meant it.

"Alec," he said. "My Alec. You have to know that's impossible."

Alec looked stunned and horror-struck. Magnus began to speak, the words tumbling out of his mouth faster and faster, trying to get Alec to see.

"Shadowhunters can marry Downworlders, in Downworlder or mundane ceremonies. I've seen it happen. I've seen other Shadowhunters dismiss those marriages as meaning nothing, and I've seen some Shadowhunters bow under pressure and break the vows they made. I know you would never bow or break. I know that type of marriage would mean just as much to you. I know that any promises you made me, you would keep. But I was alive before the Accords. I sat and ate and talked with Shadowhunters about peace between our people, and then those same Shadowhunters threw away the plates I ate off because they thought I irredeemably tainted whatever I touched. I will not have a ceremony that anyone looks down on as lesser. I do not want you to have any less than the ceremony you could have had, to honor your vows to a Shadowhunter. I have had enough of making compromises in the name of trying to make peace. I want the Law to change. I do not want to get married until we can get married in gold."

Alec was quiet, his head bowed.

"Do you understand?" Magnus demanded, feeling almost desperate. "It's not that I don't want to. It's not that I don't love you."

"I understand," said Alec. He took a deep breath and looked up. "Changing the Law might take a while," he said simply.

"It might," said Magnus.

They were both quiet for a little while.

"Can I tell you something?" Magnus asked. "Nobody ever wanted me to marry them before."

He'd had other loves, but none of them had ever asked, and he had known—had sensed with a cold, sinking feeling that it would be useless—not to ask them. Whether it was because they did not feel they could promise until death did them part when Magnus would not die, because they took Magnus lightly or thought, being immortal, that he took them lightly. He had never known the reasons they did not want to marry him, but there it was: There had been lovers willing to die with him, but nobody had ever been willing to swear to live with him every day for as long as they both had to live.

Nobody until this Shadowhunter.

"I never asked anyone to marry me before," said Alec. "So that's a no, then?"

He laughed as he asked, a soft laugh, worn but happy. Alec always tried to give those he loved a path or an open door; he tried to give those he loved anything they wanted. They sat there, leaning against their baby's crib together.

Magnus lifted his hand, and Alec caught it in midair, their fingers linking. Magnus's rings flashed and Alec's scars glowed in the moonlight. Both of them held on.

"It's yes, one day," Magnus said. "For you, Alec, it's always yes."

After classes the next day Simon sat in his dank dungeon room, resisted the almost irresistible temptation to go find Isabelle, and mustered up his courage.

He marched up the many flights of stairs and knocked on the door of Alec and Magnus's rooms.

Magnus answered the door. He was wearing jeans and a loose, frayed T-shirt, holding the baby, and he looked very tired.

"How did you know he'd just woken up from a nap?" Magnus asked as he opened the door.

"Uh, I didn't," said Simon.

Magnus blinked at him, in the slow way that tired people did, as if they had to think deeply about blinking. "Oh, my apologies," he said. "I thought you were Maryse."

"Isabelle's mother is here?" Simon exclaimed.

"Shhhh!" said Magnus. "She might hear you."

The baby was grizzling, not quite crying but making a sound like a small, unhappy tractor. He wiped his damp face against Magnus's shoulder.

"I'm really sorry to interrupt," said Simon. "I was wondering if I could have a word alone with Alec."

"Alec's sleeping," Magnus said flatly, and began to close the door.

Alec's voice rang out before the door was quite closed. He sounded as if he was midyawn. "No, I'm not. I'm awake. I can talk to Simon." He appeared in the doorway, pulling the door back open. "Go out and take a long walk. Get some fresh air. It'll wake you up."

"I'm great," said Magnus. "I don't need sleeping. Or waking. I feel great."

The baby waved his fat hands in Alec's direction, the gestures loose and uncoordinated but unmistakable. Alec looked startled but smiled, a sudden, unexpectedly nice smile, and reached out to take the baby in his arms. As soon as he did, the baby stopped grizzling.

Magnus waved his finger in the baby's face. "I find your attitude insulting," he informed him. He kissed Alec briefly. "I won't be gone long."

"Take as long as you need," said Alec. "I have this feeling my parents might be coming to help very shortly."

Magnus left, and Alec stepped away from the door, going to stand at the window with the baby.

"So," said Alec. His shirt was rumpled, clearly slept in, and he was bouncing a baby. Simon felt bad even bothering him. "What did you want to talk to me about?"

"I'm really sorry again about yesterday," Simon told him.

Then he wondered if it was terrible that he had referenced sex in front of Alec's baby. Maybe Simon was just doomed to mortally offend Alec, over and over again. Forever.

"It's okay," said Alec. "I once walked in on you and Isabelle. I guess turnabout's fair play." He frowned. "Although you two were in my room at the time, so actually I think you still owe me."

Simon was alarmed. "You walked in on me and Isabelle? But we haven't . . . I mean, we didn't . . . Did we?"

It would be typical of Simon's life, he thought. Of all things in the world, he would forget that.

Alec looked upset to be having this discussion, but Simon fixed him with a pleading stare and Alec apparently took pity on Simon's great patheticness.

"I don't know," Alec said at last. "You were in the process of taking your clothes off, as I remember. And I try not to remember. And you seemed to be engaging in some sort of role-play."

"Oh. Whoa. Like advanced role-play? Were there costumes? Were there props? What is Isabelle going to be expecting here, exactly?"

"I won't discuss this," said Alec.

"But if you could just give me a tiny hint . . ."

"Get out of here, Simon," said Alec.

Simon yanked himself back from the edge of role-playing panic, and pulled himself together.

This was more words than he had spoken to Alec in years.

Though Alec had just ordered him out of the room, so Simon had to admit things were not exactly going well.

"I'm sorry," said Simon. "I mean, I'm sorry for the inappropriate questions. And I'm sorry for walking in on you, er, yesterday morning. I'm sorry for everything. I'm sorry for whatever it is that went wrong between us. Whatever you're angry about. I honestly don't remember, but I do remember how you are when you're angry, and I don't want things to be like that between us. I remember you don't like Clary."

Alec looked at Simon as if he was crazy.

"I like Clary. Clary's one of my best friends."

"Oh," said Simon. "I'm sorry. I thought I remembered . . . I must have gotten it wrong."

Alec took a deep breath and admitted: "No, you didn't get it wrong. I didn't like Clary at first. I got—rough with her once. I slammed her up against a wall. She hit her head. I was a trained warrior and she didn't have any training at all, back then. I'm twice her size."

Simon had come here to conciliate Alec, so he was unprepared for the strong urge to take a swing at him. He couldn't do it. Alec was holding a baby.

All he could do was stare at him in furious silence, at the very idea someone would touch his best friend.

"It's no excuse," Alec continued. "But I was afraid. She knew about me being gay, and she told me that she knew. She wasn't telling me anything I didn't already know, but I was scared of her because I didn't know her. She wasn't my friend then. She was just some mundane invading my family, and I knew Shadowhunters, I was friends with Shadowhunters, who if they'd ever guessed—they would have gone running to tell my parents, so my parents could talk sense into me. They would have told everybody. They would have thought they were doing the right thing."

"It wouldn't have been the right thing," said Simon, still furious but shaken. "Clary would *never* do that. She never even told me."

"I didn't know her then," said Alec. "You're right. She never told anyone, about any of it. She had every right to say that I'd gotten rough with her. Jace would have punched me in the face if he'd known. I was terrified she would tell Jace that I was gay, because I wasn't ready for Jace to know about me. But you're right. She would never, and she didn't." He looked out of the window, patting the baby on the back. "I like Clary," he said simply. "She always tries to do what's right, and she never lets anyone else tell her what right is. She reminds my *parabatai* that he wants to live. Occasionally I wish she'd take fewer mad risks, but if I hated reckless crazy-brave people, I'd hate . . ."

"Let me guess," said Simon. "His name rhymes with Face Herringfail."

Alec laughed and Simon mentally congratulated himself.

"So you like Clary," said Simon. "I'm the only one you don't like. What did I do? I know you have a lot on your plate, but if you could just tell me what I did so I can apologize for it and so we can maybe be okay, I'd really appreciate it."

Alec stared at him, then turned and walked toward one of the chairs in the attic. There were two rickety wooden chairs, both of which held cushions with peacocks embroidered on them, and there was a sofa. The sofa was a little slanted. Alec took one of the chairs, and Simon decided not to risk the sofa and took the other.

Alec put the baby on his knee, one arm carefully around his small, round body. With his free hand he played with the baby's tiny hands, tapping them with his fingertips, as if he were teaching the baby how to play patty-cake. He was clearly getting ready for a confession.

Simon drew in a deep breath, preparing for whatever it was. He knew it might be really bad. He had to be ready.

"What did you do?" Alec asked. "You saved Magnus's life."

Simon was at a loss. An apology seemed inappropriate.

"Magnus was kidnapped, and I went into a hell dimension to save him. That was my whole plan. All I wanted to do was rescue him. On the way, Isabelle was badly hurt. My whole life, I always wanted to protect the people I loved, to make sure they were safe. I should have been able to do it. But I couldn't. I wasn't able to help either of them. You did. You saved Isabelle's life. When Magnus's father was intent on taking him and there was nothing I could do about it, nothing at all, you stepped in. I'd undervalued you, in the past, and you did everything I ever wanted to do, and then you were gone. Isabelle was a wreck. Clary was worse. Jace was so upset. Magnus felt guilty. Everyone was so hurt, and I wanted to help them, and you came back but you didn't remember what you had done. I'm not really good with strangers, and you were a really complicated stranger. I couldn't talk to you. It wasn't that you did anything wrong. It was that there was nothing I could do to make it even between us. I owed you more than I could ever repay, and I didn't even know how to thank you. It wouldn't have meant anything. You didn't even remember."

"Oh," said Simon. "Wow."

It was weird to think of faceless strangers thinking of Simon as a hero. It was even weirder to have Alec Lightwood, who he'd thought did not even like him, talk about him as if he was a hero.

"So you don't hate me, and you don't hate Clary. You don't hate anyone."

"I hate people forcing me to talk about my feelings," said Alec.

Simon stared at him for a moment, an apology on his lips, but he did not speak it. Instead he grinned, and Alec grinned shyly back.

"I've been doing it way too much since I got to the Academy."

"I can imagine," said Simon.

He had not been sure what would happen with the baby Alec and Magnus were taking care of, but from everything Isabelle had said, she was sure they were keeping him. That must have required a conversation.

"I would like," Alec said, "not to talk about feelings again for about a year. Also maybe to sleep for a year. Do babies ever sleep?"

"I used to babysit sometimes," Simon said. "As I recall, babies do sleep a lot, but when you least expect it. Babies: more like the Spanish Inquisition than you think."

Alec nodded, though he seemed confused. Simon made a mental note that it was his duty now, as Alec's established friend, to introduce Alec to Monty Python as soon as possible. The baby crowed as if he were pleased by the comparison.

"Hey," said Alec. "I'm sorry that I made you think I was mad at you, just because I didn't know what to say."

"Well," Simon said. "Here's the thing. I was helped along in my assumption."

Alec stopped playing patty-cake with the baby. He went still all over. "What do you mean?"

"You didn't talk to me a lot, and I was a little worried about it," Simon explained. "So I asked my friend, between us guys, if you had a problem with me. I asked my good friend Jace."

There was a pause as Alec absorbed this news. "You did."

"And Jace," said Simon. "Jace told me that there was a big, dark secret issue between us. He said it wasn't his place to talk about it."

The baby looked at Simon, then back at Alec. His small face looked thoughtful, as if he might shake his head and go: *That Jace, what will he do next?*

"Leave this to me," Alec said calmly. "He's my *parabatai* and we have a sacred bond and everything, but now he has gone too far."

"That's cool," said Simon. "Please exact awful vengeance for both of us, because I'm pretty sure he could take me in a fight."

Alec nodded, admitting this very true fact. Simon could not believe he had been so worried about Alec Lightwood. Alec was great.

"Well," Alec said. "Like I said . . . I do owe you."

Simon waved a hand. "Nah. Call it even."

* ✱ *

Magnus was so tired, he stumbled into the Shadowhunter Academy dining room and thought about eating there.

Then he actually looked at the food and came to his senses.

It was not quite dinnertime, but there were a few students gathered early, even though Magnus did not anticipate there would be a rush on the slime lasagna. Magnus saw Julie and her friends at one table. Julie looked him up and down, taking in the wrecked hair and Alec's T-shirt, and he read deep disillusion-ment on her face.

So a young girl's dreams died. Magnus admitted, after a sleepless night and wearing one of Alec's shirts because Isabelle had destroyed several of his own and the baby had been sick on several others, he might not be at his most glamorous.

It was probably good for Julie to face reality, though Magnus was determined to, at some point, take a shower, wear a better shirt, and dazzle the baby with his resplendence.

Magnus had visited Ragnor at the Academy, and he knew how the meals there worked. He squinted, trying to figure out which tables belonged to the elites and which to the dregs, the humans who aspired to be Nephilim but were not accepted by the Nephilim as good enough until they Ascended. Magnus had always thought the dregs showed enormous self-restraint by not rising up against Shadowhunter arrogance, burning down the Academy, and fleeing into the night.

It was possible that the Clave was right when they called Magnus an insurgent.

He could not work out, however, which tables belonged to whom. It had been very clear, years ago, but he was certain the blonde and the brunette Simon knew were Nephilim, and almost sure the gorgeous idiot who wanted to raise a baby with Simon in a sock drawer was not.

Magnus's attention was attracted by the sound of a throaty, imperious voice coming from a Latina girl who looked all of fifteen. She was a mundane, Magnus knew at a glance. Something else he could tell at a glance: In a couple of years, whether she Ascended or not, she would be a holy terror.

"Jon," she was saying to the boy across the table from her. "I am in so much pain from stubbing my toe! I need aspirin."

"What's aspirin?" asked the boy, sounding panicked.

He was obviously Nephilim, through and through and through. Magnus could tell without seeing his runes. In fact, he was prepared to bet the boy was a Cartwright. Magnus had known several Cartwrights through the centuries. The Cartwrights all had such distressingly thick necks.

"You buy it in a pharmacy," said the girl. "No, don't tell me, you don't know what a pharmacy is either. Have you ever left Idris in your whole life?"

"Yes!" said Jon, possibly Cartwright. "On many demon-hunting missions. And once Mama and Papa took me to the beach in France!"

"Amazing," said the girl. "I mean that. I'm going to explain all of modern medicine to you."

"Please don't do that, Marisol," said Jon. "I did not feel good after you explained appendectomies. I couldn't eat."

Marisol made a face at her plate. "So what you're saying is, I did you a huge favor."

"I like to eat," said Jon sadly.

"Right," said Marisol. "So, I don't explain modern medicine to you, and then a medical emergency occurs to me. It could be solved with the application of a little first aid, but you don't know that, and so I die. I die at your feet. Is that what you want, Jon?"

"No," said Jon. "What's first aid? Is there a . . . second aid?"

"I can't believe you're going to let me die when my death could so easily be avoided, if you had just listened," Marisol went on mercilessly.

"Okay, okay! I'll listen."

"Great. Get me some juice, because I'll be talking for a while. I'm still very hurt that you even considered letting me die," Marisol added as Jon scrambled up and made for the side of the room where the unappetizing food and potentially poisonous drinks were laid out. "I thought Shadowhunters had a mandate to protect mundanes!" Marisol shouted after him. "Not orange juice. I want apple juice!"

"Would you believe," said Catarina, appearing at Magnus's elbow, "that the Cartwright kid was the biggest bully in the Academy?"

"Seems like he met a bigger bully," Magnus murmured.

He congratulated himself on the correct Cartwright guess. It was hard to be sure, with Shadowhunter families. Certain traits did seem to run in their family lines, inbred as they were, but there were always exceptions.

For instance, Magnus had always found the Lightwoods rather forgettable. He'd liked some of them—Anna Lightwood and her parade of brokenhearted young ladies, Christopher Lightwood and his explosions, and now Isabelle—but there had never been a Lightwood who touched his heart, as some Shadowhunters had: Will Herondale or Henry Branwell or Clary Fray.

Until the Lightwood who was unforgettable; until the Lightwood who had not only touched but taken his heart.

"Why are you smiling to yourself?" Catarina asked, her voice suspicious.

"I was just thinking that life is full of surprises," said Magnus. "What happened to this Academy?"

The mundane girl could not bully the Cartwright boy unless the boy cared about what happened to her—unless he saw her as a person, and did not dismiss her the way Magnus had seen countless Nephilim dismiss mundanes and Downworlders, too.

Catarina hesitated. "Come with me," she said. "There's something I want to show you."

She took his hand and led him out of the Academy cafeteria, her blue fingers intertwined with his blue-ringed hands. Magnus thought of the baby and found himself smiling again. He had always thought blue was the loveliest color.

"I've been sleeping in Ragnor's old room," Catarina said.

She mentioned their old friend briskly and practically, with no hint of feeling. Magnus held her hand a little tighter as they went up two flights of stairs and down through stone corridors. The walls bore tapestries illustrating Shadowhunters' great deeds. There were holes in several of the tapestries, including one that left the Angel Raziel headless. Magnus feared sacrilegious mice had been at the tapestries.

Catarina opened a large, dark oak wood door and led him into a vaulted stone room where there were a few pictures on the walls Magnus recognized as Ragnor's: a sketch of a monkey, a seascape with a pirate ship on it. The carved oak bed was covered in Catarina's severe white hospital sheets, but the moth-eaten curtains were green velvet, and there was a green leather inlay on a desk placed under the room's single large window.

There was a coin on it, a circle of copper turned dark with age, and two yellowed pieces of paper, turning up at the edges.

"I was going through the papers in Ragnor's desk when I found this letter," Catarina said. "It was the only really personal thing in the room. I thought you might like to read it."

"I would," said Magnus, and she put it into his hands.

Magnus unfolded the letter and looked at the spiky black writing set deep into the yellow surface, as if the writer had been annoyed by the page itself. He felt as if he were listening to a voice he had thought silenced forever.

> To Ragnor Fell, preeminent educator at Shadowhunter Academy, and former High Warlock of London:
>
> I am sorry but not surprised to hear the latest crop of Shadowhunter brats are just as unpromising as the last lot. The Nephilim, lacking imagination and intellectual curiosity? You astonish me.
>
> I enclose a coin etched with a wreath, a symbol of education in the ancient world. I was told a faerie placed good luck on it, and you are certainly going to need luck reforming the Shadowhunters.
>
> I am as ever impressed by your patience and dedication to your job, and your continuing optimism that your students can be taught. I wish I could have your bright outlook on life, but unfortunately I cannot help looking around at the world and noticing that we are surrounded by idiots. If I were teaching Nephilim children, I imagine I would sometimes feel forced to speak to them sharply and occasionally feel forced to drain them entirely of blood.

*(Note to any Nephilim illegally reading Mr. Fell's letters
and invading his privacy: I am, naturally, joking. I have a
very droll personality.)*

*You ask how life in New York is and I can only report the
usual: smelly, crowded, and populated almost entirely by
maniacs. I was almost knocked over by a party of warlocks
and werewolves on Bowery Street. One particular warlock
was in the front, waving a glittering purple ladies' feather
boa over his head like a flag. I am so embarrassed to know
him. Sometimes I pretend to other Downworlders that I do
not. I hope they believe me.*

*The main reason I am writing to you is, of course, so that
we may continue your Spanish lessons. I enclose a fresh list
of vocabulary words, and assure you that you are coming
along very well. If you should ever make the terrible decision to accompany a certain badly dressed warlock of our
acquaintance to Peru again, this time you will be prepared.*

Yours most sincerely,

Raphael Santiago

"Ragnor would not have known the Academy was going
to be shut down after Valentine's Circle attacked the Clave,"
Catarina said. "He kept the letter so he could learn the Spanish,
and then he was never able to come back for it. From the letter,
though, it seems like they wrote to each other quite frequently.
Ragnor must have burned the others, since they contained
comments that would have gotten Raphael Santiago into
trouble. I know Ragnor was fond of that sharp-tongued little
vampire." She leaned her cheek against Magnus's shoulder. "I
know you were, as well."

Magnus shut his eyes for a moment and remembered Raphael, who he had once done a favor; Raphael, who had died for him in return. He had known him when he was first turned, a snippy child with a will of iron, and known him through the years as Raphael led a vampire clan in all but name.

Magnus had never known Ragnor when Ragnor was young. Ragnor had been older than Magnus and, by the time Magnus met him, had become perpetually cranky. Ragnor had been yelling at kids to get off his lawn before lawns were invented. He had always been kind to Magnus, willing to fall in with any of Magnus's schemes as long as he could complain throughout while they did it.

Still, in spite of Ragnor's dark outlook on life in general and Shadowhunters in particular, Ragnor had been the one who came to Idris to teach Shadowhunters. Even after the Academy was closed, he had stayed in his little house outside the City of Glass and tried to teach the Nephilim who were willing to learn. He had always hoped, even when he refused to admit it.

Ragnor and Raphael. They were both supposed to be immortal. Magnus had thought they would last forever, as he did, down the centuries, that there would always be another meeting and another chance. But they were gone, and the mortals Magnus loved lived on. It was a lesson, Magnus thought, to love while you could, love what was fragile and beautiful and imperiled. Nobody was guaranteed forever.

Ragnor and Magnus had not gone to Peru again, and never would now. Of course, Magnus was banned from Peru, so he could not go anyway.

"You came to the Academy for Ragnor," Magnus said to Catarina. "For the sake of Ragnor's dreams, to see if you could teach the Shadowhunters to change. It seems a pretty different place, this time around. Do you think you succeeded?"

"I never thought I would," said Catarina. "This was always Ragnor's dream. I did it for him, and not the Shadowhunters. I always thought Ragnor teaching was foolish. You cannot teach people anything if they do not want to learn."

"What changed your mind?"

"I didn't change my mind," said Catarina. "This time, they did want to learn. I could not have done this alone."

"Who helped you?" asked Magnus.

Catarina smiled. "Our former Daylighter, Simon Lewis. He's a sweet boy. He could have skated by on being a hero of the war, but he declared himself a member of the dregs, and he kept speaking up even though he had nothing to gain from it. I tried to help him along, but that was all I could do, and I could only hope it would be enough. One by one, the students followed his lead and started to fall from strictly Nephilim ways, like a set of rebellious dominoes. George Lovelace moved to the dregs dormitory with Simon. Beatriz Velez Mendoza and Julie Beauvale sat with them at mealtimes. Marisol Rojas Garza and Sunil Sadasivan started fighting with the elite kids at every opportunity. The two streams became a group, became a team—even Jonathan Cartwright. It was not all Simon. These are children who know Shadowhunters fought side by side with Downworlders when Valentine attacked Alicante. These are children who saw Dean Penhallow welcome me to their Academy. They are the children of a changing world. But I think they needed Simon here, to be their catalyst."

"And you here, to be their teacher," said Magnus. "Do you think you have found a new vocation in teaching?"

He gazed down at her, slim and sky blue in their friend's old stone-and-green room. She made a terrible face.

"Hell no," said Catarina Loss. "The only thing more terrible than the food is all the horrible, whiny teenagers. I'll see Simon safely Ascended and then I am out of here, back to my hospital, where there are easy problems to deal with like gangrene. Ragnor must have been crazy."

Magnus lifted Catarina's hand, which he was still holding, to his lips. "Ragnor would have been proud."

"Oh, stop it," said Catarina, shoving him. "You're so mushy since you fell in love. And now you're going to be even worse, because you have a *baby*. I remember what it was like. They're so small, and you put so much hope into them."

Magnus glanced at her, startled. She almost never mentioned the child she had raised, Tobias Herondale's child. Partly because it was not safe: It was not a secret the Nephilim could ever know, not a sin they would ever forgive. Partly, Magnus had always suspected, Catarina did not speak of him because it hurt too much.

Catarina caught the glance. "I told Simon about him," she said. "My boy."

"You must really trust Simon," Magnus said slowly.

"Do you know?" said Catarina. "I really do. Here, take these. I want you to have them. I'm done with them."

She picked up the old coin on the desk and put it in Magnus's palm, in the hand that already held Raphael's letter to Ragnor. Magnus looked at the coin and the letter.

"Are you sure?"

"I'm sure," said Catarina. "I read the letter a lot during my first year in the Academy, to remind myself what I was doing here and what Ragnor would have wanted. I've honored my friend. I've almost completed my task. You take them."

Magnus tucked away the letter and the good-luck charm, sent by one of his dead friends to another.

He and Catarina walked out of Ragnor's room together. Catarina said she was going to eat dinner, which Magnus thought was extremely reckless of her.

"Can't you do something safe and soothing, like bungee jumping?" he asked, but she insisted. He dropped a kiss on her cheek. "Come by the attics later. The Lightwoods will be there, so I need protection. We'll have a party."

He turned and left her, unwilling to enter the dining hall and behold the slime lasagna again. As he made his way up the stairs, he met Simon on his way down.

Magnus looked at Simon consideringly. Simon seemed alarmed by this.

"Come with me, Simon Lewis," Magnus commanded. "Let's have a chat."

Simon stood at the top of one of the towers in Shadowhunter Academy with Magnus Bane, looking out at the gathering twilight and feeling vaguely uneasy.

"I could swear this tower used to be crooked."

"Huh," said Magnus. "Perception's a funny thing."

Simon was just not sure what Magnus wanted. He liked Magnus. He'd just never had a heart-to-heart with Magnus, and now Magnus was giving him a look that said *what is your deal, Simon Lewis?* Magnus even made the tatty gray shirt he was wearing look faintly stylish. He was fairly certain Magnus was too cool to care about his deal.

He glanced over at Magnus, who was standing at one of the large, glassless windows in the tower, the night wind blowing his hair back.

"I said to you once," Magnus offered, "that one day, of all the people we know, the two of us might be the only ones left."

"I don't remember," said Simon.

"Why should you?" Magnus asked. "Barring some freak tornado that sweeps away everyone we love, that is no longer true. You're mortal now. And even the immortal can be killed. Maybe this tower will collapse and leave everyone to mourn us."

The view from the tower, the stars over the woods, was beautiful. Simon wanted to get down.

Magnus reached into his pocket and took out an old, carved coin. Simon could not see the inscription on it in the dark, but he could see that there was one.

"This belonged to Raphael once. Do you remember Raphael?" Magnus asked. "The vampire who turned you."

"Only in bits and pieces," Simon said. "I remember him telling me Isabelle was out of my league."

Magnus turned his face away, not quite successfully hiding a smile. "That sounds like Raphael."

"I remember—feeling him die," said Simon, his voice sticking in his throat. That was the worst of his stolen memories, that the weight of the memory remained when all else was gone, that he felt loss without knowing what he had lost. "He meant something to me, but I don't know if he liked me. I don't know if I liked him."

"He felt responsible for you," Magnus said. "It occurred to me today that maybe I should have felt responsible for you in the same way. I was the one who performed the spell that brought you back your memories; I was the one who set you on the path to Shadowhunter Academy. Raphael was the first one to place you in another world, but I placed you in another world as well."

"I made my own choices," Simon said. "You gave me the chance to do that. I'm not sorry you did. Are you sorry you restored my memories?"

Magnus smiled. "No, I'm not sorry. Catarina filled me in on a little of what's been going on at the Academy. It seems like you have been doing just fine making your choices without me."

"I've been trying," said Simon.

He had been shocked by Alec praising him, and it was not as if he had expected Magnus to do it. But he felt warmed by Magnus's words, suddenly warm all over, despite the wind sweeping in from the crystalline coldness of the sky. Magnus was not talking about the bits and pieces of his half-forgotten past but about what he was now and what he had done with his time since then.

It wasn't anything remarkable, but he had been trying.

"I also heard you had a little adventure in Faerieland," said Magnus. "We've been having trouble in New York with faerie fruit sellers as well. Part of the faeries running wild is the Cold Peace itself. People who are not trusted become untrustworthy. But there is something else wrong as well. Faerie is not a land without rules, without rulers. The Queen who was Sebastian's ally has vanished, and there are many dark rumors as to why. None of which I would repeat to the Clave, because they would only impose harsher punishments on the faeries. They become harsher, and the fey wilder, and the hate between both sides grows day by day. There are storms behind you, Simon. But there is another and a greater storm coming. All the old rules are falling away. Are you ready for another storm?"

Simon was silent. He didn't know how to answer that.

"I've seen you with Clary, and with Isabelle," Magnus continued. "I know you are on the path to Ascension, to having a *parabatai* and a Shadowhunter love. Are you happy with it? Are you certain?"

"I don't know about being certain," Simon said. "I don't know about being ready, either. I can't say I haven't had doubts, that I haven't thought about turning back and being a kid in a band in Brooklyn. I think sometimes it's too hard to believe in yourself. You just do the things you're not sure you can do. You just act, in spite of not being certain. I don't believe I can change the world—it sounds stupid to even talk about it—but I'm going to try."

"We all change the world, with every day of living in it," Magnus said. "You just have to decide *how* you want to change the world. I brought you into this world, the second time around, and though your choices are your own I do take some responsibility. Even if you are committed, you have other choices. I could arrange for you to be a vampire again, or a werewolf. Both are risky, but none as risky as Ascension."

"Yes. I want to try changing the world as a Shadowhunter," said Simon. "I really do. I want to try and change the Clave from the inside. I want that particular power to help people. It's worth the risk."

Magnus nodded.

He had meant it, Simon thought, when he said that Simon's choices were his own. He had left it up to Simon, that day in

Brooklyn when he and Isabelle had approached Simon outside his school. He did not question Simon now, even though Simon was afraid that choosing to be a Shadowhunter and not a Downworlder might have offended him. He didn't want to be like the Shadowhunters who acted as if they were better than Downworlders. He wanted to be an entirely different kind of Shadowhunter.

Magnus did not look offended. He stood on the tower top, on stone in starlight, turning the coin that had belonged to the dead over and over in his fingers. He looked thoughtful.

"Have you thought about your Shadowhunter name?"

"Um . . . ," Simon said shyly. "A little bit. I was wondering, actually—what's your real name?"

Magnus sent him a sidelong glance. Nobody gave side-eye like someone with cat's eyes. "Magnus Bane," he said. "I know you've forgotten a lot, Smedley, but *really*."

Simon accepted the subtle reproof. He understood why Magnus would object to the implication that the name he had chosen to define himself by, kept over long years and made both infamous and illustrious, was not real.

"I'm sorry," he said. "It's just that my mind does keep coming back to names. If I survive Ascension, I'll have to pick a Shadowhunter name. I don't know how to pick the right one—I don't know how to pick one that will mean something, mean more than any other name would."

Magnus frowned.

"I'm not sure I'm cut out for this wise-advice business. Maybe I should wear a fake white beard to convince myself I am a sage. Pick the one that feels right, and don't worry too much," Magnus said eventually. "It's going to be your name.

You're going to live with it. You're going to give it meaning, not the other way around."

"I'm going to try," said Simon. "Is there any reason why 'Magnus Bane' was the one that felt right?"

"Magnus Bane felt right for a lot of reasons," Magnus said, which was not really an answer. He seemed to sense Simon's disappointment and take pity on him, because he added: "Here's one."

Magnus flipped the coin over and under his fingers, the circle of metal moving faster and faster. Blue lines of magic seemed to spring from his rings, a tiny storm rising in Magnus's palm and catching the coin in a net of lightning.

Then Magnus threw the coin off the tower, into the night wind. Simon could see the falling coin, still touched with blue fire, going beyond the limits of the Academy grounds.

"There's a scientific phenomenon to describe something that happens when an object is in motion. You think you know exactly what path it will take and where it will end up. Then suddenly, for no reason you can see . . . the arc changes. It goes somewhere you would never have expected."

Magnus snapped his fingers, and the coin zigzagged in the air and returned to them as Simon stared, feeling like he was seeing magic for the first time. He dropped the coin in Simon's hand and smiled, a blazing rebel's smile, his eyes as gold as newly discovered treasure.

"It's called the Magnus effect," he said.

"Fzzzz," Clary said, her bright red head hovering over the baby's small dark-blue one. She pressed little kisses onto the baby's cheeks, buzzing like a bee as she did so, and the baby chuckled and grasped at her curls. "Fzzzz, fzzz, fzzzz. I don't know what I'm doing. I have never had a close relationship with any babies. For sixteen years I thought I was an only child, baby. And after that, baby, you don't want to know what I thought. Please forgive me if I'm doing this wrong, baby. Do you like me, baby? I like you."

"Give me the baby," Maryse said jealously. "You've had him for four whole minutes, Clarissa."

It *was* a party in Magnus and Alec's suite, and the game of choice was Pass the Baby. Everyone wanted to hold him. Simon had shamelessly tried to curry favor with Isabelle's father by teaching Robert Lightwood how to use Simon's digital watch as a timer. Robert was now holding the watch in a death grip and studying it carefully. It would be Robert's turn with the baby again in sixteen minutes, and he had clasped Simon's shoulder and said, "Thanks, son," which Simon took as a blessing to date Robert's daughter. He did not regret the loss of his watch.

Clary surrendered the baby, and leaned back against the sofa between Simon and Jace. The sofa creaked dangerously as she settled back. Simon might have been safer in the formerly crooked tower, but he was willing to be in danger if he could stay next to Clary.

"He's so sweet," Clary whispered to Jace and Simon. "It's strange to think he's Alec and Magnus's, though. I mean, can you imagine?"

"It's not that strange," Jace said. "I mean, I can *imagine*."

A flush rose on his high cheekbones. He edged into the corner of the sofa as Simon and Clary both turned and stared at him.

Clary and Simon continued to stare judgmentally. It made Simon very happy. Judging people together was an essential part of best friendship.

Then Clary leaned forward and kissed Jace.

"Let's pick up this conversation in about ten years," she said. "Maybe longer! I'm going to dance with the girls."

She went to join Isabelle, who was already dancing to the soft music in the midst of a circle of admirers who had come because they heard she was back. Foremost among them was Marisol, who Simon was pretty sure had determined to be Isabelle when she grew up.

The Lightwood baby celebration was in full swing. Simon smiled, watching Clary. He could remember a couple of times she had been wary around other girls, and they had stuck together instead. It was nice to see Isabelle hold out her hands to Clary, and Clary grasp them without hesitation.

"Jace," said Simon as Jace watched Clary and smiled. Jace glanced at him and looked annoyed. "Remember when you told me that you wished I could remember?"

"Why are you asking me if I remember things?" Jace asked, sounding definitely annoyed. "I'm not the one who has problems with remembering. Remember?"

"I just wondered what you meant by that."

Simon waited, giving Jace a chance to take advantage of his demon amnesia and tell him another fake secret. Instead, Jace looked incredibly uncomfortable.

"Nothing," he said. "What would I mean? Nothing."

"Did you just mean you wanted me to remember the past generally?" Simon asked. "So I'd remember all the adventures we had and the manly bonds we formed together?"

Jace continued to make an uncomfortable face. Simon remembered Alec saying Jace was so upset.

"Wait, was that actually it?" Simon asked incredulously. "Did you *miss* me?"

"Obviously not!" snapped Jace. "I would never miss you. I, um, was talking about something specific."

"Okay. So, what specific thing did you want me to recall?" Simon asked. He eyed Jace suspiciously. "Was it the biting?"

"No!" said Jace.

"Was that a special moment for you?" Simon asked. "One that you wanted me to remember that we shared?"

"Remember this moment," said Jace. "At the very next opportunity that offers, I am going to leave you to die at the bottom of an evil boat. I want you to remember why."

Simon smiled to himself. "No, you won't. You would never leave me to die at the bottom of an evil boat," he muttered as Alec strolled over to the slanted sofa and Jace looked outraged by what he was hearing.

"Simon, normally it's a pleasure to talk to you," Alec said. "But could I have a word with Jace?"

"Oh, right," Simon said. "Jace, I'd forgotten what I was trying to talk to you about. But now I remember very clearly. Alec and I had a little talk about his problem with me. You know, the one you told me he had. The terrible secret."

Jace's golden eyes went blank. "Ah," he said.

"You think you're hilarious, don't you?"

"Though I realize that you are both a little annoyed with me, and this might not be the time to shower myself with praise," Jace said slowly, "honesty compels me to tell you: Yes. Yes, I do think I am hilarious. 'There goes Jace Herondale,' people say.

'Cutting wit, and also totally cut. It's a burden Simon could never understand.'"

"Alec's going to kill you," Simon informed him, and patted Jace on the shoulder. "And I think that's fair. For what it's worth, I'll miss you, buddy."

He got up from the sofa. Alec advanced on Jace.

Simon trusted Alec to exact terrible vengeance for both of them. He had wasted enough time on Jace's dumb joke.

George was dancing with Julie and Beatriz, clowning around to try and get them to laugh. Beatriz was already laughing, and Simon thought Julie would soon.

"Come on, dancing with me isn't so bad," George told Julie. "I may be no Magnus Bane . . ." He paused and looked over at Magnus, who had changed into a black gauze shirt with blue sequins twinkling underneath. "I definitely could not pull that off," he added. "But I do work out! And I have a Scottish accent."

"You know that's right," said Simon. He high-fived George and smiled at the girls, but he was already moving past them, on his way to the center of the dancers.

On his way to Isabelle.

He came up behind her and slid his arm around her waist. She leaned back against him. She was wearing the dress she'd worn the day he'd first met her for the second time, reminding him of the starry night over Shadowhunter Academy.

"Hey," he whispered. "I want to tell you something."

"What is it?" Isabelle whispered back.

Simon turned her toward him, and she let him. He thought they should have this conversation face-to-face.

Behind her, he could see Jace and Alec. They were hugging, and Alec was laughing. Jace was patting him on the back in a congratulatory way. So much for terrible vengeance, though Simon couldn't really say he minded.

"I wanted to tell you before I try to Ascend," he said.

The smile dropped off Isabelle's face. "If this is an in-case-I-die speech, I don't want to hear it," she said fiercely. "You're not going to do that to me. You're not going to even consider dying. You're going to be fine."

"No," Simon said. "You've got it all wrong. I wanted to say this now, because if I Ascend, I get my memories back."

Isabelle looked confused instead of angry, which was an improvement. "What is it, then?"

"It doesn't matter if I get my memories back or not," Simon said. "It doesn't matter if another demon gives me amnesia tomorrow. I know you: You'll come find me again, you'll come rescue me no matter what happens. You'll come for me, and I'll discover you all over again. I love you. I love you without the memories. I love you right now."

There was a pause, broken by irrelevancies like the music and the murmur of the people all around them. He could not quite read the look on Isabelle's face.

Isabelle said in a calm voice: "I know."

Simon stared at her. "Was that . . . ," he said slowly. "Was that a *Star Wars* reference? Because if it was, I would like to declare my love all over again."

"Go on, then," said Isabelle. "I mean it. Say it again. I've been waiting awhile."

"I love you," said Simon.

Isabelle was laughing. Simon would have thought he would be appalled to say those words to a girl and have her laugh at him. But Isabelle was always surprising him. He could not stop looking at her. "Really?" she asked, and her eyes were shining. "Really?"

"Really," said Simon.

He drew her to him, and they danced together, on the top floor of the Academy, in the heart of her family. Since she'd been waiting awhile, he told her again and again.

Magnus kept misplacing his baby. This did not seem a good sign for the future. Magnus was sure you were meant to keep a firm grip on their location.

He eventually located the baby with Maryse, who had seized him in triumph and run away to coo over her treasure in the kitchen.

"Oh, hello," said Maryse, looking a little guilty.

"Hello, you," said Magnus, and curved a hand around the small blue head, feeling the crisp curls. "And hello, you."

The baby let out a fretful little wail. Magnus thought he was learning to distinguish between the different wails, and he magicked up a bottle of formula, ready-made. He held out his arms and Maryse visibly summoned up the willpower to surrender the baby.

"You're good with him," Maryse offered as Magnus tucked him into the corner of his arm and popped the bottle into his small mouth.

"Alec's better," Magnus said.

Maryse smiled and looked proud. "He's very mature for his age," she said fondly, and hesitated. "I . . . wasn't, at his age, when I was a young mother. I didn't . . . behave in a way I would want any of my children to see. Not that it's an excuse."

Magnus looked down at Maryse's face. He remembered facing off on opposite sides against her once, long ago, when she had been one of Valentine's disciples and he had felt as if he would hate her and everyone to do with her forever.

He also remembered choosing to forgive another woman who had been on Valentine's side, and who had come to him holding a child in her arms and wanting to make things right. That woman had been Jocelyn, and that baby had become Clary, the first and only child Magnus had ever seen grow up.

He had never thought he would have his own child, to watch grow up.

Maryse looked back at him, standing very tall and straight. Perhaps his assumption about how she had felt for all these years was wrong; perhaps she had never decided to ignore the past, and thought with Nephilim pride that he had to follow her lead. Perhaps she had always wanted to apologize and always been too proud.

"Oh, Maryse," Magnus said. "Forget it. I'm serious, don't mention it again. In one of those turns I never expected, we're family. All the beautiful surprises of life are what make life worth living."

"You still get surprised?"

"Every day," said Magnus. "Especially since I met your son."

He walked out of the kitchen with his son in his arms and Maryse behind him, back to the party.

His beloved Alec, paragon of maturity, appeared to be hitting his *parabatai* repeatedly around the head. Last time Magnus had seen them, they had been hugging, so he presumed Jace had made one of his many unfortunate jokes.

"What is wrong with you?" Alec demanded. He laughed and kept raining down blows as Jace flailed on the sofa, sending cushions flying, a vision of Shadowhunter grace. "Seriously, Jace, what is wrong with you?"

This seemed a reasonable question to Magnus.

He looked around the room. Simon was dancing with Isabelle, very badly. Isabelle did not seem to mind. Clary was jumping up and down with Marisol, barely taller than the younger girl. Catarina appeared to be fleecing Jon Cartwright at cards, over by the window.

Robert Lightwood was standing right beside Magnus. Robert had to stop creeping up on people like this. Someone was going to have a heart attack.

"Hello, little man," said Robert. "Where did you go off to?"

He shot a suspicious look at Maryse, who rolled her eyes.

"Magnus and I were having a talk," she said, touching Magnus's arm.

Her behavior made perfect sense to Magnus: win over the son-in-law, gain more access to the grandchild. He had seen these kind of family interactions before, but he had never, never thought he would be part of them.

"Oh?" Robert said eagerly. "Have you decided on his name?"

The latest song stopped playing just as Robert asked the question. His booming voice rang out in the hush.

Alec leaped off Jace and over the back of the sofa, to stand beside Magnus. The sofa collapsed, gently, with Jace still trapped in the cushions.

Magnus looked at Alec, who looked back at him, hope shining in his face. That was one thing that had not changed about Alec in the time they had been together: He had no guile, used no tricks to hide how he really felt. Magnus never wanted him to lose that.

"We did talk about it, actually," Magnus said. "And we thought that you had the right idea."

"You mean . . . ," Maryse said.

Magnus inclined his head, as close as he could come to a sweeping bow while holding the baby. "I am delighted to introduce you all," he said, "to Max Lightwood."

Magnus felt Alec's hand rest, warm as gratitude and sure as love, against his back. He looked down at the baby's face. The baby seemed much more interested in his bottle than his name.

The time might come when the child, being a warlock, would want to choose his own name to bear through the centuries. Until the time came when he was old enough to choose who he wanted to be, Magnus thought he could do a lot worse than this name, this sign of love and acceptance, grief and hope.

Max Lightwood.

One of the beautiful surprises of life.

There was a humming, delighted hush, with murmurs of pleasure and approval. Then Maryse and Robert began to fight about middle names.

"Michael," Robert repeated, a stubborn man.

Catarina strolled up, tucking a roll of money into her bra and thus not looking like the most appropriate teacher in the history of time. "How about Ragnor?" she asked.

"Clary," said Jace from the fallen sofa. "Help me. It's gone all dark."

Magnus wandered away from the debate, because Max's bottle was almost empty and Max was starting to cry.

"Don't magic a bottle, make a real one," Alec said. "If he

gets used to you being faster at feeding him, you have to feed him all the time."

"That is blackmail! Don't cry," Magnus urged his son, going back into the kitchen so he could make up a bottle by hand.

It was not so difficult, getting the formula ready. Magnus had watched Alec do it several times now, and he found that he was able to follow along by doing what Alec had done.

"Don't cry," he coaxed Max again as the milk heated up. "Don't cry, and don't spit up on my shirt. If you do either of those things, I will forgive you, but I will be upset. I want us to get along."

Max cried on. Magnus wiggled the fingers of his free hand over the baby's face, wishing there was a magic spell to make babies hush that would not be wrong to cast.

To his surprise Max ceased crying, in the same way he had in the hall yesterday when transferred to Alec's arms. He stared with a liquid, interested gaze at the sparkles cast on his face by Magnus's rings.

"See?" Magnus said, and restored Max's bottle to him, full again. "I knew we were going to get along."

He went and stood in the kitchen doorway, cradling Max in his arms, so he could watch the party. Three years ago, he would not have thought any of this was possible. There were so many people he felt connected to, in this one room. So much had changed, and there was so much potential for change. It was terrifying, to think of all that might be lost, and exhilarating to think of all he had gained.

He looked to Alec, who was standing between his parents, his stance confident and relaxed, his mouth curved in a smile at something one of them had said.

"Maybe one day it will be just you and me, my little blueberry," Magnus said conversationally. "But not for a long, long time. We'll take care of him, you and I. Won't we?"

Max Lightwood made a happy burbling sound that Magnus took as agreement.

This warm, bright room was no bad starting place for his child's path to knowing there was more to life than many people ever learned, that there was limitless love to be found, and time to discover it. Magnus had to trust that for himself, for his son, for his beloved, for all of the shining, fading mortals and enduring, struggling immortals that he knew, there would be time enough.

He put the bottle down to one side and pressed his lips to the fuzzy curls covering his son's head. He heard Max make a small murmuring sound in his ear. "Don't worry," Magnus murmured back. "We're all in this together."

Angels Twice Descending

By Cassandra Clare and Robin Wasserman

Simon knew if he looked up he could meet Isabelle's eyes, or Clary's, and draw strength from them. He could silently ask them if this was the right path, and they would reassure him.

But this choice couldn't belong to them.
It had to be his, and his alone.

—Angels Twice Descending

"I think we should have a funeral," George Lovelace said, voice trembling on the last word. "A proper one."

Simon Lewis paused in his labors and peered up at his roommate. George was the kind of guy Simon had once loathed on sight, assuming anyone with that bronze glow, those six-pack abs, that maddeningly sexy (at least, according to every girl and more than a few of the guys Simon had checked with) Scottish brogue, must have a brain the size of a rat turd and a personality about as appealing. But George turned Simon's assumptions on their head on a daily basis. As he was doing right at this moment, wiping away something that looked suspiciously like a tear.

"Are you . . . *crying?*" Simon asked, incredulous.

"Of course not." George gave his eyes another furious

wipe. "Well, in my defense," he added, sounding only slightly abashed, "death is a terrible thing."

"It's a dead rat," Simon pointed out. "A dead rat in *your shoe*, I might add." Simon and George had discovered that the key to a happy roommate relationship was clear division of labor. So George was in charge of disposing of all creatures—rats, lizards, cockroaches, the occasional odd-shaped mishmash of the three whose ancestor had, presumably, once insulted a warlock— found in the closets or beneath the beds. Simon handled all those that had crawled inside items of clothing and—he shuddered to remember the moment they realized this labor needed assigning—under pillows. "Also, for the record, only one of us has actually *been* a rat—and you'll note he's not the one crying."

"It could be the last dead rat we ever find!" George sniffled. "Think about it, Si. *This* could be the last shared dead rat of our entire lives."

Simon sighed. As Ascension Day approached, the day they would officially stop being students and start being Shadowhunters, George had been mournfully noting every last time they did anything. Now, as the moon rose over their last night at the Academy, he'd apparently lost his mind. A little nostalgia made sense to Simon: That morning, at their last-ever calisthenics session, Delaney Scarsbury had called him a spaghetti-armed, four-eyed, bow-legged demon-snack-in-waiting for the last time, and Simon had almost said *thank you*. And that night's final bowl of "meat-flavored" custard had admittedly gotten them all a little choked up.

But losing it over a rat with stiffening limbs and athlete's foot? That was taking things too far.

Using the torn-off cover from his old demonology textbook, Simon managed to scoop the rat out of the shoe without touching it. He dropped it into one of the plastic bags he'd had Isabelle bring him specifically for this purpose, tied the bag tightly, then—humming taps—dropped it into the trash.

"RIP, Jon Cartwright the Thirty-Fourth," George said solemnly.

They named all their rats Jon Cartwright—a fact that drove the original Jon Cartwright nuts. Simon smiled at the thought of it, their gallingly cocky classmate's forehead flush with anger, that vein in his disgustingly muscled neck starting to throb. Maybe George was right.

Maybe, someday, they would even miss the rats.

Simon had never put much effort into imagining his graduation day, much less the night before. Like prom and homecoming, these seemed like rituals meant for a very different kind of teenager—the school-spirited, letter-jacketed jocks and cheerleaders he knew mostly from bad movies. No keg parties for him, no weepy farewells or ill-advised hookups fueled by nostalgia and cheap beer. Two years ago, if he'd bothered to think about it at all, Simon would have assumed he'd spend that night like he'd spent most of his nights in Brooklyn, hanging with Eric and the guys in Java Jones, guzzling coffee and brainstorming names for the band. (*Dead Sneaker Rat*, Simon mused out of habit. *Or maybe Rodent Funeral.*)

Of course, that was back when he'd assumed high school would lead to college, which would lead to rock stardom . . . or at least a moderately cool job at a moderately cool record label. Before he knew there was such a thing as demons, before he knew there was a race of superpowered, angel-blooded warriors eternally pledged to battle them—and definitely before he'd volunteered himself up to be one of them.

So instead of Java Jones, he was in the Academy's student lounge, squinting through candlelight, sneezing from two centuries' worth of dust, and dodging the intimidating glares of noble Shadowhunters past whose portraits lined the room, their expressions seeming to say, *How could you possibly imagine you could be one of* us? Instead of Eric, Matt, and Kirk, who he'd known since kindergarten, he was with friends he'd met only a couple of years before, one of whom nurtured an intense affection for rats and another who shared his name with them. Instead of speculating about their futures in rock and roll, they were readying themselves for a life battling multidimensional evils. Assuming, that is, they survived graduation.

Which wasn't exactly a safe assumption to make.

"What do you think it will be like?" Marisol Garza asked now, nestled beneath Jon Cartwright's beefy arm and looking like she was almost happy to be there. "The ceremony, I mean. What do you think we'll have to do?"

Jon, like Julie Beauvale and Beatriz Mendoza, descended from a long line of Shadowhunters. For them, tomorrow was just another day, their official farewell to student life. Time to stop training and start battling.

But for George, Marisol, Simon, Sunil Sadasivan, and a handful of other mundane students, tomorrow loomed as the day they Ascended.

No one was quite sure what it meant: Ascension. Much less what it entailed. They'd been told very little: That they would drink from the Mortal Cup. That they would, like the first of the warrior race, Jonathan Shadowhunter, sip the blood of an angel. That they would, if they were lucky, be transformed on the spot into real, full-blooded Shadowhunters. That they would say good-bye to their mundane lives forever and pledge themselves to a fearless life of service to humanity.

Or if they were very unlucky, they would die an immediate and presumably gruesome death.

It didn't exactly make for a festive evening.

"I'm just wondering what's in the Cup," Simon said. "You don't think it's actual blood, do you?"

"Isn't that your specialty, Lewis?" Jon sneered.

George sighed wistfully. "The last time Jon makes a stupid vampire joke."

"I wouldn't count on it," Simon muttered.

Marisol whacked Jon's shoulder. "Shut up, idiot," she said. But she said it rather too lovingly for Simon's taste.

"I bet it's water," Beatriz said, always the peacemaker. "Water that you're supposed to pretend is blood, or that the Cup turns into blood, or something like that."

"It doesn't matter what's in the Cup," Julie said in her best obnoxiously knowing way, even though she clearly didn't know any better than the rest of them. "The Cup's magic. You could probably drink ketchup out of it and it would still work."

"I hope it's coffee, then," Simon said with a wistful sigh of his own. The Academy was a caffeine-free zone. "I would be a much better Shadowhunter if I got to Ascend well-caffeinated."

"Sunil said he heard that it's water from Lake Lyn," Beatriz said skeptically. Simon hoped she was right to be skeptical; his last encounter with Lake Lyn's water had been unsettling, to say the least. And given that some unknown percentage of mundanes died upon Ascending, it seemed to him like the Cup didn't need any additional help on the occasionally fatal front.

"Where is Sunil, anyway?" Simon asked. They hadn't exactly made a plan to meet up tonight, but the Academy offered limited recreational options—at least if you didn't enjoy spending your free time accidentally getting locked in the dungeons or stalking the giant magical slug rumored to slither through the corridors in the predawn hours. Most nights for the last couple of months, Simon and his friends had ended up here, talking about their futures, and he'd expected they would spend this last night the same way.

Marisol, who knew Sunil the best, shrugged. "Maybe he's 'considering his options.'" She curled her fingers around the phrase. This was how Dean Penhallow had advised students on the mundane track to spend their final evening, assuring them there was no shame in backing out at the last moment.

"Humiliation. Lifelong embarrassment over your mundie cowardice and guilt for wasting all of our very valuable time," Scarsbury had growled at them, and then, when the dean shot him a disapproving look, "But yeah, sure, no shame."

"Well, shouldn't he be 'considering'?" Julie asked. "Shouldn't you all be? It's not like going to doctor school and taking the Hypocritical oath or something. You don't get to change your mind."

"First of all, it's the Hippocratic oath," Marisol said.

"And it's called *medical* school," Jon put in, looking rather proud of himself. Marisol had been schooling him on mundane life. Against his will, or so Jon had led them to believe.

"Second of all," Marisol added, "why would you think any of us would be likely to change our minds? Are *you* planning to change your mind about being a Shadowhunter?"

Julie looked affronted by the idea. "I *am* a Shadowhunter. You might as well have asked if I'm planning to change my mind about being alive."

"So what makes you think it's any different for us?" Marisol said fiercely. She was the youngest of them by two years and the smallest by several inches, but Simon sometimes thought that she was the bravest. She was certainly the one he'd bet on in a fight. (Marisol fought well—she also, when necessary, fought dirty.)

"She didn't mean anything by it," Beatriz said gently.

"I really didn't," Julie said quickly.

Simon knew it was true. Julie couldn't help sounding like a mundane-hating snob sometimes, any more than Jon could help sounding like—well, like an asshole sometimes. That's who they were, and Simon realized that, inexplicably, he wouldn't have it any other way. For better or worse, these were his friends. In two years they'd faced so much together: demons, faeries, Delaney Scarsbury, the dining hall "food." It was almost like a family, Simon reflected. You didn't necessarily like them all the time, but you knew, push come to shove, you'd defend them to the death.

Though he very much hoped it wouldn't come to that.

"Come on, aren't you a little nervous?" Jon asked. "Who can remember the last time anyone Ascended? It sounds utterly ridiculous when you think about it: One drink from a cup and—poof—*Lewis* is a Shadowhunter?"

"It doesn't sound ridiculous to me," Julie said softly, and they all fell silent. Julie's mother had been Turned during the Dark War. One drink from Sebastian's Infernal Cup, and she'd become Endarkened. A shell of a person, nothing more than a hollow vessel for Sebastian's evil commands.

They all knew what one drink from a cup could do.

George cleared his throat. He couldn't stand a somber mood for more than thirty seconds—it was one of the things Simon would miss most about living with him. "Well, I for one am entirely ready to claim my birthright," he said cheerfully. "Do you think I'll become unbearably arrogant on first sip, or will it take a little time to catch up with Jon?"

"It's not arrogance if it's accurate," Jon said, grinning, and just like that, the night righted itself again.

Simon tried to pay attention to his friends' banter and did his best not to think about Jon's question, about whether or not he was nervous—whether he should be spending this night in sober consideration of his "options."

What options? How, after two years at the Academy, after all his training and study, after he'd sworn over and over again that he wanted to be a Shadowhunter, could he just walk away? How could he disappoint Clary and Isabelle like that . . . and if he did, how could they ever love him again?

He tried not to think about how it would be even harder for them to love him—or at least for him to appreciate it—if something went wrong in the ceremony, and he ended up dead.

He tried not to think about all the *other* people who loved him, the ones who, according to Shadowhunter Law, he was supposed to pledge never to see again. His mother. His sister.

Marisol and Sunil didn't have anyone waiting for them back home, something that had always seemed unbearably sad to Simon. But maybe it was easier, walking away when you were leaving nothing behind. Then there was George, the lucky one—his adopted parents were Shadowhunters themselves, even if they'd never picked up a sword. He would still be able to go home for regular Sunday dinners; he wouldn't even have to pick a new name.

George had been teasing him lately, saying that Simon shouldn't have much trouble picking a new name, either. "'Lightwood' has quite a ring to it, don't you think?" he liked to say. Simon was getting very good at feigning deafness.

Secretly, though, a blush rising to his cheeks, he would think: *Lightwood . . . maybe.* Someday. If he dared let himself hope.

In the meantime, though, he had to come up with a new name of his own, a name for his new Shadowhunter self—which was approximately as unfathomable as everything else about this process.

"Um, can I come in?" A scrawny, spectacled girl of around thirteen stood in the doorway. Simon thought her name was Milla, but he wasn't sure—the Academy's new class was so large, and so inclined to goggle at Simon from a distance, that he hadn't gotten to know many of them. This one had the eager but confused look of a mundane, one who, even after all these months, couldn't quite believe she was really here.

"It's public property," Julie said, a haughty—or rather, even-haughtier-than-usual—note entering her voice. Julie loved lording it over the new kids.

The girl crept toward them skittishly. Simon found himself wondering how someone like her had ended up at the Academy—then caught himself. He knew better than to judge by appearances. Especially given how he'd looked when he showed up two years before, so skinny he could only fit into girl-size gear. *You're thinking like a Shadowhunter,* he chided himself.

Funny how that almost never sounded like a good thing.

"He told me to give this to you," the girl whispered, handing a folded paper to Marisol, and then quickly backing away. Marisol, Simon gathered, was somewhat of a hero to the younger mundanes.

"Who did?" Marisol asked, but the girl was already gone. Marisol shrugged and opened the note, her face falling as she read the message.

"What?" Simon asked, concerned.

Marisol shook her head.

Jon took her hand, and Simon expected her to slap him, but instead she squeezed tight. "It's from Sunil," she said in a tight, angry voice. She passed the note to Simon. "I guess he 'considered his options.'"

I can't do it, the note read. *I know it probably makes me a coward, but I can't drink from that Cup. I don't want to die. I'm sorry. Say good-bye to everyone for me? And good luck.*

They passed the note around one by one, as if needing to see the words in black and white before they could really believe it. Sunil had run away.

"We can't blame him," Beatriz said finally. "Everyone has to make his own choice."

"I can blame him," Marisol said, scowling. "He's making us all look bad."

Simon didn't think that was why she was really angry, not exactly. He was angry too—not because he thought Sunil was a coward, or had betrayed them. Simon was angry because he'd put so much effort into trying not to think about what could happen, or how this was his last chance to walk away, and now Sunil had made that impossible.

Simon stood up. "Think I need to get some air."

"Want company, mate?" George asked.

Simon shook his head, knowing George wouldn't be offended. It was another thing that made them such good roommates—each knew when to leave the other alone.

"See you guys in the morning," Simon said. Julie and Beatriz smiled and waved good night, and even Jon gave him a sardonic salute. But Marisol wouldn't even look at him, and Simon wondered whether she thought he'd be the next to run.

He wanted to reassure her there was no chance of that. He wanted to swear that, in the morning, he'd be there beside the rest of them in the Council Hall, ready to take the Cup to his lips without reservation. But swearing was a serious thing for Shadowhunters. You never promised unless you were absolutely sure.

So Simon just said a final good night and left his friends behind.

Simon wondered whether, in the history of time, anyone had ever said, "I need to get some air," and actually meant it. Surely it was only ever used as code for "I need to be somewhere else." Which Simon did. The problem was, nowhere felt like the right place to be—so, for lack of a better idea, he decided his dorm room would have to do. At least there he could be alone.

This, at least, was the plan.

But when he stepped into the room, he found a girl sitting on his bed. A petite, redheaded girl whose face lit up at the sight of him.

Of all the strange things that had happened to Simon in the last couple of years, the strangest had to be that this—beautiful girls eagerly awaiting him in his bedroom—no longer seemed particularly strange at all.

"Clary," he said as he encompassed her in a fierce hug. It was all he needed to say, because that's the thing about a best friend. She knew exactly when he most needed to see her and how grateful and relieved he was—without his having to say a thing.

Clary grinned at him and slipped her stele back into her pocket. The Portal she'd created was still shimmering in the decrepit stone wall, by far the brightest thing in the room. "Surprised?"

"Wanted to get one last look at me before I go all buff and demon-fightery?" Simon teased.

"Simon, you do know that Ascending isn't going to be like getting bitten by a radioactive spider or something, right?"

"So you're saying I won't be able to leap tall buildings in a single bound? And I don't get my own Batmobile? I want my money back."

"Seriously, though, Simon—"

"Seriously, Clary. I know what Ascension means."

The words sat heavily between them, and as always, Clary heard what he didn't say: That this was too big to talk about seriously. That joking was, for the moment, the best he could do.

"Besides, Lewis, I'd say you're buff enough already." She poked his biceps, which, he couldn't help but notice, were very close to bulging. "Any more and you'll have to buy new clothes."

"Never!" he said indignantly, and smoothed out his T-shirt, which had a baker's dozen holes in the soft cotton and read I'M COSPLAYING AS MYSELF in letters nearly too faded to read. "Did you, uh, did you happen to bring Isabelle with you?" He tried to keep the hope out of his voice.

Hard to believe that two years ago, he'd come to the Academy in part to escape Clary and Isabelle, the way they'd looked at him like they loved him more than anyone else in the world—but also like he'd drowned their puppy in a bathtub. They'd loved some other version of him, the one he could no longer remember, and that version had loved them, too. He didn't doubt it; he just couldn't feel it. They'd been strangers to him. Terrifyingly beautiful strangers who wanted him to be someone he wasn't.

It felt like another life. Simon didn't know if he'd ever get all of his memories back—but somehow, despite that, he'd found his way back to Clary and Isabelle. He'd found a best friend who felt like his other half, who would someday soon be his *parabatai*. And he'd found Isabelle Lightwood, a miracle in human form, who said "I love you" whenever she saw him and, incomprehensibly, seemed to mean it.

"She wanted to come," Clary said, "but she had to go deal with this rogue faerie thing in Chinatown, something about soup dumplings and a guy with a goat head. I didn't ask too many questions and—" She smiled knowingly at Simon. "I lost you at 'soup dumplings,' didn't I?"

Simon's stomach growled loudly enough to answer for him.

"Well, maybe we can grab you some on the way," Clary said. "Or at least a couple slices of pizza and a latte."

"Don't toy with me, Fray." Simon was very touchy these days on the subject of pizza, or the lack thereof. He suspected that any day now his stomach might resign in protest. "On the way where?"

"Oh, I forgot to explain—that's why I'm here, Simon." Clary took his hand. "I've come to take you home."

* ✳ *

Simon stood on the sidewalk staring up at his mother's brownstone, his stomach churning. Traveling by way of Portal always made him feel a bit like puking up his lower intestine, but this time he didn't think he could blame the interdimensional magic. Not entirely, at least.

"You sure this is a good idea?" he said. "It's late."

"It's eleven p.m., Simon," Clary said. "You know she's still awake. And even if she's not, you know—"

"I know." His mother would want to see him. So would his sister, who, according to Clary, was home for the weekend because *someone*—presumably a well-meaning, redheaded someone with his sister's cell number—had told her Simon was stopping in for a visit.

He sagged against Clary for a moment, and, small as she was, she bore his weight. "I don't know how to do it," he said. "I don't know how to say good-bye to them."

Simon's mother thought he was away at military school. He'd felt guilty lying to her, but he'd known there wasn't any other choice; he knew, all too well, what happened when he risked telling his mother too much truth. But this—this was something else. He was forbidden by Shadowhunter Law to tell her about his Ascension, about his new life. The Law also forbade him from contacting her after he became a Shadowhunter, and though there was nothing saying he couldn't be here in Brooklyn to say good-bye to her forever, the Law forbade him from explaining why.

Sed lex, dura lex.

The Law is hard, but it is the Law.

Lex sucks, Simon thought.

"You want me to go in with you?" Clary asked.

He did, more than anything—but something told him this was one of those things he needed to do on his own.

Simon shook his head. "But thanks. For bringing me here, for knowing I needed it, for—well, for everything."

"Simon . . ."

Clary looked hesitant, and Clary never looked hesitant.

"What is it?"

She sighed. "Everything that's happened to you, Simon, everything . . ." She paused, just long enough for him to think through how much that everything encompassed: getting turned into a rat and then a vampire; finding Isabelle; saving the world a handful of times, at least so he'd been told; getting locked in a cage and tormented by all manner of supernatural creatures; killing demons; facing an angel; losing his memories; and now standing at the threshold of the only home he'd ever known, preparing himself to leave it behind forever. "I can't help thinking it's all because of me," Clary said softly. "That I'm the reason. And . . ."

He stopped her before she could get any further, because he couldn't stand for her to think she needed to apologize. "You're right," he said. "You are the reason. For everything." Simon gave her a gentle kiss on the forehead. "That's why I'm saying thank you."

"Are you sure you don't want me to heat that up for you?" Simon's mother asked as he shoveled another heaping spoonful of cold ziti into his mouth.

"Mmff? What? No, it's fine."

It was more than fine. It was tangy tomato and fresh garlic and hot pepper and gooey cheese, and better than leftover pasta from the corner pizza place had any right to be. It tasted like actual *food*, which already put it head and shoulders above what he'd been eating for the last several months. But it wasn't just that. Takeout from Giuseppi's was a tradition for Simon and his mother—after his father died and his sister went away to school, after it was just the two of them knocking around an apartment that felt cavernous with just the two of them left in it, they'd lost the habit of having daily meals with each other. It was easier to just grab food whenever they thought of it, on the way in or out of the apartment, his mother heating up TV dinners after work, Simon picking up some pho or a sandwich on his way to band practice. It was, maybe, easier not to face the empty chairs at the table every night. But they made it a rule to eat together at least one night each week, slurping down Giuseppi's spaghetti and drenching garlic knots in spicy sauce.

These cold leftovers tasted like home, like family, and Simon hated to think of his mother sitting in the empty apartment, week after week, eating them on her own.

Children are supposed to grow up and leave, he told himself. He wasn't doing anything wrong; he wasn't doing anything he wasn't meant to do.

But there was a part of him that wondered. Children were supposed to leave home, maybe. But not forever. Not like this.

"Your sister tried to wait up for you," his mother said, "but apparently she's been up for a week straight studying for exams. She was passed out on the couch by nine."

"Maybe we should wake her up," Simon suggested.

She shook her head. "Let the poor girl sleep. She'll see you in the morning."

He hadn't *exactly* told his mother he was staying over. But he had let her believe it, which he supposed amounted to about the same thing: yet another lie.

She settled into the chair beside him and stabbed a ziti onto her fork. "Don't tell my diet," she stage-whispered, then popped it into her mouth.

"Mom, the reason I'm here . . . I wanted to talk to you about something."

"That's funny, I've actually—I've been wanting to talk to you about something too."

"Oh? Great! Uh, you go first."

His mother sighed. "You remember Ellen Klein? Your Hebrew school teacher?"

"How could I forget?" Simon said wryly. Mrs. Klein had been the bane of his existence from second grade through fifth. Every Tuesday after school, they'd fought a silent war, all because, in an unfortunate playground incident, Simon had accidentally dislodged her wig and sent it flying into a pigeon's nest. She'd spent the next three years determined to ruin his life.

"You know she was just a nice old lady trying to get you to pay attention," his mother said now with a knowing smile.

"Nice old ladies don't throw your Pokémon cards in the trash," Simon pointed out.

"They do when you're trading them for kiddish wine at the back of the sanctuary," she said.

"I would never!"

"A mother always knows, Simon."

"Okay. Fine. But that was a very rare Mew. The only Pokémon that—"

"Anyway. Ellen Klein's daughter just got married to her

girlfriend, a lovely woman, you'd like her—we all like her. But . . ."

Simon rolled his eyes. "But let me guess: Mrs. Klein is a raging homophobe."

"No, it's not that—the girlfriend's Catholic. Ellen had a fit, wouldn't go to the wedding, and now she's wearing mourning clothes and telling everyone that her daughter might as well be dead."

Simon opened his mouth to crow about how he'd been right all along, that Mrs. Klein was indeed a horrible shrew, but his mother held up a finger to stop him.

A mother, apparently, always knows.

"Yes, yes, it's horrible, but I'm not telling you so you can feel vindicated. I'm telling you . . ." She knitted her fingers together, looking suddenly nervous. "I had the strangest feeling when I heard the story, Simon, like I knew she would regret it—because *I* regretted it. Isn't that strange?" She let out a nervous little giggle, but there was no humor in it. "Feeling guilty for something you haven't even done? I can't say why, Simon, but I feel like I've betrayed you in some terrible way I can't remember."

"Of course you haven't, Mom. That's ridiculous."

"Of course it's ridiculous. I would *never*. A parent should have unconditional love for her child." Her eyes were glossy with unshed tears. "You know that's how I love you, Simon, don't you? Unconditionally?"

"Of course I know that."

He said it like he meant it—he did mean it. But, of course, it was just another lie. Because in that other life, the one that had been wiped clean from both their minds, she *had* betrayed him. He'd told her the truth, that he'd been turned into a vampire, and she had thrown him out of the house. She had told him he was no longer her son. That her son was dead. She'd proven, to both of them, the conditions of her love.

He couldn't remember it happening, but on some level deeper than conscious thought, he remembered the feeling of it—the pain, the betrayal, the loss. It had never occurred to him she might remember too.

"This is silly." She brushed away a tear, gave herself a little shake. "I don't know why I'm getting so emotional over this. I just . . . I just had this *feeling* that I needed to tell you that, and then you showed up here like it was meant to be, and . . ."

"Mom." Simon pulled his mother out of her chair and into a tight hug. She seemed so small to him suddenly, and he thought how hard she'd worked all these years to protect him, and how he would do anything to protect her in return. He was a different person now than he'd been two years before, a different Simon than the one who'd confessed to his mother and been turned out of the house—maybe his mother was different too. Maybe making that choice once was enough to ensure she would never make it again; maybe it was time to stop holding it against her, this betrayal neither of them could quite remember. "Mom, I know. And I love you, too."

She pulled away then, just far enough to meet his gaze. "What about you? What did you have to tell me?"

Oh, nothing much, I'm just joining a supernatural cult of demon-fighters who've forbidden me to ever see you again, love ya.

It didn't have quite the right ring to it.

"I'll tell you in the morning," he said. "You look exhausted."

She smiled, exhaustion painted across her face. "In the morning," she echoed. "Welcome home, Simon."

"Thanks, Mom," he said, and miraculously managed to do so without getting choked up. He waited for her to disappear behind her bedroom door, waited for her soft snores to begin. Then he scribbled a note apologizing for having to leave so abruptly. Without saying good-bye.

His sister snored too—though, like their mother, she denied it. He could, if he stayed very silent, hear her all the way in the kitchen. He could wake her up, if he wanted, and he could probably even tell her the truth, or some version of it. Rebecca could be trusted—not just to keep his secrets, but to understand them. He could do what he'd come here to do, what he was *supposed* to do, say good-bye to her and tell her to love and protect their mother enough for both of them.

"No." He'd spoken softly, but the word seemed to echo in the empty kitchen.

The Law was hard, but it was also riven with loopholes. Hadn't Clary taught him that? There were Shadowhunters who found a way to keep their mundane loved ones in their lives—Simon himself was proof. Maybe that was why Clary had brought him here tonight—not to say good-bye, but to realize that he couldn't. Wouldn't.

This isn't forever, Simon promised his mother and sister as he slipped out the door. He promised himself it wasn't cowardly, leaving without saying anything. It was a silent promise—that this wasn't the end. That he'd find a way. And despite the fact that there was no one to appreciate his flawless Schwarzenegger accent, he swore his oath aloud: "I'll be back."

Clary had said to give her a call when he was ready to head back to the Academy, but he wasn't ready yet. It was strange:

In another day, there'd be nothing keeping him from returning to New York for good. After his Ascension, he'd be a Shadowhunter for real. No more school, no more training missions, no more long days and nights in Idris missing his morning coffee. He hadn't given much thought to what would happen next, but he knew he'd come home to the city and stay in the Institute, at least temporarily. There was no reason to feel so homesick for New York when he was *this close* to being back for good.

Except he wasn't quite sure who he'd be when he came back. When he Ascended. *If* he Ascended, if nothing terrible happened when he took his drink from the Mortal Cup.

What would it mean to become a Shadowhunter, really? He'd be stronger and swifter, he knew that much. He'd be able to bear runes on his skin, see through glamours without a warlock's help. He knew plenty about what he'd be able to do—but he didn't know anything about how it would feel. About who he'd be when he was a Shadowhunter. It's not that he thought one drink from a magic cup would instantly turn him into an egomaniacal, preternaturally handsome, wildly reckless snob like . . . well, like almost all the Shadowhunters he knew and loved. Nor did he expect that turning into a Shadowhunter would make him automatically disdain D&D, *Star Trek*, and all technology and pop culture invented after the nineteenth century. But who could know for sure?

And it wasn't just the confusing transformation from human to angel-warrior. He'd been assured that, in all likelihood, if he survived Ascension, he would get back all his memories. All those memories of the original Simon, the "real" Simon, the one he'd worked so hard to persuade people would be gone forever, would come flooding back into his brain. He supposed this should make him happy, but Simon found he felt rather territorial of his brain as it was now. What if that Simon—the Simon who'd saved the world, the Simon whom Isabelle had first fallen in love with—didn't much like this Simon that he'd become? What if he drank from the Cup and lost himself all over again?

It gave him a headache, thinking of himself as so many different people.

He wanted one last night in the city as just this one: Simon Lewis, myopic, manga-loving mundane.

Also, he still wanted some of those soup dumplings.

Simon wandered down Flatbush, soaking in the familiar noises of New York at night, sirens and construction drills and road-rage honking, along with the slightly less familiar sounds of glamoured faerie hounds barking at the pigeons. He crossed the Manhattan Bridge, metal rattling beneath his feet as the subway roared past, the lights of the Financial District glittering through the fog. Even before he'd known anything about demons and Downworlders, Simon thought, he had always known New York was full of magic. Maybe that was why it had been so easy for him to accept the truth about the Shadow World: In his city, anything was possible.

Conveniently, the bridge dumped him off in the heart of Chinatown. As he popped into his favorite hole-in-the-wall and scarfed a to-go order of dumplings, Simon's mind strayed to Isabelle, wondering if she was close by, slashing evildoers with her electrum whip. It boggled his mind—if you thought about it, he was basically dating a superhero.

Of course, the thing about dating a superhero was that you

couldn't exactly ask them to take a break from saving the world just because you were in the mood for a last-minute date. So Simon kept walking, soaking in the rhythm of the midnight city, letting his mind wander as aimlessly as his feet. At least, he thought he was wandering aimlessly, until he found himself on a familiar block of Avenue D, passing a bodega where the milk was always sour but the guy behind the counter would give you free coffee with your morning doughnut, if you knew enough to ask.

Wait, how did I know that? Simon thought. The answer came to him on the heels of the question. He knew that because, in some other forgotten life, he had lived here. He and Jordan Kyle had shared an apartment in the crumbling redbrick building on the corner. A vampire and a werewolf living together—it sounded like the beginning of a bad joke, but the only bad joke was that Simon had practically forgotten it ever happened.

And Jordan was dead.

It hit him now almost as hard as it had when he first heard: Jordan was dead. And not just Jordan. Raphael was dead. Isabelle's brother Max, dead. Clary's brother Sebastian, dead. Julie's sister. Beatriz's grandfather and father and brother, Julian Blackthorn's father, Emma Carstairs's parents—all of them dead, and those were only the ones Simon had been told about. How many other people he had cared about, or people the people he loved had cared about, had been lost to one Shadowhunter war or another? He was still a teenager—he wasn't supposed to know this many people who had died.

And me, he thought suddenly. *Don't forget that one.*

Because it was true, wasn't it? Before life as a vampire, there'd been death. Cold and bloodless and underground.

Then, later, there'd been the forgetting, and that was a kind of death too.

Simon wasn't even a Shadowhunter yet, and already, this life had taken so much from him.

"Simon. I thought you'd be here."

Simon turned around and was reminded that for all the losses, there'd also been some very significant gains. "Isabelle," he breathed, and then, for quite a while, his lips were too occupied to speak.

They went back to Magnus and Alec's apartment. The couple had taken their new baby on vacation to Bali, which meant Simon and Isabelle could have the place to themselves.

"You sure it's okay for us to be here?" Simon asked, looking nervously around the apartment. The last time he'd seen it, the decorating ethos had been part–Studio 54, part-bordello: lots of disco balls, velvet curtains, and some appallingly placed mirrors. Now the living room looked like something puked up by a Babies"R"Us—blankets and diapers and mobiles and stuffed bunnies everywhere you looked.

He still couldn't believe *Magnus Bane* was someone's dad.

"I'm sure," Isabelle said, stripping off her dress in one smooth motion to reveal the unending stretches of smooth, pale skin that lay beneath. "But if you want to leave . . ."

"No," Simon said, struggling for enough breath to speak. "Definitely. No. Here's good. Very good."

"Well, then." Isabelle swept a family of stuffed kittens off the couch, then stretched across like a very satisfied and very dangerous cat. She looked pointedly at Simon's shirt, which was still on his body.

"Well. Then." Simon stood above her, unsure what to do next.

"Simon."

"Yes?"

"I'm looking pointedly at your shirt."

"Uh-huh."

"Which is still on your body."

"Oh. Right." He took care of that. Dropped down beside her on the couch.

"Simon."

"Yes? Oh. Right." Simon leaned toward her and pulled her close for a kiss, which she indulged for about thirty seconds before extricating herself.

"What's wrong?" he asked.

"You tell me," she said. "I, your incredibly sexy girlfriend that you never get to see, am prostrating myself before you half-naked, and you seem like you'd rather be watching a base-ball game."

"I hate baseball."

"Exactly." Isabelle sat up—though, mercifully, she didn't put any clothes back on. Not yet. "You know you can talk to me about anything, right?"

Simon nodded.

"So if, hypothetically, you were feeling a little nervous about this whole Ascension thing tomorrow, and wondering whether you still wanted to go through with it, you could talk to me about that."

"Hypothetically," Simon said.

"Just picking a topic at random," Isabelle said. "We could also talk about *Avatar: The Last Airplane*, if you want."

"It's the Air*bender*," Simon said, suppressing a grin, "and I love you even if you are nerd-clueless."

"And I love you, even if you are a mundane," she said. "Even if you stay a mundane. You know that, right?"

"I . . ." It was easy for her to say, and he thought she probably even meant it. But that didn't make it true. "You think you would? *Really?*"

Isabelle let out her breath in an irritated puff. "Simon Lewis, are you forgetting that you were a mundane when I first kissed you? A rather scrawny mundane with terrible fashion sense, I should point out. And then you were a *vampire*, and I started dating you. Then you were a mundane again, but this time with freaking amnesia. And still, inexplicably, I fell in love with you all over again. What could possibly make you think I have any standards left when it comes to you?"

"Uh, thank you, I think?"

"'Thank you' is the correct response. And also 'I love you, too, Isabelle, and I would love you even if you lost your memory or grew a mustache or something.'"

"Well, obviously." Simon tugged at her chin. "Though I'd draw the line at a beard."

"Goes without saying." Then she looked serious again. "You do believe me, right? You can't be doing this for me."

"I'm not doing it for you," Simon said, and that was true. He may have gone to the Academy, in part, because of Isabelle— but he'd stayed for himself. When he Ascended, it wouldn't be because he needed to prove something to her. "But . . . if I did back out, which I would never do, but if I did, wouldn't that make me a coward? You'd date a mundane, maybe. But I know you, Izzy. You couldn't date a coward."

"And you, Simon Lewis, couldn't *be* a coward. Not if you tried. It's not cowardly to make a choice about what you want your life to be. Choosing what's right for you, maybe that's the bravest thing you can do. If you choose to be a Shadowhunter, I will love you for it. But if you choose to stay a mundane, I'll love you for that, too."

"What if I just choose not to drink from the Mortal Cup because I'm afraid it will kill me?" Simon asked. It was a relief to finally say it out loud. "What if it had nothing to do with how I want to spend the rest of my life? What if it's just being scared?"

"Well, then, you're an idiot. Because the Mortal Cup could never hurt you. It will know what I do, which is that you'd make an amazing Shadowhunter. The blood of the Angel could *never* hurt you," she said, intensity blazing in her eyes. "It's not possible."

"You really believe that?"

"I really do."

"So the fact that we're here, and you're, you know—"

"Partially disrobed and wondering why we're still making small talk?"

"—has nothing to do with the fact that you think this might be our last night together?"

This earned him another exasperated sigh. "Simon, do you know how many times I've been almost certain one of us wouldn't survive the next twenty-four hours?"

"Um, several?"

"Several," she confirmed. "And on not one of those occasions have we ever had any sort of desperate, angsty farewell sex."

"Wait—we haven't?"

Over the last several months, Simon and Isabelle had gotten very close. Closer, he thought, than they'd ever been before, not that he could quite remember. At least conversationally. As for the other kind of close—talking on the phone and writing each other letters wasn't exactly conducive to losing your virginity.

Then there was the excruciating fact that Simon wasn't certain he still had a virginity to lose.

All this time he'd been too embarrassed to ask.

"Are you kidding me?" Isabelle asked.

Simon could feel his cheeks burning.

"You're *not* kidding me!"

"Please don't be mad," Simon said.

Isabelle laughed. "I'm not mad. If we'd had sex, and you'd *forgotten*—which, by the way, I assure you would not be possible, demon amnesia or no demon amnesia—maybe I'd be mad."

"So we really never . . . ?"

"We really never," Isabelle confirmed. "I know you don't remember, but things were a little hectic around here, what with the war and all the people trying to kill us and such. And like I said, I don't believe in 'farewell sex.'"

Simon felt like the whole night—possibly the most important night of his young and sorrowfully inexperienced life—was hanging in the balance, and he was very afraid of saying the wrong thing. "So, uh, what kind of sex do you believe in?"

"I think it should be a beginning of something," Isabelle said. "Like, say, hypothetically, if your entire life were going to change tomorrow, if it were going to be the first day of the rest of your life, I'd want to be a part of that."

"The rest of my life."

"Yep."

"Hypothetically."

"Hypothetically." She took off his glasses then and kissed him hard on the lips, then very softly on the neck. Exactly where a vampire would sink its fangs in, some part of him thought. Most of him, though, was thinking, *This is actually going to happen.*

This is going to happen tonight.

"Also, most of all, I believe in doing it because I want to do it," Isabelle said plainly. "Just like anything else. And I want to. Assuming you do."

"You have no idea how much," Simon said honestly, and thanked God that Shadowhunting blood didn't bestow telepathy. "I should just warn you, I don't, I mean, I haven't, I mean, this would be the first time I, so—"

"You'll be a natural." She kissed his neck again, then his throat. Then his chest. "I promise."

Simon thought about all the opportunities here for humiliation, how he had absolutely no idea what he was doing, and how usually when he had no idea what he was doing, he screwed things up. Riding a horse, wielding a sword, leaping from a tree—all these things people kept saying would come naturally to him usually came with bumps, bruises, and, more than once, a face full of manure.

But he had tried none of those things with Isabelle by his side. Or in his arms.

As it turned out, that made all the difference.

"Good morning!" Simon sang, stepping out of the Portal and into his bedroom at the Academy—just in time to catch Julie slipping out the door.

"Er, good morning," George mumbled, tucked beneath the covers. "Wasn't sure you'd be back."

"Did I just see—?"

"A gentleman doesn't kiss and tell." George grinned. "Speaking of which, should I ask where you've been all night?"

"You should not," Simon said firmly. As he crossed the room to his closet to find something clean to wear, he tried his best to keep a silly, moony, heartsick smile off his face.

"You're *skipping*," George said accusingly.

"Am not."

"And you were *humming*," George added.

"I most definitely was not."

"Would this be a good time to tell you that Jon Cartwright the Thirty-Fifth seems to have done his business in your T-shirt drawer?"

But this morning nothing could dampen Simon's mood. Not when he could still feel the ghost of Isabelle's touch. His skin buzzed with it. His lips felt swollen. His heart felt swollen. "I can always get new T-shirts," Simon said cheerfully. He thought that from this point forward, he might say everything cheerfully.

"I think this place has officially driven you round the bend." George sighed then, sounding a bit heartsick himself. "You know, I'm really going to miss it here."

"You're not going to cry again, are you? I think there may be another sentient slime mold growing in the back of my sock drawer, if you want to get really choked up."

"Does one wear socks to get transformed into a half-angel superhuman fighting machine?" George mused.

"Not with sandals," Simon said promptly. He hadn't dated

Isabelle all these months without learning something about proper footwear. "Never with sandals."

They got dressed for the ceremony—choosing, after some deliberation, their most Simon-like and George-like outfits. Which meant, for George, jeans and a rugby shirt; for Simon, a faded tee that he'd had made back when the band was called Guinea Pig Death Posse. (This, fortunately, had been lying on the floor for a week, so was rat crap free.) Then, without much talking, they started packing up their belongings. The Academy wasn't much for big celebrations—probably a good thing, Simon mused, since at the last all-school party, one of the first-years had misfired his flaming crossbow and accidentally set the roof on fire. There would be no graduation ceremony, no mugging for cameras with proud parents, no yearbook signings or tossing of mortarboard caps. Just the Ascension ritual, whatever that meant, and that would be it. The end of the Academy; the beginning of the rest of their lives.

"It's not like we'll never see each other again," George said suddenly, in a tone that suggested he'd been worrying about exactly that.

Simon was going back to New York, and George was going to the London Institute, where, they said, a Lovelace was always welcome. But what was an ocean of distance when you could Portal? Or at least e-mail?

"Of course not," Simon said.

"But it won't be the same," George pointed out.

"No, I guess it won't."

George busied himself with neatly tucking his socks into a suitcase compartment, which Simon found alarming, since it was the first time in two years George had done anything neatly. "You're my best friend, you know," George said without looking up. Then, quickly, as if to forestall argument, "Don't worry, I know I'm not *your* best friend, Si. You've got Clary. And Isabelle. And your bandmate mate. I get it. I just thought you should know."

On some level, Simon had already known this. He'd never bothered to think much about it—he didn't think much about George, period, because that was the beauty of George. Simon never had to *think* about him, to puzzle out what he would do or how he would react. He was just steady, dependable George, always there, always full of cheer and eager to spread it around. Now Simon did think about him, about how well George knew him, and vice versa—not just in the big ways: their dead-of-night fears about washing out of the Academy, Simon's hapless pining for Isabelle, George's even more hapless, if more halfhearted, pining for most girls who crossed his path. They knew each other in the little ways—that George was allergic to cashews, that Simon was allergic to Latin homework, that George had a paralyzing fear of large birds—and somehow, that seemed to matter even more. Over the past two years, they'd developed a roommate shorthand, almost a silent language. Not exactly like a *parabatai*, Simon thought, and not exactly like a best friend. But not something *less than*. Not something he ever wanted to leave behind for good.

"You're right, George. I do have more than enough best friends."

George's face fell, so slightly that only someone who knew him as well as Simon would have noticed.

"But there's something else I've never had," Simon added. "At least until now."

"What's that?"

"A brother." The word felt right. Not someone you chose—someone the fates assigned you, someone who, under any other circumstances, might never have given you a second look, nor you him. Someone you would die for and kill for without a second thought, because he was family. Judging from George's radiant smile, the word sounded right to him, too.

"Are we going to have to hug now or something?" George said.

"I think that may be inescapable."

The Council Hall was intimidatingly beautiful, morning light streaming in through a window in its high domed ceiling. It reminded Simon of pictures he'd seen of the Pantheon, but this place felt more ancient than even ancient Rome. This felt timeless.

The Academy students huddled together in small clumps, all of them looking too nervous and distracted to do much more than comment blandly on the weather. (Which was, as the inhabitants always agreed, perfect.) Marisol gave Simon a bright smile and a sharp nod when she saw him enter the chamber, as if to say, *I never doubted you . . . almost.*

Simon and George were the last to arrive, and shortly after they did, everyone took their places for the ceremony. The seven mundanes were arranged in alphabetical order in the front of the chamber. There were meant to be ten of them, but apparently Sunil wasn't the only one who'd reconsidered at the last moment. Leilana Jay, a very tall, very pale girl from Memphis, and Boris Kashkoff, an Eastern European with ropy muscles and ruddy cheeks, had both slipped away sometime in the night. No one spoke of them, not the teachers, not the students. It was like they never existed, Simon thought—and then imagined Sunil, Leilana, and Boris out there in the world somewhere, living alone with their knowledge of the Shadow World, aware of evil but without the will or ability to fight it.

There's more than one way to fight evil in this world, Simon thought, and it was Clary's voice in his head, and it was Isabelle's, and his mother's, and his own. *Don't do this because you think you have to. Do it because you want to.*

Only *if you want to.*

The Academy's Shadowhunter students—Simon never thought of them as the "elites" anymore, just as he no longer thought of himself and the other mundanes as the "dregs"— sat in the first two rows of the audience. The students weren't two tiers anymore; they were one body. One unit. Even Jon Cartwright looked proud of, and a little nervous for, the mundanes at the front of the chamber—and when Simon caught him locking eyes with Marisol and pressing two fingers to his lips and then his chest, it seemed almost right. (Or, at least, not a total crime against nature, which was a start.) There were no family members in the audience—those mundanes with living relatives (and there were depressingly few of them) had, of course, already severed ties. George's parents, who were Shadowhunters by blood if not by choice, could have attended, but he'd asked them not to. "Just in case I explode, mate," he'd confided to Simon. "Don't get me wrong, the Lovelaces are hardy folk, but I don't think they'd enjoy a faceful of liquefied George."

Nonetheless, the room was almost full. This was the first class of Academy mundanes to Ascend in decades, and more than a few Shadowhunters had wanted to see it for themselves. Most of them were strangers to Simon, but not all. Crowded in behind the rows of students were Clary, Jace, and Isabelle, and Magnus and Alec—who had made a surprise return from Bali for the occasion—tag-teaming their squirming blue baby. All of them—even the baby—were intensely fixed on Simon, as if they could get him through the Ascension with sheer force of will.

This, Simon realized, was what Ascending meant. This was what being a Shadowhunter meant. Not just risking his life, not just carving runes and fighting demons and occasionally saving the world. Not just joining the Clave and agreeing to follow its draconian rules. It meant joining his *friends*. It meant being a part of something bigger than himself, something as wonderful as it was terrifying. Yes, his life was much less safe than it had been two years ago—but it was also much more full. Like the Council Hall, it was crowded with all the people he loved, people who loved him.

You might almost call them a family.

And then it began.

One by one the mundanes were summoned to the dais, where their professors stood in a somber line, waiting to shake their hands and wish them luck.

One by one the mundanes approached the double circles traced on the dais and knelt in their center, surrounded by runes. Two Silent Brothers stood by just in case something went wrong. Each time a mundane took position, they bent over the runes and scratched in a new one to symbolize that student's name. Then they returned to the edges of the dais again, statue-still in parchment robes, watching. Waiting.

Simon waited too as one by one his friends brought their lips to the Mortal Cup. As a blinding flare of blue light encompassed them, then faded away.

One by one.

Gen Almodovar. Thomas Daltrey. Marisol Garza.

Each student drank.

Each student survived.

The wait was interminable.

Except that when the Consul called his name, it felt much too soon.

Simon's feet were cement blocks. He forced himself toward the dais, one step at a time, his heartbeat pulsing like a subwoofer, making his whole body tremble. The professors shook his hand, even Delaney Scarsbury, who murmured, "Always knew you had it in you, Lewis." A blatant lie. Catarina Loss gripped his hand tightly and pulled him close, her brilliant white hair sweeping his shoulder as her lips brushed his ear. "Finish what you started, Daylighter. You have the power to change these people for the better. Don't waste it."

Like most things Catarina said to him, it didn't quite make sense, but some part of him still understood it completely.

Simon knelt at the center of the circles and reminded himself to breathe.

The Consul stood over him, her traditional red robe brushing the floor. He kept his eyes on the runes, but he could sense Clary out there rooting for him; he could hear the echo of George's laughter; he could feel the ghost of Izzy's warm touch on his skin. At the center of these circles, surrounded by runes, waiting for the blood of the divine to run through his veins and change him in some unfathomable way, Simon felt profoundly alone—and yet, at the same time, less alone than he'd ever been in his life.

His family was here, holding him up.

They would not let him fall.

"Do you swear, Simon Lewis, to forsake the mundane world and follow the path of the Shadowhunter?" Consul Penhallow asked. Simon had met the Consul before, when she'd delivered a lecture at the Academy, and again at her daughter's wedding to Helen Blackthorn. On both occasions she had seemed like your basic mom: brisk, efficient, nice enough, and none too surprising. But now she seemed fearsome and powerful, less an individual than the walking repository of millennia of Shadowhunter tradition. "Will you take into yourself the blood of the Angel Raziel and honor that blood? Do you swear to serve the Clave, to follow the Law as set forth by the Covenant, and to obey the word of the Council? Will you defend that which is human and mortal, knowing that for your service, there will be no recompense and no thanks but honor?"

For Shadowhunters, swearing was a matter of life and death. If he made this promise, there was no turning back to the life he'd once had, to Simon Lewis, mundane nerd, aspiring rock star. There were no more options to consider. There was only his oath, and a lifetime's effort to fulfill it.

Simon knew if he looked up he could meet Isabelle's eyes, or Clary's, and draw strength from them. He could silently ask them if this was the right path, and they would reassure him.

But this choice couldn't belong to them. It had to be his, and his alone.

He closed his eyes.

"I swear." His voice did not shake.

"Can you be a shield for the weak, a light in the dark, a truth among falsehoods, a tower in the flood, an eye to see when all others are blind?"

Simon imagined all the history behind these words, all the Consuls before Jia Penhallow stretching back for decades and centuries, holding this same Cup before one mundane after another. So many mortals, volunteering to join the fight. They had always seemed so brave to Simon, risking their lives—sacrificing their futures to a greater cause—not because they'd been *born* into a great battle between good and evil, but because they had *chosen* not to live on the sidelines, letting others fight for them.

It occurred to him, if they were brave for making the choice, maybe he was too.

But it didn't feel like bravery, not now.

It simply felt like taking the next step forward. That simple. That inevitable.

"I can," Simon answered.

"And when you are dead, will you give up your body to the Nephilim to be burned, that your ashes may be used to build the City of Bones?"

Even the thought of this didn't frighten him. It seemed suddenly like an honor, that his body would live on in usefulness after death, that from this time forward, the Shadowhunter world would have a claim on him, for eternity.

"I will," Simon said.

"Then drink."

Simon took the Cup into his hands. It was even heavier than it looked and curiously warm to the touch. Whatever was inside it didn't look much like blood, fortunately, but it didn't look like anything else he recognized either. If he didn't know better, Simon would have said the Cup was full of light. As he peered down at it, the strange liquid almost seemed to pulse with a soft glow, as if to say, *Go ahead, drink me.*

He couldn't remember the first time he'd seen the Mortal Cup—that was one of the memories still lost to him—but he knew the role it had played in his life, knew that if it weren't for the Cup, he and Clary might never have discovered the existence of Shadowhunters in the first place. It had all begun with the Mortal Cup; it seemed fitting that it should all end here too.

Not *end*, Simon thought quickly. Hopefully not *end*.

It was said that the younger you were, the less likely drinking from the Cup was to kill you. Simon was, subjectively, nineteen, but he'd recently learned that by Shadowhunter rules, he was only eighteen. The months he'd spent as a vampire apparently didn't count. He could only hope the Cup understood that.

"Drink," the Consul repeated quietly, a note of humanity creeping into her voice.

Simon raised the Cup to his lips.

He drank.

He is tangled in Isabelle's arms, he is curtained by Isabelle's hair, he is touching Isabelle's body, he is lost in Isabelle, in her smell and her taste and the silk of her skin.

He is onstage, the music pounding, the floor shaking, the audience cheering, his heart beating beating beating in time with the drumbeat.

He is laughing with Clary, dancing with Clary, eating with Clary, running through the streets of Brooklyn with Clary, they are children together, they are one half of a whole, they hold hands and squeeze tight and pledge never to let go.

He is going cold, stiff, the life draining out of him, he is below, in the dark, clawing his way to the light, fingernails scraping dirt, mouth filled with dirt, eyes clogged with dirt, he is straining, reaching, dragging himself up toward the sky, and when he reaches it, he opens his mouth wide but does not breathe, for he no longer needs to breathe, only to feed. And he is so very hungry.

He is sinking his teeth into the neck of an angel's child, he is drinking the light.

He is bearing a Mark, and it burns.

He is raising his face to meet the gaze of an angel, he is flayed by the fury of angel fire, and yet still, impudent and bloodless, he lives.

He is in a cage.

He is in hell.

He is bent over the broken body of a beautiful girl, he is praying to whatever god that will listen, please let her live, anything to let her live.

He is giving away that which is most precious to him, and he is doing so willingly, so that his friends will survive.

He is, again, with Isabelle, always with Isabelle, the holy flame of their love encompassing them both, and there is pain, and there is exquisite joy, and his veins burn with angel fire and he is the Simon he once was and the Simon he then became and the Simon he now will be, he endures and he is reborn, he is blood and flesh and a spark of the divine.

He is Nephilim.

Simon didn't see the flash of light he'd expected—he saw only the flood of memories, a tidal wave that threatened to drown him in the past. It wasn't simply a lifetime that passed before his eyes; it was an eternity, all the versions of himself that ever could have been, that ever would be. And then it was over. His mind stilled. His soul quieted. And his memories—the parts of himself he'd feared were lost forever—had come home.

He'd spent two years trying to convince himself that it was okay if he never remembered, that he could live with piecing together the fragments of his past, relying on others to tell him about the person he'd once been. But it had never felt right. The empty hole in his memory was like a missing limb; he'd learned to compensate, but he'd never stopped feeling the absence or its pain.

Now, finally, he was whole again.

He was more than whole, he realized, as the Consul said proudly, "You are Nephilim now. I name you Simon Shadowhunter, of the blood of Jonathan Shadowhunter, child of the Nephilim." It was a placeholder name, until he chose a new one for himself. Moments before, that had seemed unthinkable, but now it simply felt true. He was the same person he'd always been . . . and yet. He wasn't Simon Lewis anymore. He was someone new.

"Arise."

He felt . . . he didn't know how he felt, except stunned. Filled with joy and confusion and what felt like a flickering light, growing brighter by the second.

He felt strong.

He felt ready.

He felt like his abs were still pretty much only a two-pack, but he supposed even a magic cup could get you only so far.

The Consul cleared her throat. "Arise," she said again. Then she lowered her voice to a whisper. "That means you stand up and give someone else a turn."

Simon was still trying to shake off his joyous daze as he made his way back to the others. George was next, and as they passed each other, he gave Simon a surreptitious high five.

Simon wondered what George would see inside the light, if it would be as wondrous. He wondered whether, after the ceremony was over, they would compare notes—or if this was the kind of thing you were supposed to keep to yourself. He supposed there was probably some kind of Shadowhunter protocol to follow—the Shadowhunters had a protocol for everything.

We, he corrected himself wryly. *We have a protocol for everything.*

This would take some getting used to.

George was on his knees inside the circles, the Mortal Cup in his hands. It was strange, being a Shadowhunter while George was still a mundane, as if there was now an invisible divide between them. *This is the farthest apart we'll ever be,* Simon thought, and silently urged his roommate to hurry up and drink.

The Consul said the traditional words. George swore his oath of loyalty to the Shadowhunters without hesitation, drew in a deep breath, then jauntily raised the Mortal Cup as if giving a toast. *"Slàinte!"* he shouted, and as his friends broke into indulgent laughter, he took a slug.

Simon was still laughing when the screaming began.

The room fell dead silent, but inside Simon's mind, there was a siren of pain. An inhuman, unearthly scream.

George's scream.

On the dais, George and the Consul were engulfed in an

impossible flash of blinding darkness. When it faded away, the Consul was on her feet, the Silent Brothers already by her side, all of them peering down at something horrible, something with the shape of a person, but not its face and not its skin. Something with black veins bulging through cracking flesh, something with the Mortal Cup still clenched in its rigid fist, some withered, writhing, crumbling creature with George's hair and George's sneakers, but in place of George's smile, a tortured, toothless rictus leaking something too black to be blood. *Not George,* Simon thought furiously as the thing stopped jerking and trembling and fell still. And somehow, in Simon's head, George screamed and screamed.

The chamber was a storm of motion—responsible adults hustling students out of the room, gasps and cries and shrieks—but Simon barely registered any of it. He was moving forward, toward the thing that couldn't be George, pressing toward the dais with Shadowhunter strength and Shadowhunter speed. Simon was going to save his roommate, because he was a Shadowhunter now, and that's what Shadowhunters do.

He didn't notice Catarina Loss come up behind him, not until her hands were on his shoulders, her grip light enough that he should have been able to break free—but he couldn't move.

"Let go of me!" Simon raged. The Silent Brothers were kneeling by the thing now, the body, but they weren't *doing* anything for it. They weren't helping. They were just staring fixedly at the spiderweb of inky veins spreading across flesh. "I have to help him!"

"No." Catarina's hand feathered across his forehead and the screaming in his mind fell silent. She was still holding on; he still couldn't move. He was a Shadowhunter, but she was a war-lock. He was helpless. "It's too late."

Simon couldn't watch the black veins eat up skin or the hol-low eyes melt into the skull. He focused on the sneakers. George's sneakers. One was untied, as it often was. Just that morning George had tripped over the laces, and Simon had caught him from fall-ing. "The last time you'll save me," George had said with another of his wistful sighs, and Simon had shot back, "Not likely."

The veins were popping, with a sound like Rice Krispies in milk. The body was starting to ooze.

Now Simon was holding on to Catarina too. He held tight.

"What's the point?" he said in despair, because what was the point of dying like this, not in battle, not for a good cause, not to save a fellow warrior or the world, but for *nothing*? And what was the point of living as a Shadowhunter, what was the point of skill and bravery and superhuman powers, when you couldn't do anything but stand by and *watch*?

"Sometimes there is no point," Catarina said gently. "There only is what is."

What is, Simon thought, the wave of rage and frustration and horror nearly consuming him. He would not let himself be consumed; he would not waste this moment, if this was all he had. He'd spent two years making himself strong—he would be strong for George, now, in the only way left to him. He would bear witness.

Simon summoned his will. *What is.*

He forced himself not to look away.

What is: George. Brave and kind and *good*. George, dead. George, gone.

And though he didn't know what the Law had to say about

dying by the Mortal Cup, whether the Clave would consider George one of their own and give him Shadowhunter burial rights, he didn't care. He knew what George was, what he was meant to be, and what he deserved.

"*Ave atque vale*, George Lovelace, child of Nephilim," he whispered. "Forever and ever, my brother, hail and farewell."

Simon grazed a finger over the small stone plaque, tracing the engraved letters: GEORGE LOVELACE.

"It's pretty, isn't it?" Isabelle said from behind him.

"Simple," Clary added. "He would have liked that, don't you think?"

Simon thought that George would have preferred to be interred in the City of Bones, like the Shadowhunter he was. (More to the point, he would have preferred not to be dead at all.) The Clave had refused him. He died in the act of Ascension, which in their eyes marked him as unworthy. Simon was trying very hard not to be angry about this.

He spent a lot of time these days trying not to be angry.

"It was nice of the London Institute to offer a place for him, don't you think?" Isabelle said. Simon could hear in her voice how hard she was trying, how worried she was for him.

They told me a Lovelace is always welcome at the London Institute, George had said when he heard about his placement.

After his death the Institute made good on their word.

There had been a funeral, which Simon had endured. There had been a variety of reunions, big and small, with his friends from the Academy, Simon and the others telling stories and trading memories and trying not to think about that last day. Jon almost always cried.

Then there had been everything else: Life as a Shadow-hunter, mercifully busy with training and experimenting with his newfound physical grace and energy, along with fighting off the occasional demon or rogue vampire. There had been long days with Clary, reveling in the fact that he could now remember every second of their friendship, preparing for their *parabatai* ceremony, which was only days away. There had been numerous training bouts with Jace, usually ending with Simon flat on his back while Jace stood over him, gloating about his superior skill, because that was Jace's way of showing affection. There had been evenings babysitting Magnus and Alec's son, snuggling the little blue boy to his chest and singing him to sleep, and feeling, for a few precious minutes, almost at peace.

There had been Isabelle, who loved him, which made every day glow.

There had been so much to make life worth living, and so Simon had lived, and time had passed—and George was still dead.

He'd asked Clary to Portal him here, to London, for reasons he didn't quite understand. He'd said good-bye to George so many times now, but somehow none of it felt quite final—it didn't feel right.

"I'll take you there," Clary had said. "But I'm coming with you."

Isabelle had insisted too, and Simon was glad of it.

A soft breeze blew through the Institute's garden, rustling the leaves and carrying the faint scent of orchids. Simon thought that George would be glad, at least, to spend eternity in a place where there was no threat of sheep.

Simon rose to his feet, flanked by Clary and Isabelle. Each of them slipped her hand into his, and they stood silently, bound together. Now that Simon had regained his past, he could remember all the times he'd almost lost one of them—as he could remember now, vividly, all the people he *had* lost. To battle, to murder, to sickness. Being a Shadowhunter, he knew, meant being on an intimate basis with death.

But then, so did being human.

Someday he would lose Clary and Isabelle, or they would lose him. Nothing could stop that. So what was the point? he'd asked Catarina, but he knew better than that. The point wasn't that you tried to live forever; the point was that you *lived*, and did everything you could to live well. The point was the choices you made and the people you loved.

Simon gasped.

"Simon?" Clary said in alarm. "What is it?"

But Simon couldn't speak; he could only gape at the gravestone, where the air was shimmering, and translucent light was shaping itself into two figures. One was a girl about his age; she had long blond hair, brown eyes, and the old-timey petticoats of a BBC duchess. The other was George, and he was smiling at Simon. The girl's hand was on his shoulder, and there was something kind about the gesture, something warm and familiar.

"George," Simon whispered. Then he blinked, and the figures were gone.

"Simon, *what* are you staring at?" Isabelle asked in the tight, irritated tone she used only when she was trying not to be afraid.

"Nothing." What was he supposed to say? That he'd seen George's ghost rise from the mist? That he'd seen not just

George, which would have almost made sense, but some beautiful old-fashioned stranger? He knew Shadowhunters could see ghosts when those ghosts wanted to be seen, but he also knew that grieving people often saw what they wanted to see.

Simon didn't know what to think. But he knew what he *wanted* to think.

He wanted a beautiful Shadowhunter spirit from the past, maybe even a long-dead Lovelace, to take George away with her, to wherever it was spirits went. He wanted to believe that George had been welcomed into the arms of his ancestors, where some part of him would live on.

Not likely, Simon reminded himself. George was adopted, not a Lovelace by blood. And for Shadowhunters—presumably even the dead ones who haunted British gardens—everything came down to blood.

"Simon—" Isabelle pressed her lips to his cheek. "I know how much you . . . I know he was like your brother. I wish I could have known him better."

Clary squeezed his hand. "Me too."

Both of them, Simon was reminded, had also lost a brother.

And both of them cared about more than just bloodlines. Both understood that family could be a matter of choice—a matter of love. So did Alec and Magnus, who'd taken someone else's child into their home and their hearts. So did the Lightwoods, who'd adopted Jace when he had no one else.

And so did Simon, who was now a Shadowhunter himself. Who could change what it meant to be a Shadowhunter just by making new choices. Better choices.

He understood now why he'd felt the need to come here, almost as if he'd been summoned. Not to say good-bye to

George but to find a way to hold on to a piece of him.

"I think I know what I want my Shadowhunter name to be," he said.

"Simon Lovelace," Clary said, as always, knowing his mind as well as he did. "It has a certain ring to it."

Isabelle's lips quirked. "A sexy ring."

Simon laughed and blinked away a tear. For one blurry-eyed moment, he thought he saw George grinning through the mist again, and then he was gone. George Lovelace was gone.

But Simon Lovelace was still here, and it was time to make that count.

"I'm ready," he told Clary and Isabelle, the two wonders who had changed his life, the two warriors who would risk anything and everything for those they loved, the two girls who had become his heroes and his family. "Let's go home."